PRAISE FOR THE NO

MAYA BANK

"It pulls . . . Definitely a recommended read. Filled with friendship, passion, and most of all, a love that grows beyond just being friends." —*Fallen Angel Reviews*

"Grabbed me from page one and refused to let go until I read the last word . . . When a book still affects me hours after reading it, I can't help but joyfully recommend it!" —*JoyfullyReviewed.com*

"I guarantee I will reread this book many times over and will derive as much pleasure as I did in the first reading each and every subsequent time." —*Novelspot*

"A compelling look at love between friends." —*Romance Junkies*

"An excellent read that I simply did not put down . . . A fantastic adventure . . . covers the emotional range." —*The Road to Romance*

Titles by Maya Banks

FOR HER PLEASURE

BE WITH ME

The Sweet Series

SWEET SURRENDER
SWEET PERSUASION
SWEET SEDUCTION

SWEET TEMPTATION
SWEET POSSESSION
SWEET ADDICTION

The Kelly/KGI Series

THE DARKEST HOUR
NO PLACE TO RUN
HIDDEN AWAY
WHISPERS IN THE DARK

ECHOES AT DAWN
SHADES OF GRAY
FORGED IN STEELE
AFTER THE STORM

Colters' Legacy

COLTERS' PROMISE
COLTERS' GIFT

The Breathless Trilogy

RUSH
FEVER
BURN

The Surrender Trilogy

LETTING GO

Anthologies

FOUR PLAY
(with Shayla Black)

MEN OUT OF UNIFORM
(with Karin Tabke and Sylvia Day)

CHERISHED
(with Lauren Dane)

Specials

PILLOW TALK

for her pleasure

MAYA BANKS

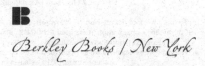

Berkley Books / New York

THE BERKLEY PUBLISHING GROUP
Published by the Penguin Group
Penguin Group (USA) Inc.
375 Hudson Street, New York, New York 10014, USA

USA | Canada | UK | Ireland | Australia | New Zealand | India | South Africa | China

Penguin Books Ltd., Registered Offices: 80 Strand, London WC2R 0RL, England
For more information about the Penguin Group, visit penguin.com.

This book is an original publication of The Berkley Publishing Group.

Library of Congress Cataloging-in-Publication Data

Banks, Maya.
For her pleasure / Maya Banks.
p. cm.
ISBN: 978-0-425-21749-8
1. Group sex—Fiction. 2. Texas—Fiction. I. Title.
PS3602.A643F67   2007   2007017298
813'.6—dc22

PUBLISHING HISTORY
Heat trade paperback edition / September 2007
Berkley trade paperback edition / April 2013

PRINTED IN THE UNITED STATES OF AMERICA

25 24 23 22 21 20 19 18 17 16 15 14

Cover design by Rita Frangie.
Cover art by Jared DeCinque/GettyImages.

ALWAYS LEARNING   PEARSON

To Amy for pushing me when I needed it and never letting me settle for less. For telling me this was *the* book. You were right.

To Roberta for making this happen.

To Karin, we've hung in there together for a lot of years. This wouldn't be nearly as fun without you.

To Jan, Liz, Edie and Michelle. I couldn't ask for a better support network.

To Holly and Fru for being my number one fans. I love you both.

To Melissa and Jennifer for such great feedback. I couldn't ask for better readers. You keep me honest.

To Jess, your support and friendship mean a lot.

To "Loo-gey" for being the best friend I could ever hope to have.

CONTENTS

what she wants

CHAPTER 1

*T*ravis "Mac" McKenzie pushed back his Stetson as he stepped into the Two Step Bar and Café. He scanned the smoky interior from left to right, taking in every person, looking for anything out of the ordinary. But all he saw was the usual crowd, mostly locals out having a good time.

The jukebox blared the latest rowdy country tune, and three couples navigated the center floor in a jerky rendition of a two-step.

As he stepped further into the bar, a few of the drunker customers sat up and took notice of his uniform. But he wasn't there to bust anyone for disorderly conduct. He was there to make sure Kit didn't have any trouble.

His eyes traveled to the back of the room where Kit Townsend was busy pouring drinks. Her back was to him, and he took in her curvy ass, outlined by a pair of too-short cutoff jeans.

His body reacted to her even across the room. It was easy to imagine those shapely legs wrapped around him, his hands cupping her perfect breasts. He curled his fingers into fists to ease the ache. He'd waited a long time for her. She was worth it, but he wasn't going to wait any longer.

She stopped every once in awhile and glanced furtively around as if she didn't trust someone not to jump out at her when she wasn't expecting it. And who could blame her after what had happened six months earlier?

His gut tightened uncomfortably, and he flexed his hands as the familiar anger surged through his veins. Someone had done his best to take Kit away from Mac, from any chance he had of making her his. She was running scared now, a fact she tried to hide, but Mac saw the shadows in her eyes every time he looked at her.

He glanced to the corner where his buddy Ryder Sinclair sat nursing a beer. He lifted his brow in silent question, and Ryder shook his head.

Mac started over in Ryder's direction. Since the attack on Kit, the two had made damn sure one of them was close by at all times. They'd been taking care of Kit since they were kids. Only they'd failed her in a big way.

"How's it going?" Ryder asked lazily, tipping his beer in Mac's direction.

Mac took off his Stetson and dropped it on the table, then settled his large frame into a chair. "Busy night or I'da been here sooner. Everything okay around here?"

Ryder shrugged. "Same ole, same ole."

Mac watched as Kit surveyed the room as if she were looking for someone or something. Her usually expressive green eyes were shadowed, reserved. Her entire demeanor had changed for the worse. The outgoing, sassy, fire-breathing spitfire he and Ryder had known all their lives had been replaced by a girl neither of them knew. Or knew how to handle.

She was afraid. And that pissed Mac off to no end. He'd love to find the bastard who had taken her spirit and kill him with his bare hands.

"Still no leads, huh?" Ryder mumbled.

Mac shook his head. "We're dumbasses, Ryder."

"Yeah well, tell me something I don't know."

"If we hadn't fucked around, played stupid games, she'da been at home in bed with us instead of where she was that night."

Ryder crooked his lip and nodded before tipping back his bottle again. "We couldn't have known. Hell, we were all having fun. Flirting. Just like old times."

"I may have fucked up any chance I have with her," Mac muttered. "She didn't have a whole lot of trust in her system to begin with, and after what happened . . . " He let his thoughts trail off. He knew he and Ryder were the only two people Kit trusted, but had that survived in the face of her attack? He didn't know, and he was afraid to press her.

Ryder arched his brow then leaned forward, his beefy arms resting on the table. The tattoo on his upper arm bulged and flexed as he gripped his beer bottle.

"Wait a minute. Just how serious about her are you?"

Mac gave him a dark look. "Come on, Ryder. You're not stupid. Just because I entertained a threesome with you and her doesn't mean she's a cheap lay."

"I never said she was," Ryder said mildly. He ran his hand through his hair and shoved it behind his left ear, baring a row of earrings.

Mac shook his head. He liked to give Ryder hell about the earrings and the tattoos, of which there were at least three, but secretly, he envied his give-a-shit attitude. And Kit was every bit the rebel Ryder was.

Growing up with the two of them was an experience in daring. Kit and Ryder had decided to go out and get tattoos one night during their senior year in high school. They'd dared Mac to get one, but he'd gone along for the ride only. Between them, they embodied a lot of the traits Mac wished he possessed himself. Maybe it was why he had gravitated toward them in their younger days.

He still remembered the night Kit had shown them just *where* she'd gotten her tattoo. It wasn't something he was likely to forget in this life time. He could get a raging hard-on just thinking about it.

She'd be a firebrand in bed, and even though a threesome had been on his and Ryder's minds for a long time, Mac knew it wasn't enough for him. Ryder was okay with good times, great sex and easy friendship, but Mac wanted more. He wanted Kit.

"Look, I'm just pissed because we fucked around and didn't act on an attraction that was obvious. She wanted us. We wanted her. And because we sat on our hands for too long, some fucking psycho hurt her. I don't like how it's changed her."

Ryder stared over at Kit, his dark eyes hooded. "No," he said slowly. "I don't like it either."

"We've waited long enough. I wanted to give her space to deal with what happened, but what I really want is to make sure no one ever hurts her again, and I can't do that unless she's home with me, in my bed."

Ryder sat back and stared at Mac for a long moment.

Mac frowned. "I don't like it when you look at me like that, bro. It usually means you're overtaxing that pea brain of yours."

Ryder grinned crookedly. "I just don't want to step on any toes. I get the feeling you're not into this for the sex only."

"She wants *us*," Mac replied. "She knows our history. She didn't pull the idea from the air, that's for damn sure. But I won't lie to you. In the end, I want to be the one she comes home to."

Ryder shrugged. "Fair enough. As long as we know where we stand. Given her attitude about relationships, I'm surprised you'd even entertain that notion."

Mac followed Kit's progress across the room. "I aim to change her mind."

Kit took in Mac and Ryder sitting across the room out of the corner of her eye. They were regular fixtures these days, and it didn't take a rocket scientist to figure out why.

She plunked down a round of beers to the table she was serving, not even bothering with her usual smile. She nodded at the guy two tables down who motioned for another beer and headed back to the bar.

She set her tray down and quickly rattled off her mixed-drink order to David, then began pouring beer out of the tap.

"Busy tonight," David shouted above the din.

She nodded and snuck another sideways look at Mac and Ryder. They were both staring at her. She blew out her breath in a mixture of irritation and sadness. Once they'd looked at her with lust in their eyes. Now she had a hard time figuring out if they viewed her with pity or disgust. Or something else entirely.

She prided herself on knowing where she stood with people. She was a no-bullshit kinda girl, but that note had changed everything. It made her question her instincts. She didn't like feeling vulnerable. It had made up entirely too much of her past, and in her adult life, she'd flipped that past the finger.

"Honey, if they stare at you any harder, they're going to eat you for dinner," Rose said beside her.

Kit looked up at the other waitress as Rose gave her drink order to David.

"I wish," she muttered.

Rose looked at her with a mixture of pity and sadness. "You can't let what happened hold you back, girl. Those men won't wait around forever."

Kit ground her teeth. Rose was well meaning, but Kit hated

when people pried into her business. She smiled through her teeth and said, "Thanks, Rose. I appreciate your concern."

She turned her back, arranged the beer and drinks on her tray and headed back into the crowd. She wished it was as simple as throwing a few veiled invitations, whispering a few bold words, then enjoying sex with two hot guys.

"Hey, darlin'," Ryder said in a low voice as she passed their table.

Despite her sour mood, she smiled as Ryder's slow sexy voice rolled over her. She felt a quiver deep in her belly, and it fanned out in waves.

"What's up, guys?" she asked lightly.

"You gonna come talk to us tonight?" Ryder asked, flashing her a grin.

It was too easy to fall back into their flirtation. She winked at him and gave him a sassy smile. "Sure. Let me deliver these drinks. Can I get you anything on my way back?"

Mac regarded her with those dark blue make-you-come-with-one-look eyes, and she felt the flutter rise from her stomach into her throat. Damn the man was sexy as hell. They both were, and there was never a time that she hadn't known it. If they both hadn't left town when they did, she would have had them years ago. But like everyone else in her life, they'd left her behind. Now that they were back, she wanted to be closer to them. They made her feel safe.

"I'll take a water," Mac said.

"You can bring me another beer," Ryder said as he downed his last swig.

She winked again and sashayed away from the table. She felt alive around those two. Like she could erase the past. Like she was the most sexy, desirable woman on earth.

She delivered her drinks then made a trip back to the bar for a glass of water and a beer. David leaned over and said in a low voice, "Trouble at six o'clock."

Before she could turn around, she felt a firm grip on her ass. She froze.

"Hey sweet thang, what do you say you and me hook up after you get off."

Gerald. Fuck.

She whirled around, but Gerald only tightened his grip on her rear. The dumbass was drunk as a skunk and didn't have the sense God gave a mule.

"If you don't get your hand off me, you're going to lose your right nut. You got me?"

He put his hands up in exaggerated surrender. "Hey now. I was just being friendly-like."

"Don't you ever fucking touch me," she hissed.

"S'cuuuuse me. How 'bout a kiss. I can apologize nicely."

It might mean her job, but at this point she didn't give a fuck. She paused only long enough to slam her tray back on the counter, then she decked him.

He went down in a heap, holding his nose and bellowing like a branded bull. David hopped over the bar and subdued Gerald before he could get back up. Suddenly a big body stepped between her and the two men on the floor. Mac.

"I'll take care of this, David."

Mac's voice was tight with anger. She glanced over to see Ryder standing a few feet away, fire in his eyes.

"I believe I can handle this," she said dryly.

Mac glanced at her but didn't stop as he hauled Gerald off the floor.

"That bitch bloodied my nose!" Gerald raged.

Kit shoved past Ryder and inserted herself in front of Gerald. "You ever touch me again, asshole, and that's not all I'll bloody."

Ryder pulled her back, and Mac shoved Gerald toward the door.

"Easy, darlin'," Ryder drawled.

She glared at him and jerked her arm out of his grasp. "I was doing just fine before you and Mac interfered."

He shrugged. "No one said you weren't. But we've looked out for you all our lives. Don't expect us to stop now."

Her heart sank. Of course they were looking out for her. Why else would they be here? Certainly not because they wanted hot, sweaty, monkey sex with her.

"I'm not a scared little girl anymore, Ryder," she said in a low voice.

He studied her for a long moment, his eyes probing her. "I think you *are* scared, Kit. And who could blame you? Someone attacked you. They hurt you."

She flinched and turned away. She and Ryder grew up in very similar situations. Rotten home life. Parents who didn't give a shit. Sometimes she thought he understood her better than anyone. They'd spent many a night with Mac out by the lake, hiding from the reality of what waited for them at home.

And then Mac and Ryder had gone away. She'd missed them terribly. When they'd returned home, she had every intention of resuming their easy friendship. Only she wanted more. She knew Ryder had the same view of relationships she did. No entanglements, no messy emotional upheavals. Sex between them should be easy. No strings. But she wasn't sure where Mac stood. Once she'd thought he wanted her every bit as much as she wanted him, but the attack changed everything. Including the way he and Ryder looked at her, and she couldn't stand it.

If she hadn't been so damn coy and stupid, she would have never found herself in the situation she had that night. It wasn't like her not to be straightforward, on the level, but she'd played a game of flirtation and hard to get, and she'd paid dearly for it.

"I don't like that look," Ryder said.

She glanced guiltily back up at him. "You shoving off?" she asked, desperate to change the subject.

He crooked his brow at her. "You trying to get rid of me?"

She sighed. "Look, it's sweet that you and Mac are hanging around so much, but it's not necessary. I'm sure you have other things you'd rather be doing. Some hot chick y'all haven't fucked yet."

She felt a warm hand slide over her bare shoulder. It sent a shiver down her spine, and her insides turned to jelly. Mac.

"Maybe the woman we want isn't ready for us," he murmured close to her ear.

She wet her lip nervously. She was tired of games. Tired of harmless flirting that didn't get them anywhere. She was tired of being scared.

"What does she have to do? Wave a sign with 'I want you' in big letters?"

"Or she could just tell us what she wants," Ryder spoke up.

"What if she's afraid?" Kit whispered.

"Afraid of what?" Mac demanded.

"Rejection?"

Mac put a finger under her chin and nudged her so she looked him in the eye. She loved the differences between him and Ryder. Ryder was dark and brooding, long hair, tattooed, earrings, a rebel in leather. Mac was a tall, muscled, gorgeous hunk of a man. His dirty blond hair was short and spiked, more often than not mussed. And when he wore his Stetson and boots, she wanted to lick every inch of his skin.

"Rejection?" His eyes bore into her. "Honey, the only reason I haven't hauled you home over my shoulder is because of what happened six months ago. I've tried to give you space. Time to heal. But I have to tell you, my patience is wearing thin. Rejection isn't an issue here. Your telling me what you want is."

Her mouth rounded to an O of shock. She swallowed, and for the first time felt the tingle of nervousness. Followed by a roll of desire. Her breasts ached from want. Need. This was it. All she had to do was reach out and take what she wanted. And she wanted them badly. She took a deep breath and went for it.

"I want *you*."

CHAPTER 2

*M*ac's eyes darkened. He curled his fingers around Kit's chin, and he rubbed his thumb up and down her jaw. "Be sure about this, Kit."

She let out a shaky breath. "I'm sure."

His lips were so close to hers now. She wanted to kiss him so badly she ached. He hovered over her for a second longer then slowly withdrew. His hand slid from her chin, and she was tempted to pull it back.

She glanced over at Ryder to gauge his reaction to her announcement. He stared back at her then cocked his eyebrow. She nodded in response to his unspoken question.

"My place. Tonight after work," Mac said.

Desire bloomed in her stomach. Her knees shook and heat rushed through her veins.

"I'll stay around until she gets off," Ryder spoke up.

Kit frowned. "I'll be fine, Ryder. I don't close up. Plenty of people will be here when I leave."

"You weren't supposed to close up *that* night either," Mac said quietly.

Her cheeks tightened as warmth flooded them. She knew all too well why she'd been so late that night.

"You better get a move on, honey," Rose said as she shoved by on her way to the bar. "Customers are starting to complain."

"I've got to go," Kit said. "But I'll see you guys after work."

She started to turn away, but Mac grasped her arm and pulled her to him. Before she could react, he tilted her head back and pressed his lips to hers. She opened her mouth in a gasp. It wasn't a light brush. It was a mark of possession.

Their tongues met and dueled, flitting forward then retreating. Blood pounded in her ears, shutting out the sounds around them.

He pulled away leaving her dazed, her lips swollen. He stroked her cheek with his hand. "I'll see *you* later."

She raised trembling fingers to her mouth as his hand dropped to his side. He retrieved his Stetson from a nearby table, clapped it on and walked toward the door.

Despite Kit's earlier protest, Ryder ambled back over to his table and sat down. Kit turned around to the bar, and for the life of her, she couldn't remember what the hell she was doing before all hell had broken loose.

"I took care of your orders," Rose said close to her ear. "But the natives are getting restless. Make the rounds. They want refills."

"Thanks, Rose."

Rose stopped and slid her a sideways smirk. " 'Bout time you lassoed that young hunk."

Kit worked to keep the smile from her face. She hadn't realized just how anxious she'd been over Mac and Ryder's reaction to her proclamation. She'd spent so much time skirting around the issue she'd worked herself into knots. After the fool she'd made of herself over that damn note, she'd sworn never again to play games.

She worked her way into the crowd, stopping at the tables and taking drink orders. Not even the fear that had hovered over her for the last six months would get her down tonight. In just a few hours, she'd be in the arms of the two people she trusted most in the world. The only people she trusted for that matter.

Two hours later, she took off her apron and dropped it behind the bar. "I'm outta here, David. You and Rose okay with closing tonight?"

He nodded and gave her a two-finger salute.

Kit looked across at Ryder, and her pulse began to race when he stood up and made his way toward her.

"You ready, darlin'?"

Her mouth went dry and her throat tightened. She wiped her hands over the back of her shorts and nodded.

"Do you need to go home first?"

"Yeah, but you don't need to follow me," she began.

He ignored her and gestured for her to precede him out of the bar. His Harley was parked close to the door, and he slung his leg over the bike. He planted his feet on the ground and knocked the kickstand back with his heel.

"I'll be behind you," he said.

She shook her head and walked over to her Bronco. She inserted the key in the door and froze. Her gaze fixed on the lock indicator. It was in the up position. The door wasn't locked.

She pulled the key from the lock. Her hands shook so badly she dropped the keys on the ground. Knowing Ryder was watching, she bent to pick them up then quickly opened the door.

Nausea seized her stomach when she saw the small piece of paper taped to her steering wheel. She whipped her head around. Was he here? Was he watching her right now?

She heard the roar of Ryder's Harley as he gunned the engine. Fumbling with the door, she slid into the seat and slammed it behind her. She jammed her hand down over the lock then looked over to make sure the passenger door was locked.

The white paper stared malevolently back at her. She reached for the switch to flip on the overhead light. Then her eyes settled on the scrawled words.

Have you forgotten that night already?

She swallowed back the rage that threatened to consume her. She yanked at the paper, balled it up in her fist and threw it at the windshield.

The keys rattled in her hand as she tried to start the ignition. Her left hand gripped the steering wheel until her fingers felt bloodless.

She forced herself to perform the motions of driving. She backed out of her parking space then pulled forward out of the lot. Ryder fell in behind her, and instead of being annoyed, she felt comforted by the single headlight in her rearview mirror.

The ten minutes to the small house she rented took forever. Her eyes never stilled. They darted from side-view mirror to rearview in rapid succession. Was he out there? Flashes of that night ricocheted in her head like a barrage of bullets.

I'm disappointed in you, Kit. I never thought you'd fall under their spell.

She shook her head to rid herself of the eerie voice.

She blinked and braked as she nearly passed her house. She took the turn too hard and ground to a halt, the tires skidding on the gravel. Ryder pulled in beside her and stared curiously at her.

She took a huge breath and stepped out of her Bronco, a wide smile plastered on her face. "I'll just be a minute," she said as she walked by Ryder.

"I like black underwear," he called out.

She didn't laugh at his humor. All her concentration was focused on getting in the house before she completely lost it. She wrenched open her door and slid her hand along the wall for the light switches. She hit them all, flooding the living room and hallway with light.

She dropped her purse on the couch then hurried to the bathroom. She winced at her reflection. No way could she face Mac and Ryder looking like this. Her face was pale, her eyes large and frightened. They'd know something was wrong in two seconds flat.

She threw water on her face and tried to even her breathing. The distant ringing of the phone pulled her up. Probably Mac making sure she got home okay. If she didn't answer, he'd worry.

She grabbed a hand towel and hurried to the kitchen as she wiped her face. She picked up the phone and said hello, priding herself on how calm she sounded.

A chill skirted up her spine as silence met her greeting.

"Hello? Mac, is that you?"

"You just don't learn do you, Kit?"

She opened her mouth to scream but nothing came out. Every muscle in her body shut down, paralyzing her. The raspy voice she'd heard so many times in her nightmares was back.

"What do you want?" she whispered. "Why are you doing this?"

"They can't have you, Kit. They won't love you like I do."

"Fuck off, you sick bastard!"

She slammed the phone down and backed away into the living room. She tripped over a pair of shoes lying on the floor and went sprawling. She reached for the edge of the sofa and hauled herself up on the cushions.

Oh God, she felt sick. She buried her face in her hands and rocked back and forth. She became aware of dim sobbing then realized *she* was making the noise.

The door opened, seemingly a mile away. She felt Ryder's hand on her shoulder. Then it left her, and she heard him a few seconds later.

"Mac, you better get over here. It's Kit."

The cushions sank beside her, and then she felt Ryder stroking her hair. A brief moment of panic hit her. Mac was on his way over. She'd have to tell them the *truth* about what happened that night.

CHAPTER 3

Mac roared into Kit's small driveway and hit the ground running. Ryder's phone call had scared the hell out of him. He could hear Kit's sobbing in the background. What the fuck had happened?

He bounded up the steps and threw open the door. Ryder looked up from the couch where he sat by Kit. His heart lurched when he took in Kit's tearstained face. Her arms were wrapped around her waist, her eyes vacant and afraid. He was immediately transported to that night six months ago when he'd found her outside the bar.

He forced himself to relax his clenched fists as rage washed over him all over again. He strode forward and went to his knees in front of Kit.

To his surprise, she threw herself into his arms, burying her face in his neck. He held her tightly against him, threading his hands into her hair.

He looked up at Ryder, but Ryder shook his head and shrugged.

Kit held onto him tightly. She was scared out of her mind. A fact he didn't like at all.

He pried her away from his neck and slid his hand over her cheek. "Kit, what's wrong? What happened?"

"I'm such an idiot," she whispered.

A tear slid down her cheek and collided with his fingers. He wiped it away but another tracked down in its place.

Unease ran circles in his chest. "Does this have to do with what we planned?"

She shook her head.

"Then tell me, Kit. What's going on?"

"He called me," she choked out.

"Who called you, darlin'?" Ryder asked.

She turned her face up, misery etched in the lines around her eyes. *"Him."*

Mac struggled to make sense of just who *he* was. Dread settled into his chest as he thought of the one person who could possibly make her this afraid.

"The man who attacked you?" he demanded.

Ryder jerked his head toward Mac as if he didn't believe it either.

She nodded.

Mac shook his head. "I don't understand. Has he called you before?"

She raised her eyes to meet his then slowly nodded again.

All the air left his lungs. He gaped at her incredulously. "And you didn't tell me?"

"I couldn't," she whispered.

Ryder sat back down on the couch beside Kit, and Mac rocked back on his heels, stunned by her announcement.

"You couldn't tell me? Why the hell not? Kit, this isn't something you can fuck around with. We assumed when we had no leads that it was some sick fuck passing through, and now you're telling me he knows enough about you that he's stalking you? That you weren't some random victim he happened on?"

The look on her face was all the answer he needed. He stared at her in shock.

"Why wouldn't you *tell* me, Kit?"

"What is it we're not seeing?" Ryder spoke up. "There's more to this than just you not telling us about this asshole."

She closed her eyes and twisted her hands in her lap. "It is . . . was someone close to me, or at least someone who knows me well."

"You *know* who did this to you?" Mac demanded.

She shook her head vehemently. "No. That's just it. I can't imagine who did it."

"Then how do you know it's someone close to you?" Mac prodded.

Her eyes flashed guiltily, and Mac knew she'd been holding back a lot more from him. That bothered him. Bothered him a lot. Kit had never had any problem confiding in him or Ryder, and by the shell-shocked look on Ryder's face, Mac knew he was just as much in the dark as Mac.

"Spill it, Kit. What the fuck is going on? What haven't you told me?"

She stood up, holding her arms around her waist in a protective manner. She paced several feet away then turned to face him and Ryder again. Mac rose to his feet and waited for her to talk.

He wasn't used to Kit looking so vulnerable. She looked positively fragile, and before six months ago, he would've sworn she didn't have a fragile bone in her body. Maybe he took her strength for granted. It wasn't a mistake he'd be making again.

She opened her mouth then wet her lips. Indecision was written on her face. Whatever it was she had to tell him had her tied up in knots. What could be worse than finding her huddled in a ball on the ground, half naked, her voice gone from screaming? He wasn't sure he wanted to find out.

He moved toward her, wanting only to comfort her, but she backed away. He gave her the space and stepped back to stand beside Ryder.

"I feel like such a fool," she said huskily. "I brought it all on myself. If I hadn't been such an idiot. If I would have just come out and told you both what I wanted."

Mac frowned. She wasn't making any sense. He glanced at Ryder to see if he was getting it any better, but Ryder looked equally baffled.

She turned and walked to the desk that sat by the window. She pulled open the drawer and rifled through the contents for a minute before she pulled out a napkin.

She smoothed the edges with shaking fingers then looked up at them both. "The night . . . the night I was attacked, Ryder had been to the bar early. But he had a job at the garage he had to finish so he only stayed a few minutes."

Ryder nodded. "I remember."

"And you had to work," she said to Mac.

Mac waited for her to continue.

She looked down again at the napkin in her hand. "We'd all been flirting. Playing a silly game of cat and mouse. I was being all coy. Wouldn't just come out and say I wanted you. After Ryder left, I found this on the bar where he'd been standing."

She held out the napkin, her hand shaking like a leaf.

Mac took the napkin and Ryder surged forward to get a look too.

Mac stared at the words, not believing what he saw. Ryder sucked in his breath beside him and let it out in a long hiss.

"Oh, darlin', tell me this isn't why you were at the bar so late," Ryder said.

"I thought you wrote it," she said in a choked voice.

Mac looked down again, his stomach tight with nausea.

Wait for us after work, darlin. Mac and I'll swing by and pick you up. Time for us to quit all this flirting and get to the point.

"Jesus Christ," Mac swore. "The bastard set you up."

Ryder put his hand out to Kit, regret plastered all over his face. "Kit. My God, I don't even know what to say."

She flinched away. "This is why I didn't tell you. I don't want your pity."

Mac exploded. "Goddamn it, Kit, we're not offering you pity. I'm pissed as hell that someone would use us against you."

He almost crumpled the napkin in his hand then stopped cold. "Kit, this is evidence and you kept it from me. What else have you concealed?"

She looked at him with pain-filled eyes. "He's left me a few notes. Called a few times."

Mac fought to control his fury. All this time he thought the fear he saw in Kit on a daily basis was all due to the attack. Now he realized it was because she continued to live in terror. The bastard wouldn't leave her alone. And he was someone who knew her, and him, very well.

"Do you have those notes?" Mac demanded.

"Only the one from tonight," she said quietly.

"Tonight?" Ryder inserted.

"In my truck. I locked it before I went in to work. When I came out, it was unlocked. There was a note on the steering wheel."

"Is that why you were acting so all-fired jumpy in the parking lot?" Ryder demanded.

"Jumpy?" Mac asked. He lifted a brow in surprise. Ryder was a man of few words, but once he got riled, he didn't mind flinging them around.

"Yeah, she dropped her keys, was acting all weird right before we left."

"Where's the note, Kit?" Mac asked softly.

"It's in the Bronco. I wadded it up."

"How many have there been?"

She shrugged. "Three or four. Most right after the attack. I thought . . . " Her voice cracked. "I thought he'd given up. It's been three months since the last note or phone call."

Ryder swore long and hard. Kit winced as the expletives cracked the air. Mac didn't feel any better.

"Why didn't you just tell us, baby?"

The question hovered in the air. Perhaps the most important question in all of this. Why hadn't she trusted them, come to them right from the start?

A dull flush worked its way across her cheeks. "When I realized Ryder hadn't written the note . . . I'd made such a fool of myself—" She broke off and looked away. "He said things. He knew I was interested in you two. He taunted me with the fact you didn't return that interest. Told me I was making an ass of myself, that I was a whore, and that he wouldn't stand by and let me throw myself at you two."

Mac stared at her in horror. Then he looked up, his mouth open. Beside him Ryder swore again.

"He hurt you because of us," Mac finally managed to get out. The words had stuck in his throat. The bastard had gone after her because of him and Ryder. He wanted to goddamn puke his guts up.

He grabbed Kit and yanked her to him. He wrapped his arms around her and held her as tightly as he could. Her heart pounded against his chest, her body quivered, and he wanted to fucking howl in rage.

"Jesus, baby, I'm so sorry. I'm so goddamn sorry."

Her arms crept around him, holding onto him as her body shook against him.

"Who would do this?" Ryder growled.

Mac looked over at his friend. Ryder's face was dark with anger, his expression menacing. As many years as they'd spent protecting Kit, they'd failed her when she'd needed them most. That was one thing that wasn't going to happen again.

"Get some clothes together, whatever you need from here," Mac said above her head. "You're going to my place."

She stiffened slightly and pulled away. "You make it sound like it's more than just tonight."

"You guess right," he said. "You're not staying here with that sick fuck out there waiting for you. You'll stay with me, and if I can't be there, Ryder will stay."

He looked to Ryder for confirmation. Ryder, usually the most easygoing of the group, nodded, his face set into a hard mask.

"I just don't know how he knew," she whispered. "How did he know it was tonight?"

"Hell, anyone in the bar knew after Mac kissed you," Ryder pointed out.

Mac pressed his lips together. He was seething on the inside. By laying claim to Kit for God and the world to see, he'd made her a target. Again.

Well, that was fine. He didn't give a shit who knew that she was his. From now on, the whole goddamn town could know it, because the sooner the bastard who'd attacked her realized it, the sooner he'd realize just how badly he'd fucked up by hurting Kit.

"You're mine, Kit," he murmured as he pulled her into his arms again. "And I protect what's mine."

CHAPTER 4

*K*it splashed water onto her face and dabbed at her cheeks with a towel. After wiping her eyes, she picked her head up and looked into the mirror. She still looked like hell.

With a sigh, she dropped the towel on the counter. She shrugged out of her clothes and turned on the shower. Maybe a full run under the water would alleviate some of the fear that seemed engraved in her eyes.

She eyed the duffel bag she'd hurriedly packed, then plucked out clean underwear, a T-shirt and a pair of shorts while she waited for the water to heat.

Despite Mac's clear-cut order that she stay with him indefinitely, the mere thought gave her the hives. It was too close to a semblance of a relationship for her comfort level. She'd stay until she was sure it was safe, but she had no intention of making it long term. They may never catch her attacker, and hiding forever wasn't in her game plan.

She stepped into the hot spray and closed her eyes as the heat rushed over her. Already, she felt ridiculous for losing control in front of Mac and Ryder. No wonder they looked scared to death. Emotional breakdowns weren't in character for her.

She scrubbed her hair, every inch of her skin. The attacker's touch was fresh in her memory, brought to the surface by hearing his scratchy voice, remembering the taunts he'd thrown at her as she lay helpless beneath him.

Another tear rolled down her cheek, shocking her. She swiped the back of her hand over her eye and shook her head angrily. She had to get it together. The guys were waiting in Mac's living room, and unless she could convince them she was okay, they'd hover over her forever.

She turned her face up into the spray and let the water run over her for several long minutes. Finally, she reached for the knobs and turned the shower off.

She hurriedly dried off and pulled her clothes on. She didn't bother blow-drying her hair, opting to run a towel over it and give it a quick comb-through.

With nervous bubbles scuttling around in her stomach, she left the bathroom and eased her way into the living room where Mac and Ryder sat waiting for her.

They looked her way as she stepped into the room, concern mirrored in their eyes. Her heart sank. This wasn't the way she'd envisioned her evening going. They were supposed to be having mind-blowing sex, and instead she'd been forced to come clean and humiliate herself.

"Are you all right?" Mac asked gently.

She nodded with more confidence than she felt. She walked over to the couch where Ryder sat and plopped down beside him. Ryder wrapped an arm around her and pulled her against him. She rested her cheek on his hard chest and glanced nervously at Mac.

She had purposely taken refuge in Ryder. There was something in Mac's eyes, in his earlier statements that screamed a warning to her. Even now, his gaze slid possessively over her as if staking his claim.

Yes, Ryder was safe. Mac . . . was not.

Mac sighed and ran a hand though his short cropped hair. Kit was running from him sure as shootin'. Oh, she wanted him. He had no doubt of that, but she was trying to hide from what they both knew to be true. She was his.

He tried to muster irritation that she was wrapped so sweetly around Ryder, but he knew she was scared. Ryder was safe and comfortable to her, and Mac didn't want to ruin that.

"Ryder and I have talked. One of us is going to be at the bar with you at all times."

Kit's eyes flared in surprise, and she raised her head from Ryder's chest. "But you can't do that. I have to work five nights a week. You guys both have jobs."

"We'll work around your schedule," Mac said firmly.

Kit sat forward, her face drawn into a cloud of confusion and anger.

"I won't let that creep run my life, and I certainly won't let him upend yours and Ryder's."

"Hey now, darlin'," Ryder said as he leaned forward beside her. "You can't fuss because Mac and I want to look out for you. We've been doing it too long for you to get all riled about it now."

She turned vivid green eyes on Ryder. They were chock-full of things Mac didn't like. He wanted Kit to sparkle. She'd had too many moments in life where she'd lived in fear or sadness.

"But that's just it, Ryder. You guys have been looking out for me too long. It's time I did it myself. I did just fine when you both left."

The hurt in her voice twisted Mac's gut. He knew she'd felt betrayed when he and Ryder had left the town they all grew up in, Mac to join the service, and Ryder to roam the country.

It still surprised him that Ryder came back. But Mac, well, he always knew he was coming back for Kit. If he had to do it all over again, he'd have taken her with him.

"I'm not leaving again, Kit," Mac said quietly.

She flinched and refused to meet his gaze.

Ryder laid a hand on Kit's knee. "Mac and I have it worked out. One way or another, one of us will be at the bar when you're working, and when you aren't working, you'll be here."

"I can't stay here," she said. "I have a house. My life."

"Relax, darlin'. It's not like we weren't planning to be spending a whole lot of time together anyway, right?"

Kit flushed, her cheeks turning pink. She stole a look at Mac and flushed all over again. It was all Mac could do not to carry her to bed here and now.

Mac held her gaze, meeting her eye to eye. "Have you changed your mind?"

Indecision briefly flickered and skirted across her face. She licked her lips nervously, then she slowly shook her head. "No," she whispered.

"Then it shouldn't be a big deal if we want to be around you. As long as you're in my bed, I'll be damned if I let anyone take a shot at you."

He didn't add that he planned to keep her there on a permanent basis. She'd run like a scalded cat if she got so much as a hint he wanted something more than a casual fling.

"And when it's over?" she asked quietly. "What then?"

Ryder raised one eyebrow in Mac's direction. A clear warning to tread carefully.

"By then we'll have nailed the son of a bitch. But baby, surely you don't think one night is all we're interested in, do you?" he asked silkily.

She glanced between Mac and Ryder almost in panic.

"We've waited a long time for this, Kit. One night won't even begin to satisfy our needs."

"I'll stay. Temporarily," she added.

Mac nodded and fought back his smile of triumph. It was a step in the right direction at least. "We'll head over to your place tomorrow to pick up anything you might need. In the meantime, why don't you get some rest?"

She looked surprised, as if she'd expected something else all together.

He crooked an eyebrow at her. "Surely you didn't think we'd jump your bones tonight?"

She nibbled on her bottom lip. Obviously she had.

Mac sighed. "Don't get me wrong, babe. All I've thought about is peeling every piece of your clothing off and licking every inch of your skin, but not tonight. You're in no state for what we want to do."

He could swear disappointment flashed across those green eyes of hers. He smiled to himself. Maybe one more night would have her wanting and needing them every bit as much as he needed her.

She sat there in silence for several long seconds. The awkwardness was thick between the three of them. Mac shifted in an attempt to alleviate the strain.

Finally, Kit's lips thinned and she stood up, hands on her hips. "Look. If us having sex is going to cause so much goddamn tension, then I vote we hang up the idea and call it good."

Ryder chuckled. "Always blunt and to the point, darlin'. That's what I love about you."

"Can't we kick back and watch some TV? Isn't there a fight on tonight? God, anything but this sitting around staring at each other like a bunch of deer in the headlights."

Mac relaxed into a smile. "I'll get us a couple of beers out of the fridge."

He trudged into the kitchen and retrieved three bottles from the refrigerator, grabbed a bag of chips then headed back into the living room where the others were.

"I'm gonna go take a quick shower and change out of my work clothes," he said as he handed Kit and Ryder their beers. "I'll be out shortly."

Once in the bathroom, he turned on the water, sliding the knob over to its coldest setting. His zipper was putting a permanent tattoo on his dick, and it was getting damn uncomfortable. He'd been rock hard ever since Kit entered the living room.

He stepped under the cold spray and winced as it sluiced over his body. He closed his eyes and tried to calm the rage that had settled into his mind like a long-lost companion.

Whether Kit knew it or not, tonight marked a ninety-degree turn in their otherwise casual relationship. He was tired of teasing, joking and innuendo, and he was sure as hell tired of sleeping in an empty bed.

He finished quickly and toweled off. He flexed tired muscles, trying to work the knots of tension from his shoulders. He'd been one gigantic pretzel ever since leaving Kit's house.

He pulled on a T-shirt and a pair of gym shorts then scrubbed the dampness from his hair with the towel. He ran a quick hand through the spiky length just to make it lay down right then headed to join Ryder and Kit in the living room.

When Mac entered the room, Kit's breath left her body as if someone had landed a punch to her stomach. God, the man was one sexy beast. He padded over to the couch in bare feet and flopped down beside her.

He reached forward to pluck his beer off the coffee table before leaning back and propping his feet up. He glanced sideways at her for a moment before placing an arm behind her shoulders.

"Come here," he directed, pulling her against his chest.

She didn't resist and soon found herself absorbing his scent as she burrowed deeper into his body. Her gaze flitted downward to the juncture of his legs. She'd have to be blind to miss his hard-on.

Her hands itched to touch him, to take his length in her hands and caress him. How would he taste? As sexy as he looked and smelled, she'd bet her next paycheck.

"Sugar, if you don't quit staring at me that way, we're never going to make it like this."

The words rumbled out of his chest, vibrating against her ear. Her cheeks warmed, but she smiled as she saw his cock swell even larger, straining against his shorts.

She grinned impishly, the devil taking over. She slid her hand over the solid wall of muscle on his chest, down toward his taut abdomen. The man was built like a brick wall.

Her hand drifted lower.

"Kit," Mac warned.

She ignored him and slipped her fingers into the waistband of his shorts. Hmmm. No underwear. His crisp curls tickled her palm as she delved lower.

"Kit, for God's sake," Mac said in a strained voice.

His rock-hard erection flinched in reaction when her hand curled around it. His shorts had to go.

She moved off the couch and settled between Mac's legs. Without looking once into his eyes, she pulled at his shorts. She smiled a tiny smile when he raised his hips to aid her.

God, the man was built for pleasure. A woman's pleasure. His cock jutted upward, straining and swollen. She cupped her hands around the base, stroking upward in gentle motions.

Out of the corner of her eye, she saw Ryder watching them intently, desire glittering in his dark eyes. He'd shoved closer once Kit had gotten out of her place. If the bulge in his jeans was any indication, he was as turned on as Mac was.

She continued the slow up and down movements of her hands, then she leaned forward, letting her hair fall across Mac's thighs.

With only a little hesitation, she slid her mouth down the length of his penis, sucking him against the back of her throat.

Mac let out a long hiss. He thrust a hand in her hair, gathering it away from her face. His fingers ran gently over her cheek, stroking the skin before delving deeper into her hair.

"God, baby, that feels so good."

Encouraged by his approval, she picked up her pace, sliding her lips up and down his length. She cupped his balls in her hands, squeezing and massaging as she sucked him deeper into her mouth.

His hips began arching to meet her, and his hand tightened in her hair as he held her in place to meet his thrusts.

"Kit, you gotta stop or I'm going to come."

His words came out breathless, edged with lust and need.

She pulled away, and for the first time, met his gaze head on. "I want you, Mac. It took me long enough to say it, but I'm saying it now. I don't want to wait. I'm not some fragile piece of glass that'll break if you touch it."

She turned her head to Ryder so he'd know he was included in her declaration. His dark eyes probed her. He reached out a hand to cup her chin, and he rubbed his thumb over her bottom lip.

"Darlin', if you'll run that sweet mouth of yours over my dick like you did Mac's, I'll give you damn near anything you want."

His words sent sharp tingles of need straight to her pussy.

"Then you'd better get those pants off," she directed.

CHAPTER 5

*K*it sat back on her heels and watched in appreciation as Ryder pulled his shirt over his head. His muscles rippled across his abdomen. He tossed the shirt aside then began unbuttoning his jeans.

He peeled them down his hips, and Kit quivered as his cock sprang into view. He stood before her, a wild thing, all hard muscle and badass attitude. His dark hair curled wildly at his shoulders, and she itched to dive into it with her hands, wrap the strands around fingers as he fucked her.

Ryder stepped forward, a clear invitation for her to taste him. Using Mac's leg to brace herself, she rocked forward until she was on her knees in front of Ryder.

She reached up with one hand and circled the rigid cock just an inch from her lips. Slowly, teasingly, she wet her lips and gently tucked the head into her mouth.

Ryder groaned above her. "Easy darlin'."

She sucked him farther into her mouth, sliding her tongue over the vein down the back of his penis. Light sucking noises filled the room as she took him in and out.

Mac took her hand from his knee and guided it to his own cock. She curled her fingers around the base and let him ease her hand up and down with his.

Ryder's hands tangled in her hair, holding her tightly as he began moving in and out of her mouth. Then Mac cupped her chin and guided her gently away from Ryder. Mac leaned back against the couch and urged her back to his straining erection.

"You have too many clothes on, darlin'."

Ryder's hands skimmed over her back, shoving her shirt up and unclasping her bra. She closed her eyes and sucked Mac's dick deep inside her mouth. Warm, firm hands slid over her bare skin, around to her breasts.

Mac pulled her away, then Ryder urged her to her feet. Mac stood up so that they flanked Kit. Four hands reached for her shirt and shorts, pulling, peeling until she stood naked before them.

"You are every bit as beautiful as I imagined," Mac said huskily.

She closed her eyes and leaned into his arms. How she loved their strength, the raw power that exuded from them in waves. Here, between them, she felt safe. Protected.

"We're going to take you to bed, Kit. Do you want that? Do you want what's about to happen?" Mac asked.

She opened her eyes and found her lips hovering a heartbeat from Mac's. "I want you to kiss me," she whispered. "Like you did in the bar."

His hands cupped her face, and he leaned down to capture her lips in a hot embrace. "I'm going to kiss you, baby. And a whole lot more. Before this night's over with, there isn't a place on you that won't have felt my lips."

Kit shivered and went limp against him. How his voice had the power to rob her of all strength she didn't know, but she was a mass of jelly.

Ryder's hands gripped her hips and pulled her back against his chest. His large arms encircled her body. She leaned her head into the curve of his neck to give him better access to whatever parts of her body he wanted to explore.

One hand palmed her breast. The other hand slid down her belly to the quivering flesh between her legs. He slid his fingers into the soft folds of her pussy, parting them as he stroked a finger over her clit.

Her body jolted as waves of electric pleasure snaked through her lower body.

"I love that your pussy is bare," Mac growled. "So soft and pretty. Did you do this for us, Kit?"

She swallowed and nodded. Yeah, she knew their predilection for shaved pussies. She'd heard their rowdy talk enough to know precisely what it was they liked in their women.

Mac leaned in to kiss her again, his body meshing against hers, pushing her further into Ryder. Then he stepped back long enough to pull his shirt over his head and toss it aside.

"Time to go to the bedroom," Mac said.

Ryder let his hands fall down her body. Mac reached for her, pulling her close then lifting her into his arms. Ryder walked ahead of them, flipping the light on in Mac's bedroom. Mac carried her through the doorway and laid her gently on the bed.

She gazed up at the two men who stood over her, two hulking, prime specimens of manhood, and tonight they were all hers. Damned if she wasn't going to make the most of it.

"I've wanted to taste you all night," Mac murmured as he crawled between her legs.

A full body shiver took over her as Mac spread the folds of her pussy with gentle fingers. The bed dipped beside her as Ryder spread out next to her. His fingers chased the chill up her belly to her breasts as Mac's lips kissed the soft flesh between her legs.

"You're beautiful, darlin'. We've waited a long time for this."

She closed her eyes and threw back her head as Mac's tongue delved deeper. Her clit quivered and shook as his tongue traced lazy circles around the taut peak. His fingers sank lazily into her cunt, sliding in and out with exquisite care.

Ryder's warm breath blew over one nipple just as he sucked it between his teeth. She bucked and writhed as the two mouths performed delicate surgery on her body.

Mac spread her legs wider, baring her completely to the two men's view. He pressed a tender kiss to her clit before sliding his big body up her abdomen and settling his hips over hers.

Ryder rolled to the side, his hand tangled in Kit's hair. Mac reached between them, grasped his cock in his hand and guided it toward her waiting pussy.

Kit's breath caught in her throat as Mac probed her entrance with the head of his cock. She moaned low in her throat and twisted restlessly. She wanted him inside her, a part of her.

Slowly, reverently almost, he slid into her. Her body welcomed him like a long lost part of her. His frame encompassed her, covered every inch of her as his hips surged against hers. She was stretched to her limits, her body seeking to accommodate what he demanded of her.

"Move with me," Mac whispered as he bucked forward, seating himself deeper.

She wrapped her leg around his hips, holding him tightly. She arched her body into him as his cock came to rest against her cervix. It was hard to breathe. She struggled to control the overwhelming tide of pleasure. It threatened to consume her, and she didn't want to let go yet. She wanted it to last.

Mac gathered her in his arms, held her tight as he sank into her again and again. Every muscle in his body tightened until he felt like stone against her. Then he pulled away, withdrawing from her.

She cried out in protest, reaching for him. But then Ryder covered her, and her pulse sped up all over again. Ryder was more impatient than Mac. He spread her legs in one swift motion and thrust into her.

Unlike Mac, Ryder gripped her hips in his hands, knelt between her legs, pumping into her with greater force and speed. Mac fused his mouth to hers as Ryder filled her again and again. Mac's hand drifted down her belly. His finger found her clit as Ryder withdrew. He began to manipulate the throbbing bead as Ryder picked up his pace.

"Oh . . . " Her voice gave out in an unintelligible gasp.

"That's it darlin'," Ryder encouraged. "Let it go."

Noooo. She didn't want it to end. Not yet. But her release started a slow crawl as she ascended the peak.

Ryder thrust harder. Mac continued the rapid circular motion of her clit. His mouth dropped from her lips to suck at first one nipple, then the other.

Kit squeezed her eyes shut and let out a high keening wail. Her belly exploded in pleasure. Fireworks went off around her. She bucked underneath the men but Ryder's hands never left her hips. Mac held her tightly. He murmured encouragement, words she didn't understand in her ear as the world swirled around her.

Finally, she sagged, her body coming off the tight spin. She sank into the covers, her muscles as limp as a bowl of overcooked pasta.

Ryder leaned over her and kissed her tenderly on the forehead. Only then did she register that he was still embedded deeply within her, and still very hard.

He pulled away, shifting his weight off her. She focused her bleary vision on him trying to understand why he and Mac had both quit before they'd reached their orgasm.

Mac chuckled lightly in her ear as if he'd heard her unspoken question. "The night is still young, babe."

She shifted, turning on her side to cuddle into Mac's arms. Ryder slid behind her until she was cradled between him and Mac.

"Rest a minute, darlin'," Ryder murmured. "Because then it starts all over again."

CHAPTER 6

$\mathcal{K}$it awoke to warm lips nuzzling her breast. She blinked sleepily, enjoying the feeling of complete and utter peace that enveloped her. Soft light poured from the bedside lamp, bathing their naked bodies in warmth.

Ryder's hand rested on her hip, and he squeezed lightly as he kissed the back of her neck. Mac sucked at her nipples until she moaned softly in response.

"You're awake," Ryder said.

Mac didn't take his head from her breasts. He sucked harder, alternating between the tips. He grazed the stiff peaks with his teeth as he sucked hotly.

Kit wrapped her arm around Mac's shoulders, running her hand to the back of his neck. Her fingers brushed through his short hair as she pulled him closer to her chest.

The bed swayed as Ryder sat up. Kit looked at him over her shoulder when he rose and walked to the dresser a few feet away.

"Where you keep the condoms, bro?" Ryder asked.

Kit frowned slightly. "I'm on birth control," she said in a low voice.

Ryder turned dark eyes on her, staring intently. Mac's lips stilled, her nipple on his tongue.

"You not want me to wear a condom, darlin'?"

"No, I mean unless you think you should?"

"I've never gone bareback with a woman. You'd be the first."

"Mine too," Mac whispered against her breast.

"I trust you," she said. They were the only people she trusted. Then another thought occurred to her, and embarrassment rolled hot over her cheeks. "Unless you want to wear one because of . . . because of what happened," she finished quietly.

Mac's hand tightened around her waist. Anger flashed in Ryder's eyes.

Mac slid his hand up to cup her chin, forcing her to look at him. "You had all the tests, Kit. You checked out fine. We're not afraid of you. We're just trying to protect you. You're the only woman I've even considered not wearing condoms with. It's your call."

She looked back at Ryder then shook her head. "I don't want them. Not with you. I trust you both."

Ryder slid back onto the bed and spooned against her back. He rubbed his hand over her hip and up to her breasts. "Kit, we don't think any less of you for what happened, and if I ever find the bastard who hurt you, I'm going to kill him."

The promise lay heavy over them. No dramatics from Ryder. He wasn't the dramatic type. He meant business. She shivered, knowing Ryder would indeed kill her attacker. She imagined the same thought was running through Mac's head even though he remained quiet. Too quiet.

She'd seen the look of rage in his eyes that night. Violence had blown like an out-of-control fire through his big body. She'd known in that moment that cop or no cop, Mac would have foregone the very laws he'd sworn to uphold. It was one of the many reasons she hadn't told him about the stalking.

She sighed, feeling a little deflated. Since the attack, Mac and Ryder *had* treated her differently. She just wanted to go back to the way things were before. They were careful around her now. Quieter. As if the attack had changed them as much as it had her.

Mac fingered a lock of her hair. He'd pulled his head up until he was eye level with her. His blue eyes blazed with a multitude of emotions.

"I can pretty much guarantee I won't like whatever it is you're thinking right now."

She smiled. "I'd rather not be thinking at all."

Mac stared into her eyes for a long moment before he slowly lowered his head to hers. His lips touched her lips. Gently at first. So tenderly she wanted to cry. Then he deepened the kiss, sliding his tongue over hers.

"Don't wear those lips out," Ryder said. "I have plans for that sweet mouth."

Kit smiled as Mac grumbled.

"Ride me, Kit?" Mac asked.

He stretched to his full length beside her, turning flat on his back. Her gaze wandered down his chest to where his swollen cock lay against his stomach.

Ryder helped her up, his hands drifting over her skin as she threw one leg over Mac's body. She reached between them, grasped Mac's heavy erection in her hand and positioned it at her pussy entrance.

She closed her eyes as she sank down onto him. Mac emitted a long hiss of air. His hands gripped her hips, holding her down against his body.

"You feel so damn good, Kit."

She opened her eyes to see Ryder stretched on the bed beside her and Mac, his hand sliding up and down his cock as he watched Kit fuck Mac. She held his gaze as she began riding Mac. Then she threw back her head, struggling to breathe as her stomach tightened unbearably.

Mac shifted beneath her, rotating their bodies. She opened her eyes as Mac turned until his legs hung over the side of the bed. Ryder moved from the bed to stand behind her. His hands splayed over her back, pushing her toward Mac.

She understood the command and leaned into Mac. Mac wrapped his arms around her, holding her against his chest as he continued to thrust between her legs.

Ryder stepped between Mac's legs and palmed her buttocks in his large hands. Kit nearly came right there. She knew what was next. Shards of pleasure cut into her abdomen, tightened her pussy until she gripped Mac's cock so tightly, he moaned in pleasure.

Ryder's cock butted against the tight seam of her ass. She trembled in Mac's arms.

"Easy, baby," Mac whispered. His hands soothed up and down her body. "Relax. Let us do all the work."

The head of Ryder's cock pushed forward until she felt the tight muscle give way under his persistence. He paused, giving her body time to adjust to his invasion. Then he sank all the way into her.

She bolted forward in Mac's arms, her body as tight as a bow at full draw. Two cocks deeply embedded within her. She felt full, engorged, and never had she experienced such pleasure in her life. She danced a fine line between pain and ecstasy. Her vision swam as she tried to process the barrage of sensations that pelted her.

The two men began to move, alternating thrusts, in a rhythm she knew they were familiar with. Oh yeah, they'd had plenty of practice taking the same woman.

Ryder's hands gripped her waist, aiding her movement as the two men pumped in and out of her. Mac tangled his fingers in her hair, pulling her down to meet his demanding kiss.

This time neither man stopped as they had before. She could feel them tense as they neared their release. Her body was doing its own rapid climb up a very steep hill.

She panted, trying desperately to squeeze more oxygen into her burning lungs. She was running. She was flying. She was hurtling out of a plane in a ninety-mile-an-hour freefall.

"That's it baby, let go. Just let go."

Mac's voice seemed a mile away. But she grabbed on tight and held on just as her body exploded with the force of an atomic bomb.

Ryder surged forward, burying himself deep into her ass. His entire body trembled and shook against her. Then Mac stiffened beneath her, bucked up, trying to find his way deeper into her pussy. They met in a powerful tangle of bodies. Hot jets of semen rushed into her body.

She heard someone cry out then realized it was her. She collapsed onto Mac's chest, holding him as tight as she could. Hot tears rolled down her cheeks, spilling onto Mac's skin.

She was dimly aware of Ryder easing from her then of him wiping her sensitive skin with a cloth. She lay limply over Mac, his cock still buried in her pussy.

Mac kissed her temple and ran his fingers tenderly over her cheek.

"I'm gonna go jump in the shower," Ryder rumbled behind her.

Mac nodded and continued stroking over her face. He rolled her over and gently withdrew from between her legs.

"Are you all right?"

She nodded, not certain she was capable of speech. She burrowed deeper into Mac's arms and closed her eyes.

A few minutes later she heard Ryder walk back into the room. He bent over the bed, his head close to her ear. "You all right, Kit? I wasn't too rough, was I?"

Kit smiled. "No, in fact if you two treated me with any more care, you'd have to unwrap me from a wad of cellophane."

"Want to jump in the shower with me?" Mac asked.

She sighed. "I'm not sure I can move."

He chuckled. "I'll take care of the moving."

Mac rolled out of bed then bent and picked her up. He carried her into the bathroom and set her on the counter. The mirrors were fogged from Ryder's shower, and the air hung warm over her.

Mac leaned in to turn the water on, then he collected her in his arms. The warm spray sent a groan of pleasure straight out of her throat.

He gently soaped her body and rinsed the suds from her skin. Kit stood there as he took care of her, marveling at this puzzling side of Mac.

She wasn't used to him being so tender. So utterly gentle. In all the years she'd known Mac and Ryder, neither one of them had ever been the sensitive type. They were too busy being badasses.

Honestly, she'd expected hot, rough, scorch-the-sheets sex, and what she'd gotten was . . . Well, she wasn't sure she wanted to dwell on the feelings their lovemaking had elicited.

Lovemaking. Just the fact she was calling sex some frilly, girly moniker was a huge warning sign.

Mac turned off the shower and stepped out. He reached back in for her, a towel in his other hand. Soon she was wrapped in a fluffy towel. She stood for a moment while Mac dried himself off, and she took the opportunity to admire the work of art that was his body.

Muscles rippled across his back as he slid the towel over his shoulders. His legs, long, thick, leading up to the tightest ass she'd ever seen on a guy. Not one ounce of fat marred his body. She knew he worked out daily, but damn, nothing could have prepared her for the reality of his physique up close and personal.

Unable to resist, she moved closer and ran her hand over his ass. He turned around, a wicked gleam in his eye.

"I'd much rather that hand be here," he said, guiding it to his semi-aroused cock.

His flesh was still slightly damp. She curled her hand around the thick base and slowly pumped up and down.

"Are you two going to fuck in the bathroom or what?" Ryder called from the bedroom.

Kit laughed. She dropped the towel and walked past Mac into the bedroom. Ryder was on the bed, sprawled on his back, his hand curled around his cock.

His eyes gleamed in the lamplight. "Come over here, darlin'. I want to sample that pretty mouth of yours again."

Mac's hand slid over her bare ass as he walked up behind her. She smiled at Ryder and sauntered over to the edge of the bed. She crawled onto the covers and slowly made her way between his legs.

"Don't tease," Ryder said in a strained voice. "Just wrap those lips around my dick before I come all unglued."

Instead of complying, she bent her head and ran her tongue slowly up the length of his shaft. His hips bucked and jerked as she reached the tip, and she closed her mouth around it.

"Take it deep," he said raggedly.

She sank her mouth down until she could take no more. She paused then slowly slid her lips upward again.

Ryder moaned. "Goddamn, woman. You're killing me!"

She wrapped her fingers around the base of his cock and began working her hand up and down as her mouth followed suit.

Ryder's hands plunged into her hair, gripping her tightly. He held her as he bucked his hips, fucking her mouth with urgency. He trembled beneath her, and the first jet of cum hit the back of her throat. She swallowed and took more of him until finally he went limp against the bed.

His hands stroked through her hair, smoothing it from her face.

She looked up to see him staring at her with lust-filled eyes, their dark orbs brimming with approval.

"It's your turn, darlin', and don't think I won't enjoy every minute of it."

Kit's mouth went dry. Behind her, Mac put his hands on her shoulders and eased her backward. She let him control the flow of her movement until she was flat on her back, her head dangling over the edge of the bed.

His cock nudged her lips, and she opened her mouth to accept him. The position seemed awkward at first, but she was at the perfect level for Mac to fuck her mouth, and he did so with gentle strokes.

Ryder spread her legs and ran his fingers lightly over the folds of her pussy. His tongue flicked over her tight bud, and she jerked in reaction.

He spread her wider and delved his tongue over her opening, then began to fuck her with his tongue. His thumb found her clit and began to massage it in a circular motion.

She cried out around Mac's thick cock, the sound escaping in a soft echo. He stroked in and out, his cock reaching farther into the wetness of her mouth. He tasted as masculine as he looked, and she couldn't get enough.

She was like an addict in need of a fix. She wanted more and didn't want them to stop. She sucked loudly and registered Mac's desperate moans.

Ryder slid two fingers into her writhing pussy then sucked her clit into his mouth and stroked his tongue repeatedly over the quivering flesh.

She bowed her back in one long continuous arc as her orgasm crashed hard over her. The explosion rocked her and continued rocking her even as Mac flooded into her mouth.

She twisted her hips in a desperate plea for mercy, but Ryder continued his assault with his mouth.

Mac withdrew from her mouth and bent over her body to suck sharply at her nipples. She felt something pop within her, and unbelievably, on the heels of the most awesome orgasm of her life, she began a fast climb toward another.

She cried out and clenched her fists into balls. Then Ryder threw open her legs, and in one forceful thrust, he lunged into her.

The room went dark. She couldn't see. All she could do was feel. Mac sucked her nipples. Ryder fucked her pussy with long, hard strokes. Mac's hands covered her body. Ryder gripped her hips. He plunged again and again until she honest to God thought she was going to pass out.

Ryder tightened between her legs just as Mac pinched one nipple between his fingers. He bit the other, and she gave herself over to the cataclysmic volcano that was threatening to consume her.

Several long minutes later, she lay there gasping for breath. Every muscle in her body had the consistency of Jell-O. She couldn't move if she wanted.

Ryder was slumped over her, the last quivers of his orgasm jerking his hips. He withdrew, and she felt the warm flood of his cum leave her.

Mac collected her carefully in his arms. He moved her up the bed until she lay in the middle. Then he simply pulled the covers over them and reached to turn out the light.

Ryder threw one leg over her, and Mac curled his arm over her waist. She fell asleep with both men wrapped around her.

CHAPTER 7

he bed dipped, and one of the warm bodies surrounding Kit went away. She made a disgruntled sound and heard a soft chuckle close to her ear. Ryder kissed her temple.

"I've got to go into the garage, darlin'. But I'll be around tonight. Why don't you let me take you into work?"

"On the motorcycle?"

"Uh-huh."

"Deal," she said with a grin.

He tweaked her on the ass and headed for the bathroom. She yawned and closed her eyes again. Several minutes later, she heard Ryder come out of the bathroom. She turned in his direction and smiled as he blew her a kiss. After he left the room, she turned back to Mac to see he was awake and staring at her.

"You're staring," she said.

"That's because you're gorgeous."

She ducked her head shyly.

"How are you this morning? Sore?" Mac asked as he snuck an arm around her waist.

She grinned. "Think that highly of yourself, big boy?"

"Babe, you took on two very large, very aroused men. It ain't about my ego. You're a tiny thing. Ryder and I are not."

She chuckled. "Yes, I'm a bit sore, but I have to say, if I couldn't walk, I wouldn't care."

"That good?"

She leaned in and kissed him. "Yeah, that good."

His beard scratched across her chin as he kissed her back.

"You need to shave."

Mac rolled over onto his back and stared up at the ceiling. "What say we get dressed, go eat some breakfast down at the café then head over to your place to pick up some more of your things?"

She paused. She didn't want to piss off Mac after an otherwise spectacular night by informing him she had no intention of hiding out at his house forever. But she would stay a few days, at least until he could investigate her stalker.

"Sounds good," she finally said. No sense making an issue before it was necessary.

Mac relaxed beside her as if he'd expected her to argue. He swung his legs over the side of the bed and stood up. He walked naked to the bathroom, giving Kit a prime view of his backside. And damn, when he turned sideways, she could see how very well hung he was when he *wasn't* hard. Jesus.

"Like what you see?"

His blue eyes twinkled as a sexy grin spread across his face. She hurled a pillow across the room at him.

"You know damn well I do."

"It's yours, babe. All you gotta do is ask."

He turned and disappeared into the bathroom, leaving her to ponder the implication of his statement.

She rolled out of bed and wrinkled her nose at the sheets. Rumpled, wadded and probably sticky to boot. She yanked them off the bed and headed for the washing machine.

When she returned to the bathroom, Mac had just stepped out of the shower. He reached back in and turned the water back on.

"All yours," he said.

Ten minutes later, she left the bathroom in a towel and nearly collided with Mac as she entered his bedroom.

He caught her in his arms and whistled appreciatively. He slid a finger under the band of the towel. "Come on, just one peek," he said as he yanked downward.

The towel fell to the floor, baring her body. Tiny prickles danced up her spine as Mac's fingers trailed down her skin. They came to rest below her hip bone where her dragon tattoo was displayed.

"Have I ever told you how much I love your tattoo?" Mac asked.

She chuckled. "You'd only seen it once before last night."

He grinned wickedly. "But I've thought about it a thousand times."

She stepped around him and reached for her duffel bag on the floor. She could feel him watching her as she dressed, and she purposely teased him by pulling her underwear up her legs as slowly as she could. She turned around to face him then pulled a T-shirt over her head.

He raised an eyebrow. "No bra?"

She shrugged. "I don't have that much."

He snorted. "Your breasts are perfect, and I have to tell you, I don't like the idea of everyone getting such a spectacular view of them."

She raised her head in surprise.

The distance between them closed as he stepped forward. He cupped her breasts through the thin T-shirt and thumbed her nipples until they stood pointy and erect.

"Oh yeah," he muttered. "Fucking perfect."

Her legs trembled, and her pussy throbbed. "Mac," she whispered. "If we don't leave now, we'll never get breakfast."

Regret shadowed his eyes as he withdrew. He reached for her hand, twining his fingers with hers. "You definitely need to eat if you're going to keep your strength up."

He winked and pulled her along out of the bedroom.

Despite the fact that Kit had eaten in the café with both Ryder and Mac on more occasions than she could count, today with Mac it felt awkward.

Mac eyed her possessively, and he touched her often, light brushes across her skin. One time he even reached across the table to take her hand.

It made her uncomfortable as hell. She didn't want their easy camaraderie to change just because they were having sex. And she sure as hell didn't want Mac or Ryder to get the wrong idea. Sex was fine. After what happened, she wasn't sure she could trust anyone but Mac or Ryder to touch her, but that didn't mean she wanted more.

If she had to choose between keeping the sex or keeping their friendship, it was a no brainer. She'd just have to start abstaining.

"Hey, there's David," Mac said.

Kit turned around to see David enter the café. She smiled and waved. Mac motioned him over.

David ambled over, a warm smile on his face. "Hey, you two."

Mac kicked one of the available chairs out from under the table. "Have a seat."

David plunked down and motioned for the waitress.

"I'm glad to see you, David. I have a few questions for you if you don't mind," Mac said.

"Sure, no problem. What's on your mind?"

The waitress poured David a steaming cup of coffee, and David set to work sweetening it with four packets of sugar.

Kit tensed and looked away. She knew Mac was going to ask him about what had happened last night. An uncomfortable, itchy sensation crawled over her skin. The idea of anyone knowing humiliated her even more.

"Before I got to the bar last night, did you see anything out of the ordinary? Anything unusual? Maybe someone paying a little too close attention to Kit?"

David frowned and shook his head. He glanced over at Kit, concern creasing his brow. "What's going on?"

Kit closed her eyes and lowered her head.

"I have reason to believe that Kit's attacker is still around," Mac muttered.

David blinked. "You're serious."

"As a heart attack."

Kit reached for her juice and knocked it over with shaky fingers. Damn it.

David leaped up to retrieve napkins, and Mac reached across the table and gripped Kit's hand. The waitress hurried over with a dish towel, and soon the mess was cleaned up.

Mac stared at Kit, his blue eyes shadowed with concern. "Are you all right?"

"Can we . . . can we please talk about something else?" she pleaded.

His expression softened. "Baby, if David saw anything I need to know it. I can't protect you if I don't ask questions."

She shoved back from the table and stood, rigid from head to toe. "Then do it when I'm not around," she choked out.

She turned and ran for the door.

Mac cursed and slammed his fist on the table. Running scared. He couldn't remember a time when she wasn't running. From her past. From her present.

"What's going on, Mac?" David asked.

Mac sighed. "The son of a bitch who raped Kit is still out there. He's been stalking her ever since the attack. I only found out last night."

David's eyes widened in surprise. "But I thought there were no leads? That the attacker was someone passing through?"

Mac grunted. "Yeah, so did I."

He looked toward the entrance of the café where Kit had fled just moments before. He scrubbed his hands over his face. "Look, David, I need to go, but do me a favor, okay? Keep a close watch at the bar. The bastard was there last night. He left a note in Kit's truck. She isn't safe."

David's face darkened. "I'll do everything I can, Mac. I'll let you know if I see anything that doesn't add up."

Mac stood and shoved his Stetson on his head. He extended his hand to David. "Thanks, man. I appreciate this a lot."

"No problem."

Mac stalked out to the small parking lot and over to his Dodge truck. He slid into the driver's seat and put his hands on the steering wheel.

Beside him, Kit sat huddled in the passenger seat, staring blindly out the window. He let out a small sigh and reached across the seat to touch her arm.

"Kit, I didn't do that to hurt you," he said softly.

She stared at him with haunted eyes. "I know, Mac."

Silence lay heavy between them. He let his hand fall away from her, and he twisted back in his seat. He started the engine and backed out of the parking lot.

He drove toward her house, occasionally glancing over at her. Her body language screamed vulnerability, and again, he was flummoxed by how to handle this unfamiliar side of Kit. What he wanted to do was wrap himself around her so tightly she'd never feel threatened again, but that would likely scare her as badly as the demons she hid from did.

He pulled into her driveway and parked behind her Bronco. He reached over and took her hand. Slowly, she turned her head until she looked at him. The raw emotion in her eyes was nearly his undoing. It took all of his control not to crush her into his arms.

Instead he smiled lazily, as if he hadn't a care in the world. "You ready to go in, babe?"

She tensed, paused a second then reached for the door handle. He got out and walked around the front of the truck to wait for her.

They mounted the steps to her porch, and Mac hung back as she went to insert the key in the lock. But as soon as she touched the door, it eased open.

She dropped the keys and stepped back, bumping into Mac. In a second, he whirled her behind him and reached for his off-duty weapon.

"Go sit in the truck and lock the door," he ordered.

She stumbled back down the steps, her legs so shaky she looked like a newborn colt. When Mac was sure she was in the truck, he eased the front door open and peered inside.

"Son of a bitch," he swore.

Shit was scattered from one end of the house to another. He stepped inside the doorway, his gun raised. His neck prickled, the hairs standing at attention.

Not a single thing lay untouched in her house. Her sofa was ripped to shreds, the stuffing littered across the room. Pictures, books, plants lay broken and torn.

He walked into the kitchen only to see every single dish, glass and plate in a million pieces on the floor. He continued to her bedroom, afraid of what he'd find.

The door was flung wide. All her clothing lay scattered on the floor. Oddly enough, her bed was in pristine condition. In fact, he'd swear the intruder had made it, because Kit wasn't nearly as tidy as the bed appeared.

He walked over, glancing over the tightly creased linens. Then he froze. Bile rose in his throat, and he swallowed convulsively against the urge to vomit.

There in the center of the bed lay a picture of Kit. Huddled in a ball, on the ground, just as Mac had found her six months ago. Only he damned sure hadn't taken pictures of her.

Below the picture, a single piece of paper with one word scrawled. *Mine*.

The attacker was making his statement. He wasn't going anywhere.

Mac yanked up his cell phone and dialed the station. He quickly explained his location and what had gone on. Then he strode back through the house and outside where Kit sat in the truck.

She jumped out of the truck when he hit the steps. She ran up to him, would have run past him, but he caught her in his arms and held her tight.

"Don't go in there, Kit," he said firmly.

"What has he done?" Kit demanded.

Mac looked down at her eyes rapidly filling with tears, and he felt as though someone had torn his heart right out of his chest.

"It's a crime scene, baby. You can't go in there. I've called it in. They'll be here soon."

"What did he *do?*" she asked in a voice that made Mac ache.

"He tore the place up," Mac said. No way was he going to tell her about the picture on her bed.

Kit slowly tore her gaze from the house and looked back up at Mac. "I'm scared, Mac," she whispered.

Mac knew how much the words had cost her, but more than that, he knew how very terrified she must be in order for her to make such an admission.

He shook with rage. "I'm going to call Ryder to come get you. I'll need to be here for awhile. If I'm not there by the time you go to work, Ryder's going to take you in. I'll be there later on. I promise."

"He's not going to leave me alone, is he?" Kit said in a voice so low he almost didn't hear her.

Mac pulled her into his arms. He held her tightly, pressing his lips into her hair. "I'll find him, Kit. I swear to you, he's going to pay for what he's done."

CHAPTER 8

*R*yder arrived five minutes later, his face a mask of rage. Kit watched as he strode over to Mac, and the two talked, their expressions growing angrier by the minute.

She should be there, demanding to know what all had happened. She knew from the filtered bits of conversations she'd managed to grasp that her house was completely destroyed. But still, she hung back. She wasn't sure she could face the full scope of what Mac had found. He'd kept things from her. She knew it, but she was afraid to find out what they were.

A few minutes later, Ryder walked over to her, his black hair swinging over his shoulders. His expression softened when he reached her, and he put out a hand to cup her cheek.

"Let's get out of here, darlin."

"Where are we going?" she managed to croak out.

"For a ride. Anywhere but here."

She let him guide her over to his Harley. He straddled the bike then patted the space behind him. She got on and hugged her arms around Ryder's waist.

They tore out of her driveway and hit the main road out of town. Once outside the city limits, Ryder gunned the engine and opened it up.

The road stretched ahead of them through the dense green woods and over the hills surrounding their small town. Kit closed her eyes and allowed the wind to blow at her hair. She relished the feeling of freedom. For a brief moment, she could forget her worries.

A good twenty minutes later, Ryder turned onto a dirt road and sped down it in a cloud of dust. It was then she realized where they were going. The lake.

The road narrowed until all it became was a small trail through the woods. Ryder eased the bike along, using his arm to block tree branches from hitting Kit. A few minutes later, he pulled to a stop beside a huge oak tree.

"Remember this place?" he asked.

She smiled. "Yeah. Our tree." How many nights had they sat nestled among the roots, staring out over the lake, drinking beer and running from their reality?

She got off the bike and walked closer to the where the tree met the edge of the lake. So many nights spent here. She laid her hand against the rough bark and stared out over the sparkling water.

She heard Ryder behind her, then felt his arms sneak around her until she was nestled against his chest, his chin on top of her head.

"Why does he hate me?" she whispered. "What did I do?"

Ryder's arms tightened around her. He kissed the hair above her ear. "You didn't do anything, darlin'. He's a sick bastard who gets his kicks terrifying women."

She broke away from Ryder's embrace and sank down between

two of the roots. Ryder walked closer to the edge and looked down the embankment where the water lapped gently.

"What did Mac find at my house?" she asked. "He kept something from me, and at the time I didn't want to know, but I need to."

Ryder turned to look at her, anger flashing in his eyes. "No good can come of rehashing it, Kit."

"Tell me," she said quietly.

Ryder squatted on the ground in front of her. He looked back and forth between her and the lake, indecision making a crisscross pattern over his face.

"He took a picture of you. After . . . after he raped you," he said in a strangled voice. "He put it on your bed."

All the blood drained from her face. Panic surged and swelled, did battle with the rising nausea in her belly.

"Did—did you see it?"

God, until now, only Mac had seen her that night. He'd wrapped a blanket around her so no one would see.

"No, darlin', I didn't see," Ryder said softly.

She closed her eyes and hugged her knees to her chest. "I wish Mac hadn't seen either," she whispered.

"You think it bothers him?" Ryder asked sharply.

"It bothers *me*," she replied.

"Kit, look at me," Ryder directed. His voice was uncharacteristically harsh.

She blinked in surprise and dragged her eyes up to meet his gaze.

"You can't think it matters to him. Or to me. Kit, you know us better than that."

Her hands fluttered up in defense. "Ryder, I didn't think you thought badly of me. I do know you better than that. I just didn't want anyone to see me like that. Especially you and Mac," she finished lamely.

Ryder crawled over to where she sat. He hunkered down behind her against the tree and pulled her back against his chest until she rested between his legs, her ass tucked against his groin.

He trailed his fingers through her hair, smoothing the tangles. "You'll never know just how sorry I am that happened to you, darlin'. If I could take it away, I'd do it, no matter the cost. But at the same time, it doesn't change one damn thing about you and me, and I know it doesn't change anything between you and Mac."

She sighed and leaned deeper into his arms. "How many times have we sat here, staring out over the water wishing we were anywhere else?"

He chuckled. "Too many to count."

"So why are we still here?" she asked softly.

"I know why I'm here, and I know why Mac's here, but why are you here, Kit?"

She stiffened in his arms. "Because no one ever asked me to leave."

He trailed his hand through her hair again. Here, in the place they'd spent so much of their youth, there was nothing sexual about their embrace. Just two friends holding on, one drawing comfort from the other.

"Don't let this destroy you, Kit. And don't push me and Mac away because you're scared of your feelings. It doesn't make you weak to admit you're afraid."

"When did you become so in touch with your feminine side?" she muttered.

He chuckled close to her ear. "You know I'm right."

"I still hear him, Ryder. In my dreams. When I'm awake. He never goes away."

Ryder's hand stilled in her hair. "Mac and I'll find him, darlin'. This I swear. And when we do, he's a dead man. You won't ever have to hear him again."

Kit relaxed against Ryder, content to exist only in the moment. Her eyes fluttered, and she felt the overwhelming urge to close her eyes.

Ryder's hand smoothed the hair away from her cheek. "Go to sleep, darlin'. I'm not going anywhere."

Mac pulled into the busy parking lot of the Two Step and cut the engine to his truck. It had been one hell of a day, beginning with Kit's house and not stopping since. And the bitch of the thing was not a single print had been lifted from the break-in.

He walked into the bar and immediately sought out Kit. She was across the room, delivering drinks. Ryder watched closely from his perch at the bar.

He started in Ryder's direction. When he got to the bar, David slid a beer over the counter to him.

"Thanks, man," Mac said, picking up the cold brew.

"No problem."

"Where'd you and Kit go all afternoon?" Mac asked as he slid onto the stool beside Ryder.

"Out to the lake," Ryder replied.

Mac tilted back the bottle and took a long swig. "Been awhile since we all went out there."

Ryder nodded. "Still looks exactly the same."

Mac paused and set his beer down on the rough surface of the wooden bar top. He felt like a jealous teenager, but he had to know.

"Did you have sex with her?"

Ryder blinked in surprise. "What the hell kind of question is that?"

Mac shrugged. "Just a question."

"I know how you feel about her, man. I wouldn't do that to you. Or her. She wasn't in any shape to be having sex this afternoon."

Mac clenched his fist, pissed at himself. He knew Ryder would never cross the line with him or Kit, and yet he'd had to ask.

"I know, man. I guess . . . I guess I wanted to know if she was any more open with you than she is with me, because between you and me, she's got a wall a foot thick stuck right in the middle of me and her."

"You knew it wouldn't be easy," Ryder said. "And no, she isn't any more open with me. In some ways she's still a scared little girl playing at being an adult. Other times she's every man's wet dream. All grown up and exotic. And you never know which one will show up to see you."

Mac nodded his agreement. "I won't let her go, Ryder. I don't know how to make her see I'd never hurt her, but I won't let her go."

"What are you two talking so serious about?" Kit asked as she set her tray down on the bar.

Mac turned to her, a smile on his face. He tugged her into his arms. "How you doing, babe?"

She returned his smile but eased from his arms. She rattled off her drink order to David then turned her attention back to Mac.

"Find out anything?"

His smile disappeared and he shook his head. "Sorry."

Her lips trembled before she pasted on a bright smile. "Oh well, I'm sure it's only a matter of time, right?"

"We'll find him, Kit. I promise."

She put her small hand on his arm. "I know you will, Mac."

"What time you get off?" Mac asked.

Kit turned her arm up to look at her watch. "One more hour. You going to stay?"

"Not going anywhere. You want to ride home with me?"

She glanced sideways at Ryder then slowly nodded. She dipped her head in David's direction as he plunked the last drink on her tray. She almost looked nervous as she turned back to Mac once more.

"What's on your mind, babe?"

She hesitated and wiped her palms down her shorts. "I don't want you and Ryder to treat me different," she whispered. "I don't want us to go home and for you to treat me like I'm broken."

Mac leaned in close and tipped her chin up with one finger. "Kit, we'll do whatever it is you want us to. No pressure. No expectations. No disappointment. You're in control."

"And if I want you to take me home and make me forget?" she asked.

"Then we'll take you home and make love to you all night," he said huskily.

Her green eyes flared and gleamed a brilliant emerald in the low light. To his surprise, she walked into his arms and pressed her lips against his.

His entire body went rigid. Hot. It was hot. All the breath left his body. How a little slip of a woman could make him so weak he didn't know, but she brought him to his knees.

"I need you to understand," she murmured close to his lips. "I have so many fantasies, but none that I can trust anyone with. Except you and Ryder. When I look at another man, I can't be sure he won't hurt me."

Mac slipped his hand to the back of her neck. "Tell me what you want, baby. I'll make it happen."

"I want you to call the shots," she whispered. "I trust you. I want you to handcuff me, tie me up, whatever it is you cops do. I want one night where what happened six months ago isn't lying between us."

Mac's breath hitched and escaped him in fits and jerks. She was handing him her trust on a silver plate. He'd been waiting for this moment a long time, and he'd be damned if he fucked it up.

He tried to keep his voice light, casual, a little teasing. "I'm always up for a little role playin'," he drawled.

She shivered in his arms. Then she slipped away from him and retrieved her tray. He watched as she walked back into the crowd to deliver the drinks.

Ryder shifted beside him. "That mean what I think it does?"

Mac smiled. "You up for it?"

Ryder snorted. "For her? You don't need to ask. I've never had anyone like her, and I doubt I ever will again."

"I hear you," Mac murmured.

He glanced over at Ryder and caught his eye. "Look man, I'm sorry about before. It was a stupid question."

"It's forgotten," Ryder said.

Mac clenched his fist and offered it to Ryder. Ryder cracked a grin and bumped his fist to Mac's.

CHAPTER 9

*K*it leaned back in the seat and tried to relax. Mac sat next to her, his hands gripping the steering wheel as he navigated his way to his house. It had been such a long day. For all of them. Mac still wore his uniform, not that she minded.

The only thing she liked better than his uniform was when he wore his faded, broken-in pair of blue jeans. They adhered to his ass and outlined every muscle in his long legs. She could imagine unzipping the fly, loosening his belt and pulling out his cock.

She closed her eyes and squirmed around in her seat to alleviate the burn between her legs.

Mac looked sideways at her. "You okay, babe?"

Her heart did odd little flips in her chest. Butterflies danced in her stomach and made her breath come out in short hiccups. She couldn't wait for them to get home.

A few minutes later, Mac pulled into the drive of his house. Before she could open her door all the way, Mac hopped out and hurried around. He caught her in his arms and eased her to the ground before closing the door behind her.

Ryder roared in behind them and parked the bike a foot away from where they were standing.

Kit looked nervously between them and nibbled at her bottom lip. She'd never anticipated something so much in her entire life.

Ryder walked by and trailed his hand over her cheek before heading into the house ahead of them. Mac smoothed his hand over her hair.

"You ready to go in?"

She took a deep breath and nodded.

Mac walked ahead of her and opened the door. She followed him in, and the first thing she saw was Ryder standing in the middle of the living room, his shirt already off.

Before she could fully appreciate his physique, Mac spun her around, pulling one arm behind her back. She found herself face against the wall, and she heard the unmistakable rattle of handcuffs.

The cool metal clapped around her left wrist. Mac reached for her other arm, twisting it behind to meet the other. His breath blew hot in her ear, and he leaned in close to her body.

"Listen to me, baby. If at any time, you want us to stop, if you aren't comfortable, for any reason, you say so, okay?"

She nodded.

The click of the other handcuff locking jolted her into awareness. God. She was handcuffed and at the mercy of two gorgeous men.

"Then let the games begin," Mac murmured.

He turned her around, his hand gripping her manacled wrists. Ryder was naked in front of her, his dark eyes gleaming in the light.

Her eyes ran appreciatively up and down his well-muscled body. His midnight hair hung wildly over his shoulders. The dragon tattoo that matched her own spread across his upper chest.

Two more marked his arms. A dagger on his left arm. A coiled serpent on his right.

Her gaze dropped between his legs to the dark nest of hair. His cock stood swollen, distended, a testament to his arousal.

A pocketknife flashed in front of her as Mac came around to stand, momentarily blocking her view of Ryder. He eyed her hungrily, the knife moving closer to her shirt.

She shivered, her skin puckering as he slid the knife underneath her shirt to rest against her skin. He moved the knife upward until the point came out of the neck of her shirt. Then he pulled it outward until the material gave way under the strain. He pulled downward, cutting her shirt open.

He pushed the shirt over her shoulders until it fell down her arms to dangle from the handcuffs.

"Kick off your shoes," he ordered.

She slipped her sandals off, and he kicked them across the floor, out of the way.

He hooked his fingers in the waistband of her shorts and unsnapped the fly. He peeled the shorts down her legs, leaving her in only her underwear. He looked up and smiled before setting the point of the blade at the curve of her hip. The material gave way, and soon the panties fell to the floor in a heap of scrap.

Mac stepped away and put his hand to her bare back. He let his hand wander down until he palmed the curve of her ass in his hand. Then he pushed her toward Ryder.

"On your knees," Ryder said gruffly.

Kit sank gracefully to her knees.

"Knees apart, chest out."

Again she complied.

He smiled down at her. He circled his cock with his hand and pumped slowly up and down. "I swear, darlin', I don't think I've ever seen anything so beautiful. You're every man's fantasy come to life."

His words skittered over her, and she was shocked by her reaction. Tears welled in her eyes. Never would she feel this way with any other man. Not as safe. Not as cherished. Mac and Ryder made her examine emotions she'd long ago locked inside her.

Ryder cupped her chin and rubbed his thumb gently over her cheek. "You have such a sweet mouth. Now be a good girl and open it for me."

Her mouth fell open, and Ryder slid his hand behind her head just as he used the other to guide his cock between her lips.

Every nerve ending in her body screamed for release. She was pulled tighter than a rubber band at full stretch. She was completely and utterly at their mercy, and it made her hotter than she'd ever been in her life.

Ryder pumped in and out of her mouth, slowly, softly, but he held her head firmly. He was in control. She wanted to come right then and there.

He groaned, the sound torn from his throat. Both hands crept around her head, tangled in her hair, held her as he gently fucked her mouth.

"I'm going to come, darlin'," he said huskily. "And I want you to swallow every drop."

She closed her eyes and moaned softly around his thrusts as they became more urgent. His hands tightened in her hair. His thrusts became more dominant. Then he buried himself in her wet mouth and held her tightly as he began to jet his cum to the back of her throat.

She swirled her tongue around his pulsing cock and swallowed as he spilled himself in her mouth. Long after his release, he rocked back and forth as she sucked and licked at his softening erection.

He withdrew, letting his hands fall from her face. Behind her, Mac curled his hands under her armpits and lifted her upward.

"Can you stand by yourself?" Mac asked.

She nodded.

His hand caressed her ass again as he directed her to the bed-room. Probing fingers slid between her cheeks and feathered over her anal opening.

Her legs trembled and threatened to buckle.

"Get on the bed," Mac directed. "On your knees, lay your cheek on the mattress."

She crawled awkwardly onto the covers and slowly leaned for-ward until her face pressed against the bed. Her ass stuck in the air, leaving her completely exposed. She flexed and extended her fin-gers, testing the cuffs.

"Now that's a pretty sight," Mac murmured.

"Doesn't get any prettier," Ryder agreed.

Her pussy clenched and quivered. If Mac so much as touched her in the right spot, anywhere *near* the right spot, she'd explode.

"I want to fuck your ass, Kit."

She screwed her eyes shut and bit her bottom lip. Her breath came in small pants, and she began to tremble from head to toe.

Large hands cupped and fingered her ass, spread her. The broad head of a cock settled between her cheeks. Mac rubbed his dick over her entrance. The slippery coolness of lubricant eased his passage.

He pressed forward. Unbearable pressure fired into her belly. The tight opening flared and began to accept Mac's cock. Then with a gentle plop, the head slipped past the tight muscle.

She moaned when he stilled behind her.

"Do you want it, Kit? Do you have any idea how fucking sexy you look, your ass clutching at my dick, sucking me inside?"

"Please," she whispered.

He reached underneath her and slid his fingers over her slick pussy. He found her clit and began to finger the small bud.

"Mac!" she wailed.

He bucked his hips forward, his cock thrusting deep into her ass. Every muscle in her body shrieked, tightened, convulsed as he began pumping in and out of her body.

His fingers tweaked and plucked at her pussy, plunging in unison with his cock then sliding upward to tease her clit. Mindless pleasure consumed her. So wicked and forbidden. Only in her darkest fantasies had she given light to having her ass fucked.

"I'm going to come, Kit, but not you. Not yet."

She groaned. Her body was so rigid, so wanting. She needed release. Couldn't take much more of the electric sparks igniting over her body.

Just when she thought she'd come anyway, his hands left her, and his motions stilled. He stood there, embedded tightly within her. His hands smoothed over her back, touching, caressing.

Then he withdrew, ever so slowly. He let out a growl, so possessive sounding, so erotic. He rammed forward, once, twice. His body strained against her as he sought to get deeper. And she felt the hot flood of his release in the darkest recesses of her body.

He leaned against her for a long moment before carefully pulling away. A warm cloth soothed the tender flesh and cool air blew over her skin.

Gentle hands eased her over until she lay on her back, her hands pressed firmly against the bed beneath her.

"I want to taste that pussy," Ryder said as he settled between her legs.

Her pussy twitched and spasmed in response. She stared down at Ryder's dark eyes, so alight with desire.

He bent over and ran his tongue up the folds of her cunt.

Oh my God!

She bucked and writhed, cursing the fact she was in such a helpless position. She was open to whatever Ryder wanted to do, however he wanted to touch her.

He nibbled gently at the sensitive skin, nuzzled beyond the

outer flesh, then nipped sharply at her clit. Feather light, he licked and sucked. He ran his tongue over and over the tight bud.

He lapped downward, circling her entrance with his lips then his tongue. His teeth grazed the plump folds.

"Ryder!" she cried out.

"Feel good, darlin'?"

His tongue swirled then plunged into her. He was fucking her with his tongue!

She arched her back trying desperately to get closer to him. She was so close. Just one more touch. She was poised on the brink, ready to go over the edge. Just a little push and she'd be there.

Ryder pulled away, and she let out a sound of distress.

He chuckled above her. His fingers plucked and strummed her nipples, eliciting another moan from her.

"You're such wicked teases," she protested.

"Not at all, darlin'. We just want to give you the most incredible night of pleasure you've ever had."

No chance that wouldn't happen. She'd already experienced more hedonistic ecstasy than she had in her entire life.

Mac walked back over, his skin damp from a recent shower. She glanced down to see he was very much aroused again. His thick erection stood stiff from the blond patch of hair in his groin. Her mouth watered as she imagined him sliding it past her lips.

Mac grinned. "I like the direction of your gaze, babe."

Ryder reached forward and turned her to her side. Mac fiddled with the cuffs and her hands came free. She moved them around and rubbed at her wrists.

Mac frowned. "Did we hurt you?"

She smiled over at him. "Uh-uh."

"Then don't get too used to your freedom," Ryder drawled.

CHAPTER 10

An adrenaline-induced wave rolled through Kit's belly. A thousand butterfly wings fanned in rapid succession and swooped through her chest and into her throat.

Mac leaned into her, pressed his big body against her and pressed her down to the bed. A thickly muscled thigh wedged between her legs and spread her knees. His cock, swollen and heavy, slid between the slick folds of her pussy and rubbed teasingly against her clit.

Her breasts tingled and tightened against Mac's chest. Desire blazed in his eyes, making them burn a darker blue. Once, twice he kissed her, the light smooching sound echoing softly in the stillness. She could hear their heartbeats, feel every pulse and jump.

She raised her lips for more, fusing her mouth to his. Their tongues met and tangled. Breathless. Hot. Impatient.

He growled softly. "I want you so damn much. You make me crazy."

She laughed soft and low. "Make you crazy? What do you think you've been doing to me all night?"

He nudged impatiently at her pussy. "I want inside you."

"Then what are you waiting for?" Kit murmured.

He thrust into her in one hard movement.

Her breath caught in her chest and hung there as he lodged himself deep inside her. Finally she released the air, it all escaping in a sigh of contentment.

"Like that do you?"

"Oh yes."

He grinned and withdrew only to thrust even deeper.

She arched into him, wrapping her legs tightly around him. He stroked back and forth until she writhed beneath him. Maybe now he would assuage the burning ache inside her.

Mac dropped his weight onto her and gathered her in his arms. Then he shifted and rolled her with him until she sat astride him, her body sprawled across his chest. Then Ryder curled his hand around her wrist and gently pulled it behind her.

The snap of the cuffs sounded loud in her ears. Ryder swept her other arm behind her back and handcuffed it as well.

She lay helpless on Mac, his cock buried in her pussy, her cheek pressed against his chest and her hands securely bound behind her.

"We'll take care of you," Mac whispered.

Ryder lifted her up, pulling on her cuffed hands. Mac supported her upper body by cupping her breasts and holding her in place. He grinned wickedly at her, knowing she was completely at his and Ryder's mercy.

The bed dipped and swayed as Ryder climbed onto the mattress. She felt the nudge of his cock at the seam of her ass. She leaned forward onto Mac, allowing Ryder easier access.

Blood hummed through her veins so rapidly she felt faint. Her body tightened, and for a moment, she thought she would orgasm before Ryder ever gained entrance. But he paused.

Two sets of hands ran soothingly over her body. Ryder stroked her back, ran his palms over her hips. Mac slid his hands over her taut belly and up to her breasts. His fingers nipped and plucked at her aching nipples. Ryder paused as she stiffened further.

"Relax, darlin'. Not yet. Make it last. Make it good."

She forced her body to relax around Mac's invasion even as she prepared for Ryder's cock to tunnel into her.

Ryder cupped her ass and slid his thumbs down to open her. She closed her eyes when she felt the head of his penis press inward. So much pressure. Such exquisite pleasure and pain. Just when she was sure she couldn't stand it any longer, her body gave way, and he sank into her.

Both men groaned. She let out her own cry as she felt herself come apart in their arms.

Ryder held her arms, supporting her, not letting her fall. Mac gripped her waist, encouraged her to ride him as Ryder sank into her over and over.

They were in control of her pleasure. They set the pace. She threw back her head and let them.

"You have the sweetest ass, Kit darlin'. So tight. A man could lose his mind fucking you."

His words sent whipping strands of pleasure into the deepest center of her body.

"Please," she whispered.

"Please what?" Mac rasped.

"Make me come," she begged. "I need you so much."

Ryder flexed his hips, and the hard muscles of his thighs slapped against her ass. He was deep within her, she couldn't differentiate between the two men who possessed her. All she could do was feel the mindless pleasure they gave her.

"Come then, darlin'," Ryder murmured close to her ear.

They both began pumping into her, their hands gripping her tight, their cocks working in unison.

"Oh God!" she cried brokenly.

"Let go, baby," Mac encouraged.

She heard him seemingly miles away. A dull roar sounded in her ears as the fire burned higher in her abdomen. They rocked her between them. Her body jerked and heaved as they plunged over and over.

Her eyes shut tight and her teeth clamped together. They were going to kill her.

Ryder stiffened behind her, and he gripped her arms tightly as his release flooded hot into her. Then she felt Mac, so hard and tight inside her, swell with his orgasm.

She panicked for a moment as her body seemed to fly out of control. Never before had she felt so helpless, so out of touch with her body. She flew in forty directions. Her vision blurred and she screamed as her world exploded around her. The sensation went on and on, and impossibly built again rapidly. She never came down from the first orgasm when the second starting burning inside her.

"No, nooo! I can't take it again," she said weakly.

"We've got you, baby. Just go with it," Mac said.

They held her, stroked her, caressed her, murmured words of encouragement. Mac slipped a hand to her pussy where they were still joined. He flicked a finger across her clit and stroked as her second orgasm swept over like an out-of-control firestorm.

"Mac!" she cried out.

Her muscles seized and convulsed. Ryder pressed his lips to the back of her shoulder. The gentle kiss shattered her control. She melted into a puddle in Mac's arms. She fell forward and rested her cheek against Mac's heaving chest.

She fought to try and regain control of her breathing.

"You were magnificent," Mac whispered as he stroked her hair.

She nearly moaned in protest when Ryder gently picked her up and cradled her in his arms. He held her close as he walked toward the bathroom. She snuggled deeper into his chest, and he kissed the top of her hair.

Ryder turned the shower on and waited as the water warmed. Then he stepped in with Kit and carefully washed her body and hair. She clung to him, loving his strength and the safety his embrace offered.

Long after he was finished rinsing the soap from her, they stood in the shower, her locked in his arms. Finally he turned the water off and eased her out of the stall.

Mac was waiting with a towel, and she went willingly into his arms. He wrapped the towel and himself around her and held her close.

As he guided her back into the bedroom, a disturbing thought filtered through her mind. She didn't want to go back to her house, her life the way it was before. She felt safe with Mac here in his house. She felt safe in Ryder's arms.

She shook her head as panic overtook her. No. This wasn't supposed to happen. She wasn't supposed to depend on them. She wasn't supposed to *need* them so badly.

Mac eased her down on the bed and pulled the towel away from her naked body. Ryder walked in behind them, a bottle of baby oil in his hands.

Ryder settled down on the other side of her and handed the bottle to Mac. They divided her body right down the middle and began massaging her weary muscles, rubbing the baby oil into her skin.

She closed her eyes, willing the panic to diminish. She was being stupid. These two men were her best friends in the entire world. She loved them, and she knew they loved her. They took care of her, and whether she wanted them to or not, they'd continue to.

Get over it, Kit. Enjoy the moment. Don't ruin it by overthinking things.

Bubbles of pleasure rose and floated within her body. She gave herself over to their care, and her last conscious thought was that she was finally where she truly belonged.

CHAPTER 11

Kit puttered around Mac's kitchen, her mind at ease for the first time in days. She set about making Mac's favorite for breakfast, homemade hash browns, grits and eggs.

She raised her brow when Ryder ambled into the kitchen, fully dressed. He stopped long enough to open the fridge and grab a drink.

"You not going to stick around for breakfast?" she asked.

He walked over to her, wrapped his arms around her and gave her a quick kiss on the forehead. "No darlin'. Y'all go on and eat without me. I've got to get down to the garage."

Kit shook her head as she watched him go. He never failed to keep her off balance. When his father died, he'd left Ryder a very wealthy man, but Ryder still tooled around in his run-down garage, restoring motorcycles.

She dug around for a whisk and began beating the eggs. She had started the grits and arranged her hash browns on the skillet when the phone rang. She wiped her hands on a dish towel and reached for the receiver.

"Hello?"

She frowned when silence returned her greeting. She started to hang it back up when a voice made her freeze.

"You're mine, Kit."

Fear, hot and desperate, raced through her system. She dropped the phone and backed away.

"Kit, what the hell's wrong?" Mac demanded.

She looked up to see him standing in the kitchen door in just a pair of shorts. His hair was damp from a recent shower. Her mouth opened, but no words would come out.

Mac strode over and yanked the phone off the floor. He put it to his ear then frowned. "It's just a dial tone."

She began to shake.

"Baby, what's wrong?"

Mac's voice was gentler, and he pulled her into his arms.

"It—it—it was him."

His body went rigid against her. "He called here?"

She nodded, her head buried against his chest.

Mac let loose a string of expletives. He pulled away from her and yanked up the phone. He punched in a series of numbers then put the receiver to his ear.

She only half listened as he spoke to someone at the station. He wanted a trace. He wanted results. He was furious.

She reached for one of the chairs at the small table. She sank down and buried her face in her hands. No matter how many times she escaped in the arms of Mac and Ryder, reality always came back to bite her on the ass immediately after. She couldn't continue to hide.

Mac's hand curled around her shoulder, and he sat down beside her. She looked up at him and recoiled from the violence she saw in his expression.

"I don't want you going back to work," he said. "Not until we've found this son of a bitch."

She gaped at him. "Mac, I don't have a choice. I can't afford not to work, and I won't let him ruin my life. I won't!"

"Kit, we'll work something out. You can stay here as long as you need. You know Ryder and I will help out any way we can."

She took in several calming breaths. "Mac, you know I appreciate you and Ryder. More than you'll ever know. God knows I would have gone crazy without y'all. You're the best friends I've ever had."

Mac held up his hand to interrupt her. "I don't want to hear what a good *friend* I am, damn it." He placed his hands on her shoulders, forcing her to look at him head on. "Kit, I love you. You're mine. *Mine.* There's never been a time when you weren't. I've waited all this time because I knew you weren't ready, but damn it, baby, I'm not going to stand back anymore. I need you here with me, in my bed. Every night."

She stared at him in horror. She brushed away his hands. Got up and backed hastily away from the table.

"*Goddamn* you, Mac! Why did you have to ruin everything? This wasn't supposed to happen. You of all people should know . . ."

She trailed off, her throat knotting with sobs. Not giving him a chance to respond, she whirled around and ran.

"Kit!" Mac stood up. Damn it. He raced after her, but she was out the door and gone.

He watched her run down the street. "Fuck me."

He went back into the kitchen and snatched up the phone to call Ryder.

"Hey, man, look. Kit's on the run. I think she's headed your way. I'm going to go out and look for her, but if she comes by, keep her there. And let me know she's safe, okay?"

Mac hung up then pounded his fist into the wall. He couldn't lose her now. Not when he was so close. Not after all that had happened. He had to find a way past her stubborn defenses.

Kit ran until her body screamed in protest. And she kept on running. Tears blinded her. Angry tears. Scared tears. She'd never felt more betrayed. Or helpless.

She rounded the street corner and found herself in front of Ryder's garage. She hadn't consciously come here, but here she was, nevertheless. Her breath spilled torturously from her lips, and she doubled over to try and catch up.

Strong arms wrapped around her and pulled her upright. "Ahh darlin', don't cry. You know I can't stand it when you cry."

She let Ryder guide her inside the musty garage, and he sat her down on the same ragged couch that had been there since high school. He left her for a moment then returned with tissues and a cold beer.

A few seconds later, she heard him on the phone.

"She's here, man. You can stand down. Yeah, I'll keep an eye on her."

She closed her eyes. What was Mac thinking? Feeling? She hadn't wanted to hurt him, but he'd yanked the rug out from under her completely.

Ryder shuffled over and flopped down on the couch beside her. He popped the top of his beer and took a long swallow. He was silent for a long moment. She liked that. Gave her time to think. To breathe.

Finally he looked over at her. "Mac drop the bomb on you?"

Her eyes widened. "You knew?"

He shrugged. "Knew what? That he cared about you?"

She shook her head vigorously. "It goes deeper than that, Ryder. He said . . . he said he loves me."

"Why should that bother you, darlin'? Everyone loves some-one, and everyone wants to *be* loved."

"He's ruined everything," she whispered.

Ryder sighed. "Kit darlin', do you honestly think we could fuck you and not have any feelings for you? Do you think that little of us?"

"No! I mean, of course I don't think little of you. Either of you."

"Mac's held a torch for you since high school. That's a long time for a man to love a woman and not act on it."

"But he left. You both left," she said brokenly. "Everyone I've ever cared about left."

"Ahh, Kit girl."

He scooted over and put his big arms around her. He leaned back on the couch taking her with him. Her head rested on his chest, and he stroked through her hair with a comforting hand.

"Mac came back, Kit."

She stiffened.

"He came back for you. Think about it, darlin'. He could have gone anywhere after the service. Good cops are in demand all over the country. But he came back here to this Podunk hole-in-the-wall town we all swore we'd get out of because you were here."

Her heart sped up and did a peculiar thunking against the walls of her chest. She elbowed up until she faced Ryder.

"Why did you come back, Ryder?"

"Why did you never leave?" he asked softly.

She stared at him a long moment, fear circulating her head in a dizzy rotation.

"I was afraid."

"Afraid of what, darlin'?"

"If I left—" She broke off and sucked in a deep breath. "If I left, you and Mac wouldn't know where to find me. I was afraid I'd never see you again."

"So you waited for us," he said quietly.

She closed her eyes as the realization rolled over her. She'd never voiced her reasons aloud.

"Why did you come back?" she asked again.

"After my old man died, there was nothing to hate here any longer," Ryder said simply. "Mac was coming back, you were here, and you're the only two people I ever gave a damn about."

"But Ryder . . . if me and Mac . . . where does that leave you?"

He smiled gently. "I'll always be here for you, Kit. But I've known how Mac feels about you, and if you're honest with yourself, you'd realize how you feel about him is not the same thing you feel for me."

"I love you, Ryder. I do."

"I know you do, darlin'. I love you too. You're the only woman I've ever cared about beyond a casual fuck. If something ever happened to Mac, I'd step up in a minute to take care of you, and I'd never have a single regret. But Mac loves you in a way you and I don't love each other. And I think you love him that way too."

"Nobody ever understood me the way you did," she whispered.

"I know you're scared, Kit. I know you're still hurting over your mother leaving you with your bastard stepfather. I know me and Mac hurt you when we took off, but we were kids, Kit. You can't hold that against us. We all had our soul-searching to do, and it brought us back to you. That ought to mean something. Mac won't leave you again, darlin'. You have to trust in that."

"Why is it I can tell you I love you, but the mere thought of saying it to Mac scares me so badly?" she asked.

"Because I'm safe. You know I won't hurt you. And you don't feel the same way about me as you do Mac."

His last statement made her suck in her breath as if he'd punched her in the stomach.

"I do love you," she said stubbornly.

He chuckled. "I love you too, darlin'."

"Where does this put you?" she asked in a miserable tone. "I'm not ready to let what we have go. Not after waiting for it for so long."

"Sugar, no one said we had to end things. You, me and Mac, well we've always had a different relationship. We're closer than any other three people on earth. You're assuming too much. Just because Mac loves you doesn't mean things have to be different between the three of us. It just means at the end of the day, he wants to be the man you go home to. In his bed. Every night."

"What if he leaves?" she whispered. "What if one day he wakes up and decides he doesn't want me anymore?"

Ryder's hold tightened on her. "Life doesn't offer any guarantees, darlin'. It wouldn't be near as fun if it did. You have to decide if you trust him."

"I do trust him."

"Then what's holding you back?" he asked. "You can't run scared forever, Kit. At some point, you've got to take a chance. You just have to decide which risks are worth it."

Kit turned in his arms and wrapped herself around him as tight as she could get. She melded her lips to his, absorbing his taste, his scent. He returned her kiss, hot, gentle, loving, and it was then she understood.

With Mac, the kisses scorched. There was an element of the wild and unpredictable, like two wild animals coming together. With Ryder, it was comfortable, safe and exquisite, like a fine piece of artwork. She loved them both so very much, but Mac held a piece of her heart no other man ever would.

"I'm not ready to let go of you, Ryder," she whispered.

He kissed her again, letting his tongue linger over hers. "That's good, darlin', because I'm not ready to let go of you either."

For the second time in as many days, she retreated in Ryder's arms, but this time . . . this time was different. The beginnings of something new and beautiful lay just beyond her reach. If only she'd take it. Take a chance.

CHAPTER 12

Mac shoved the truck into park then gripped the steering wheel in both hands, his fingers curled as tight as they'd go. Kit was here at work. She'd insisted on Ryder taking her in. Mac was supposed to be working, but he'd called in for the first time since he'd become a cop. There was too much unresolved.

He closed his eyes and blew out his breath in a weary sigh. He couldn't stand the thought of losing Kit. He'd tried so hard to be patient, to wait until the time was right, but now he realized there probably wasn't ever going to be a right time.

He got out of his truck and headed for the bar entrance like he'd done so many other nights. Only now he didn't look forward to seeing Kit. Didn't know if he could stand the look on her face.

Ryder saw him across the room and stood up. They met halfway across the floor.

"How is she?" Mac asked quietly. His eyes found Kit even as he focused on Ryder.

"She's okay I think. Look, I'm gonna split, leave y'all to it. Call me if you need anything."

Ryder connected his fist to Mac's then slipped past and out the door. Mac looked over at Kit again to see her staring at him. Her emerald gaze held steady. There was a mixture of emotion reflected in the orbs. A little fear, confusion and something else he couldn't quite name.

He stared back at her until she was forced to turn her attention to a table she was tending. David motioned him over to the bar and plunked down a draft beer in front of him.

"You look like you could use a drink," David said.

Mac lifted one corner of his lip. "Yeah, I could. Thanks."

"Kit told me the son of a bitch called her this morning at your house. Any idea who it is yet?"

Mac shook his head. "Not a damn clue."

"That's too bad. Kit deserves better than that."

"You got that right," Mac muttered.

"She'll come out all right. She's a tough girl. Anyone who can get a tattoo of a dragon where she did has more balls than I do," David said with a chuckle.

Mac nodded absently, his attention focused on Kit through the crowd. His pulse picked up a beat when she headed in his direction. Her eyes kept falling away as if she couldn't meet his gaze.

She stopped beside him and gave her order to David. Then she turned to look at him. Her eyes were hooded, her actions hesitant.

"Mac, we need to talk," she said in a soft whisper.

"Yeah, we do."

"After work? Can we go somewhere alone? Just the two of us?"

He put a hand to her cheek. "Yeah, baby. Just you and me."

She smiled a nervous smile and turned back to the bar to get her drink order.

Mac tried not to panic. Tried not to guess what was going

through Kit's mind. This might be his only chance to keep her. He couldn't afford to fuck this up.

He nursed the same beer for most of the evening. Getting wasted was the last thing he needed. Not when he faced the most difficult obstacle of his life.

It was getting on in the evening when David held up the phone and motioned for Mac.

Mac raised a brow in question but took the phone. After a brief conversation with headquarters, he hung up and swore long and hard. Goddamn it. Of all nights. He thought hard for a moment, trying to come up with a solution.

He glanced up at David and waved him over.

"What time do you and Kit get off tonight?"

"I'm closing. Kit's supposed to leave at eleven. Why do you ask?"

Mac swore again. "I've got to go in. There's a big drug bust going on right on the county line. They need everyone."

"I can run Kit home for you," David offered. "If that's what you needed."

"What about the bar?" Mac asked.

David shrugged. "I can call Pete in to cover for me."

"That's okay. I can call Ryder right quick."

"Suit yourself. The offer's still open."

David walked off to help a customer who had signaled, and Mac picked up the phone to call Ryder. He swore when he got no answer on Ryder's cell.

He walked over to where David was pouring a round. "David, if your offer's still open, I'd appreciate you running Kit over to my house. Make sure she locks all the doors if you don't mind."

David gave him a two-finger salute. "No problem."

Mac turned around in search of Kit. When he saw her, he parted the crowd and made his way across the floor. She looked up in surprise when he touched her arm.

"I've got to go. Been called in."

She nodded her understanding.

"But, Kit, we'll talk, okay? David's offered to drive you to my house after you get off. Will you go there and wait for me?"

Their eyes locked, and his voice was too close to pleading for his comfort, but he needed her to be there when he got home.

"I'll wait," she said softly.

He dropped his hand from her arm and turned away before he did something foolish like drag her into his arms and kiss the breath from her.

Kit watched him walk away when what she wanted to do was beg him to stay. *He came back for you.* Ryder's words echoed in her heart.

Take a chance. Take a chance. It repeated like a litany in her mind. She didn't want to lose Mac. Would do anything to prevent it. Even if it meant taking the biggest risk of her life.

She trudged back over to the bar and checked the clock. Two more hours.

"You okay?" David asked.

She smiled at her friend. "Yeah, thanks for giving me a ride. Mac said you were taking me home."

David looked confused for a moment. "Home? He wanted me to take you to his place."

Her cheeks flamed, and she felt a little silly. "Yeah, his place. Home."

Or it would be if she could take the leap.

"As soon as Pete gets in, we'll take off. Business is slow tonight. Rose can handle the remaining customers."

"Thanks, David."

She worked to keep on top of orders as she waited for Pete. If she could satisfy most of the orders, Rose would be left in good shape, and Kit could go home to wait for Mac.

An hour and a half later, David motioned to her from the bar, and she walked over to shed her apron.

"You ready?" he asked.

Oh yeah, she was ready. She nodded and followed him out back where his truck was parked. She slid into the passenger seat and waited as he cranked the engine and backed out of the small alley.

"I really appreciate this, David," she said again. "It was totally unnecessary, but it made Mac feel better."

David threw her a curious glance. "What's between you and him anyway?"

Kit blinked in surprise. "I'm not sure that's any of your business."

David frowned but didn't say anything further.

"Hey, you missed the turnoff," Kit said, turning around in her seat to look back.

David remained silent and accelerated down the street.

"David, you missed the turn."

He stared at her, anger rolling off him in waves. "I didn't miss the turn, Kit. I'm not taking you to Mac's."

"Where the fuck are you taking me then?" she demanded.

"Somewhere I can make you realize they won't love you like I will."

Kit sucked in her breath and panic exploded like a Fourth of July fireworks display. Bile rose in her throat and she gagged to keep it back.

"Oh my God. It was you."

"Yes, Kit, it was me," David hissed. "You're too fucking stupid to put two and two together."

"I trusted you, you son of a bitch. You raped me!"

He glared at her. "I didn't rape you, Kit. You wanted me just as bad as I wanted you."

"Let me out of this truck!" she yelled. Her hand went to the handle. She was prepared to leap out at high speed if she had to.

David's arm snaked across the truck seat and grabbed her arm. He yanked her to him, swerving wildly on the road as she kicked and fought. He howled in pain when she punched him in the ear. He slammed on the breaks and backhanded her viciously.

Tears swam in her vision. He slapped her again, and the world faded around her.

Mac sighed in relief when Ryder answered his cell phone.

"What's up?" Ryder asked. "You and Kit at home?"

Mac sighed. "I wish. I got called in. Big drug bust over on 107. Look, I got David to run Kit home. Can you go over and stay with her until I get done here?"

"Sure, she already there?"

Mac checked his watch. "Yeah, she should be. She got off at eleven."

"I'll head over now."

"Thanks, Ryder. I'll be there as soon as I'm done with all this freaking paperwork."

Mac hung up and turned his attention to the parade of hand-cuffed prisoners being stuffed into the array of cruisers. What bad fucking timing. They'd been after the drug dealers running their shit over the county line for over a year. And tonight of all nights, the break had to come. Just when he was on the cusp of the most important conversation of his life.

He holstered his gun and climbed into his truck. He'd run by the station, finish up his shit, and then he was heading home to Kit.

Ten minutes later, he turned into the parking lot of the station and shut off the engine. Before he could get out, his cell rang. It was Ryder.

"Talk to me," he said.

"Mac, when did you say Kit got off from work?"

Mac frowned. He didn't like the worry he heard in Ryder's voice. Ryder didn't get worried unless there was a damn good reason.

"Eleven." He checked his watch again. Damn, it was almost midnight.

"She's not here," Ryder said. "I don't think anyone's been here all night."

Mac's blood ran cold. "Did you try her house?"

"Yeah, I ran by there a minute ago. No one's been there either. I tried her cell and got no answer. I called the bar, and Rose said she and David left at ten thirty."

A loud roar began in Mac's ears. An hour and a half? No where David could possibly have driven her would take an hour and a half.

"Hang tight. I'm on my way over," Mac said.

He tore out of the parking lot, leaving a layer of rubber six feet long. Exactly three minutes later, he skidded to a halt in his drive. Ryder leaped down from the porch where he'd waited and strode over, his expression grim.

"No one's seen David or Kit since they left. David isn't home."

An eerie tingle skirted up Mac's spine. Something David said earlier. Only now did it sink in. Realization hit him square in the chest, sucking his breath right out of his lungs.

"Son of a bitch. *Son of a bitch!*"

"Tell me," Ryder demanded.

"It was him. It was him all along," Mac shouted.

"Who?"

"David! Earlier tonight, he said something about her tattoo. He knew exactly what it looked like and where it was on her body."

Ryder's eyes glittered in the night. "She never showed it to any-one but us, and I know she damn well wouldn't have spread that kind of information about herself."

"Exactly. Which means the son of a bitch has seen it firsthand. Goddamn, Ryder, he raped her. The bastard raped her!"

Mac's fury spiraled out of control. He punched the door of his truck, putting a fair size dent where his fist landed. "We've got to find her, Ryder. The bastard is out of his mind. I don't like to think of what he could do to her."

"We'll split up. I'll go west on my bike. You take the east. I'll keep my phone ready. Call me if you see anything."

Mac nodded. "I'm calling into the station. Get the other men out there looking."

Kit crawled from the cobwebs surrounding her brain. She could feel hands on her. Unfamiliar hands. They stroked her flesh, and she shivered in revulsion.

She opened her eyes and blinked as she tried to see through the curtain of dark. She tried to move, but found she was awkwardly positioned. Her hands were tied behind her at her waist, and they dug painfully into her back as she laid on them. Her chest bowed unnaturally, and she tried to roll over so she could regain feeling in her numb arms. God, where was she?

It was dark. Only the soft gleam from the cab light illuminated the night. Then she saw him. David stared menacingly down at her, promise in his eyes. Promise to hurt her once again.

Cool metal pressed into her shoulders. She glanced around to see she was lying in the bed of his truck, her legs dangling off the tailgate. A quick appraisal of her clothes revealed he'd stripped her of her jeans and shirt. Only her bra and underwear kept her from being completely nude.

"You're awake," he said.

"No shit, Sherlock."

He slapped her across the face, and she saw stars.

"Keep a civil tongue," he warned.

"Or what?" she taunted. "Like you haven't already done your worst."

He looked so seriously at her, she fell silent.

"Oh no, Kit, I haven't done my worst. Far from it. I made love to you. Showed you what we could have together. But you threw it all away to become Mac and Ryder's slut."

"You *raped* me," she spit out.

He shook his head. He reached down and grabbed her knees with his hands, his grip bruising. He yanked her legs apart and moved closer to her. Lord help her. She was completely vulnerable in this position.

"I'm going to give you a chance, Kit. A chance to see how good it can be."

"Oh, is that why you tied me up?" she said scornfully. "You know, David, if you have to tie a woman up to have sex with her, chances are she isn't too crazy about you."

"Shut up!" he screamed.

But she wouldn't be silenced. She'd been a victim six months ago, but she'd be damned if she remained one. The sorry bastard was going to regret betraying her friendship. It wasn't something she offered to many people.

His hand yanked at her bra, pulling it down until one of her breasts was bared. He inched his fingers up her body, and she struggled to keep away from him. When his thumb brushed across her nipple, she lost control and let her rage fly.

She pulled her legs back to her chest and kicked him right in the face. He stumbled back, holding his nose. She didn't give him any more time to react. She rolled toward the tailgate, and when he loomed over her again, she kicked again.

It gained her enough time to scramble off the end of the truck. She hit the ground hard, her breath leaving her in a painful thud. Her hands, still bound together, sought purchase on the soil below. She pushed herself up and ran for her life.

Behind her, David bellowed in rage and took off after her.

She ran headlong into the woods surrounding her. She had no idea where she was or where she was going, but she wasn't going to stay there and take what he had planned for her.

Tree limbs slapped her in the face. Vines and thorns clutched at her legs, and still, she ran. Blindly, her blood humming in her veins, she pushed harder into the suffocating darkness. Complete panic flooded her mind. She couldn't see.

Her foot caught on a root, and she went flying. She landed on her chest, her forehead slamming against the ground. She lay there, robbed of breath, trying desperately to summon the strength to get back up and run again.

Think, Kit, think! She had to keep a level head if she was going to stay ahead of David. Running around like a chicken with its head cut off was not going to help her. She had to outsmart him.

She managed to get to her knees and hoist herself up. She looked up to the sky, trying to find even one star amongst the black cover. She needed a sense of direction. Something to keep her from going in circles and getting caught. And she had to be quiet.

But then she heard the heavy sound of a man thrashing through the woods, and she forgot all about her plan to outwit him. She ran.

How long she continued her grueling pace, she didn't know. Her lungs burned as if someone had turned a blowtorch on them. Her legs spasmed and convulsed. She fell too many times to count, but she forged ahead, deeper into the thick, overgrown forest.

Finally, the floor opened up so her path wasn't as impeded. She put on a burst of speed. Just as hope began to beat a steady rhythm in her heart, she stepped in a hole. Her ankle popped and twisted, and she went headlong into a pile of leaves.

She cried out at the pain lashing up her leg. Tears of frustration streamed down her face. Her eyes closed in exhaustion as she went limp. She couldn't stop now.

She began dragging herself along the rough ground. Finally, she couldn't go another inch. Spots flashed across her eyes, and her head lolled back.

CHAPTER 13

$\mathcal{M}$ac drove down the old dirt county road like a man possessed. Five minutes ago, they'd gotten a report of a truck matching the description of David's vehicle at one of the turnouts.

Ryder was behind him on his motorcycle, and Mac had called for backup. Two more squad cars were enroute.

He'd let her down again. He'd gift wrapped and delivered her right into her attacker's hands. Mac pounded the steering wheel in fury and drove his truck to its limits.

Ahead he saw a glint. His headlights bounced off the reflector of a taillight. He slammed on his brakes and fishtailed on the gravel road, finally coming to a stop near the ditch.

He leaped out of the truck, pulling his gun. Ryder ran over as well, and in the distance, Mac could hear sirens.

"It's his truck," Mac said.

He and Ryder ran over to the parked truck only to find it empty. Mac circled the vehicle and found the tailgate opened. He grabbed his flashlight from his belt loop and shined it over the bed. He froze when he saw the unmistakable smear of blood on the edge of the tailgate.

Two seconds later, two squad cars roared up, their floodlights shining toward Mac.

Ray Hartley and Sean Gardner, two sheriff's deputies, stepped out of their cars and hurried toward David's truck.

"You find anything, Mac?" Ray asked as they approached.

"Negative," Mac returned.

"Think they could be in the woods?" Sean asked.

A sound behind Mac whirled him around. He threw up his flashlight, and to his shock saw David stumble from the woods. Mac's heart stopped. Blood was smeared down the front of David's shirt. He looked rough and bloodied, scratches on his face. His clothing was torn. As if he's just gone through the fight of his life.

The three deputies pulled their weapons simultaneously.

"Down on your knees!" Sean barked.

Mac ran to where David had sunk to the ground, rage pumping through his veins. "Where is she?" he demanded. "Where is she?"

He pulled David to his feet and gathered his bloodied shirt in his hands. "What did you do to her?"

David smiled. It was a vacant expression, eerie and evil. "Wouldn't you like to know?"

Mac lost all control. He slammed his fist into David's jaw, and the other man crumpled. Mac went down after him. Behind him, Ryder, Sean and Ray made no move to stop him.

Mac hit him again and again. "Tell me where she is!"

But David remained silent.

Finally the others pulled Mac off David's wilted form. Mac struggled and fought like a madman. David had killed her. He knew it. He just knew it.

Tears streamed down his face as the three men pinned him against the truck and held him.

"It's all right, man. We'll find her, I swear," Sean murmured close to his ear.

But what would they find? Mac jerked away and buried his face against the side of the truck. God, he had to find her. He wouldn't let her stay out there alone.

"You don't know that he killed her," Ray said quietly. "He didn't try to kill her last time. Chances are she's out there. Hurt, but alive."

Mac's fists clenched as hot fury poured over him like molten lava. "Call everybody out," he said hoarsely. "I won't rest until she's found."

He turned to Ryder, whose expression was as haunted as his own had to be. Ryder nodded.

Ray walked over to his squad car and returned with a duffel bag. "Here's a couple of floodlights and a flare. Sean's radioed in for a search party. We'll take the scumbag in and be back out to help. Keep your radio on you and send up a flare if you find her."

Mac threw one of the lights to Ryder. "Let's split up."

Ryder nodded and headed into the woods.

As Mac tromped through the heavy brush, his hopes sank further. How on earth would they ever find her in this shit? Sweat lay thick on him. The evening air, humid and suffocating, hung like a cloak of doom.

For hours he waded through heavy brush, swinging his spotlight in a radius around him. He'd shouted Kit's name until he was hoarse.

Sean and Ray had long ago radioed that they'd joined the search along with a group of volunteers. As time passed, Mac became more and more convinced they'd find a body.

The radio crackled beside him, and he paused to rest a moment. He mopped the sweat from his forehead and grabbed the radio. "Ryder, any luck?"

He knew the futility of the question. Ryder would have radioed immediately if he'd found anything, but the silence was driving Mac insane.

"Nothing."

The one word, so full of despair, nearly sent Mac over the edge. He closed his eyes and screamed her name, willing there to be an answer.

The only sound that resonated through the forest was the chirping of crickets and the sound of tree locusts.

Above him the sky was starting to lighten the tiniest bit, and he knew dawn wasn't far off. They should have found her by now.

He stumbled off again, refusing to concede defeat. The way became easier as the undergrowth thinned. He picked up his pace, scanning the area with his flashlight.

He almost missed the flash of pale skin as he swung the light to the right. In a flash, he yanked the light back to the two trees he'd scanned by. His heart plummeted when he finally saw what it was.

Huddled in the underbrush, nearly concealed by the mound of leaves and downed branches, lay Kit. She faced away from him, so still. Her hands were tied behind her back. She wore only panties—torn panties—and a bra.

His throat closed. He ran for her.

"Kit! Oh my God, Kit!" He rolled her over and gathered her in his arms. Her face, oh God, so pale, bruised. Blood. Whose blood? "Kit, baby, sweetheart, oh my God, please be alive."

He didn't know what to do first. With trembling fingers, he felt for a pulse. His heart soared, and breath he hadn't realized he'd been holding escaped in a whoosh when he felt the slight tremor at her neck.

He yanked his pocketknife out and sawed the ropes at her hands until they fell away. With extreme care, he rolled her over until she lay in his arms. His bag. He needed his bag.

Easing her down to the ground, he crawled over to his bag and ripped a blanket and the flare gun out. He moved back to Kit and arranged the blanket around her near-naked body. He fumbled with his radio, dropping it once in his haste. A muffled curse slipped from his lips as he snatched it up again.

"I've found her. She's alive. I'm sending up a flare."

He dropped the radio and aimed the flare skyward. It arced above the trees, leaving a bright red trail in the air.

Ryder's voice carried over the radio. "On my way."

"We'll have an ambulance on standby," Ray broke in.

Mac cradled her body to him, holding her close, rocking her back and forth. "Kit, baby, please be all right," he whispered. "Wake up, baby. I need you. God, be okay."

He smoothed her matted hair from her dirty face, his fingers trembling as he touched the dark bruise on one cheek. What had David done to her? He buried his face in her neck and felt hot tears slide down his cheeks.

"Goddamn it, Mac, shine a light or something!"

Mac picked his head up as Ryder let loose a string of curses in the distance. He picked up his floodlight and began waving it frantically. "Over here!" he yelled.

Seconds later, he heard Ryder thrashing through the woods, the sound coming closer until finally Ryder burst into the clearing. He stumbled over to Mac and sank down on the ground.

"How is she?" he demanded, his voice raspy.

"She's alive," Mac said. "We have to get her out of here, but I don't have a prayer of doing it myself. I need you to lead me."

"Let's go," Ryder said grimly.

Ryder collected Mac's light and flare then reached for Kit. Mac handed her up to Ryder while he struggled to his feet. Mac's heart lurched at the sight of Kit lying so limply in Ryder's arms.

Mac arranged the blanket tighter around her then gently took her back, hoisting her up in his arms. Her head lolled against his chest, and he rested his cheek on the top of her head.

"How far do you think we are from where we came in?" Mac asked.

"Not too far. She must have run a straight line."

"If she ran," Mac said quietly.

"She fought him," Ryder said in a hard voice. "The blood on David wasn't hers."

Kit began to tremble and stir in Mac's arms. She moaned low in her throat, a sound of fright and anguish. Mac gripped her tighter.

"Kit, Kit, baby, can you hear me? I've got you, honey. You're safe now." He pressed his lips to her forehead. "Talk to me, baby," he whispered.

Kit heard a sound, and she tensed. Oh God, he'd find her. She had to be quiet and still. He'd find her. How long had it been since she'd fallen? Had she given him time to catch up to her?

The sound got louder. It was a voice. She whimpered as terror took firm hold of her. Tears streaked down her cheeks.

"Baby, don't cry, I've got you. I swear he can't hurt you."

Mac. She blinked tired eyes. It was dark. So dark. Then she saw light. Moving light.

"Darlin', listen to me. You're safe now."

Ryder?

She opened her mouth and blinked harder. "Mac?" she croaked out. "Ryder?"

"We're here, Kit."

"Mac!"

Tears flooded her already fuzzy vision, and she began to sob in earnest. She felt his arms around her, and suddenly she realized he held her. Mac. Not David.

She swayed back and forth, and she knew he rocked her in his arms. A gentle hand wiped the tears and the dirt from her eyes, and finally she could see the face looming over hers.

Warm lips kissed her forehead, her eyes, her cheeks.

She shook violently as reality settled in. Somehow Mac had found her. He'd saved her. David couldn't hurt her now.

"Kit, talk to me, sweetheart. Are you hurting anywhere?"

She was aware of movement, of a light bobbing in front of them. She furrowed her eyebrows as she tried to make sense of their surroundings.

"My ankle," she said in a cracked voice. Her hand slid to her throat, and she massaged it, flinching at the discomfort caused by talking. Had she screamed so much?

Mac stopped, and Ryder turned around with a flashlight. He shined it on her ankle as Mac gently examined her. She hissed in pain when he hit a tender spot.

"I'm sorry, baby."

"I don't think it's broken," Ryder spoke up. "But it's pretty swollen."

"She's not going to walk anyway," Mac said tightly.

She clutched tightly at Mac's neck. "David," she whispered. They needed to know who had done this.

Mac stiffened, his arms like steel bands around her.

"Don't worry about him, Kit. Never again. He'll never hurt you."

"Y-you know?"

"Yes, baby, I know. Rest now. Ryder will have us out of the woods soon."

She bounced slightly against his chest as they continued moving forward. Sweat dampened his shirt. His heart thudded comfortingly in her ear, and she nuzzled closer. She closed her eyes and let the tears seep from underneath her lids.

CHAPTER 14

$\mathcal{M}$ac sped up when he caught the first glimpse of flashing lights through the trees. His breath came heavy. Sweat rolled down his brow, and he blinked as the salty moisture stung his eyes.

"Do you need me to take her?" Ryder called back.

"I'm fine," Mac said. Kit's weight was negligible. And he wasn't about to let her go. Even for a second.

Several long minutes later, the two men burst out of the woods. Ray and Sean hurried over, both offering to take Kit. Mac shook them off and headed for the waiting ambulance.

"I'm going to put you down, sweetheart. The medics are here to check you out."

"No," she whispered. "Don't let them see."

Mac's throat tightened, and he swallowed back the heavy emotion knotting there. He kissed her forehead. "You need to go to the hospital, baby."

"Come with me. I don't want to go alone."

"I won't leave you, Kit. I promise."

Her lips formed a smile. He'd never seen anything so glorious. "I know," she said.

He set her down on the waiting stretcher and arranged the blanket around her. The paramedic approached and Mac held out his hand when the medic would have removed the blanket to examine her.

"It can wait," Mac said in a quiet voice.

The paramedic nodded his understanding and motioned to his partner to help load the stretcher onto the ambulance.

"I'll be behind you," Ryder said.

Mac nodded and climbed into the back of the ambulance. As they pulled away, he looked down at Kit. She looked completely vulnerable, her pale, bruised face resting on the small pillow at the head of the stretcher.

He reached down and curled his fingers around her hand. She latched on, holding tightly as they bumped and swayed. Beside Mac, the paramedic kept close watch on Kit, but he didn't move to disturb her.

Mac raised her hand and pressed her palm to his lips. "I love you," he whispered. "I don't know what I would have done if I lost you. I thought I *had*."

Tears filled her green eyes and spilled over the rims. "I'm so stupid," she croaked out.

He stroked the hand he held. He wasn't entirely sure what she was talking about, but it didn't matter. All that mattered was that she was here, touching him, looking at him with her beautiful eyes.

"We're here," the paramedic said as he braced himself for the turn into the hospital.

Mac put a hand down so that Kit wouldn't be jostled. Soon the doors swung open and hospital personnel reached in for the stretcher. Kit's hand tightened around his, and he saw fear in her eyes.

"I'm not going anywhere, baby. I swear."

She relaxed her grip.

Mac jumped down from the truck and hurried after the stretcher as it was wheeled into the emergency room. No one tried to prevent him from entering the exam room with Kit, which was just as well, because he wasn't budging.

An older nurse clucked and fussed over Kit, managing to get her into a hospital gown in the process. After promising the doctor would be in soon, the nurse exited, leaving Mac alone with Kit.

Mac pulled a chair close to the edge of Kit's bed and settled down. He twined his fingers with hers, and with his other hand, he stroked the skin of her arm.

Ryder burst in seconds later, and he immediately went to Kit. Mac eased back to give Ryder room.

Ryder gathered Kit in his arms and hugged her tight.

"You scared me, darlin'."

Mac kicked another chair closer to the bed so Ryder could sit down. As Ryder took a seat, Kit's hand crept back into Mac's.

"How did you find me?" Kit asked.

Mac exchanged glances with Ryder. He wasn't sure how much he wanted to tell her right now. She'd have to make a statement, and he was dying to hear her version as well, but he didn't want to upset her before it was necessary.

He was saved any response when the doctor walked into the exam room. The same nurse who had fussed over Kit before walked in on the doctor's heels, and she made to shoo Mac and Ryder out.

"We need to examine her, then we're sending her to get that ankle x-rayed. When she gets back, you're welcome to come back in," the nurse said.

Mac reluctantly followed Ryder to the outside waiting room. Sean and Ray motioned them over to where they stood.

"How is she?" Ray asked.

"The doctor's with her now," Mac said. "She's awake and talking."

"That's great. Hey look, Sean and I are going to go grab a shower and change. We'll be back up to see how she is, and if she's up to giving us a statement."

"Thanks for all the help," Mac said.

Mac watched as the two men left then slumped into a nearby chair. Ryder slid into the seat next to him and heaved a big sigh. Weariness rolled off them in waves, their dirty, sweat-stained clothing just adding to the mix.

"How was she when you found her?" Ryder asked quietly.

Mac rubbed some of the crud from his eyes and noticed his hands shook. God almighty, he never again wanted to endure the kind of paralyzing fear he'd experienced tonight.

"I found her on the ground, unconscious, half-dressed, her arms tied behind her back," he muttered.

Ryder let out a hiss of anger. "God, you don't think he . . ."

"I don't know, man. I don't know!" Mac thumped his fist into his palm. "How can I ever expect her to trust me when I've let her down so many times?"

"You couldn't have known what a sick fuck David was," Ryder pointed out.

Mac closed his eyes. He was tired, so goddamn tired, and he wanted the doctor to hurry the fuck up so he could return to Kit.

"I need a cigarette," Ryder muttered.

Mac opened one eye. "Thought you quit?"

"Yeah, I did. Bad idea."

"Have a drink with me when this is all over instead."

"You're on. Getting wasted sounds like a hell of a good idea."

Thirty minutes later, Sean and Ray walked back through the ER entrance in clean uniforms. Before they could make it across to where Mac and Ryder sat, the doctor pushed open the swinging doors to the waiting room.

Mac and Ryder both jumped up and met the doctor halfway.

"How is she?" Mac demanded.

The doctor smiled. "She's going to be just fine. She suffered a rather nasty sprain, but her ankle isn't broken. A few days on crutches, and she'll be as right as rain."

"Excuse me, doctor," Ray cut in. "Did you do a rape kit? We'll need to log it in as evidence."

The doctor looked curiously at him. "There was no need. The young lady said she wasn't assaulted."

Mac let out his breath in a long whoosh. His legs went weak, and he stumbled slightly before he caught his balance.

"Thank God," he whispered. He looked back up at the doctor. "Can we see her now?"

"I don't see why not. She's demanding to go home, and frankly, there isn't a reason to keep her. The nurse is seeing about her discharge now."

"Mind if we go in and ask her a few questions?" Ray asked Mac.

"If she's up to it," Ryder broke in.

"Of course. We won't bother her," Sean assured.

Mac strode toward Kit's room, anxious to be close to her again. He knocked softly on the door before opening it a crack and peering in.

She smiled tiredly at him and motioned for him to enter.

"Hey baby," he said huskily. He dropped a kiss on her forehead and ran his hand through her hair. "Ray and Sean want to know if you're up to answering a few questions."

She frowned but nodded.

"You don't have to," Ryder said.

Mac looked up to see a protective scowl darken Ryder's face.

"No, it's fine," she said. "Have they caught him? David?"

"Yes, baby, he's in custody. He's not going anywhere. I promise."

She sank back onto her pillows in relief. "You can let them come in."

Mac went to the door and gestured for Sean and Ray. As they passed, Mac murmured in a low voice, "Don't overdo it guys. Just the basics."

Ryder pulled a chair up to the opposite side of Kit's bed and plopped down unceremoniously. Mac stifled a smile at the way he glared at Ray and Sean. Ryder was fiercely protective of Kit. A feeling Mac knew all too well.

Mac settled down in the chair on the near side of Kit's bed and took her hand. He couldn't stop touching her. Couldn't stop thinking about the fact he could have lost her forever. As Kit recounted her story, Mac's chest grew tighter, his throat swelled and rage blew through his system like a Texas summer thunderstorm.

When she had finished, Mac looked over at Ryder to see the same anger brewing.

Sean stepped forward and took Kit's hand. "We appreciate your help, Kit. We'll make sure the son of a bitch doesn't get away with this."

"Thank you," she said quietly.

When they left, Kit closed her eyes, weariness etched across her brow.

"Are you sure you shouldn't stay the night, darlin'?" Ryder asked.

She shook her head. Then she looked at Mac. "I want to go home," she said softly.

Mac threaded his fingers through hers and held on tight. "I'll take you wherever you want to go, sweetheart."

She smiled.

Ryder stood up and leaned over to kiss Kit. Mac watched idly as he gathered Kit in his arms and held her close. If any other man had touched her as intimately as Ryder was, Mac would've seen red, but he didn't feel threatened by Ryder. The only thing he felt threatened by was not knowing how Kit felt about Mac.

"I love you, Kit girl. You take care of yourself."

"Where're you going?" Kit asked.

Ryder glanced over at Mac. "I'm going to scoot home and get cleaned up. Leave you two to sort things out."

Mac's brow went up and a delicate blush colored Kit's cheeks. She was *not* a blusher.

"Thanks for coming for me, Ryder," she whispered.

"Anytime, darlin', anytime."

Ryder held a fist out to Mac as he started to walk to the door. "Good luck, man," Ryder said in a low voice.

CHAPTER 15

*K*it waited nervously for Mac to drive his truck around to the ER exit. She stood just inside the automatic doors under the cool air of a vent and shivered despite the oppressive humidity that hit her every time the doors opened.

Her stomach had managed to tie itself in a variety of knots a Boy Scout would be proud of. After escaping the clutches of the sick, twisted former *friend* of hers, a man who'd raped her once already, all she could think about was whether she'd screwed things up with Mac.

She leaned heavily on the crutches as she shifted so her injured ankle wouldn't bear the brunt of her weight. The thin pair of scrubs the nurse had given her to wear home hung loose on her, and with only a little provocation would slide right off. She looked like a ragamuffin. Mac had offered to go get her clothes, but in the time it would take him to go home to get them, she could be away from this place.

Mac roared up and quickly got out. She started forward, her movements awkward as she tried to learn the crutches. He stopped her before she went two feet.

He held out his arm to her. "Hold on to me for a sec," he said.

When she complied, he took the crutches and leaned them against the side of the building. Then he swung her into his arms and carried her the remaining distance to the truck.

"Careful not to bump your foot," he cautioned as he eased her into the passenger seat.

She melted into the seat, her muscles lacking any sort of tone. Fatigue rippled through her body, and she fought to keep her eyes open.

Mac got into the driver's seat and eased away from the ER.

"You get my crutches?" she asked, not opening her eyes.

"In the back."

She nodded, too tired to say anything else.

"We'll be home in a minute," he said softly.

She must have dozed off because the next thing she knew, Mac shook her gently. She roused as he cradled her in his arms and lifted her from the seat.

When he walked into his house, she sighed as a blast of cool air hit her.

"Where do you want to be?" he asked.

In your arms. Next to you. Close to you. God, anywhere he was.

"I need to change," she said.

He took her into the bedroom and set her down on the bed.

"Sit tight. I'll get you some shorts and a shirt."

"Just a T-shirt."

He smiled. "Okay. Just a T-shirt. Want one of mine?"

"Please?"

He rummaged in his drawer and pulled out a large red T-shirt. He returned to where she sat on the bed.

"Want help?"

She thought for a moment and quickly decided she didn't have the strength to hold her arms up much less get out of the hospital scrubs.

With infinite care, he tugged the scrubs from her body then quickly pulled his T-shirt over her head and settled it over her shoulders.

It smelled of him. She clutched her arms around her, hugging his scent close to her. Then she slowly raised her gaze to him, looked into his blue eyes.

"Hold me?"

"Ahh, sweetheart."

He crawled onto the bed with her and pulled her gently into his arms. He tucked her into his side and rested his chin on top of her head.

Safe. She felt safe and protected, like nothing could hurt her in his arms. God, she never wanted to move. Could she stay this way forever?

"I love you, Mac," she whispered.

His entire body stiffened. He went so still, she couldn't even feel him breathe. Then he pulled slightly away from her. He stared down at her, his eyes intense.

"Say that again."

"I love you."

His body deflated like a balloon. His breath tore out of his chest in one explosion of movement.

"Do you mean that?"

Hunger flooded his expression. And vulnerability like she'd never seen before in Mac. She lifted her hand to his face and cupped his beard-roughened cheek. "I never say something I don't mean."

He closed his eyes then lowered his forehead to hers until their noses brushed. "God, Kit. I never thought I'd hear you say those words."

Tears welled and threatened to spill over the rims of her eyes. "I'm sorry, Mac. I've been such a fool. I've let fear rule me for so long, I don't know how to live any way else."

Mac cupped the side of her neck, threading his hand through her hair, up behind her ear.

"You don't have to be afraid, Kit. I'm not going to leave you. I'm never going to leave you."

"I know," she said softly. She smoothed a hand over his rumpled hair. "You look like hell."

He grinned. "So do you."

She sobered and grew silent.

He feathered his hand over her cheek then ran his fingers across her lips. "What's wrong, baby?"

"What do we do now?"

His smile was so gentle it made her chest ache.

"We take it one day at a time. Me and you. Together. I love you, Kit. So much it makes me crazy sometime."

"I love you too."

"Say it again."

She smiled and kissed him full on the lips. "I love you. I always have."

what she needs

CHAPTER 1

*R*yder Sinclair eyed the shapely blond onstage as she wound down her routine. She dipped and swayed, keeping perfect time with the music. Not as tall as most of the other strippers, she was still dynamite. Her naked breasts bobbed and swayed, and Ryder wished to God he could muster enthusiasm for the sight.

He sighed and threw back the rest of his beer in a long swallow. Mia would be done soon. They'd have a few beers, shoot the shit and both go home alone. What a fucking way to spend a Friday night.

The music stopped, and he glanced up to see Mia collect a few eager tips, then she stepped off the stage and pulled on a large T-shirt. She made her way through the crowd then slid onto the bar stool next to him.

"Beer," she said, motioning toward the barkeep.

"Hot stuff as usual, darlin'," Ryder said.

She snorted and rolled her eyes then stared ahead, focusing on the bartender as he plunked a beer down in front of her.

Ryder shook his head. She was young to be so damn cynical. Somewhere, sometime, someone had hurt that little girl but good.

Mia slid him a sideways glance. "You not hanging out at Mac's this weekend?"

Ryder slowly shook his head.

Her eyes softened in sympathy. "You going with avoidance mode now?"

"I don't know what I'm doing," Ryder muttered.

Mia raised an eyebrow and nodded slightly. "That much is evident."

He reached over and smacked her on the ass. "Watch it, little girl."

She laughed then quickly sobered. "You know, it would have made things a lot easier if we could have been attracted to each other."

"No shit," Ryder agreed.

They'd certainly tried. A few months earlier, they'd made it all the way to Mia's tiny apartment. Had even shed their clothes before they realized what a huge mistake they were making. Instead, they'd gotten roaring drunk and exchanged sob stories.

Ryder winced. He still wished he hadn't bared his soul. It made him damned uncomfortable for Mia to know his feelings for Kit Townsend.

"How long's it been since you got together with Kit and Mac?" Mia asked softly.

"Awhile."

Several weeks to be exact. He'd found it increasingly hard to make love to Kit when he knew at the end of the night he'd be leaving and Kit would sleep in Mac's arms.

"Any chance they might split up?" Mia asked.

Ryder shook his head. "No, and I'd never try to do it. Kit loves Mac. He loves her. She needs him."

"You said she loves you too, though."

He nodded. "Yeah, she does. Just not like she does Mac."

Mia shook her head. "That is one fucked-up situation, Ryder."

"Yeah, tell me about it."

He motioned for another beer. The barkeep slid a cold bottle across the bar to him, and Ryder picked it up and took a long swallow. After several long moments, he turned back to Mia.

"What about you, little girl? You ever going to stop carrying a torch for that asshole who hurt you and find yourself a decent man?"

Pain darkened her blue eyes, so much so that Ryder immediately felt bad for bringing the subject up.

"Nice try," she muttered. "But changing the subject won't work. And I'm over him."

Uh-huh. And Ryder might sprout wings and start clucking.

Ryder's cell phone rang, and he looked down to see the name and number on the LCD screen. Mac. Fuck.

"Hey, man," Ryder said as he put the phone to his ear.

"Hey," his friend greeted. "What's going on?"

"Nada. What about you? How's Kit?"

Mac paused for a moment. "She's good. The trial has been hard on her, though. Thought I might take her to the coast for the weekend. Wondered if you wanted to come."

Ryder didn't respond right away. He knew what the invitation involved. Sex. Between the three of them. Just like so many times before. It hadn't used to be a problem.

He closed his eyes. "Nah, you two go on ahead. Maybe another time."

"Okay, man. If you change your mind, you know where to find us."

"Give Kit a kiss for me," Ryder said.

Mac laughed. "I'll do more than that."

Ryder closed his cell phone and shoved it back into his pocket. Hell's bells.

Mia looked at him, her eyes soft with sadness. "That Mac?"

Ryder nodded. "Yeah. He wanted me to go down to the coast with him and Kit."

"Why don't you go?"

He stared back at her. "It's hard for me to make love to her and pretend it's just casual sex. I don't think I can do it anymore."

Mia put out her hand to touch him on the arm. "I'm sorry, Ryder."

He shrugged. "She's happy. She's had a lot of hurt in her life. I just want what's best for her."

"And what if you're what's best?" Mia asked.

Ryder shook his head. "She's got Mac. He loves her."

Mia set her beer back down with a tired sigh. "I'm going to scoot on out of here. It's been a long day, and I'm tired. I'll catch you later though, okay?"

Ryder leaned down and kissed her on top of the head. "You be careful, little girl. I'll stop in to check on you soon."

She smiled cheekily at him and headed for the dressing room.

Ryder headed out to the parking lot and straddled his Harley. A few seconds later, he gunned the engine and roared out onto the highway toward home. He was hungry and restless. If Mac was taking Kit out of town, she must not be working at the Two Step tonight. It should be safe to stop off and grab a bite.

Then again he could be very wrong. Fifteen minutes later, Ryder stood at the entrance to the Two Step staring across the room at Kit.

It was a hell of a note when he started avoiding a girl he'd considered his best friend for over half his life. She was more than his best friend. And that was the problem.

He shook his head and forced himself to walk in as casually as he used to. When things had gotten so fucking complicated he didn't know. Had he always felt so deeply for her? He honestly couldn't separate the way he felt about her now and the way he felt for her even six months ago. It all ran together in one long string.

"Ryder!"

Shit.

He looked up, unable to keep from smiling at her. "Hey darlin'," he said huskily.

She threw herself in his arms and proceeded to wrap herself completely around him. God, she felt good in his arms. He held onto her for a second before lifting her away.

"How you doing?"

She smiled. "I'm good. Hey, did Mac call you?"

An uneasy sensation crept up his spine. "Yeah, he called."

"And? Are you going?"

Excitement shown in her green eyes, and her lips were split into a wide smile. It was good to see her smiling. She'd been through a hell of a lot in the past months.

"Uh, not this time, darlin'."

Her lips turned down into a pout. "Why not?"

"You and Mac need the time alone. You don't need me tagging along like a third wheel."

Something indiscernible flashed in her eyes. "I want you to come, Ryder," she said quietly. "You said that me and Mac . . . that me being with him didn't change things between us. I've missed you."

"Ah hell, darlin'."

He dragged a hand through his hair and fiddled with his row of earrings. He didn't want to disappoint her, and she was right. It was him who'd reassured her that her relationship with Mac wouldn't change things between the three of them. It was a lie, but not one he'd intended to tell. It was *his* fault things were changing.

"Will you come?"

The pleading in her eyes was his undoing. Kit didn't ever ask for a lot, and he'd cut off his right arm before denying her pretty much anything.

"You know I never could turn you down when you pout," he said by way of concession.

She threw herself around him again, and he felt himself harden instantly. She reached up on tiptoe and brushed her lips across his. He caught her before she withdrew and deepened the kiss, his tongue melting hot against hers.

Her breathing sped up, and her hand tangled in his long hair. Man, he loved it when she got her hands in his hair. Almost as much as he loved wrapping his hands in *her* hair while she sucked his cock.

"You've missed me too," she whispered against his lips. Her mouth curved into a smile of satisfaction.

Hell yeah, he'd missed her. He'd thought of little else for the last several weeks.

"Yeah, darlin'. I've missed you."

She smoothed a hand through his hair then let it slip until it was centered on his chest. "Mac's going to be here in a little while to get me. Why don't you go home and grab a bag and meet us back here? We have to stop by the house to get my things and let Mac change. You could drop your bike there."

He caught her hand and raised it to his lips. He tasted her palm then kissed it before letting it fall once more. He must be out of his fucking mind to agree to this. He was as hard as a fucking rock, and it was a long-ass drive to Galveston.

"All right, darlin'. I'll be back in a bit."

He turned to go but Kit slid into his arms once more.

"I'm glad you're going, Ryder," she said softly.

He smiled down at her and tried real hard not to kiss her again. Mac was a reasonable guy, but he might not be pleased that Ryder was putting his mark on his girl in public.

His girl. Mac's girl. Fuck.

He squeezed Kit's hand then walked toward the door.

Kit watched him go, her chest tight. She missed him. He hadn't been around much in the last weeks. Oh, he'd been a steady source of support during the trial of the man who'd raped her over a year ago, but he hadn't been to Mac's.

What a twisted mess. She should be the happiest woman alive. She no longer lived in constant fear now that her attacker had been jailed. Mac loved her and they enjoyed a terrific relationship. But she missed Ryder. Missed his big body wrapped around hers, his lips and hands on her skin. Missed the comfort of having the two people she loved most in the world close to her heart at all times.

She headed back to the bar and set her tray down. A quick survey of the room told her the customers were satisfied for the moment. She leaned against the worn countertop and took a breather.

Fifteen minutes later, she headed back into the crowd, her tray full of beers and mixed drinks. Her pulse sped up when she spied Mac standing in the doorway. She grinned and blew him a kiss.

No matter how many times he walked through that door, she got a ridiculous thrill, like it was the first time she'd laid eyes on him.

Tall, big, broad shouldered, looking like the sexiest man alive in his police uniform and Stetson. His blue eyes positively smoldered as he raked his gaze over her.

Oh, this weekend was going to be fun.

He strode toward her, and her pussy tightened painfully. Figures she could get wet, and he was still ten feet away.

"Hey, baby," he said huskily as he came to a stop in front of her.

She shivered at the raw sexuality in his voice. She reached up on tiptoe and kissed him. "Hey yourself."

"You about ready to go?"

She checked her watch. "Ten more minutes and I'm yours."

"I'll wait for you by the bar," Mac said.

She nodded and set about finishing her drink deliveries.

A few minutes later, she walked back over to the bar and plunked down her tray. Mac slid an arm around her and began untying her apron for her.

"I missed you today," he murmured against her ear.

She leaned in against him, resting her cheek on his chest. He smelled delicious. Felt even better.

Suddenly she picked her head back up. "Have you talked to Ryder?" she asked.

"Yeah, he couldn't make it. Sorry, baby."

"Oh, he came by here and I talked him into going. He's headed home to grab a bag, and he'll be back in a few minutes. I told him he could catch a ride with us. Is that okay?" she asked anxiously.

"Of course it's all right. I wouldn't have invited him if I didn't want him to go."

She relaxed into a smile. "You're the best, Mac. I can't believe you planned this whole weekend. I can't wait for it to just be us. I've missed you both."

"I know you have, baby," he said quietly.

"Hey, there he is," Kit said as she looked beyond Mac to the door.

Mac's hand tightened at her waist.

Ryder approached them at the bar, and Mac held out a fist. Ryder bumped it with his. "How's it going?"

"Great now that you're here," Mac said lazily. "We can get this party started if Kit's ready to leave."

Kit looked between the two men, and her nipples hardened to points. Her stomach clenched with heady anticipation. Oh yeah, she was ready. A whole weekend rocked between the two sexiest men alive? What girl wouldn't orgasm just thinking about it?

CHAPTER 2

*R*yder looked over his shoulder to see Kit curled up sound asleep in the back seat of Mac's extra-cab Dodge truck. She looked fragile, delicate, and he knew she was anything but. The last year had taken its toll on her in more ways than one.

"She asleep?" Mac asked in a low voice.

Ryder turned back to Mac. "Yeah. Crashed hard."

Mac shook his head. "She needs this weekend to decompress." He paused for a long moment and gripped the steering wheel tighter. "She's still having nightmares."

Ryder clenched his jaw until it ached. "Are you sure you wanted me along? You guys probably need the time together."

Mac stared curiously at him. "Is there something going on with you, bro? You've been acting weird lately. I could swear you've been avoiding us. Kit's missed you being around."

Ryder swallowed and looked away. "Nah," he lied. "Just been

busy at the garage. Besides, I figured you guys had enough to deal with without me hanging around."

"Cut that shit out. You know you're welcome at our place any time. Kit's going to kick your ass if you continue to blow us off."

Ryder grinned. Yeah, she was feisty. It was what he loved about her most. She was strong willed, a free spirit. She was beautiful.

"Yeah, she latched onto my ass like a pit bull when I got to the bar," Ryder said.

Mac chuckled. "That's my girl. Won't take no for an answer."

"I've missed her too," Ryder admitted before he could think better of the statement.

Again Mac looked sideways at him. "Then don't be a stranger."

"Who's being a stranger?" Kit asked in a sleepy voice.

Ryder turned to see her sit up in the seat and rub her eyes.

"No one, darlin'. You get a good sleep?"

She yawned then frowned. "I should have made one of you sit in the back with me so I could snuggle."

Both he and Mac laughed. Kit was a total snuggle bug. She wasn't content unless she was wrapped around him or Mac, and the truth was, Ryder was more than happy to accommodate her most of the time.

She leaned forward until her arms rested on the seat between him and Mac. "So who's the stranger?"

"Ryder is, baby."

She snorted. "That's the truth. If I didn't know better, I'd say he doesn't love me anymore."

"Fat chance," Ryder said, flicking his finger under her chin.

She leaned over the seat and kissed Ryder full on the mouth. He was so surprised he didn't react immediately. And before he could, she pulled away.

"Kit," Mac growled. "Don't start something you can't finish. I'm driving for God's sake."

She grinned mischievously. "You don't complain when I give you a blow job on the road."

"Hell," Mac said.

"Well now, darlin', had I known that little tidbit, I most definitely would have ridden in the back seat with you."

"It's not too late," she said innocently. "Mac could always pull over."

"The hell I will," Mac muttered. "Maybe you think driving with a hard-on is a piece of cake."

She laughed and leaned back once more. "You guys are in so much trouble when we get there."

"Darlin', is that supposed to be a threat? Because I have to tell you, I hope to hell it's a promise."

"Amen," Mac said as he exhaled.

Ryder tensed when he felt her fingers dig into his hair. Her small tips smoothed over the strands, pulling and separating them.

"I love your hair," she said huskily. "So long and wild. Like you."

Ryder groaned. Fuck on a stick. How the hell was he supposed to maintain any sort of distance? Kit was a goddess. There wasn't anything he didn't like about this woman.

Her hands continued to knead in his hair, and he leaned back to give her better access.

"I can't wait to have my hands in your hair while you fuck me," she whispered.

"Jesus, Kit. You have to stop or I swear to God, I'm gonna make Mac pull over while I fuck your brains out."

"And that's supposed to warn me off?" she deadpanned.

Mac laughed again. "I told you, man. She's really missed you."

"How much further, Mac?" Kit asked as she let her hands fall from Ryder's hair.

"We're about an hour out of Houston, baby. Then another forty-five minutes or so to Galveston."

Ryder turned around in his seat. Despite her short nap, she still looked tired. Fatigue rimmed those beautiful green eyes, dark smudges resting in the hollows.

"Why don't you go back to sleep, darlin'? We'll wake you when we get there."

"You bored with my company already?" she teased.

"Do as he says, Kit," Mac rumbled from the driver's seat. "You're gonna need all the rest you can get."

"I'd sleep better if I had someone to snuggle," she grumbled.

But she lay back down and curled into the seat with a yawn.

Ryder and Mac drove the rest of the way in silence. Ryder snuck a peek at Kit every once in a while, but she slept soundly.

They arrived in Galveston and drove along the seawall until they came to their hotel. Mac parked in front and quietly opened his door to go check in. Kit remained asleep as Ryder waited with her.

A few minutes later, Mac slid back into the truck and pulled it into the parking lot adjacent to the hotel.

"I'll get the bags. You wake Kit up," Mac said in a low voice. "We're on the top floor."

Ryder eased out of the truck and opened the back door. Kit's silky hair splayed out over the seat, and her soft breathing filled the interior. Ryder stroked fingers over her cheek, and she stirred restlessly.

"Time to wake up, darlin'," he murmured.

She stretched and emitted a low groan. "We're here?"

She rose up on her elbow and peered around. As if struggling with the heavy fog of sleep, she blinked and shook her head.

He reached his hand out to help her down. When she stepped from the cab, she melted into his arms, burrowing her face into his chest.

He gripped her tightly with one arm, squeezing her against him. "Come on, darlin'. Mac's waiting for us in the lobby."

He ushered her inside where Mac was holding the elevator. She immediately nestled into Mac's side, and Mac wrapped a possessive arm around her. Mac kissed the top of her head, and she turned her lips up, offering her kiss to him.

Ryder glanced away, the intimacy between them making him uncomfortable.

The elevator doors swooshed open, and they stepped into the hallway. Mac led the way to the room at the very end and set the baggage down long enough to insert the card in the door.

Kit opened the door and walked in ahead of them, flipping on the lights as she went. Mac had booked a suite, Ryder noted. There was a small living area with a sliding door to the outside balcony.

He and Mac followed Kit into the bedroom.

"Ohhh, one king bed," she said as she bounced onto the mattress. "I like!"

Mac chuckled and set the luggage down near the bed. "I'm going to take a quick shower. I'll be back in five."

Mac shuffled into the bathroom and closed the door, leaving Ryder and Kit alone.

Kit sat on the edge of the bed, her expression hesitant. Ryder cocked an eyebrow, curious as to why she'd be unsure.

"What's going on in that pretty head of yours, Kit girl?"

She flushed guiltily and looked away. Her fingers flexed and curled against the bed spread, almost nervouslike. Then she turned her green eyes back on him.

"I guess it's just been awhile," she said huskily. "Maybe I'm not sure you want me anymore."

Ryder sighed. What a mess he'd made of things. Instead of enjoying a good thing, he'd done his best to screw it up. He walked over to the bed where she sat and cupped her head in his hands. He shoved his fingers deep into her hair.

He bent his head and captured her lips in a deep kiss. He feasted on her mouth. Gone were the warm, comfortable kisses they used to share. It was hot, breathless, and it sent a jolt to his groin that had his dick paying quick attention.

He licked at her lips, nipped with his teeth, gave her no choice but to respond.

"Get out of those clothes, darlin'. It's been a long time since I got to taste that pussy, and I'm as hard as a jackhammer at the idea."

Kit shivered as she stood in front of Ryder and began pulling her shirt over her head. There was something different about him. She couldn't put her finger on it, but there was enough sexual tension in the room to float a small barge.

She let her shirt drop to the floor then slid her hands down to the waistband of her jeans. Slowly, she peeled the denim down her legs until she stood in only her underwear.

Ryder sucked in his breath. "Black underwear. My favorite."

She smiled. "I remembered."

"Of course, darlin', you'd look good in a sackcloth."

She leaned into Ryder and wrapped her arms around his neck. "You've got too many clothes on, and if you want to see the rest of me, you better get to shucking."

His hands drifted down to cup her ass through the silky material of her panties. Then he walked her backward until the back of her knees hit the edge of the mattress. She went down onto the bed, his arms around her. He came with her, until their bodies tangled together.

"You're not calling the shots tonight, darlin'," he murmured close to her ear.

He proceeded to lick and nibble at the delicate skin surrounding her ear. Forty thousand chill bumps did the river dance over her skin as he sucked the lobe between his teeth.

The straps to her bra slid down her shoulders. He pushed impatiently at the cups until her breasts sprang free. A growl echoed through the room just before he latched onto a nipple.

She sucked in breath after breath but couldn't manage to catch up. The rasp of denim scratched between her legs as Ryder thrust a big thigh between her knees and spread. His body, hard, urgent, mimicked fucking motions, and she felt the bulge suppressed by his jeans cradle into her pussy.

He rubbed again, denim against silk. The sensation set her clit on fire.

"Please," she whispered.

"Please, what, darlin'? Kiss you? Suck you? Fuck you?"

"Yes, yes and yes!"

He chuckled then slid his big body down hers until his lips pressed against the waistline of her panties. He nipped until he caught the edge in his teeth then slowly began to pull down.

His fingers feathered over her tattoo as her underwear moved lower. Cool air blew over the bare skin of her cunt and she shivered.

With a light tug, she was free of the underwear, and she lay naked on the bed, sprawled out for Ryder to do as he wanted. And that made her hot as hell. It had been awhile. Too long. She wanted him desperately. Wanted to be touched and loved by the two men so important to her.

Gentle fingers spread her pussy lips. A fingertip dipped into the folds and trailed around her swollen clit. She jumped and bucked, arching her back.

"Easy, darlin'."

The finger slid downward to her opening. Slid in the barest little bit then retreated, leaving her moaning with want. He bent his head and feathered his tongue over the throbbing button.

"Ryder!"

He sucked it into his mouth just as he sank two fingers deeply into her pussy. She wrapped her legs around his shoulders and hung on for dear life.

"You taste so damn good, darlin'. Just like I remember. All sweet and pretty."

His words combined with the magic of his tongue and fingers sent a spasm through her pelvis, deep into her stomach. She arched and convulsed again.

"Come for me, darlin'. Let it go," he murmured against her skin.

He plunged three fingers into her. He sucked then nipped at her clit.

She closed her eyes and let out a loud wail. Her orgasm raced over her, tightening every muscle in her abdomen. He gripped her ass in both hands and feasted on her pussy, his tongue and teeth covering every quivering inch of her skin.

Her hands plunged into his hair, and she gripped his head tightly, holding him to her as shards of pleasure splintered and spread out over her body.

He carefully pulled free of her clutching hands, and smiled wickedly at her from between her legs. "Like that, did you, darlin'?"

"You beast," she muttered. "What woman alive wouldn't have liked it?"

He pushed off the bed and quickly stripped his shirt over his head. She lay back, lazily taking in his bulging muscles and admired the dragon tattoo that splayed out over his upper chest. An exact replica of the one on her lower abdomen near her pelvis.

Whoever dreamed up the word "sexy" had to have had him in mind. He exuded strength and confidence. That, combined with the wild that surrounded him, would cause any woman with half a libido to turn to jelly.

His hands fell to his fly, and he unbuttoned his jeans then slid them down his thighs. Then he reached into his underwear and pulled out his cock.

She sucked in her breath. God, she'd never get tired of that move. He stood there a moment, stroking his rigid length. He stared at her, promise in his eyes.

Her legs fell open in unconscious invitation. She squirmed when he moved to kneel back on the bed. He towered over her, one hand on his cock, the other hand shoving her thighs further apart.

She opened her arms to welcome him as he settled over her. He covered every inch of her, his skin hot against hers. His hand between their bodies nudged and brushed against the inside of her thigh.

Then he sank into her in one forceful stroke. He settled both his elbows on either side of her head, holding his weight slightly off her. He flexed and rocked his hips against her, burrowing deeply into her pussy.

She wasn't used to the patient, gentle side of him. He was usually demanding in bed. Forceful and hot.

He kissed her lightly on the lips, the soft smooching sound echoing in her ears. He licked at her mouth, sucked her bottom lip between his teeth then thrust his tongue over hers.

They moved together, his hips rolling against hers, his thighs urging hers wider apart with every thrust.

She curled her hands into his black hair, threading the strands over her fingers. She kissed him back, allowing the heat of her passion to bleed through. She held nothing back.

"Wrap your legs around me and hold on tight, darlin'," Ryder whispered.

She did as he asked and locked her ankles around his waist. He held her tightly against him, sliding his arms around her back, lifting her slightly from the mattress. Their lips met again as he rocked against her.

"I've missed you, Kit girl."

"I've missed you too, Ryder. So much. I don't want you to go away again."

"I'm not going anywhere, darlin'."

He squeezed her tighter, and his hips bucked forward more

forcefully. She knew he was close. Her hands skimmed over his back, feeling the dips and ridges of the muscles. Her palms slid down to his tight waist, and then she merely hugged him as close as she could and closed her eyes as she felt him pour himself into her.

He panted softly and dropped his head until his forehead rested against hers. He kissed her again. "You're so beautiful."

She ran a hand through his hair, stroking repeatedly through the wild locks as he shuddered against her.

The bed dipped beside her, and she looked over to see Mac recline beside her, naked. Hard. Very aroused. Had he watched while she and Ryder had made love?

She reached a hand out to him, and he captured it, bringing it to his lips until he pressed a kiss to her palm. Ryder moved off of her and to the other side so that she lay between the two men.

Mac smoothed a hand over her body, cupping her breast and running a thumb over her nipple. On her other side, Ryder laid a possessive hand on her hip, slid his fingers over her tattoo and lower to her pussy. He stroked gently, petting and stroking the tender flesh between her legs.

She moaned and closed her eyes.

"That feel good, baby?" Mac said in his sexy husky voice.

"Mmm hmmm."

He laughed. "You sound pretty content. Ryder been treating you good?" He cupped her cheek with his hand.

She turned into his palm, nuzzling against his hand. "I'd be more content if you'd shut up and fuck me."

CHAPTER 3

"Is that so?" Mac asked with a smile.

Kit stretched then let her hand drift down to cup Mac's heavy sac in her hand. She squeezed and massaged then circled his cock with her fingers.

"Mmmm hmmm. What are you waiting for?"

"Up on your knees, baby. I want your ass."

Her stomach clenched and rolled. She shook so badly she could barely manage to follow his command. Ryder's warm hands helped her, easing her over and coaxing her to her knees. He pressed a gentle kiss to her back before rising from the bed.

Mac settled behind her, his hands firmly on the globes of her behind. He squeezed then leveled a sharp smack to her left cheek. She jumped and moaned.

"You're wet, baby."

"No shit, Sherlock," she muttered.

He smacked her again, this time closer to her pussy. Spasms

weakened her legs and she swayed. He caught her at the waist to steady her then pressed his body against hers.

The heat of his breath blew over her neck, then he sank his teeth into the soft flesh at her nape.

"Maaac!"

He drew away. Then his hot tongue touched the small of her back. Slowly, he slid up her spine, leaving a damp trail. When he reached her neck, he kissed and nuzzled where he'd bitten just moments ago.

Ryder cupped a hand to her cheek and forced her gaze upward. She blinked in surprise. For the space of a moment, she'd forgotten all about him. Forgotten everything but the delicious sensations Mac wreaked on her body.

"Open your mouth, darlin'."

Her lips parted at his command, and she felt his thumb smooth over her cheek. He held her jaw firmly as he positioned his cock between her lips.

"Hold still now, Kit girl. Let me fuck that mouth."

She closed her eyes as he thrust to the back of her throat.

Mac's hands stilled as if he was giving her a chance to adjust to Ryder's demands before he went any further.

"Relax, darlin', you can take it deeper. Swallow and breathe through your nose."

She opened her eyes and looked up to see approval burning in his eyes. His expression was tender and so loving. He stroked her face with his hands as he gave her time to adjust to his request.

He withdrew and paused for a moment. "This time, take it all, Kit. Show me you can."

He slid back in, pushing to the back of her throat. She relaxed her mouth and breathed in through her nose.

"Oh, fuck yeah, that's the way, darlin'."

He began a series of short and longer strokes, alternating, giving her room to breathe in between the deep thrusts. Then she felt her ass cheeks part and Mac's dick lodge against her tight entrance.

She moaned as Mac pressed forward, exerting pressure on the small opening. Slowly, she felt it give way. Twinges of pain mixed with unbearable pleasure swirled in her deepest regions.

"Oh, baby," Mac moaned. "You're so fucking tight. You feel so good. I love the way you look, all flared around my dick, holding on so tightly."

They began to move in unison, fucking her ass and mouth. She reveled in the sensation, being filled by the gorgeous men. Ryder's hand tangled in her hair, pulling her head to meet his thrusts. Mac gripped her waist, plunging over and over, his muscled abdomen smacking against her behind.

Ryder slowed his thrusts, and she made a sound of protest when he slid from her mouth. Before she could say anything, Mac picked her up, holding her tightly against his abdomen, his cock still firmly embedded in her ass.

"Trust me, baby," Mac murmured close to her ear.

He rotated until his back was to the bed. Then he slowly settled onto the bed, first sitting with her in his lap then leaning until he was flat on his back, his legs dangling over the edge of the bed.

He gripped her hips, holding her firmly in place. Ryder walked around the bed from the other side until he stood in front of her. He smiled and gently parted her legs. He climbed on top of her, holding his weight off her by placing his palms down on the mattress.

He flexed his hips, teasing her with his cock. Mac nibbled at her shoulder then twitched his hips until her ass squirmed between him and Ryder.

"Please," she gasped. "Fuck me!"

Ryder swooped down and captured her lips in a passionate kiss. He eased one hand between them, guiding his dick toward her pussy entrance. His thumb found her clit and rubbed just as he sank inside.

"Wrap those legs around me, Kit girl. We're going for a ride."

She readily complied and he and Mac began moving. Ryder's thrusts pushed her further down onto Mac's cock, and Mac thrust back, pushing her up into Ryder's thrusts. She was caught between two forces of nature, each determined to bring her to the ultimate pleasure.

"You okay, baby?" Mac whispered in her ear.

She smiled at his concern. He was so loving. So protective. How could she not be okay? Here, between two men she loved so dearly. She hadn't been this okay in a long time.

Ryder bent to suck one nipple between his teeth. He nipped sharply, upping the bite of pain. She arched into him, wanting more. Needing more.

He thrust harder into her, forcing her into Mac. She gasped at the fullness. Her body felt stretched in a dozen directions.

Mac's hand crept around her waist, between her and Ryder until his seeking fingers found her clit. He rubbed in a circular motion as Ryder plunged and strained against her.

"Oh!"

The sound escaped her in a breathy exclamation. The room blurred around her. She felt sudden wetness between her legs and knew it was her. The orgasm burst on her so unexpectedly. No warning, no build up, just a microburst of stunning pleasure.

She'd never felt anything like this. The orgasm buzzed but didn't fade. Instead it built higher, stretching her to impossible limits. It was painful in its intensity and yet, she didn't achieve her limit. Not yet.

"Oh God! It hurts," she groaned.

"It hurts good though, darlin'," Ryder said with a chuckle. "That was one hard orgasm you just had. I've never felt you get so wet."

The slick sounds of flesh meeting flesh filled the room. Ryder's body made a sucking sound as he continued to pump in and out of her soaked pussy.

"Switch," Mac called.

Before she could react, Ryder hauled her into his arms, pulling her ass from Mac's cock. He stood, her legs still wrapped around him while Mac scrambled up. Then he turned and fell back on the bed, her on top of him.

Mac straddled her body from behind and slid back into her ass in one long movement. He began riding her hard while Ryder held her in his arms.

"Mac! Mac!" she chanted over and over as her pleasure built and spiraled out of control.

Ryder sucked her nipple into his mouth and latched on with a vengeance. He twisted her arms behind her back and held them firmly. She was completely captive to whatever pleasure they wanted to give her. And pleasure her they did.

She let out a long scream as her pussy exploded. Her nerve endings tingled and spasmed painfully. Mac shouted his own release and went rigid behind her. One, two, three spurts of hot fluid filled her. One more thrust and a bigger flood. Then Mac collapsed against her back, breathing heavily in her ear.

He lay there a moment catching his breath, then he moved off of her, pulling out of her with a slight plop. Ryder immediately rolled her over and continued to thrust into her pussy. He closed his eyes above her and continued to pump.

"Oh darlin,' hold onto me. I'm coming."

She wrapped her arms tightly around him and held on for dear life. He clenched his teeth and screwed his eyes shut as if he was in the worst sort of pain. Then he let out a shout and surged against her one last time.

He remained rigid against her, his hips bucking as he spurted deep inside her. He fell onto her, wrapping his big arms tightly around her. He held her as his chest heaved against her. He kissed her neck, her ear, then fused his lips to her mouth.

She held him, stroking her hand over his hair as his shoulders rose and fell with his exertion. Finally he slipped from her pussy, and she felt a flood of fluid leak down her leg.

As Ryder rolled away, Mac curled an arm over her waist and pulled her up next to him. "I love you, baby," he whispered.

"Mmmm, I love you too," she said drowsily.

Mac leaned up then plucked her from the sheets, cradling her against his chest. "Come on, I'll shower you, then we'll get some sleep."

Ryder opened his eyes, not sure what had woken him up. The room was dark, and he blinked to give his eyes time to adjust. He glanced to the middle of the bed only to find Kit gone. A few feet away, Mac slept soundly on the other side of the bed.

Quietly, he slipped out of bed and checked the bathroom. It was empty. He shuffled into the living room and heard the sounds of the ocean filter through the room. The sliding door to the balcony was open, and he could make out Kit's outline as she bent over the railing.

The lights from the street offered enough illumination that he could see she wore one of the Harley T-shirts she'd stolen from him. And nothing else.

Despite the workout he'd gotten earlier, his dick hardened, strained outward. He'd never get enough of her.

He walked silently to the balcony and stepped outside. She hadn't heard him. He reached out to cup the globe of her ass then slid his hand underneath her shirt and pushed until her entire ass was bared.

She let out a small sigh but didn't look back at him.

He wrapped one hand around his cock and used his other to spread her thighs until her pussy was opened to him. In two seconds, he was balls-deep inside her.

She moaned and pushed back against him.

His hands slid up her back, gentle and soothing. "Why are you up, darlin'? You having nightmares again?"

She stiffened against him, and he withdrew only to plunge deeply inside her again. He loved the sight of his dick sliding into her body, the width of his cock spreading her, her wet flesh grasping him so tightly.

He withdrew and pressed forward until her ass cheeks flattened against his abdomen.

"Yes," she whispered.

"Ahh darlin', you know Mac and I won't let anything hurt you again. The bastard who hurt you will be in jail a long, long time."

"I'm glad you came, Ryder," she said, her voice catching as he pumped into her again.

"But I haven't come yet, darlin'," he teased.

She laughed softly. "I've missed you, Ryder. Promise me you won't stay away anymore."

He stilled against her and closed his eyes. Goddamn, he couldn't make that kind of promise, could he? Ah hell. He didn't reply. Instead he slid his hands underneath to palm her breasts. He rolled her nipples between his thumb and forefinger and felt her suck in her breath.

He smiled. "Like that, darlin'?"

"Ohhh."

He loved how responsive she was, how uninhibited she was, and the fact she wasn't afraid of what she wanted, of taking what she wanted.

He pushed into her and stood there, embedded in her. She moved restlessly against him.

"Ryder, please," she begged.

He gripped her hips, holding her against him. "You ready for me to go for a ride, darlin'?"

She moaned and shivered. She was close to her orgasm. He could feel her tighten around his dick, her body emitting tiny little spasms.

"Do you have any idea how good you feel, Kit? You drive me crazy."

"Shut up and fuck me," she wailed.

He laughed. But he gave her what she wanted. Foregoing his soft and slow approach, he began thrusting hard.

She gripped the railing as the sound of his thighs slapping against her ass filled the air. In the distance, the sound of the ocean echoed in the night.

He was close. His dick swelled painfully. All the blood rushed to his groin. With effort, he ripped himself from her clinging pussy. She immediately made a sound of protest and tried to straighten herself.

His hand in the middle of her back prevented her moving. "Oh no, darlin', I'm not done with you yet."

He fisted his cock in his hand and guided it to the puckered opening above her pussy entrance. As soon as the head touched her anal opening, Kit jerked in response.

"Oh my God," she groaned. "I can't stand anymore. My legs are jelly."

He chuckled. "Oh yes, darlin', you don't have a choice. You just stand there and take it like a good girl. I've been wanting to fuck this ass all night."

Her body quivered and shook as he pressed against the tight opening. Her body was slow to accept him, and he didn't rush it. Finally he felt the muscle give way, and he sank inside her an inch.

"Ryder!" she gasped.

"Stay with me, darlin'. Give it a minute."

She pushed back, trying to seat him further, but he held her off with a light slap on her ass.

He remained where he was for a long moment, loving the feel of her ass surrounding the head of his cock. Finally, he bucked forward, sinking himself all the way.

She bolted forward against the railing, and he caught her hips, holding her in place. Over and over he retreated only to plunge back into her ass.

He slid his hand around to her stomach and lower to her pussy. His fingers strummed at her clit, and she bucked wildly against him.

"Please, Ryder, finish it!"

He pinched the taut flesh between his fingers then began fucking her ass in earnest. The friction of her tender flesh over his cock sent him into a frenzy. His orgasm swelled and bolted like fire through his gut. Every ounce of feeling was trapped between his legs, and he strained to bury himself deeper still.

"God, darlin'!"

He poured into her in a hot rush of fluid. His legs shook and he pounded against her as the firestorm blew out of control. He jerked and closed his eyes tight as he finished.

Her entire body trembled and shook as he gently pulled away from her. Her body slumped against the railing, and he pulled her upright then into his arms.

"Come inside, darlin'. Let me take care of you."

She nodded and he led her inside the door and shut it behind them.

"Go lie down on the couch. I'll be right back with a towel," he said gently.

Kit knelt on the couch then slid onto her belly, closing her eyes as her cheek met the cushion. Her body hummed in satisfaction. An empty part of her had been filled. Filled in only the way Ryder could.

She loved Mac dearly. Would never betray his love. But she loved Ryder too. Maybe not as deeply—she stopped herself at the thought.

She was reminded of a conversation between her and Ryder so many months ago. The one where he'd told her she didn't love him in the way she loved Mac. She'd assumed at the time that it meant not as *much*. But no, that wasn't it at all.

Warm hands gently cupped her ass, separated the cheeks, pressed a wet washcloth to the sensitive skin there.

"You all right, darlin'?" Ryder asked close to her ear.

She shifted and sat up. "I'm fine."

Ryder sat down beside her and pulled her against his muscled chest. She snuggled into his body and ran her fingertips over the dragon tattoo on the upper left portion of his chest.

"Now tell me about these nightmares," he prompted.

She sighed. "It's crazy I know. But sometimes when I close my eyes, I see him. He's real, he's there. And I'm back in those woods running as fast I can, crazy with fear, afraid I'll never see you and Mac again."

Ryder swallowed against the anger swelling his throat and tightened his hold on her. He rubbed his hand up and down her arm. "He can't hurt you, darlin'. Not anymore."

A sound across the room made him look up. Mac was standing in the doorway to the living room.

"Everything okay?" Mac asked as he walked over to the couch. A concerned look creased his brow.

Kit slid from Ryder's grasp and stood up. She walked into Mac's arms, and he wrapped his big body around her much smaller one.

"Bad dream?" Mac asked.

She nodded and Mac stroked her hair in a soothing motion. Ryder suddenly felt awkward, as if he had no right to have been here offering comfort to Kit.

"Come back to bed, baby," Mac said in a gentle voice.

As Mac guided Kit back toward the bedroom, he turned his head over his shoulder. "You coming, bro?"

Ryder shook his head. "Nah, you go on. I'm wide-awake." He knew Mac would take her to bed and make love to her, try to banish her demons. Ryder didn't want to stand out like a sore thumb.

As Mac and Kit disappeared into the bedroom, Ryder stood up and walked out to the balcony where he and Kit had fucked just minutes ago. He leaned forward, looking at the ocean across the highway.

What the fuck was he going to do? If he was smart, he'd run as far and as fast as he could. Kit would be hurt, but she'd get over it, and she'd have Mac.

But Ryder wouldn't have her, and right now, anything, any part of her was better than nothing.

CHAPTER 4

*R*yder woke when he heard Mac shuffling through the living room. He cracked open an eye to see Mac standing by the sliding doors staring out over the ocean.

"Kit still sleeping?" Ryder asked from his position on the couch.

Mac turned around and nodded. "Yeah, she didn't even move when I got up."

Ryder yawned and stretched. "We heading to the beach today?"

"Yeah, Kit brought her suit." Mac grinned. "If you can call it that."

"Ah hell, man, don't tell me she brought those two strings she calls a bikini."

Mac chuckled. "You know I can't refuse her anything."

"Yeah, well, when our asses are tossed into jail for beating other men's asses, you'll think differently," Ryder grumbled.

"Hey, you want a beer?" Mac asked as he bent over the cooler they'd brought.

"Fuckin' A," Ryder said as he sat up further. "Never too early."

Mac tossed him a can then slumped into the chair across from the couch.

"So what's been up your ass lately?" Mac asked as he flipped the top to his beer.

Ryder raised a brow. "What do you mean?"

Mac shrugged. "You haven't been yourself, man."

Ryder felt an uncomfortable prickle down his spine. He shifted and chugged half his beer. "I'm not sure what you mean by that," he said, forcing casualness to his tone.

"Are you pissed at Kit about something?" Mac asked. A protective scowl darkened his face as he stared over at Ryder.

"God no. What could Kit girl possibly have done to get my underwear in a bunch?"

Mac's expression relaxed, and he went back to his beer. "I dunno, man, but it looks like you've been avoiding us. I mean if you no longer want the sort of relationship we have, all you need to do is say so."

Fuck me. What to say to that? Yes. No. Yes. No. Or even better. I want your girl, Mac. Mind stepping aside?

Ryder stuck a hand in his hair and rubbed his head. "It's nothing like that, Mac. You know I love Kit."

"I hear a 'but' in there."

Mac sat forward and eyed Ryder with a light of revelation in his eyes. Ryder tensed. Had Mac figured it out?

"You aren't still worried about how I feel about this, are you?" Mac asked.

A slow crawl of relief swept through Ryder's chest. He latched onto the offering like a starving dog to a rib-eye steak.

"Well, hell, man. She's your girl and I'm fucking her. Yeah, I worry sometime."

Mac sat back. "If it were anyone else, it would be twisted. No doubt. But you and I both know we go way back with Kit. We've both loved her forever, and it's not like we've never shared a woman before."

"Not one we've both cared about so much," Ryder said cautiously. Stupid fuck. He needed to just shut the hell up before he blurted out the wrong damn thing.

"I think that's what makes it all right," Mac said quietly. "Look, I trust you, and I sure as hell trust Kit. She loves me. She'd never betray me, and you wouldn't either. The fact is, I like knowing that if something ever happened to me, you'd be there for her. As a cop I have no guarantees of a long and happy life. Besides, it's not like you're off fucking her when I'm not around."

Ryder paused and again considered the wisdom of shutting the fuck up. Too bad he never listened to good advice.

"I fucked her last night while you were asleep."

Mac laughed. "Dude, is that what has you all in knots? You feel guilty because you fucked Kit while I was asleep?"

Ryder shrugged. "It wasn't planned."

Mac shook his head. "Do you think I would have invited you to come with us if I didn't know you'd be making love to her? I was in the next room, man. Not across town. Not in secret. There's a huge difference. Kit was up with nightmares. I'm glad you could offer her some comfort. I only wish I'd been awake."

"What are you two talking about?" Kit asked sleepily.

Ryder turned to see Kit standing in the doorway, still wearing his Harley Davidson T-shirt. Her hair was rumpled and she had a soft, sleepy look. She looked sexy as hell. Like she'd just come from the arms of a lover and wanted more.

Mac held out his arms, and Kit trudged over to where Mac sat. She slid onto his lap and curled up like a contented cat. Mac's entire demeanor softened. He stroked his hand through her hair and looked over the top of her head at Ryder.

There was unspoken approval, a determined look that Ryder

knew meant the conversation was closed. Mac was okay with the dynamics of the relationship between the three of them.

A ball of regret settled into Ryder's stomach. He could never ever step between Mac and Kit. No matter how much he loved Kit, how much he longed to have a bigger part of her heart. He wouldn't betray his friendship with Mac, and he wouldn't hurt Kit by making her choose.

"I'm hungry," Kit mumbled against Mac's chest.

"So am I, but it's not for food," Mac replied.

Ryder chuckled despite his dark thoughts. Kit had the same effect on him. All she had to do was walk in the room and his body jumped to attention.

"Ma-ac," Kit protested. "You guys wore me out. Now feed me before I fall over."

Mac gave an exaggerated sigh. "All right. I suppose I can put off my needs in order to feed my woman. Get dressed, baby. Ryder and I'll take you out for breakfast."

She kissed him full on the mouth then scampered back into the bedroom.

When she was gone, Mac stood up and held his fist out to Ryder. "So are we good?"

Ryder stood up and bumped his fist to Mac's. "Yeah, man. We're good."

"All right then. Let's go get our girl something to eat and take her to the beach for awhile."

Ryder nodded and headed into the bedroom to get dressed.

Kit stepped out of the hotel lobby and breathed in the warm, salty air. God it felt good to be in the sun, not a care in the world.

Her floral sarong swished at her feet as they walked to the truck. She'd worn just her bikini underneath, wrapping the light material around her waist and letting it hang loose. She didn't have much to hold the bikini top up, but Mac and Ryder didn't seem to mind.

Her eyes flitted across the guys as she waited for them to open the truck. They were dressed similarly in shorts and muscle shirts. Mac's short-cropped, dirty blond hair gleamed in the sunlight, and more than ever, he presented the image of a beach bum. A completely hard-assed, muscle-bound, *buff* prime specimen of a man.

Ryder just looked as badassed as ever. She doubted anyone would ever try to fuck with him without a few weapons in their arsenal. His arms rippled and bulged with muscles. He had the tightest abdomen she'd ever come across on a man, and his tattoos and multitude of ear piercings just added to his bad-boy appearance.

Ryder's black hair blew in the breeze, lifting slightly from his shoulders. Her fingers itched to delve into it, wrap it around her hands and hold on.

"You coming, darlin'?"

She smiled at Ryder, who was holding the door open for her. She slid into the front seat and moved all the way over against Mac so Ryder could shove in beside her.

A sinful, delicious tickle churned in her stomach as they drove down the seawall. She loved going places with both the guys. Loved the thrill it gave her to have two gorgeous, forceful men surrounding her, protecting her, loving her.

She sighed and leaned her head back to catch a ray of sunshine beaming through the windshield.

"You look content, baby," Mac said.

She smiled but kept her eyes closed. "I am. This was such a great idea, Mac. I can't thank you enough." She opened her eyes and turned to look at Ryder. She put her hand out to his tattooed arm. "And thanks for coming, Ryder. It wouldn't have been the same without you."

"Anything for you, darlin'," he said huskily.

She leaned over and kissed him, allowing her lips to linger warmly over his. He shoved a hand into her hair and held her in place while his tongue flicked out to meet hers. Then he pulled away from her with seeming reluctance.

She smiled then turned to kiss Mac. "You guys are the best. I don't deserve you."

Mac cocked his head sideways at her. "Whatever makes you say a crazy thing like that, baby?"

"I'm just glad y'all came back," she added quietly.

Mac pulled into the parking lot of a café serving breakfast and killed the engine. As if completely oblivious to Ryder's presence, Mac turned in his seat and cupped her face in his hands.

"There was never a question of me coming back for you, Kit. If I had it to do all over again, the only thing I'd change is that I would have taken you with me. I'll live with that regret for the rest of my life."

Her cheeks warmed and her heart lightened. Was there another woman luckier than she? She didn't think so.

She melted into Mac's embrace and brushed her cheek lovingly across his chest. "I am so lucky," she whispered.

Mac hugged her back. "You say some of the craziest things, baby."

He let go of her and opened his door. She opted to scoot the other way since Ryder was already out of the truck. Ryder reached up for her, and she went willingly into his arms. He swung her down, and she immediately settled into his side. Ryder wrapped his arm around her waist and urged her toward the entrance.

There she was, between two to-die-for men, walking into a restaurant. As far as fantasies went, this was heady stuff.

"What's that shit-eating grin for, darlin'?" Ryder asked in a low voice.

"I'm just feeling a little sassy," she said.

"God help us," Mac muttered.

She elbowed Mac in the stomach and smiled brightly at the waitress waiting to seat them.

They spent an hour in the restaurant laughing, joking and eating. The tension and fear that had eaten at Kit for so long dissipated under the comfortable rapport the three enjoyed. She was looking forward to a day soaking up the rays on the beach.

When she finally shoved her plate aside, Mac motioned for the check.

"Get enough to eat, baby?"

She nodded and groaned. "Too much."

"You needed to eat. You've lost weight," he reproached.

"Let's go," she said impatiently, tugging at Ryder's arm. "I'm ready to feel the sand between my toes."

Mac laughed. "You two go on to the truck. I'll be along as soon as I pay out."

She grabbed Ryder's hand and pulled him toward the entrance. He smiled indulgently at her, but his expression remained shuttered. Her smile faded as they walked toward the truck.

She leaned against the door, refusing to allow Ryder to open it. She looked up at him, studying his eyes. Then she reached up and put her palm to his cheek.

"Are you going to tell me what's wrong?" she asked softly.

In a way she wasn't sure she wanted to know. She wasn't used to Ryder keeping secrets from her, and she had a feeling whatever he was thinking wasn't something she wanted to hear. Was she crazy for wanting to do anything to ruin the weekend?

His eyes softened and he reached a hand up to capture hers. "Nothing's wrong, darlin'. You know I love being around you and Mac."

Her eyes furrowed doubtfully. "Are you sure? Because—"

"Because what, Kit girl?"

"Because I haven't been so sure you've wanted to be around me lately."

He cursed under his breath then reached out to frame her face in his hands.

"Look at me, darlin'."

His eyes bore into her and he lowered his head until their foreheads touched.

"I'm sorry I've been such an ass. You know I'd never do anything to hurt you. I've never not wanted to be around you."

Her chest caved in a bit with relief. In the back of her mind, she'd wondered if they were reaching the end of the unique relationship they shared. Selfishly, she had no desire to see Ryder slip away. She'd made a commitment to Mac. She loved Mac. But she loved Ryder too. Would always love him.

She smiled a bit shakily. "I'm glad. I didn't want you to go away."

Ryder folded her into his big arms and hugged her tight. "No one's leaving you, Kit girl. Not ever again. Now let's go have some fun."

"Come on you two, don't make me call the cops on your asses," Mac drawled as he walked up.

"You are the cops," Kit grumbled.

"That's right, baby. Don't forget it either. I'll use my handcuffs if I have to."

Her body tightened, and red hot need splintered through her abdomen. Damn but he was good with handcuffs. She remembered with vivid detail the last time Mac and Ryder had used those cuffs.

"Jesus, Mac, cut it out or we'll never make it to the beach," Ryder growled.

Mac laughed and sauntered around to the driver's side. "I think she liked the handcuff idea, man."

CHAPTER 5

*K*it dug her toes into the wet sand at the edge of the surf. She closed her eyes, threw back her head and took in a deep breath. Then she opened her eyes and stared out over the gulf. A shrimp boat dotted the horizon, and a smaller pleasure boat jetted parallel to the shore.

It was a perfect day. A blue-water day. Rare along the Texas shore. A fisherman's wet dream, according to Mac. Usually the gulf waters were muddy or stained. The green water usually held well off the shores, but today, the blue stretched as far as the eye could see.

She waded a little further into the water until the gentle swells lapped at her knees. She glanced over her shoulder and smiled. The men were several feet back, their eyes fastened to her backside. She turned back around and jiggled her ass the slightest bit for effect.

Her bikini, if it qualified as one, was practically scandalous. It was basically a thong with a tiny scrap of material for a top. If she hadn't gotten an all-over tan at the local salon back home, she would have never flaunted her shiny white ass to the world, but the creamy brown tint to her skin made her feel sexy, and she didn't mind making the guys squirm.

She forged ahead into the warm water until finally she dove forward, slicing through the water with lazy strokes. She swam until the water shallowed again, and she dug her feet into the second sandbar.

With a contented sigh, she lay back in the water and floated lazily on her back. The sun was high overhead, and she squinted against the glare, but she enjoyed the warmth. The freedom. The fact that for the first time in longer than she could remember, she didn't feel weighted down by fear or indecision.

"You look like the cat who got the cream, darlin'."

She kicked her feet downward and stood up, her heart thumping in her chest.

"Sorry, didn't mean to scare you."

She smiled. "What are you doing out here. I didn't think you'd come swimming."

"Oh, like I could resist following that luscious ass anywhere," Ryder said.

He reached around her and slid his hands along the bare expanse of her buttocks. His finger slid along the crack as the water lapped against the sensitive tissue there.

"I had no idea you noticed," Kit said innocently.

He pulled her up tight against him so she had no choice but to feel his erection against her belly.

"Then again . . ."

"You're a miserable tease," he growled.

"And what do you plan to do about it?"

"I'm going to fuck you all night long," he said, his eyes glittering with need. And promise. "I'm going to fuck you in every con-

ceivable position. I'm going to have your mouth, your pussy and
your ass. You're going to be begging for mercy."

She went weak against him. He had to catch her and hold her
up. Her stomach fluttered and turned somersaults at the images he
painted.

He kissed her. Hard. Demanding. Taking her breath away.
Then just as quickly, he let her go and backed away.

"Just wanted to give you a little something to think about," he
drawled.

She watched as he dove back into the surf and swam toward
the beach. Damn the man. She was so horny she could get off with
one touch. But he hadn't touched her. He'd just made her so crazy
that she couldn't wait to get back to the hotel. And whatever
pleasures awaited her there.

She dove under the water, swimming a good length before
coming up for air. She loved the water. Felt weightless, graceful,
carefree. Soon she reached a depth where she could stand again
and made her way toward the beach.

As she approached, she noticed that Ryder was lying on the
sand, propped up on one elbow. She frowned and looked around
for Mac. She glanced up to the seawall where the truck was
parked, only to find it gone.

She walked over to Ryder. "Where's Mac?"

He grinned at her. "Gone to the hardware store."

"Hardware store? What on earth for?"

"Supplies," Ryder said shortly.

She gaped at him like he'd lost his mind. Supplies from a hardware store? She didn't even want to know what the two of them
had going on. She was better off not knowing.

Ryder patted the sand beside him. "Come lie down, darlin'."

She went down on her hands and knees and crawled up against
him. She turned her body until she cradled her behind into his
pelvis then laid her head on his outstretched arm.

He curled a hand around her hip, his fingers resting just inches from her pussy. She loved it when he touched her. He and Mac both were very possessive of her. They liked to touch her frequently, put their stamp on her. And that was more than fine with her.

His chin brushed against her shoulder as his lips nuzzled in against the curve of her neck. "You taste good," he murmured. "A bit salty, but always sweet."

The ridge of his cock felt heavy in the crack of her ass. He was aroused. Very much so. He shifted, rubbing his dick against her, burrowing deeper between her ass cheeks. His erection strained against the wet material of his shorts. She'd never been so tempted to roll over and reach inside those shorts. Take his cock out and suck it until he begged for mercy.

But this was a public beach, damn it. Despite the fact they'd driven well down the seawall, away from the more popular spots, there were still a few people milling around.

"When is Mac going to be back," she said grumpily.

Ryder chuckled in her ear. "Patience, darlin'. I promise it'll be worth the wait."

She sighed and snuggled deeper into his body. The sun felt warm and comforting on her skin, and Ryder's body felt good wrapped around hers. Patience wasn't one of her finer virtues, but she'd just have to enjoy the present until Mac returned.

Kit heard her name, and she mumbled something in return. A laugh brought her more fully awake.

"Come on, baby, we need to get you out of the sun before you burn."

She opened her eyes to see Mac squatting over her, his body shielding the sun from her face.

"You're back," she said, a wide smile taking over her face.

His expression softened and fire built slowly in his eyes. "I love it when you look at me that way, baby."

"What way is that?" she asked. She struggled to sit up, and Ryder's arms came around her to help push her up.

"Like you're glad to see me," he said.

"But I am. I missed you."

She leaned forward and wrapped her arms around him, hugging him close to her. As she hooked her chin over his shoulder, she could see a couple of people down the beach staring at them.

She nearly smiled. It probably did look strange for her to be sleeping in the arms of one man one minute then wrapped around the body of another man the next.

Ryder's hand came up to caress her ass, and she grinned wider. If anyone ever thought she'd be embarrassed by the attentions of two men in public, they could go suck an egg. It was a huge turn-on. She loved it when the two of them got demonstrative in front of others. Maybe it made her a slut, but she didn't give a shit.

She drew away from Mac then planted a scorching kiss right on his lips. In response, Mac stood up, hauling her with him. His hands went behind her to cup her ass as he shifted her up higher. They stood there, her legs hooked around his waist, his hands on her ass, and her lips solidly fused to his.

Let the damn locals ogle all they wanted.

"Let's go back to the hotel," Mac rasped.

"Yes, let's," she responded. "I need a shower to get all the sand off."

Mac set her down, and Ryder stood up behind her. He slid a hand over her backside then allowed his hand to rest possessively on one cheek as they started toward the steps.

A few minutes later, they stepped into the cool interior of their hotel room, and Kit shivered slightly.

"I'll start us a shower, baby."

She followed along behind Mac and waited as he stepped into the shower stall to start the water.

"Turn around. I'll untie you," he directed.

She presented him her back, and he untied the thin string holding her top on. When it loosened, she let it fall to the floor. Then she hooked her fingers in the string of her thong and pulled it down her hips until she stood naked.

Mac pulled her into the shower, and she sighed as the warm water pulsed over her. He soaped her hair first and rinsed. Then he soaped her body, paying special attention to her pussy. Before he was finished, she was awash in need. She could barely stand. Her legs trembled and shook as his fingers slid over her clit again and again.

She reached up and hooked her arms around his neck to steady herself. He stared at her for a long moment, his blue eyes burning into her.

"Are you enjoying yourself, baby?"

She nodded. "It was so great of you to think of this, Mac. I've had so much fun." She pulled his head down to hers and kissed him, the spray from the shower sluicing over their lips. "I love you so much."

He gripped her tightly, hugging her to him. "I love you too, baby. Always."

He reached behind her and turned off the water. Then he stepped out and retrieved two towels, handing one to her. They dried off and walked into the bedroom. Ryder stepped around them and headed for the shower. He shot Mac a sly grin before closing the door behind him.

"What was that all about?" she demanded.

Mac merely smiled. "I told him I'd prepare everything for when he got out of the shower."

She arched an eyebrow at him. "Prepare what?"

"You."

Her pulse sped up, and she licked her lips nervously.

"We have something special planned tonight," he continued.

"I see. And when does this start?"

"Now," he said.

He reached over and tugged her towel down her body until it fell in a heap on the floor. She stood there naked, her legs trembling with anticipation.

He walked over to a bag lying on the floor. A bag she hadn't noticed until now. A bag that hadn't been there before.

He pulled out a length of rope and a knife. Her eyes widened as he turned to her, carrying both with him.

"Lie down on the bed," he directed.

His voice had lost its soothing quality. This was the cop Mac. Not her gentle lover. This was the voice of a man in control. Of a man used to being in control.

"Don't make me tell you again," he said softly.

She took a shaky step and nearly stumbled. God, she was turned to complete jelly. Moisture pooled between her legs, and she ached to touch herself there, to alleviate the burning vibration she felt.

Mac gripped her arm and helped her onto the bed. He tumbled her over onto her back then pulled both hands above her head. "Don't move them."

She nodded her understanding. She didn't trust herself to speak.

He cut a length of rope from the coil then quickly wrapped it around her wrists. Then he secured the rope and her wrists to the bedpost, effectively trapping her there.

He stood back and smiled a satisfied smile. "You look beautiful all tied up, at our mercy. How does it feel to know we can do what we want? To know there's not a damn thing you can do about it?"

She shivered in response and licked her dry lips. God she needed to come. "Touch me," she begged.

"Not a chance, baby. We've got all night. I'm not ending things as soon as we've started."

"Bastard," she muttered.

He reached down and smacked her lightly on the pussy. "Watch your mouth."

Fire spread through her pelvis, and she jerked at the small blow. Oh God, if only he'd done it a little harder she could have orgasmed right then. She moaned low in her throat.

He grinned then began cutting another length of rope. Her eyes flickered toward his hands. What would he do with more rope? She was already a prisoner to the bed.

He took his time coiling the rope around one of her ankles. A long piece dangled and he picked it up and stretched it back toward the head of the bed until her leg was forced high in the air. He spread it as it stretched, making her leg move to the side. Then he secured it tightly to the bedpost.

He moved to the other side of the bed and repeated the process until she lay there, legs spread, her pussy and ass completely bared.

"Mac, I can't stand it, I need to come," she whispered.

He leaned forward and kissed her lips, nipping and sucking at her bottom lip. "I love that you're so receptive to the things we want to do. You know I'd never do anything to scare you. I want this night to be good for you. I know you have fantasies about this. Me and Ryder decided it was time to let them play out for you."

She kissed him back, the sting of tears on her lids. God, she loved this man. Trusted him with her whole being.

Mac backed away to stare at her. Lust blazed in his eyes. Her gaze flickered down to his cock, and she smiled. He was as affected by her new position as she was.

"Goddamn, Mac. I don't think I've ever seen such a gorgeous sight in my life," Ryder said from the doorway.

She looked over to see Ryder standing there, toweling his hair dry. He was naked and as aroused as Mac was.

He dropped the towel and stepped forward. "I hope you're comfortable, Kit girl, because you're in for a long night."

CHAPTER 6

Kit swallowed as Ryder came closer to the bed.

"I swear I don't know where to start," Ryder murmured.

His gaze ripped up and down her bound body.

"So many possibilities. Your ass. Your pussy. Or I could climb up and take your mouth."

She let out a gasp. If they didn't touch her soon, she was going to go insane. She didn't care where, but this could not go on.

"Decide quickly," Mac drawled. "Because wherever you don't go is where I'm starting."

Ryder crawled onto the bed and positioned himself between her legs. "Hmm, I don't know what to choose first. She's got the finest ass and the prettiest pussy I've seen in my life."

"Ryder!" she said through clenched teeth.

Mac emitted a deep chuckle then got onto the bed close to her head. "I want to fuck that mouth of yours, baby."

She closed her eyes for a second. They were going to torture her. And goddamn if she wouldn't enjoy every minute of it.

She opened her eyes to see him standing over her, his legs on either side of her shoulders. He crouched down, his cock brushing across her lips. He fisted his dick in his hand and guided it toward her mouth.

"Take it, baby. Take it all the way," Mac encouraged.

He slid forward, parting her lips with his broad head. She loved the taste of him. So strong and masculine. She ran her tongue down the thick vein on the underside of his penis.

He twisted his hands in her hair. "I want you to lick my balls, baby. Take it all the way. Stick that pretty tongue of yours out and lick me."

She struggled to accommodate his length, but he gave her time, easing further into her mouth until she could feel the puckered skin of his sac against her tongue.

He groaned as she swirled her tongue and lapped at the skin. He withdrew to give her a breath then sank slowly back in.

Between her legs, Ryder positioned himself at her ass. The broad head of his dick pressed relentlessly against her opening. Her entire body tensed. She opened her mouth to cry out, but Mac took advantage and pressed home.

She was buffeted between their bodies, powerless against whatever they chose to do. She reveled in their power and her ability to give up such power to them. In their arms, she was completely safe to be anything and anyone she wanted. She was loved and cherished.

Mac's cock slid in and out of her mouth, gently at times, more forcefully at others. He kept her off balance with his pace. Ryder gripped her hips and sank repeatedly into her ass. Then his fingers dipped into her pussy. His thumb brushed her clit and his fingers plunged and explored.

She cried out as Mac's cock retreated, but her voice was cut off as he thrust against the back of her throat.

"Suck me, baby," he said in a strained voice. "I'm about to come. I want you to come with me. I want you to swallow me whole."

Ryder sped up, the friction he created nearly unbearable. His fingers pressed harder, his thumb circled and massaged.

Mac leaned over her, positioning his cock deeper. He gripped the headboard with his hands and began thrusting into her mouth in earnest.

Warm, salty spurts filled her mouth. She swallowed quickly then felt her own release build and fan out of control. She bucked wildly against the ropes, straining and pulling. Mac's thrust became gentle while Ryder's became more frenzied.

Mac pulled from her mouth and allowed the last of his ejaculation to spill onto her chin. Then he rolled off her and Ryder leaned further into her. At the last possible moment, he ripped himself from her ass and held his straining cock to her belly, spilling his seed over her smooth skin.

He melted against her for a long moment before moving back. He stood beside the bed as Mac did and they both looked her over, desire and approval glittering in their eyes.

"I love the way you look, all tied up, our cum on you," Mac growled. "You're the sexiest thing I've seen in my life."

"You got that right," Ryder breathed.

"Are you all right, Kit?" Mac asked. He leaned over to check the ropes around her ankles and wrists.

She nodded, still too numb from her orgasm to speak.

He kissed her forehead then sauntered across the room, Ryder right behind him. They pulled on their clothes and left the room.

She crinkled her forehead. Where the hell were they going? Probably to get something to clean her up. They always took care of her. She could feel the cum on her chin so close to her mouth. And on her belly. Some had even splattered onto her breasts.

She smiled. How primitive it made her feel. Never in a million years could she explain the sensation, but she got an indecent thrill from them marking her, putting their stamp of possession on her.

When several minutes passed, she began to wonder what the hell was taking them so long.

"Mac?" she called out.

The ropes weren't uncomfortable, but she felt vulnerable here alone, trussed up like a Christmas turkey.

A few seconds later, Mac stuck his head in the door. "Yes, baby?"

"What are you doing?" she asked.

"Drinking a beer with Ryder and watching TV."

She stared at him in disbelief. "What?"

He smiled, his eyes glinting with mischief. "Hush, baby. Ryder and I will be back in awhile. We like the idea of you being there unable to move, having to wait for us to come back." His voice dropped lower. "Wondering what we'll choose to do next."

She swallowed hard. Holy moly. They were taking this to entirely new limits. Before their role playing had been fairly short-lived. She'd spent plenty of time in cuffs, one of their favorite scenarios, but never had they left her to go do something else.

Mac disappeared back into the living room, and Kit lay there, her pussy already throbbing again. Her breath came in ragged spurts as she imagined what they *would* do next. She was so turned on, she could go off like a rocket at any second.

She forced herself to relax. As much as she could in the ropes that bound her. She closed her eyes and relived the exotic experience of being tied hand and foot and fucked senseless by both men at the same time. A smile curved her lips upward. She could die tonight and go a very happy woman.

* * *

She must have dozed because the next thing she knew, she was being shaken awake by Mac. She opened her eyes to see both men standing over her, naked again. Very aroused. She licked her lips. She couldn't help it.

"Have a nice rest, darlin'?"

"Mmm hmm."

She tried to stretch but the ropes pulled her up quick.

Mac leaned over in concern. "Are they hurting you, Kit?"

She smiled and shook her head. If he only knew how very much she liked the little game they'd come up with for their last night in the hotel.

Mac climbed up on the bed and positioned himself at the junction of her thighs. He curled his hands around her buttocks and placed his cock at her pussy entrance.

"I love the way your body sways with the ropes," he said tightly. "The way you can't move. How you're so spread out for me. So perfect and beautiful."

He slid inside her in one stroke. God he felt so good. Ryder smoothed a thumb over her chin, a smirk on his face when he felt the dried evidence of Mac's ejaculation. Then his hand went to her stomach and breasts where he'd spilled himself on her.

Mac didn't play around this time. He began a hard pace and set her pussy on fire. Ryder bent over to suck at her nipples, alternating between the two taut peaks.

This was no sweet lovemaking session. This was raw sex. Her orgasm flashed on her with breathtaking speed. She'd never gotten off so fast before, but within a minute she was panting and screaming Mac's name.

"Move," Mac said in a guttural voice.

Ryder stood back while Mac tore himself from her spasming pussy. He rolled away and came to stand on the side of the bed where Ryder had stood seconds before.

As Ryder moved to take his place, Mac positioned himself at her head.

"Open your mouth, baby."

She obeyed and he pumped his hand over his cock. He leaned forward, placing the tip close to her lips. Once, twice he jerked then a hot jet of semen hit the inside of her cheek.

Ryder thrust into her as Mac pumped his seed into her mouth.

"Swallow," Mac whispered. "Every drop."

Again, she obeyed. He caressed her cheek with his hand. "Good girl, baby."

The bed rocked and swayed as Ryder worked his way in and out of her pussy. She was so sensitive after the mind-blowing orgasm she'd experienced with Mac. Too sensitive. She felt every thrust of Ryder's cock in every nerve ending.

"Take care of her," Ryder grunted at Mac as he pulled out and stood up next to the bed.

Mac moved down and slipped a hand to her quivering pussy. He fingered her, swirling around her entrance, tweaking her clit then sinking his fingers deep.

Ryder assumed Mac's earlier position, his cock gripped tightly in his hand. "Open," he said.

She opened her mouth and he jerked at his dick, directing it past her waiting lips. A warm flood filled her mouth, and she marveled at the difference in Mac's and Ryder's tastes.

As Ryder continued to direct his cum into her mouth, Mac bent and sucked her clit into his mouth. Impossibly, a second orgasm blew over her like a bolt of lightning. She nearly choked on the fluid in her mouth as she cried out.

"Don't swallow," Ryder commanded. "Let it spill out of your mouth. I want to watch it run down your lips."

She allowed it to leak over her lips and down the side of her face, watching as Ryder's eyes roved over her.

"You are so damned sexy," he said hoarsely. "You're every man's wet dream come to life."

He reached over to untie her hands. Mac walked to the other side and began untying her legs. Then he scooped her up and carried her to the bathroom. He held her in his arms while they showered then carried her back to the bed where Ryder was waiting.

He laid her on the mattress then pulled her arms up to once more tie them above her head. But this time he left her legs free.

"Get some rest, baby. We'll be back."

Kit turned on her side and curled her legs up to her chest. She sighed with contentment and closed her eyes again. Three more times they'd come to her, bringing her to unbelievable heights. Each time they'd made her wait, leaving then returning to surprise her with what came next.

She was exhausted, her body sated. Mac crawled into bed beside her, fresh from another shower. Tenderly, he enfolded her into his arms and pulled her close.

She cuddled against him, loving his warmth, his strength. Maybe she'd never get over the feeling of being so fortunate. Surely everyone wasn't as happy and as cherished as she was. After waiting for so long, she finally felt complete.

The bed dipped and Ryder pressed his body against her back. He ran a hand over her waist down to her ass, smoothing over the tender skin that had endured so much use that night.

"You're incredible, Kit," he whispered.

She reached between her and Mac, down to where his cock pressed into the V of her legs.

"Baby, don't," he muttered. "We've been too hard on you as it is."

She smiled and guided his cock into the folds of her pussy. "Please."

It was the soft-uttered "please" that seemed to do it. He gently pushed up her leg and slid his dick into her wetness. She looked over her shoulder to where Ryder stared at her. "Please," she said again. And she knew he could refuse her nothing.

As Mac held her leg up, Ryder used his hand to part her ass cheeks. He nudged and pushed, his movements so careful. He flexed his hips against her and shoved past the resisting muscle of her anus.

She closed her eyes and laid her head on Mac's chest. This was heaven. Lying between them, being held so lovingly. They both whispered kisses over her skin as they thrust so lightly into her body.

Hands smoothed and petted. They murmured words of love and approval. Told her how beautiful she was and how they'd always take care of her.

Tears welled in her eyes and slid down her cheeks as they continued their slow movements. Half a year ago, she would have resisted any idea that they made love. She would have gone to her grave swearing it was just sex. But she'd been wrong. This was love. How could it be anything else when she stood at the center of two hearts?

They were both such a part of her soul that she'd die before losing either of them. She couldn't imagine being without them. Thank God, Mac understood that, didn't allow it to threaten their relationship.

"Why are you crying, baby?" Mac asked as he thumbed away one of her tears.

"I feel so safe," she whispered back.

He looked into her eyes, his expression so serious. "I'll never allow anyone to hurt you again, Kit. You *are* safe. Believe that if you believe anything else. I'll protect you with my life."

She smiled as the tears fell even faster. Their motions stilled and they just laid there, all connected, Mac and Ryder deeply seated in her body.

"I could stay this way forever," she said.

Ryder nibbled at her neck sending chills racing down her spine. "And I could taste you forever," he said. "You have the sweetest skin."

"That she does," Mac agreed as he bent to taste her himself.

She sighed and let herself melt into their embrace. They would take care of her. Of that she had no doubt. It was a comforting feeling after everything that had happened in the last year.

In the morning, they'd pack up and return home. She'd go back to work, and life would resume as normal. Only now Ryder was back, or at least she hoped he was. He'd promised her he wouldn't stay away again.

She smiled a small smile. She'd just have to make sure he didn't wander too far.

CHAPTER 7

*R*yder congratulated himself for the way he'd handled things since they'd returned from the beach. Nearly two weeks had passed, and he'd made it over to Mac and Kit's four times, not that it had been a hardship to have sex with Kit, but each time he felt another piece of himself fall away in the process.

Today he was working in the garage, piecing together an old Harley for a client who couldn't accept that he'd turned the bike into road pizza.

Usually, he could lose himself in his work. He liked working with his hands, making a beautiful machine from old parts and torn-up dreams. Today, though, he just couldn't get into the process.

A soft clicking sound alerted him to the fact someone had just walked into the garage. He looked up to see Kit standing there, tension radiating from her in waves. He could tell she was agitated, like something big was bothering her. But then she'd always run to him when she had a problem.

He dropped the wrench and stood up, reaching for a towel to wipe his hands. Then he walked silently over to her and held out his arms.

She rushed into them, burying her face in his chest. Worry plagued him. Had something gone wrong with Mac?

"Don't go crying now, darlin'. You know I can't stand it when you cry."

She sniffled against his T-shirt. He sighed.

"Come over here and sit down," he said, directing her toward the worn-out couch a few feet away.

She plopped down on the sofa, and he settled down beside her, turning so he faced her.

"Now tell me what's wrong."

"M-Mac . . . he asked me to . . . he asked me to marry him," she said quietly.

A fist knotted in his gut, just like someone had punched him. He sucked in his breath and tried like hell not to let her know how affected he was by her announcement.

Married. Jesus. Mac was moving fast.

He was pissed off and gut shot all at the same time. Mac should know better than to push Kit like this. She wasn't ready for marriage and the whole shebang, and Mac ought to damn well know it. Hell, maybe she'd never be ready.

He reached out a hand, wanting to touch her, then he pulled away. Touching her right now probably wasn't the best idea. Not when he ached so goddamn much to have her as close to him as he could get her.

Shit on a stick, this was a disaster.

He willed himself to calm down and do what he'd always done. Be there for Kit. However she needed him.

"And what did you say, darlin'?"

His pulse sped up as he prepared himself for her response.

She moaned softly, a torturous sound of someone in deep conflict. "I didn't say anything."

Ryder blew out his breath. "Hoo boy. I'm guessing Mac didn't take that too well."

"I don't know," she said miserably. "I left before he could say much. But no, he didn't look too thrilled."

Ryder sat back and carried her with him, settling her against his chest in the crook of his arm. "So tell me then, darlin'. Do you want to marry him?"

She got real quiet. So still in his arms that he could feel her heart beating against his side.

"I s-suppose if I ever got married, I'd marry him. I mean I don't object to marrying *him*, just to getting married period."

Ryder nodded his understanding. He opened his mouth to speak then snapped it shut. He wasn't going to do it. He wasn't going to try and talk her into something that might very well kill them both. Wasn't going to be the good guy and speak up for Mac. Mac could damn well fight his battles himself.

How on earth could he possibly speak positively of Kit getting married when it was the last thing on earth he wanted her to do?

It was one thing for the three of them to share an intimate relationship when they were all single, but if Mac and Kit got married, not only would that make things awkward as hell, but it would also close the door to any hope Ryder ever had of being a permanent part of Kit's life.

Goddamn Mac. Damn him to hell. Why now? What had changed? Why was he pushing Kit to make a commitment above and beyond the relationship they had now?

It wasn't like he was afraid of losing Kit, or was he? Ryder had never seen two people more committed to each other. Why was he pushing for marriage, something he knew Kit was afraid of?

"I'm being stupid, aren't I?" Kit whispered, her voice muffled by his chest.

Ryder stroked a hand over her hair. "No, darlin', I don't think you're being stupid at all. Marriage is a big leap. Not worth rushing into."

"Kit."

Ryder looked up to see Mac standing across the garage. Kit pulled away from his arms and turned her eyes toward Mac.

"Baby, we need to talk," Mac said in a heavy voice.

Kit stiffened, and Ryder could see the fear in her eyes. Fear of losing Mac. Ryder clenched his fingers into fists and looked away. Mac was a goddamn fool.

Kit's small hand curled around Ryder's leg. "Thank you," she whispered as she stood up from the couch.

Ryder watched as Kit trudged over to Mac. She stopped a foot away, and Ryder could see the strain between them. He glared at Mac, letting the full brunt of his disapproval show.

Mac returned his stare, bleakness dulling his expression. Ryder flinched. There was pain in Mac's eyes. No ulterior motive. Just his love for Kit. Guilt weighed in Ryder's gut like a bad case of food poisoning.

Finally Mac put an arm around Kit and led her toward the door. Ryder watched them go, a sick feeling in his chest. If Mac convinced her to tie the knot, Ryder would be left standing in the cold.

You'll come, won't you, Ryder?

Kit's anxious question echoed in his alcohol-dulled brain. Ryder set his beer down, adding to the growing collection of empty bottles.

"Ryder, maybe we should leave," Mia said in a low voice.

He looked up at her and shook his head. "Nah, not yet. The happy couple hasn't even made their announcement yet."

"You're a fool," Mia hissed. "I can't believe you're just going to stand by and let her go."

Her comment landed like a knife in the chest. Ryder glanced over to where Mac and Kit stood by the bar, all wrapped up around each other and glowing.

"Have you looked at them?" he demanded. "Do you see how fucking happy they look? I can't destroy that, Mia. I can't. No matter how much I love Kit."

Mia sat back in her chair and pushed a hand through her blond hair. She pinned him with those ice blue eyes of hers until he looked away.

"You, my friend, are a coward."

He jerked his gaze back to her. "Fuck you."

She smirked. "You tried, remember?"

Ryder ran a hand through his tangled hair and sighed. God save him from smart-mouthed women.

"Look, little girl. I know you mean well, but you're not helping here, okay?"

"Why did you want me to come, Ryder?" she asked quietly. "Was it so they wouldn't see you bleed? Was it to make Kit think you found a new piece of ass?"

"I wouldn't hurt her like that," Ryder growled.

Mia lifted one eyebrow. "You think showing up with a stripper won't bother her? You think I haven't seen how many times she's looked over here with hurt in her eyes? If you don't think she has feelings for you, Ryder, you're smoking some fucked-up weed."

Ryder glanced over to where Kit stood, waiting at the bar for Mac to announce their engagement. Everyone knew what the party was about, but the official announcement hadn't been made. For a moment, her eyes met his, and all the breath left his body. She *did* look hurt.

Kit's gaze skittered over Mia then back to Ryder, and the smile she'd worn for Mac just moments earlier faded. She turned away, but not before Ryder saw the uncertainty and anguish in her eyes.

"See what I mean?" Mia spoke up.

Ryder looked away from Kit and gripped his beer tightly in his hand. Goddamn it. He hadn't so much as touched Kit since the day she'd come to the garage. He'd given her and Mac a wide berth as they'd sorted out their differences. Successfully it would seem since Kit had called him to ask if he'd come to their engagement party at the Two Step.

Only from the looks of things, Mac was the only person who seemed happy.

Mac held up his hands and shouted for attention. Ryder froze, unable to look away, as much as he want to. It was like a train wreck.

The mixture of local cops, EMS personnel, rescue crew and the regular patrons of the bar quieted as Mac looked tenderly down at Kit and squeezed her to his side.

"I've invited you all here to celebrate the fact that Kit has agreed to marry me," Mac said with a broad smile.

The room erupted in a chorus of cheers and whistles as Mac bent to kiss Kit. Ryder could see the hunger. Mac's body language screamed possession. He was putting his stamp on her for all the world to see.

Somehow, Ryder managed to get up and go along with the flow of well-wishers pushing toward the happy couple. When finally he drew abreast of Mac and Kit, he stood there, unsure of what to say or do.

Mac stuck out his fist. "Thanks for coming, man."

Ryder stuck out his hand to meet Mac's then turned his gaze on Kit. She stood there, biting her bottom lip, so much hurt and confusion in her eyes, it made his chest ache.

"Who's the woman?" Kit asked lightly.

Ryder found himself saying, "Just a friend, darlin', just a friend."

He pulled Kit into his arms and hugged her tightly. Beside him, Mac got pulled into a crowd of fellow cops as they knocked him on the shoulder and wished him well.

"I don't want things to change," Kit whispered in his ear.

He hugged her a little tighter before finally letting her loose.

"But they will, darlin'. You know things have to change now. You're getting married. You and Mac . . ."

Tears pooled in her eyes and she hastily wiped them with the back of her hand. On a night she should be as happy as a woman could be, she looked downright miserable.

Ryder cupped her chin in his hand and leaned down to lightly kiss her lips. "You know I'll always be here for you, Kit girl."

His chest ached all the more as he uttered the words that might as well have been a brush-off.

She looked away, but not before he saw a single tear trickle down her cheek.

"You should get back to your friend," she said huskily. "She looks lonely."

He opened his mouth to explain Mia again then closed it. Better to let sleeping dogs lie. Maybe if Kit thought he was involved somewhere else, it would make things easier all around.

"Congratulations, darlin'," he murmured before turning to walk away.

Kit watched him walk back to the table where his blond bimbo sat, and tried to swallow the knot in her throat. Then the blond looked up at her, and Kit read *sympathy* in her eyes. Sympathy. God. Did she know about Ryder's involvement with her and Mac?

She closed her eyes and tried like hell to get rid of the hurt eating a hole in her chest. This should be the happiest day of her life. A man she loved more than anything stood at her side proclaiming to the world that she was his and that he'd stand by her always.

On cue, Mac's arm wrapped around her waist and pulled her against him. She tried to smile up at him, but knew she failed miserably.

"What was that all about?" he murmured.

She struggled with her feelings, with the overwhelming sadness. She wanted to laugh and play it off, but she couldn't. Deceit wasn't a part of her nature. She was too direct. Too blunt.

"Did you tell him it was over?" she whispered.

Mac frowned and his brows furrowed. "I haven't said anything to him, baby. But . . ."

He dropped off and looked away with a sigh.

"But what?" she asked.

He looked back at her, his eyes stroking over her face. "Kit, it wasn't supposed to be forever. You know that, right? You and me, though. You're mine. You're going to marry me."

Kit closed her eyes and willed no more tears to leak down her face. When she opened them again, Mac studied her quietly, concern and uncertainty reflected in his face.

She smiled then, knowing it was shaky, but still, she did. It nearly killed her when all she wanted to do was cry, but she wasn't going to hurt Mac.

"I'm yours, Mac. You know that. I just thought . . . I guess I didn't expect it to end so soon," she finished quietly.

"I didn't ask him to, baby. Maybe . . . maybe he's met someone," he said carefully.

Kit jerked her gaze over to the table where the blond sat. Had he found someone? Why did that knowledge nearly flay her alive?

"Yes, maybe he has," she whispered.

CHAPTER 8

"*L*ong time, no see, man."

Ryder stiffened then slowly looked up to see Mac standing beside the bar.

"What the hell are you doing here?" Ryder asked. "Kit will kick your ass if she finds out you went to a strip joint."

Mac cracked a grin. "Mind if I sit?" he asked, gesturing toward the stool next to Ryder.

"Be my guest." Ryder motioned to the barkeep. "A beer for my friend."

Mac's eyes flitted toward the stage where Mia was dancing. He picked up the beer plunked in front of him and took a long swallow.

"That the new woman?" he asked.

Ryder bit the inside of his cheek. "Kit send you to ask?"

Mac's expression darkened. "What's that supposed to mean?"

Ryder sighed and turned to look fully at Mac. "Look, man, let's not play games. I know Kit was upset. I know I was an ass."

Mac stared for a minute then slowly nodded.

"Why did you do it, man? Why did you push for marriage?"

Mac looked away then back at Ryder. "You're pissed that I asked her to marry me."

"Yeah, you could say that."

"What's going on, Ryder? Is there something you're not telling me?"

Ryder knew he should just shut up, lie through his teeth and be done with it. But damn it, he couldn't.

"You knew she wasn't ready for marriage. Hell, she'd just gotten used to the idea of living with you. You knew she ran scared the minute she figured out how you felt about her. Are you just trying to push her away?"

Anger glinted and flashed in Mac's eyes. "Not everyone has such a shitty view of relationships, Ryder. Not everyone would prefer death to an actual commitment. Marriage is a natural progression in a relationship."

"Yeah, I suppose next, you'll be telling me you want a picket fence and two-point-five kids."

Mac remained silent.

"Jesus. I'm right aren't I?"

Mac's lips pressed together, looking as if he were holding onto his temper by a thread.

"Look, Ryder, not everyone hates their parents like you and Kit. Not everyone had a crappy upbringing. Some of us had normal, loving parents, and some of us want to carry on that tradition."

Ryder gritted his teeth and counted to five. Then he got into Mac's face.

"Listen to me, Mac. Kit has a very good reason to hate her lousy-ass parents. Even more so than I do. They hurt her more than you or I can ever understand. You should know all of this, Mac. More than that, you should respect Kit's wishes, and you know damn well she isn't ready for marriage or for kids. You should feel damn lucky she loves you and wants to be with you."

"What the fuck are you really saying, Ryder?" Mac challenged, his face growing angrier by the moment. "What gives you the right to make judgments about my relationship with Kit?"

"I love her."

Mac sighed. "I know you do, man."

"No, Mac. I *love* her."

Shocked silence descended between them. The anger completely disappeared from Mac's face. He stared hard at Ryder, his mouth slightly open.

"Jesus."

"Yeah."

Mac turned around to face ahead then drained the rest of his beer. "I don't know what to say, man."

"There's nothing to say," Ryder said grimly. "I know I'm too late, but this isn't easy for me. I've been looking out for her as long as you have. Maybe longer. I know she loves you. I'd never try to come between the two of you. But don't expect me to be all happy and wear a shit-eating grin for you when I feel like I'm fucking dying."

Mac opened his mouth to speak, but Ryder cut him off.

"And don't you breathe a goddamn word to Kit about this. She doesn't need this. It's easier this way. She has you. She'll forget me."

"No," Mac said quietly. "I'm not so sure she will."

Mac stood up and scrubbed a hand through his hair. "I guess I should go. I just wanted to stop in. I hadn't seen you in a while." He seemed at a loss for words, like he couldn't get away fast enough. Ryder couldn't blame him.

"Yeah," Ryder muttered.

He watched his longtime friend walk away and wondered if he'd irrevocably fucked up his friendship with the two people who were most important to him.

"Damn it!"

He pounded his fist on the bar, ignoring the swift flash of pain that shot up his arm. He turned back to the stage only to see Mia had already stepped off. He scanned the room and found her standing by the hallway that led to the dressing rooms.

Ryder frowned. Mia was against the wall, a uniformed cop pressing heavy into her space. He clunked his beer bottle down and strode across the crowded room, shoving people out of his way.

When he got close enough to see better, he could see that Mia was being threatened by the punk in uniform. God, he hated cops on a power trip. Too bad the strip joint wasn't in the same county Mac worked in. Ryder actually liked his sheriff's department.

"Back off, buddy," Ryder said in a menacing voice.

The cop whipped around in surprise, then his lips curled in a surly twist. "I don't believe this concerns you, *buddy*. Police business. Butt out."

"Unless you have a warrant for her arrest I suggest you get out of the lady's space," Ryder snarled. He flexed his muscles for good measure.

The cop swore under his breath then turned back to Mia. "We're not finished."

He stalked off, brushing hard against Ryder's shoulder as he passed. Mia sank against the wall, her eyes glazed with fear and disgust. She looked surprisingly vulnerable, a change from her usual cocky, smart-mouthed attitude.

"What did he want, Mia?"

She shook her head. "He's a dickhead. Don't worry about him."

"Are you all right, little girl?"

She gave him a shaky smile. "Yeah. Thanks, Ryder. I appreciate the assist."

He frowned and put his hand on her arm to steady her as she stood up straight. "Want me to take you home?"

She shook her head. "No, I've got to pull a double. One of the other girls didn't show. I've only got a few minutes to change. I'll catch you later."

Ryder's brows came together as he watched her walk down the hall toward the dressing room. He didn't know what the fuck had just gone on, but whatever it was, it wasn't on the up and up. Mia was shook up. Her usually unflappable demeanor had taken a serious beating.

He shook his head and turned to go. The entire fucking world was two shakes from insanity. He needed a ride. Something to clear his head. Maybe the open road and his Harley could provide a reprieve from all the goddamn drama.

CHAPTER 9

*I*t had begun to rain, and Ryder was soaked to the skin. Typical late summer Texas shower. Blew up from nowhere and wouldn't last long.

He rode blindly, opening up the Harley until the wind and rain lashed his face. He hadn't meant to go the old familiar route to the closed-up house high atop Barkley Hill. But here he was.

He slowed and turned into the drive then stopped and set his feet down on the ground to steady the bike. The house loomed in front of him like some goddamn bad omen. Why had he come here of all places?

You're a goddamn mess. Just look at you. Do you think anyone will ever take you seriously with all those earrings and tattoos?

His father's voice echoed so loudly in his head he flinched and looked around. But he wasn't here. He was dead. Long buried in the esteemed family plot reserved for the lofty Sinclairs.

I thank God every day that your mother isn't alive to see what you've become.

A heavy ache settled into his chest, tightening until he was sucking harder to get air into his lungs.

Mac's words echoed next to his father's in his head.

Not everyone hated their parents like you and Kit.

"And not every parent hates their child," Ryder muttered.

He should have burned the house to the ground the day his father passed away. There was no reason to keep it. No reason to sell it. He sure didn't need the money. It stood on the hill looking down on the world just like his father had.

"Fuck you," Ryder bit out. "Fuck you and your goddamn expectations."

It rained harder and still Ryder stood there, glaring up the hill. His fingers curled into fists. Mac might have had a June-fucking-Cleaver upbringing, but it didn't mean the rest of the world had. He had no right to assert his own Pollyanna view on everyone else. Or on Kit.

And what could you offer her? a voice jeered in his head.

"Understanding," Ryder muttered. "I could offer her understanding."

Kit snuggled deeper into Mac's arms and listened to the steady downpour of rain as it echoed off the roof. They were lying in bed watching the credits role on the movie that had just finished.

"I love the rain," she murmured.

"Tell me why you hated your parents," Mac said.

She reared her head in surprise and pushed away from him to stare in astonishment. "What? Why would you ask something like that? What on earth brought that up?"

He regarded her with a thoughtful expression. "Ryder says I should already know, but I don't because you've never told me."

Her heart sped up. "When did you talk to Ryder?"

An annoyed expression covered his face. "It doesn't matter

when we talked. What matters is that you tell me what happened with them. Why you hated them so much."

She slid further under the covers and turned her face away from Mac to stare out the window on the opposite wall. Rain splashed against the window and ran in rivulets down the glass.

"I don't want to talk about them," she whispered.

Mac scooted up in the bed and gently turned her chin until she faced him again. "It's important, Kit. We need to talk about them."

She closed her eyes and shuddered lightly. "There's not much to tell. My stepfather was a bastard. My mother got tired of him. And me apparently. She left when I was ten. Never said good-bye. One morning I woke up and she was gone."

Mac's hand stroked soothingly through her hair.

She sat up, pulling the covers around her waist. She pulled her knees toward her chest until her chin rested on the tops. She hugged her arms around her legs and took in several steadying breaths.

"My stepfather was furious. With me. He blamed me for her leaving. I was too whiny. Too demanding. Too high maintenance."

"Jesus, you were just a kid," Mac said.

She nodded. "At first his abuse was just verbal, but his drinking got worse and then he started hitting me."

She could hear the distant echo of smacking flesh. Feel the pain and accompanying shame. Beside her she heard Mac's sharp intake of breath and his grip tightened in her hair.

"Nothing major at first. A slap here. A kick there."

Mac swore.

"But it got worse. I learned to avoid him," she said in a dry dispassionate voice. "And then, when I was sixteen, his abuse turned sexual."

Numbness crept over her. Numbness she was used to, clung to, needed desperately in order to think back to that time.

"Goddamn!"

Mac turned her into his chest and hugged her tightly against him. "I didn't know, baby. I knew it was bad at home. I knew it was why you spent so much time with Ryder out at the lake, but I didn't *know*."

The pain and anguish in her voice managed to prick her when the memory of her abuse couldn't. She felt distant, like she was telling someone else's story. Blocked out that it had been her.

She licked her lips and pushed away from Mac. "I threatened to kill him," she murmured. "After the third time, I couldn't take it anymore. Something broke inside me. Maybe I went a little crazy. I took his shotgun and told him to get out. Told him if he ever came near me again, I'd kill him. He didn't believe me until he tried to take the gun away from me. I pulled the trigger. I think it scared him. He packed up and left. I never saw him again."

She laughed dryly, the sound unpleasant. "He was the one person I wasn't sad to see leave me."

Mac leaned into her, pressed his forehead to hers until their lips were just a breath apart. "I'm so sorry, baby. I wish I had known. I wish I had done something."

She looked at him a little sadly and reached up to touch his face so close to hers. "You were a teenager, Mac. What could you have done?"

"I would have taken you away from there," Mac said. "I swear I would have."

She smiled and closed her eyes to hold the tears back. "You're here now. That's all that matters."

Mac pulled away and cupped her cheek in his big hand. "Do you love me, Kit? I mean really love me? Do you want to marry me?"

She stared at him in astonishment. This was not like Mac at all. "What on earth has gotten into you? Do you doubt me?"

"Just answer the question, Kit. I need to know."

She reached out a hand to touch him. To somehow reassure him. "Mac, I love you with all my heart. I never want to be without you."

He let out all his breath then pulled her against him, gripping her tightly. "I never want to be without you either, baby."

CHAPTER 10

*R*yder roared into Mac's drive and skidded to a stop in the gravel. He knocked the kickstand down with his foot and eased off his bike. He stood there staring at the door for a long time.

It had been two weeks since he had blurted out to Mac that he loved Kit. Two long-ass weeks of being without his friends. He wasn't a sappy kind of guy, but he missed being around Mac and Kit.

He was through being a dumbass. Yeah, he loved Kit so much he ached, but there wasn't a damn thing he could do about it. Mac and Kit belonged to each other, and he wasn't going to begrudge them their happiness. Nor was he going to end up a bitter old bastard and sacrifice their friendship because the other man won.

He trekked up the steps to Mac's porch and walked inside just like he'd done a million times before. What met his gaze drew him up short, though.

There in the middle of the living room stood Kit and Mac. Kit's forehead rested against Mac's chest, and he held her tightly against him.

"We'll work it out, baby," Mac said softly, still oblivious to Ryder's presence.

Ryder cleared his throat. "Did I come at a bad time?"

When she heard him, she looked up and Ryder could see the evidence of her tears. His gut tightened in reaction.

"What the hell is going on?" Ryder demanded. Fear swelled in his throat. "Are you all right, darlin'?"

"I'm—I'm pregnant," she whispered.

"Ah hell," Ryder said. No wonder she was so upset. He glared over at Mac. Had he planned this? Was this one more thing he'd pushed Kit into?

Mac looked back at him, pain burning so brightly in his eyes, Ryder knew immediately something else had to be wrong.

"I take it you aren't happy about it?" Ryder asked, trying to inflect a little levity into the situation.

Kit stared at him, tears filling her eyes once more. "You don't understand, Ryder. The baby . . . it could be yours."

Ryder took a step back. He opened his mouth to speak but nothing would come out. Of all the things she could have said, this wasn't something he ever would have dreamed.

"Mine?" he finally croaked. "*What?*"

Kit looked away, and her shoulders trembled. He knew she was crying again. Fuck on a stick, what a goddamn disaster.

He stepped forward, reaching out his hand to Kit. "I don't understand. Darlin', talk to me."

She turned her head back to him, her green eyes swamped with so much pain he sucked in his breath.

"I'm pregnant," she said baldly.

"Yes, I heard that much. Go back to the part about it being mine."

She took in a wavering breath, her lips shaky. Ryder snuck a look at Mac, and he looked as shell-shocked as Ryder felt. God, what a bomb to drop. For all of them.

"I went to the doctor. He thinks I'm about six weeks along."

"The beach weekend," Ryder said, all the wind knocked right out of him.

She nodded. "I think so. I don't know." Tears flooded her eyes, and sobs welled from her throat.

Ryder looked again at Mac. Saw answering grief in his expression. Christ. He'd royally fucked things up now.

"Kit, darlin', I'm sorry. I'm so goddamn sorry."

She closed her eyes and pulled further away from Mac. Then she turned and fled from the room, leaving Ryder standing there feeling like the biggest piece of pond scum ever dredged from the mud.

Slowly, he looked over at Mac. The two men stood staring at each other in silence for a long moment. It had been a long time since Ryder had seen such torment in Mac's eyes. Not since the night Kit had disappeared and they'd thought for sure they'd lost her.

"Mac, you have to know. I never meant for this to happen," Ryder said in a low voice.

"I know, man. I know you didn't."

"I wouldn't come between you two like this." He paused for a moment then looked Mac straight in the eye. "But you have to know, I can't walk away if she's pregnant with my baby."

Mac nodded his head. He ran a hand through his hair then back down over his face. He looked tired. Like a man fighting a no-win battle.

"I've been doing a lot of thinking, Ryder." He broke off, walked around Ryder and sank down on the couch.

Ryder turned around to face him, his arms crossed over his chest.

"I've been thinking about how I'd feel and what I would have done if you had acted first with Kit. I won't lie. When you told me about your feelings for Kit, I wanted to kick your teeth in. But I don't think I could have stepped back like you did. I couldn't have been the better man. I would have fought like hell for her even if it meant ruining our friendship."

"I considered it," Ryder said honestly.

Mac leaned forward, his elbows resting on his knees. "She needs us both, man. We both love her and we both need to be there for her."

"What exactly are you saying?" Ryder asked calmly though his pulse was about to beat right out of his head.

"Just what I did," Mac said evenly. "We both need to be here for her. This isn't going to be easy. It's like you said. She isn't ready for children. Hell, she probably isn't ready for marriage either."

He looked guilty as he made the proclamation.

"Are you saying you want me around?"

"This isn't about what I want. It's about what's best for Kit. You and I, we go back, man. We understand each other, and we understand Kit. This won't hurt us. I'm cool with it."

"Really?" Ryder asked doubtfully.

"Yeah. Really. It's not the same when you aren't around. We had good times."

"I don't know what to say," Ryder said with a shake of his head.

"Say you'll be here for her. She's going to need us both to come to terms with this." Mac looked up at him then held out his fist. "We okay now?"

Ryder slowly brought his fist up to meet Mac's. "Yeah. We're cool."

"Then let's go find Kit. If I know her, she's tearing herself apart as we speak."

Ryder followed Mac to the bedroom, and when he saw Kit huddled on the bed, his heart fell. Not bothering to give Mac space, he shoved around him and settled on the bed beside Kit.

"Darlin', look at me please," Ryder pleaded.

He put his hand out and threaded it through her hair, stroking gently. She turned her tearstained face up to him, and his breath caught in his throat.

"I'm so sorry, Kit girl."

"No, I'm sorry," she whispered as more tears coursed down her cheeks.

He blinked in surprise. "What on earth do you have to be sorry about?"

She sat up in the bed and hunched her knees to her chest. She looked so damned fragile, like she'd break into a million pieces. He'd thought those days were behind them.

Mac settled on the other side of her and curled his fingers over hers. "Tell us what you mean, baby."

"It was my fault. I—I forgot to take my pill the night . . . the last night we were there," she choked out.

She looked frantically up at Ryder. "It wasn't intentional, Ryder. I wouldn't do this to you or Mac, I swear."

Ryder sat there stunned. He exchanged incredulous looks with Mac.

"Kit, look at me," Ryder demanded.

She turned sad eyes up to him.

"This is not your fault. Goddamn it, stop blaming yourself."

"He's right, baby," Mac interjected. "It's our fault. We took chances with your body. Chances we should have never taken. Birth control isn't just your responsibility."

"But I never wanted you to wear condoms," she muttered.

Ryder glanced again at Mac, wanting to know how he was taking it so far. It had to be hard after all he'd done to tie Kit to him. Now he was faced with sharing her, possibly forever if the baby turned out to be Ryder's.

The pain he saw there made him uncomfortable. If he'd only listened to his first instinct and never gone on that beach trip.

This would never have happened and the two people he loved most in the world wouldn't be hurting.

He dropped his face to his hand and rubbed wearily.

"Ryder," Mac spoke up.

He looked over at Mac again.

"I don't blame you, man. Neither does Kit."

"Thanks for that," Ryder said honestly. "But it doesn't make me feel any better." He turned his attention back to Kit. He hesitated, feeling unsure of himself, not something he was used to.

"Kit, I understand if you're angry with me. In your position I would be."

"But—" she began.

He held up a hand. "Let me finish."

She closed her mouth and looked down at her hands. He tucked a finger under her chin and forced her to look back up at him.

"I'd never do anything to hurt you, Kit girl. You have to know that. I know you aren't ready for children, and I'm so damn sorry this happened to you. Mac's right. We took chances with your body we shouldn't have, and you're left to pay the price. But you won't be alone, darlin'. This I swear. Mac and I are going to be here every step of the way for you."

He looked over to Mac for confirmation of what they'd already discussed and Mac nodded in agreement.

"You're not angry?" she asked hesitantly.

He slid his hand around to the back of her neck and pulled her up against his chest. "Never with you, darlin, never with you. I'm angry at myself for putting you in this position, but I have nothing to be angry with you about. You put your trust in our hands. You allowed us freedoms most people would never dream of giving. You can't know what that feels like, to be trusted that way, and I feel like I've betrayed it."

She shook her head. "No, Ryder. I don't blame you, I swear. I was so stupid. If I'd just remembered the damn pill."

"Don't torture yourself, darlin'. Who's to say you wouldn't still be pregnant if you'd taken the pill? Nothing's foolproof."

She pulled away from him and sat up in the bed. She reached over to take Mac's hand and looked at him with so much anguish and guilt, it nearly tore Ryder's insides out.

"What are we going to do, Mac?"

The question, so agonizingly phrased, lay heavy over the room.

Mac's expression softened, and he tucked Kit into his arms, wrapped himself around her and held on tight.

"We'll work it out, baby. I don't want you to worry. I'm not going anywhere and neither is Ryder. I promise. I love you."

"I love you too," she whispered.

Ryder ached with the need to let her know he loved her as well, but this wasn't the time. She needed his support, not to be weighed down with more baggage.

"What's important now is you," Mac continued. "Ryder and I are going to be with you every step of the way. You and me, this changes nothing, baby. Even if turns out the baby is Ryder's."

But it changed everything for Ryder. There was no way he could pretend differently. If Kit was pregnant with his child, how could he stand to step back and let Mac take over? God, what a mess.

He closed his eyes and rubbed his hand across his brow.

"I'm sorry, man. I know this is hard for you too," Mac said quietly.

A look of understanding passed between the two men. Ryder held out his fist, and Mac slowly raised his to bump it.

"We can do this for Kit," Ryder said evenly.

CHAPTER 11

"Oh man, what a cluster fuck," Mia said.

"You're telling me," Ryder muttered as he downed the last of his beer.

Mia looked tired tonight, and Ryder felt guilty for unloading his woes on her shoulders.

"You okay, little girl?" he asked.

She smiled tightly. "Oh yeah, couldn't be better."

Ryder shook his head. "I came by because . . ."

"Because you won't be around much anymore," Mia finished with a smile.

"Yeah, something like that," Ryder said softly.

"Are you happy, Ryder? Is she happy?"

He sucked in a deep breath and plunked his empty beer bottle on the bar. "If I'm completely honest, a part of me is not sad this happened. It makes me a complete and total bastard, but there you have it anyway. She's not ready for kids and marriage.

Mac and I both know this, and yet, we've fucked things up royally for her."

"But you're not terribly upset it happened," she said dryly.

"No. I'm not." He looked back up at the pretty blond. "Go on, you know you're dying to call me an asshole."

"Asshole," she said with a laugh.

He sighed. "It's twisted, I know. I tore Mac a new asshole when he pressured Kit into marriage. And then I basically do the same by knocking her up."

Mia arched a brow. "You seem so sure it's yours."

Panic curled and twisted in his gut. It had to be his. Otherwise he'd lose Kit forever.

"Let's just say the percentages are in my favor."

"Oh? Do tell."

"We did a lot of fucking that weekend. It had been awhile and I wanted her so badly. I came inside her twice as much as Mac did."

Mia colored slightly. Ryder raised a brow. Mia blushing? How on earth did a stripper blush?

"So you're going to be hanging around her a lot more now, which means you'll be spending less time here," she pointed out.

"Yeah. You okay with that?" he asked.

She gave him a strange look. "Why wouldn't I be okay with it? You've moped around for God knows how long because you couldn't be as close to Kit as you'd like, and now you're going to be spending a lot of time with her."

"I care about you, Mia. You've been a good friend. I just want you to know you can call me if you ever need me."

She smiled. "I'm a big girl, Ryder. I can take care of myself."

"Then what are you doing in a place like this?" he pointed out.

He could swear he saw fear in her eyes. Eyes that pretty didn't need to be shadowed by fear.

"Is there something you need to tell me, little girl?"

"I wish you'd stop calling me 'little girl'," she muttered. "Makes me feel all silly and immature. Like a fourteen-year-old with her first crush or something."

He laughed. "You're young and a little slip of a thing."

"But I don't feel young," she said quietly. "Sometimes . . . " A far away look entered her eyes. "Sometimes I feel so damn old, you know?"

"Yeah, I know what you mean." He reached out to cup her cheek. "If you ever need me, little girl, you just holler, okay?"

She smiled at him. "I will. Now get on home to your woman. I can see you itching to get up."

Ryder chuckled and stood up. He reached for her and grabbed her up in a hug. "Thanks for the shoulder, Mia."

"Anytime, badass. Anytime."

Ryder entered Mac's house and found it quiet. Mac's truck was gone, but Kit's Bronco was there. Strange since she was supposed to be working tonight. He'd gone over to the Two Step to see her, but he was told she hadn't come into work. Not like Kit at all. He heard a peculiar sound from the kitchen and went to investigate.

He found Kit leaning over the sink, her body convulsing with her retches.

"Ah hell, darlin'."

He gathered her hair in his hands and held it away as she heaved again. He smoothed a hand up and down her back, murmuring soothing words to her as she shook.

Finally she seemed to calm down. He waited until she'd washed her mouth out then pulled her into his arms.

"Are you okay now?" he asked.

She nodded weakly. "I'm sorry you had to come in on that."

"Hush. I'm glad I was here. That can't be any fun."

"No," she said wryly. "It isn't."

He led her over to the table where she'd been chopping vegetables for supper. When he'd settled her into a chair, he took the one next to her and sat down.

"You been sick much? I haven't noticed you doing much puking. But I went over to the Two Step and they said you'd called in sick."

She grimaced. "I don't have morning sickness as much as I have evening sickness."

"You look tired, darlin'. Too tired. And if you're sick you need to be getting even more rest."

She made a face and blew out a weary breath. "Problem is I'm sick when I need to be at work. If this would just go like a normal pregnancy, I'd be sick in the mornings, and then I'd have the rest of the day to feel better before work."

Ryder frowned, then he leaned forward and took her hand. "I want you to quit, Kit. You don't need to be working in a bar in your condition. All that smoke, being on your feet the entire time. It can't be good for the baby."

She looked at him in shock. "I can't quit, Ryder."

"I've talked it over with Mac," he continued, ignoring her outburst. "We agree we'd both feel better if you'd quit your job. At least for now."

She laid her other hand over his arm. "Ryder, I appreciate your concern, but I can't quit. Mac and I need the money. We both have bills even living together. I wouldn't feel right making him take responsibility for the things I have to pay."

Ryder pressed his lips together. "Kit, you know I have more money than I'll ever know what to do with."

He held up his hand when she would have protested.

"Let me help out, darlin'. You could be pregnant with my child. If that's the case, don't you think I'll be doing everything in my power to make sure you're taken care of? Let me do this for you, Kit. Quit your job and stay home. Take care of yourself and our baby. Let me take care of you."

He'd gotten to her. He knew when she didn't immediately respond that she was at least considering his proposal. Fear and a little uncertainty flashed in her eyes.

"I've never completely depended on anyone else," she whispered. "It scares the hell out of me."

"Then maybe it's time you started," he said firmly. "Mac and I will take care of you, darlin'. We won't let you down, I swear it."

"I'll think about it," she finally conceded.

He smiled and squeezed her hand. The silence between them lay heavy, and he cleared his throat in an attempt to alleviate the strain.

"Where the hell is Mac anyway? Shouldn't he be home by now?"

She sighed a little unhappily. "He got called in to work. Some big case that's poised to crack. I get the feelin' he'll be working a lot of hours for awhile."

"Damn. Sorry to hear that."

"I'm glad you're here," she said, a sweet smile spreading across her face. Her green eyes had regained their luster after her puking episode, and they shone with happiness now.

"I've been here, darlin'. Nothing could keep me away."

"I know, but you've been here less when Mac's around."

He shifted uncomfortably. "I didn't mean to hurt your feelings or anything, Kit girl. I just thought . . . " He broke off with a heavy sigh. "I just thought it best to give you two as much breathing room as possible given the circumstances."

She stared at him for a long moment. Her lips trembled, and she looked as if she was doing battle with the devil.

"Ryder, I love you and I want you here. Especially now."

"I know you do, darlin'," he said soothingly.

She stood up in agitation, her back to him. Then she turned around and took a deep breath. "No, Ryder, I don't think you do know. I *love* you. I feel so guilty even saying it, but it's the truth. I can't go on denying what I feel. You once told me that I didn't love you the same way I did Mac, and you were right. But at the time I thought you meant not as *much*. And that's not true. I love you and Mac both."

Her eyes filled with tears, and she wrapped her arms tightly around herself. "I fought with myself so many times. I know it could hurt Mac, and God knows I'd never do anything to hurt him. I love him so much. But I love you too, Ryder. I don't want to be without either of you."

Ryder felt downright light-headed. He gaped at her, not knowing how to respond, what to say. What could he do? And why, when she was standing there telling him everything he'd ever dreamed, was he not overjoyed?

He stood up and closed the distance between them. He pulled her into his arms and held on tight.

Tell her you love her too. Don't fuck this up.

But instead he said, "I don't want to hurt Mac either, darlin'. You know I love you. I'm always here for you. Let's just leave it at that and see what happens down the road."

She stiffened in his arms and turned her head away so he wouldn't see her tears. Goddamn it killed him to see her cry. He'd do anything to spare her pain.

He reached down to cup her stomach, marveling that his child could be nestled inside her.

"You need to take better care of yourself, darlin'. I aim to make sure you do."

"Take me to bed and hold me, Ryder. Please."

He looked down into her big green eyes and lost whatever remaining part of his soul he had. "That I can do, Kit girl. That I can do."

He bent down and gently picked her up. She looked tired and worn-out, like a woman with the weight of the world on her shoulders. He should have been here with her instead of at the strip joint whining at Mia.

He carried her into the bedroom and eased her down on the bed. Taking only a moment to strip out of his shirt and jeans, he climbed in beside her. She snuggled into his chest and closed her eyes immediately.

Soon her soft, even breathing filled the room. He stroked her hair, pulling a strand away from her face. She was so beautiful. She was tired, too. Pregnancy was taking its toll on her early. He'd make damn sure she quit her job. He wasn't going to relent until she saw things his way.

She loved him. It tore her apart, the thought of hurting Mac, but she'd said it anyway. Wanted him to know. How he got so lucky, he'd never know. He should have held her, told her that somehow they'd work it out, but he couldn't lie to her.

The future was one bitch of a cliffhanger. Who knew what the fuck would happen months down the road. Kit needed them both right now, but when the baby came . . .

What a cluster fuck indeed. If it was his baby, he'd always be between Mac and Kit. If it was Mac's baby, Ryder would be left out in the cold.

Neither option was particularly appealing.

He bent to kiss her softly on the forehead. He couldn't control the outcome. Couldn't dictate the future. But he could decide the present. Whatever happened in the end, he was going to make the next seven months the best for all of them.

CHAPTER 12

$\mathcal{K}$it settled onto the couch between Mac and Ryder, a contented smile on her face. The last few weeks had been nothing short of magical. Although Mac was working long hours, and she missed him terribly, he and Ryder watched over her constantly.

The three had settled into a comfortable routine. Ryder had all but moved in, opting to spend the majority of the nights over at Mac's. And when he wasn't working in the garage, he kept her company.

At first she'd been loathe to admit it, but quitting work had been a huge relief. Accepting help—money—from Ryder had been extremely uncomfortable, but he didn't so much as blink an eye. He wrote a check—an extremely large check—and made her deposit it into her bank account. Then he'd given her a credit card and a duplicate ATM card for his own account with instructions to use it if necessary.

"How are you feeling tonight, baby?" Mac asked as he wrapped an arm around her. His hand settled possessively on her shoulder, and he squeezed her lightly.

Tonight was one of the few nights he'd been at home for more than a few minutes to grab something to eat, shower and leave again. She missed him.

She snuggled into his arms and laid her head on his chest. "I'm feeling okay. A little queasy, but better now that you're at home."

He kissed her forehead then nuzzled down to her lips, capturing them in a long, hot, breathless kiss.

"I've missed you, baby. I'm sorry I've had to work so much lately." She smiled up at him. "It's your job. I know that."

"I'm also glad you let Ryder help out so you could quit," he said seriously. "It's a huge weight off my mind not to have to worry about you working at the Two Step anymore."

She crinkled her brow. She had no idea it worried him that much. She knew he still had nightmares about her attack and the night he thought he'd lost her, but she didn't realize he'd wanted her to quit so badly.

"I'm glad too," Ryder butted in from the other side. "It would have been damn hard on you when you're belly starts swelling along with your feet."

She smiled a satisfied smile. A ridiculous thrill fluttered in her stomach. "I love the way you two fuss over me," she admitted.

"Get used to it," Mac said as he kissed her again. "It's only going to get worse."

"Make love to me," she whispered. "It's been so long since I got to spend the night in your arms. Tonight I want to sleep between the two of you."

Mac looked over her head at Ryder and grinned. "That sounds like an invitation to me."

Ryder stood up. "You won't see me turning it down."

Mac sat forward and got up from the couch. Then he reached down for her, picking her up and cradling her in his arms.

She loved his strength. She rested her head on his chest as he walked back to the bedroom. He set her on the bed and began undressing her in gentle motions.

When she reached for his fly, he blocked her hands.

"Let us love you, baby. You just lie back and enjoy it."

She stared at him feeling so much love she thought she might burst. He pushed her back until she lay in the middle of the bed. Then he and Ryder began undressing.

Mac knelt on the bed, sliding up her body. She welcomed him with her arms, holding them out to pull him close. He held her face in his hands and kissed her reverently, as if she were a precious piece of glass.

His knee nudged impatiently at her thighs, spreading them, readying her for his swollen cock.

"Love me," she whispered.

"I do, baby. I do."

He slid easily into her. All the breath sucked right out of her lungs. He paused when he was all the way in, looking down at her with so much love in his eyes. He smoothed her hair from her face as he propped himself on his elbows.

He rocked gently against her, his hips undulating in a slow rhythm. Finally he rose up and settled between her legs on his knees.

Ryder rolled closer to her and cupped a breast with his hand as Mac continued his tender assault on her pussy. Ryder's fingers crept up to her jaw and turned her to face him. Her lips melted against his as he kissed her. His tongue slid over her lips, gaining entrance to duel with her tongue.

The kiss burned on and on, and Mac slid lazily in and out of her pussy. Never before had they shown this degree of tenderness. A knot of emotion swelled in her throat until she gasped for air.

Ryder's head lowered to her breasts. He sucked first one nipple into his mouth then moved to the other. He circled the puckered tip with his tongue, and he sucked in rhythm with Mac's thrusts.

"Please!" she cried out.

"Please what, baby? Love you? I do," Mac said. "Protect you? Take care of you always? I will."

Tears flooded her eyes.

"That goes for me too," Ryder whispered in her ear.

Her eyes flew open at his words. Did he mean them the same way Mac did, or was he just saying it in the heat of the moment? For now it didn't matter. She took them both to heart. A heart that was so full of love for both of them, she didn't think she could bear it.

Her orgasm built slowly, leisurely, like a calm wind on a summer day. She felt loved and cherished, like she was the only woman in the world.

Mac leaned further into her, his hardness causing unbearable friction in the delicate tissues of her pussy. She squeezed her eyes shut as the tension built and built. Ryder plucked at her nipples, rolling them between his fingers then nipping with his teeth.

When she opened her eyes again, Mac threw back his head and she could see his jaw straining. She arched into him, wanting him deeper. She was so close. One more time. She cried out as he sank in once more and began pulsing into her.

Ryder suckled at her breasts, alternating, his mouth sending streaks of fire straight to her clit. She shoved her hand into his dark hair and held him tightly against her as Mac gripped her hips and exploded in his orgasm.

It felt as though something popped inside her, setting her free. She floated, the room fuzzy, her vision blurred. She was dimly aware of Ryder pulling her over so Mac could settle down on the other side of her.

Then both men flanked her body, and she melted against them. "I love you," she whispered as her eyes fluttered closed.

*   *   *

Ryder walked into the house and looked around for Kit. Mac was working late again, and he'd called a minute ago to tell Ryder he probably wouldn't be home until the morning.

He smiled when he saw Kit all curled up on the couch fast asleep in just a T-shirt. He decided not to disturb her. She needed her rest. Her pregnancy had been difficult so far, and she was sick often.

He just gave thanks she'd listened to reason and quit her job. The job would have been too hard on her when she was doing all she could just to stay above water.

His stomach growled, and he headed into the kitchen to make a sandwich. Then he'd hit the hay. He had an early job to do in the morning at the garage.

After throwing together a ham and turkey sandwich, he slouched at the table with a cold beer. He was nearly finished when his cell phone vibrated then rang. He snatched it up so it wouldn't wake up Kit and muttered a hello.

"Hey, man, you at the house?" Mac asked.

"Yeah, just got done eating."

"How's Kit?" Mac sounded concerned.

"She's sleeping on the couch. I didn't wake her."

"Good. I was worried about her. I hated to leave, but we need all the men we can get. Got a lot of shit going down lately."

"I'll take good care of her," Ryder promised.

"Thanks, man."

They rang off, and Ryder tiptoed back through the living room and checked on Kit one last time before he slipped past her into the bedroom.

He shucked his boots and clothes and turned the shower on. He flexed tired muscles and stepped under the hot spray. After a quick rinse, he got out and wrapped a towel around his hips. He took another towel from the rack and began rubbing his long hair.

As he walked back into the bedroom, a peculiar sound from the living room had him frowning. He dropped the towel he was drying his hair with and headed toward the sound.

When he reached the door, he heard it again. Kit was moaning and gasping in pain. His blood ran cold as he looked across to see her doubled over on the floor by the couch. But what scared him even more was all the blood spreading out on the carpet.

"Kit!"

He launched himself across the room and dropped to the floor beside her. She looked up at him her eyes chock-full of agony.

"The baby," she gasped. "I think it's the baby."

She looked down at her hand, smeared with bright red blood, and she began to shake uncontrollably.

"Jesus." He looked frantically around and swore. "Let me get my pants, darlin'. Sit tight."

He sprinted to the bedroom, his towel falling from his hips. He yanked his pants and shirt back on and bolted back into the living room. Kneeling beside her on the carpet, he scooped her up in his arms and hurried for the door.

"It hurts, Ryder."

"I know it does, darlin'. I'll get you to the hospital. Just hold on to me tight."

He carried her to her Bronco and eased her into the passenger seat. Then he raced around and threw himself into the driver's seat.

All the way to the hospital he listened to her moans and cursed his inability to stop her pain. He rubbed her head in his lap and smoothed a hand down her body. Anything to make her feel better. To let her know he was here.

Five minutes later, he careened into the emergency-room alcove and screeched to a halt. He ran around to the passenger side and collected her in his arms. He was met at the door by an ER tech who asked the situation.

"Miscarriage," Ryder muttered.

The tech motioned him through the employees-only door and ushered him into an exam room.

"Lay her here," the tech directed. "Then wait outside."

"I'm not leaving her," Ryder ground out.

The tech looked at him for a long moment and must have realized he had no chance of throwing him out. He shrugged instead and pointed to a chair. "Park it then. I'll get the doctor."

Ryder ignored that command as well. He stood by Kit's bed, holding her hand as she moaned softly in pain.

Fear consumed him. She was losing the baby. What else could account for so much blood? This wasn't something he'd ever counted on. He knew there was a chance the baby might not be his, but he'd never expected not to be able to find out.

Her muffled sobs reached his ears, piercing his gut like someone had laid into him with a bat.

He bent to hold her, pressed his face to her hair and held her tightly. "Don't cry, darlin'. Please don't cry."

Before the doctor even made it in, Mac burst through the door like a man possessed. Ryder wondered for all of a second how he'd found out so fast, but he knew the ER personnel were tuned into the local cops. Someone had probably called him as soon as he'd hit the entrance with Kit in his arms.

"Kit, baby. What's wrong? What's happening?" Mac demanded as he bent over her curled up form.

She raised her red, splotchy face, and more tears poured down her cheeks. "It's the baby, Mac. I think I'm losing it."

Ryder stumbled back, allowing them space. He continued to back up until he was out in the hall looking in at the tender scene in front of him.

"It's okay, baby, I'm here," he heard Mac say. "We'll get through this."

The sandwich he'd eaten earlier seemed lodged in his throat. He couldn't breathe around the knot. His eyes stung like hell, and it was then he realized if he didn't get out of here soon, he'd break down and bawl like a baby.

He turned and strode down the hall and out the doors he'd come in. A few more feet and he stepped out into the Texas summer heat. But for some reason he felt frozen.

The truth hit him like a cement truck. With the baby gone, there was no place for him in Kit's life. No reason for him to hang around, intrude on her and Mac's relationship.

She was as lost to him as their baby was. Somehow he'd been so sure it was his. Something he and Kit had created together.

He got into Kit's Bronco and drove it back toward Mac's house. When he pulled into the driveway, he sat there for several long minutes. He wanted desperately to be with Kit, to soothe away her pain, but Mac was there. She had who she needed.

Feeling like he'd been sucker punched, he shuffled into the house, went to collect the few things he'd stored there then walked back out to his motorcycle. He cranked the engine and headed out onto the road. The streaks of wetness on his cheek blew dry almost before he could register their presence.

CHAPTER 13

"*J*'m worried about you, baby," Mac said.

Kit looked up from her perch by the window and flinched at the raw concern in Mac's expression. She turned away, looked out the window again and tried to keep the anguish at bay.

Mac moved across the room then settled down in the window seat beside her. He reached for her hand and brought it up to his lips. He pressed a kiss to her palm and held her fingers to his cheek.

"I wish you would talk to me," he said softly. "I know you're hurting. I am too. We need to talk about this."

Kit closed her eyes and willed the tears not to fall. It had been two weeks since she'd gone home from the hospital, an empty shell, her insides feeling they'd been scraped clean. Two weeks in which she'd not seen Ryder once. Not since he'd left the hospital the night he'd taken her in.

She was angry, but more than that she ached. Her heart ached.

Mac put a finger under her chin and gently turned her face up to meet his gaze.

"Talk to me, baby. I can't stand this silence between us."

A tear trickled down her cheek. She didn't want to hurt him. She hurt enough for both of them. And she knew what she'd say *would* hurt.

He pulled her into his arms, hesitant at first, as though he thought she'd resist. She didn't fight him, but she didn't embrace him either.

She felt a shudder roll through his big body, and she cursed herself all over again.

"Tell me what's going in that head of yours, baby."

His tone had turned pleading. God. She owed him the truth.

She pulled away and wiped at the damnable tears streaking down her cheeks. "I hurt," she croaked.

"Oh God, baby, I know you do. I know you do."

"You don't understand," she whispered.

"Then make me understand, Kit. Talk to me please."

She looked into his eyes, eyes that held so much love for her. They burned an intense blue. She reached out a hand to his cheek and he turned into her palm to kiss it.

"I didn't just lose my baby," she began. "I lost . . . I lost Ryder too, and it's killing me."

She let her hand slip from his face and turned away, not wanting to see the hurt in his eyes.

"I love him, Mac," she said quietly. "I've always loved him. Somehow I confused what I felt for you and thought I didn't love him as much, but I do. And now . . . now he doesn't want me. There's nothing to tie us together. I shouldn't be saying this, but I can't lie to you, Mac. I've lost him, and it's eating me alive."

Mac slowly pulled her into his arms. His breath came heavy. She could feel him pulling ragged breaths into his chest. God, she hadn't wanted to hurt him this way. What kind of woman was she that she could drive a knife into a man who loved her so much, who'd do anything to keep her from hurt.

They sat there for several long seconds, silence heavy between them. He gripped her tightly, and she could feel a surge of emotion in his embrace.

"I'm sorry, Mac," she said as sobs welled from her throat. Her voice was muffled by his chest but she continued on. "I don't deserve you. I don't. I'll understand if you don't want me anymore."

"Hush, baby, stop talking like that. You and me. We're forever. I promise you that."

She hauled back and looked at him in disbelief. Searching for a sign of anger, of betrayal or at least disappointment. What she found was sincerity. And love. More love than she could have imagine after what she'd just told him.

"Mac, didn't you hear what I said?"

"I have excellent hearing, baby," he said calmly.

"You're not angry?" she asked.

He cupped her face in his hands and leaned in to kiss her. "I'm a lot of things right now. But angry isn't one of them. I'm sad that you're hurting. I'm sad we lost our baby. I'm frustrated because I want so much to make your pain go away and I feel so damned helpless. But, baby, I love you. That doesn't go away in five minutes. I love you so damn much that it kills me to think of being without you."

The sobs tore out of her throat in a painful rush. She struggled to breathe as they came out faster than she could handle. All the pain and grief she'd stored up over the last two weeks flooded from her.

She sounded harsh, ugly and guttural. And still, Mac held onto her as if he'd never let her go.

He smoothed her hair with his hand. Stroked her gently, offering her comfort. They sat there for a long time as she released the pent-up emotion.

Finally her sobs quieted, and Mac leaned down to kiss her tears away.

"There's only one thing I need to know, baby. Only one important issue. Do you love me?"

She threw her arms around him and kissed his neck. "I do love you, Mac. I didn't lie about that. I love you so much, and I'd die without you."

He carefully pulled her away from him and looked down at her, his gorgeous blue eyes so serious. "Then that's all that matters. We'll work out the rest."

Ryder sat at the bar staring at the empty bottom of his sixth glass of whiskey. Or was it the seventh? He slid it across the rough surface of the countertop and motioned for another. Whatever it was, it wasn't enough.

"When are you going to stop trying to kill yourself?" Mia asked in a dry voice.

He didn't turn around. He ignored her. But she wouldn't leave him alone. She took the seat beside him.

"It won't work, you know."

He cocked his head to the side. "What's that?"

"Drinking yourself into oblivion." She motioned for a beer then turned back to him. "I've tried it. I know."

Ryder wasn't impressed. Where was his whiskey, damn it?

"Is that what you did when your asshole hung you out to dry?" he asked.

She flinched. "I tried a lot of things. But drinking didn't help."

"You sound like a damn self-help group," he said snidely.

"Uh-oh," she murmured.

"What?"

"Don't look now, but your cop friend is headed this way. He doesn't look too happy."

Ryder tensed. "Mac? Here?"

"Yeah, it would appear so. I'm gonna run. Can't say I want to be within a mile of this place when this shit blows."

She slid off the bar stool and hurried away. Chicken.

"Somehow I'm not surprised to see you here," Mac said from behind him.

Slowly, Ryder turned around until he faced Mac. Mac stood there, anger emanating from him in waves. Fuck. He didn't need this right now.

"Why are *you* here?" Ryder asked wearily.

"You've done some stupid shit in the time I've known you, Ryder. Lord knows we go way back. But I will *never* forgive you for the way you've hurt Kit. If you weren't so damn drunk, I'd lay your ass out."

Ryder surged to his feet. He was spoiling for a good fight. Maybe if he got his ass kicked he'd feel better. He doubted it, but it was worth a shot.

"Want to take it outside?" Ryder challenged.

"No, I don't," Mac said evenly. "You're a goddamn fool, Ryder. The sad thing is you don't even realize it."

Ryder stared at him in confusion. Either he'd seriously miscounted the number of drinks he'd had or Mac was talking out his ass.

He spread his arms out. "What do you want from me, Mac? I would have thought you'd be glad to see me gone. I'm in love with your girl. Go back home to her and be damned glad she loves you."

Mac shook his head in disgust then turned on his heel and stormed away.

Well fuck. What the hell was all that about? The world was going crazier by the minute.

"I don't want to leave you, baby."

Kit shook her head. "I'll be fine, Mac. You have to go. They need you. It's your job."

"My *job* is to be here for you. However and whenever you need me," he corrected.

"I'll be okay," she said softly.

He stared at her for a long minute, clear indecision ratcheting a path across his face.

"Go!" she said with a smile. "Get dressed and get your ass to work."

His features dissolved into relief. "God, it's good to see you smile again, Kit."

She leaned up on tiptoe and kissed him hard across the lips. "I'll smile even bigger when you come home to me. Now go and get changed."

He kissed her back, long and lingeringly. Reluctantly, he broke away. "I'll call you later."

She laughed. "If it makes you feel better to check up on me then by all means call."

He quickly changed into his uniform and phoned into the station to let them know he was coming in. After another long, hot kiss, he hurried out the door.

Kit sighed and plodded into the kitchen. She was hungry. Starving actually. She hadn't eaten worth a shit in the weeks since the miscarriage. She knew she'd lost weight and looked like hell, but she hadn't been able to muster any enthusiasm to eat.

Mac was worried. He fussed over her constantly. It was time to pull her head out of her ass and get on with her life. Ryder didn't want her. He'd made that abundantly clear.

She rummaged through the refrigerator and found a half-empty carton of eggs. Taking it out, she plunked it down on the counter and retrieved a bowl and a fork. She cracked two eggs then beat them stiffly with the fork. After adding some seasoning, she poured them into a skillet and waited for them to harden.

They turned out a little brown, probably too done, but she didn't care. She plated the eggs then walked back into the living

room. She was lonely. This was the first night she'd been alone
since the miscarriage. Mac had taken a leave of absence, and he'd
never left her by herself for more than five minutes.

Had she been that bad? Had he thought he needed to hide the
knives in the house or something? Was he afraid if he'd left her
alone she would have hurt herself?

She shivered, not wanting the answer to that question. Yeah,
she'd been bad. She cringed at the memory of her first few days
home from the hospital. Numb and yet filled with such agony. The
two seemed incongruous.

She managed to choke down half the eggs and plodded back to
the kitchen to dump the plate in the sink. A night in front of the
TV sounded good. She wasn't sleepy. Maybe she'd wait up for Mac.

After finding the remote, she rounded up an old quilt and settled on the couch to flip through the channels. Her eyes grew
heavy half way through. So much for not being tired. She struggled to stay awake. She focused on the TV, determined not to succumb to the fatigue settling into her body.

A knocking on the door roused her from sleep. She opened her
eyes and looked over at the TV, surprised that a completely different movie was on. She checked her watch. It was 2 A.M. Damn,
she'd really zonked out.

The knocking grew louder. What the hell? Who could be
knocking on her door at this hour of the morning?

She threw the quilt aside and stood up on shaky legs. Damn
foot was asleep. She hobbled to the door and unbolted the lock.
Leaving the chain in place, she flipped the porch light on and
opened the door a crack to peer out.

She froze, every muscle in her body tightening until she nearly
cried out in pain. On her doorstep stood two familiar faces. Sean
Gardner and Ray Hartley. Two deputies from the sheriff's department. Friends of Mac's. People he worked with. Two cops who
should be on duty, not standing at her front door.

CHAPTER 14

Kit stood staring out an inch-wide crack in the door afraid to open it. Afraid of why they were there.

"Kit," Sean began, his voice shaky. "We need to come in, sweetheart."

"Oh God!" she choked out.

She slammed the door shut and fumbled with the chain. Several long seconds later, she threw open the door.

"What is it?" she cried. "What's happened to him?"

Ray pulled her into his arms and held tightly to her. "Come inside with us, Kit. We'll talk in the living room."

She allowed him to guide her inside. Her entire body was numb. Everything moved in slow motion. This wasn't happening. She knew the reasons for late-night visits from fellow cops. They didn't come because they had good news.

Ray set her down on the couch next to Sean, backed up and took a seat in the armchair a few feet away.

"What happened?" she said desperately. Tears pricked her eye-lids, and she clenched her teeth to try and keep them back.

"Mac . . . he, uh, he was conducting a routine traffic stop. Sus-pected DUI." Sean stopped and swallowed hard.

Kit closed her eyes. God, it must be bad. Don't let him be dead. Please don't let him be dead. Why were they stalling? Why wouldn't they just come out and say it?

"When he walked up to the driver's window, the suspect pulled out a gun and shot him."

Kit bolted from the couch, swayed and would have fallen if Ray hadn't acted so quickly to catch her. Tears poured down her cheeks. Ray tugged her head until her face was buried in his chest.

"Tell me he's not dead," she cried. "Please. Tell me he's not dead!"

"He's not dead," Sean said urgently. "He's in the hospital."

She whirled around out of Ray's arms. "Take me to him, Sean." She scrambled for her shoes. Where were her goddamn shoes?

"Honey, he's in bad shape," Sean added. His eyes brimmed with sympathy. "You have to know what you're facing."

"But he's alive, right?"

"Yes," Ray said. "He's alive."

"Then take me to him," she said in a deadly quiet voice. "I won't let him die. I won't let him go."

The men exchanged glances, and Ray retrieved his keys from his pocket. "We'll take you in the police cruiser," he said.

"My shoes," she whimpered as she looked desperately around the living room. "I need my shoes."

"Here they are, sweetheart," Sean said gently.

He held out a pair of sandals to her, and she immediately tugged them from his hand and dropped them on the floor. She shoved her feet into the shoes and started for the door.

When the police car turned out of the driveway in the opposite direction to the hospital, she immediately demanded to know where they were taking her.

"Honey, they had to life-flight him to Houston," Ray said.

She thrust her knuckles into her mouth, biting painfully into the skin. "Can you take me all the way to Houston?" she asked.

"We're going to drive you the whole way," Sean said soothingly.

He reached over and switched the lights on, speeding up as the red and blue flash lit up the night air.

"We'll get you there as fast as we can, Kit. Just hang tight. Are you feeling all right?"

She looked at him in confusion. Then she realized he was referring to her miscarriage. It was the last thing on her mind right now.

"I'm fine," she managed to croak out.

The highway passed in a blur as they hit the interstate. She slumped in the back seat, tears spilling down her cheeks. What would she do if she never saw him again? Never lay in his arms or heard him call her "baby".

She covered her face with her hands and wept big noisy sobs. Sean reached over to lay a hand on her shoulder.

"I'm sorry, Kit. Mac's a fine cop. He didn't deserve to go down like this."

"Stop talking about him like he's already dead!" she said fiercely.

The look of sympathy, of pure pity, he sent her chased a chill down her spine. God, it must be bad. So bad. Sean and Ray didn't expect him to be alive when they got there. They thought they were bringing her to Houston to view a body.

She turned to look out the window, dying on the inside. She couldn't live without Mac. She simply couldn't.

When they arrived at the hospital in Houston, Ray got out at the after-hours entrance with her while Sean went to park the car. They hurried inside, stopping at the ER desk to ask where Mac was.

Kit held her breath, waiting for the look of sympathy to appear on the clerk's face, waiting to hear that he hadn't made it.

After tapping on the keys of her computer, she looked up and said, "Mr. McKenzie is still in surgery. If you walk down this hall, take the elevator on the left. Go to the second floor, get off and go right. You'll run right into the surgery waiting room. I'll let them know you're here so that when there is any news they'll notify you."

Kit gulped and stood statuelike, afraid to move. Ray guided her forward, and she stumbled against him. He caught her and steadied her before they continued on.

As they arrived at the elevator, Sean ran up behind them. He huffed as he sought to catch his breath.

"What's the word?" he asked.

"He's in surgery," Ray said shortly. "We're headed up there now."

The elevator doors opened with a swoosh, and they moved forward. Ray reached over to push the button, and they waited for the doors to close.

"He'll make it," she said fiercely.

Sean wrapped an arm around her and squeezed. "He's a fighter, Kit. If he's made it this far, he'll pull through. He has a lot to live for."

She closed her eyes. *Please, Mac. Don't die.*

She paced the waiting room for the hundredth time. She checked her watch even knowing, at the most, two minutes had elapsed since the last time she'd looked.

The waiting room had filled with off-duty cops, all waiting to hear word about Mac. Sheriff Johnson had driven in as soon as he'd heard. And their cell phones rang regularly as the on-duty personnel, state troopers and the city cops called to check in on Mac.

Every few minutes, one of the cops would ask her if she needed anything. If she wanted something to eat or drink. If she needed to sit down. She wanted to scream. She needed Mac! She needed him alive, well, loving her, touching her.

Finally exhaustion claimed her. She slumped into a chair in the corner and felt the tears begin to fall once more. Sean squatted in front of her and put a hand to her cheek.

"We've seen some tough times together, Kit."

She knew he was referring to her first attack and then that night a year ago when her attacker had struck again.

"You're tough. Mac's tough."

"I'm not tough," she whispered. "Mac's the strong one. He's always taken care of me."

"That's bullshit and there ain't a person who doesn't know it. Sure Mac takes good care of you. He'd be a fool not to. But you're the toughest woman I know, Kit. You keep that boy in line. You've kept him and Ryder both in line for years."

She froze at Ryder's name. "Someone should tell Ryder," she said quietly. It wouldn't be her. But he'd want to know. He and Mac had been friends as long as she and Ryder had.

"I'll take care of it, sweetheart. You just sit tight and get a little rest. You've been through hell lately."

"Miss Townsend?"

Kit jumped up at the sound of her name. She strode over to the desk situated at the front of the room. "I'm Miss Townsend," she said.

Behind her the cops congregated, all waiting to hear any news of Mac.

"Mr. McKenzie is out of surgery now. The doctor will come talk to you in a few minutes if you'd like to take a seat in our family room."

The receptionist gestured toward a small room a few feet away that offered privacy from the larger room.

"I'll go with you," Sean offered, squeezing her shoulder.

"Thank you," she whispered.

She walked stiffly toward the room and sat down in one of the chairs. She stared down at the floor, every second that she waited excruciating.

Finally she heard a noise at the door. She looked up to see a doctor, still in surgical scrubs, standing in the doorway.

"Are you here with Mr. McKenzie?"

She tried to speak, cleared her throat then merely nodded.

"I believe in giving it straight," the doctor began. "Mr. McKenzie suffered a massive chest wound. He's come out of surgery, but he's in a coma."

She sucked in her breath, feeling every drop of blood drain from her face.

"Will he . . ."

"Will he live?" the doctor finished. "Quite frankly, I'm amazed he made it to the hospital. Even more amazed he survived the surgery."

Tears filled Kit's eyes.

"He's in pretty bad shape, but he's alive. Despite all odds, he's fighting for life. He's got some tough days ahead, and a long recovery if he survives. I can't offer any guarantees that he'll make it. Only time will tell. Obviously the longer he lives, the better his chances are of recovery."

Kit slumped further into her chair, dazed, horrified and hopeful all at the same time. "When can I see him?" she asked.

"He'll be in recovery for awhile. Then he'll be taken to ICU. After they get everything set up, they'll let you go in for short periods of time. I feel compelled to warn you. When you first see him, it'll be a shock. He won't look anything like the man you know. You need to prepare yourself for that."

Kit nodded her understanding. "Th-thank you," she managed to stammer out.

The doctor looked at her, his expression softening. "Don't thank me until he goes home from the hospital. Then I'll have done my job right."

If Sean hadn't been holding on to her so tightly, Kit would have collapsed when she got her first look at Mac.

"I've got you," Sean said as he sought to steady her.

Tears filled her eyes at the sight of the big strong man lying so helplessly on the hospital bed. There were wires, IV lines and tubes everywhere.

He was hooked to a respirator, and the whooshing sound echoed harshly in her ears.

Hesitantly, she approached his bed. He looked so still and life-less. If it weren't for the heart monitor, she'd think he was dead.

"Oh, Mac," she choked out.

Sean held a firm hand on her shoulder as she reached out a hand to touch Mac's. She flinched. His skin felt cold, lifeless.

A nurse walked into the glassed-in cubicle and smiled kindly at her. "You'll have to leave now. You can see him in a few hours if you like. I'll come get you in the waiting room when you're al-lowed back again. Our visiting hours are from 9 A.M. to 9 P.M. daily. No more than two visitors are ever allowed in at a time."

Kit nodded, still too numb to form a coherent thought.

"Come on," Sean coaxed. "You need to eat. I'll take you down to the cafeteria. We'll come back when we can see him again."

Kit followed meekly behind Sean but paused at the door to look back at Mac. "I love you," she whispered brokenly. "Please don't leave me."

CHAPTER 15

*R*yder roared into the parking lot of the Two Step and jammed down his kickstand. He was hungry, in a foul mood and he could use a beer. Or three.

He'd pretty much come to the conclusion he was rotten company. Mia's avoidance was a good clue. She'd told him what a dumbass he was then refused to speak to him at the strip club. After that, he'd taken refuge in his garage, refusing to go anywhere he might run into Mac or Kit.

At least now that he'd gotten Kit to quit her job he wouldn't be running into her at the café, and he could get a burger in relative peace.

Despite everything, he really hadn't liked her working here. It involved way too many painful memories for them all, and he worried about her safety. The money he'd given her would last a good long while, and by the time she needed to get another job, she could find something better.

He tromped into the bar and flinched at the blare of music that greeted him. His string of hangovers was catching up to him real fast.

He moseyed up to the bar and gestured for the bartender. He ordered two beers and a burger and immediately set to drinking the first.

"Ryder? What the hell are you doing here?" Sean Gardner asked as he walked up to the bar. "I thought you'd be in Houston."

Ryder glared over at the cop in his best do-not-disturb impression.

Sean stared hard at him, his lips curled in distaste. "Look, I don't know what happened between you and Mac. Ain't none of my business."

"Damn straight," Ryder agreed.

Sean ignored him and continued.

"But you're being the worst sort of ass. He's fighting for his life, and Kit, Lord knows she could use some support. The girl's been at his side day and night for days now. Won't eat. Won't sleep. She's not going to last at the rate she's going."

Ryder's blood ran cold. He turned on Sean and hauled him up by his uniform. "What the fuck are you talking about?"

Sean drew in a deep breath, his eyes widening in shock. "You don't know, do you? How in the world could you not know?"

"Know what? Spit it out for Christ's sake."

"Have you been home to check your messages? I left several there and on your cell phone."

"I've had my cell turned off," Ryder bit out. "Now tell me what the fuck is going on before I lose my temper."

Sean's eyes glimmered in regret. "It's Mac. He was shot the other night. Had to life-flight him to Houston. Me and Ray drove Kit to Houston to be with him. But it's bad, man. And Kit's about to fall apart."

Ryder let go of Sean's shirt and sank back onto the bar stool.

Mac shot? Dear God. While he'd been off licking his wounds, Mac was fighting to hang onto life, and Kit was alone?

He closed his eyes, regret beating through his system like an overdose of steroids.

"Where?" he croaked out.

He was already running for the door, Sean on his heels.

"Ryder, damn it, don't go and kill yourself."

"I'll be careful," Ryder said as he climbed onto his bike. "Kit needs me."

Ryder hated hospitals. The cold, sterile environment reminded him too much of his father. Nothing good ever came of being in a hospital. Three times he'd been there for Kit, and each time had ripped his guts out.

He walked slowly down the polished floor toward the cubicle the nurse had pointed to. He dreaded what he'd find. He paused for a moment to take a deep breath before finally stepping through the door.

What he saw tore his heart right out of his chest.

Mac lay there, motionless, a multitude of shit running from head to toe. Kit sat beside the bed, her head resting on Mac's hip. He could hear her sobs from the doorway, each sound sending a bolt of pain through his body.

"Don't leave me, Mac," she whispered, so much agony in her voice. "You promised never to leave me."

Ryder's gut clenched. So had he. And he'd lied.

Unable to keep from touching her, he stepped forward and laid a hand on her shoulder. "Darlin', you're going to make yourself sick."

Her head came up and she whipped around to look at him. He winced at her appearance. Tired, haggard. Deep circles pitted her eyes. Her green eyes were dull with pain, and her cheeks blotchy from her crying.

"What are you doing here?" she managed to get out.

He deserved that. How many days had Mac lain here hovering between life and death while he'd been out drowning his sorrows and being an asshole? Kit had needed him more than ever, and he'd failed her miserably. Worse, he'd done it consciously. He'd run as far as he could after she lost the baby.

"I didn't know," he said quietly. "I only found out awhile ago."

A tear rolled down her beautiful face.

"I can't lose him," she said. "Not after losing everything else. He's all I have left."

Ryder bent down and folded her into his arms. He stood her up and hugged her tightly. "You have me, Kit girl."

She shook her head in denial. "You left. You left when I needed you. When I was hurting so bad I thought I'd die. You didn't care. I don't need you now. I need Mac."

Ryder closed his eyes and willed himself not to cry like a damn sissy. He kept a tight hold on her, determined not to let her go.

"We need to talk, darlin'. I need to know what's going on here. How Mac is. Then we can talk about us."

She pulled back and looked at him, her eyes flashing in anger. "There is no us, Ryder. You left me at the hospital after I'd just lost our baby. No word, no nothing. Disappeared. I haven't seen you since."

He might have believed her, but her lips trembled and tears welled in her big green eyes. He reached out a hand to touch her cheek. "I'm here now, and I'm going to make sure you take care of yourself. How long's it been since you ate last?"

She shook her head and turned away. "I'm not leaving him," she said stubbornly.

He wrapped his arms around her shaking body and rested his chin on top of her head. "You're coming down to eat with me if I have to carry you, Kit. I brought you some clothes and some toiletries, and I booked a hotel right down the street. You're going to eat, shower and get some sleep."

She went rigid in his arms. "I won't leave him, Ryder. What if he wakes up and I'm not here? I don't want him to be alone."

Ryder turned her around to face him. "Do you think he wants you here tearing yourself apart? Do you think he wants you to fade away, become a shell of yourself because you were holding vigil by his bedside? Think, Kit girl. You need to be strong. You don't know when he'll wake up, and you have to pace yourself or you're going to end up in a bed on another floor and you'll both be alone."

Her shoulders slumped in defeat. Her lips trembled and shook as more tears slid down her cheeks. He thumbed them away, soothing his hand over her face.

He led her away from the bed and out the door. They stopped by the nurse's desk, and Ryder gave his cell number with instructions to call if there was any change in Mac's condition. Then he turned her toward the elevator so they could go down and eat.

He piled a tray high with food for them both, paid for it and searched for a place to sit. Kit remained silent the entire time. When he pushed a plate of food toward her, she wrinkled her nose and poked a fork at it.

"Eat," he commanded. "We're not leaving here until you've eaten something decent."

She blew out a weary breath and slumped in her chair. But she took a bite of the food. Then another. They ate in silence. He gazed often at her, but she kept her eyes downcast as she picked at her meal.

Finally she pushed the plate away and set down her fork. When she looked up at him, her eyes were swamped with emotion.

"Why did you leave?" she asked softly. "Were you so angry with me for losing the baby you couldn't bear to be around me? Did you hate me for what happened?"

He dropped his fork with a clatter. "God no, Kit. How could you think such a thing?"

"How could I not?" she said simply. "While I was lying in a hospital bed feeling like my guts had been ripped out, you walked away."

He closed his eyes. "I deserved that." He opened his eyes and reached across the table to grip her hand. "Kit, I did what I thought was best for us all. My presence caused problems for you and Mac. You can't deny that. When you lost the baby, well, I felt like I'd lost you as well. There was no longer a reason for me to be between you and Mac, so I walked away. I wanted you to be happy."

Tears slid down her cheeks as she stared helplessly at him. "And I felt like I lost you," she said. "Mac knows . . . he knows how I feel about you. It wasn't an issue. He still loves me even knowing a part of my heart belongs to you."

"You claim to love me after I ditched you when you were miscarrying?" he asked in disbelief.

She sucked in her breath. "As Mac told me, love doesn't go away in five minutes. It's bigger than that. I can't stop feeling for you what I've felt half my life. I'm angry. I'm hurt. I feel betrayed. But I love you. And it makes me so goddamn angry that Mac is lying there in his hospital bed. I don't know if he's going to live or die, and all I can think about is I can't survive it if both of you leave me!"

Something unraveled inside him. The knowledge that he could not possibly walk away from her, no matter what happened with Mac hit him solidly in the chest. He was tired of fighting it. Tired of feeling like a goddamn martyr. Kit needed him, and he'd be damned if he let her down again.

"I won't leave you again, Kit. I know you have no cause to believe me. But I'll be here. I don't know in what capacity. We can work it out."

"I need you both, and it's tearing me apart," she said, agony seeping into her voice. "Do you have any idea how guilty it makes me feel that I can't just go on and be happy with Mac? Marry him, have a dozen babies and grow old together. I just know that if you aren't here, if you aren't somehow in that picture, I can never be completely happy."

Ryder swallowed heavily. He didn't know what to say. How could he spill his guts when his buddy lay next to death a floor away? What kind of bastard did it make him to confess his feelings to Kit, to move in on Mac's territory when he wasn't around?

He squeezed her hand again. "Kit, I swear to you, when Mac gets better we'll work this thing out between us, okay? I'm not leaving you. I need you to believe that."

She nodded slowly, so much fatigue swimming in her eyes it made his gut ache.

"Come on, darlin'. Let's get you to the hotel so you can get some rest."

He stood up and held his hand out to her. She slid her fingers into his and glanced up at him, her green eyes seeking.

"Will you hold me, Ryder? I just want you to hold me."

"Yes, darlin'. I'll hold you. All night long. I won't let you go."

CHAPTER 16

For days Kit and Ryder sat by Mac's bedside. Ryder bullied her, prodded her, forced her away to eat and sleep, but he never left her. Not even once.

She spent her days talking to Mac, holding his hand, telling him how much she loved him. Her nights were spent sleeping in Ryder's arms, trying to keep the nightmares at bay.

His breathing tube had been removed, a huge source of relief to her. Breathing on his own had to be a sign of improvement, right? But he remained stubbornly in a coma.

Two weeks after the night Mac had been shot, Ryder stood and held out a hand to Kit.

"You need to eat, darlin'. Let's go down. We can come back in a bit."

She wiped at her hair and face with her hand and let out her breath in a long discouraged sigh. She started to remove her hand from Mac's when his fingers tightened around her palm.

She forgot about Ryder, about eating, about everything else but the fact Mac had just moved. She leaned forward excitedly.

"Mac, Mac! Can you hear me?" She turned to Ryder, her emotions rioting. "He moved, Ryder. He grabbed my hand!"

Not waiting for Ryder's response, she edged closer to Mac, leaned over to brush her lips across his. "I'm here, Mac. Please come back to me. I love you so much."

A soft moan escaped Mac's lips.

"I'm getting the nurse," Ryder said behind her.

As she kissed Mac again, his eyes fluttered weakly and they opened the tiniest bit. She withdrew just enough that she could look him in the eye.

"Mac!" she cried softly. "Can you hear me?"

He opened his mouth as if trying to speak then frowned as nothing came out.

She put a finger to his lips. "Don't try to speak. I'm here."

Tears poured down her cheeks as she took both his hands in hers. "Squeeze my hands instead. Do you understand that?"

He tightened his grip on her hands. Her heart nearly burst out of her chest in her excitement.

"K-kiss me," he rasped, his voice hoarse and shaky from nonuse.

"Oh Mac," she breathed. She leaned over and kissed him tenderly, lovingly. Her tears splashed onto his face. "I thought I'd lost you."

"N-never . . . lose . . . me," he said with difficulty. "Never . . . leave you. Swear it."

She cried harder.

Ryder came in with the nurse, who let out an exclamation of delight when she saw Mac was awake. She shooed Kit away from the bed and did a quick examination of him.

"I've already called his doctor in," the nurse explained as she fiddled with the numerous IV lines and the wires to the heart monitor. "He should be here shortly."

Kit stood away, her back cradled against Ryder's chest, waiting anxiously for the nurse to finish. She wanted to be close to Mac, to reassure herself that he was okay.

When the nurse finally stepped back, Kit surged forward, taking Mac's hand again. Slowly, a little shaky, he lifted his other hand to touch her face.

"Love . . . you," he murmured.

"I love you too," she choked out.

His gaze went beyond her, to something behind her. She turned around to see Ryder standing over her shoulder. Mac's hand wavered as he took it away from her face. His face straining with the exertion it took, he balled his fingers into a fist and held it out to Ryder.

"Glad . . . you're . . . here."

Ryder stepped forward, mashing his fist to Mac's. His eyes glittered suspiciously. "I wouldn't be anywhere else, man. You scared us. Don't ever pull that shit again."

Mac grinned crookedly then let his arm fall with an exhausted sigh.

"Take . . . care of Kit."

"I will, man. I promise. You just get your ass well so we can all get the hell out of here. I hate hospitals. You know that."

Kit watched the two of them, her heart lighter with each passing second. Her relief threatened to overwhelm her. She felt faint and strong all at the same time. Her muscles ached and throbbed. She was smiling wider than she'd smiled in longer than she could remember.

Finally after so many weeks of pain and worry. First her miscarriage then Mac's accident. Finally she felt free again. Happy.

"You okay, darlin'? You look a bit shaky," Ryder said.

"I'm fine," she said around the knot in her throat. "I'm perfect." She smiled through her tears at him.

*　*　*

Ryder watched Kit sleeping in the small recliner across the hospital room. She was completely worn-out, but since Mac awakened, she'd refused to leave his side. So he'd brought her food and clothes so she could eat and change. She slept in the chair by the bed or in the chair she currently occupied.

Mac had made remarkable progress. He was still weak, but he'd shown steady improvement in the last week. If his progress continued, he'd be moved to a step-down unit in a few days.

"You need to take her ass out of here," Mac reproached.

Ryder jerked around to see Mac awake.

"Hey, man, you're looking better. You sure sound better," Ryder commented.

Mac twisted his lips and grunted. "I still feel like I met with the front end of a speeding truck."

Ryder nodded. "Well, you should. You met up with the front end of a speeding bullet."

Mac grimaced. "Yeah. I remember."

Mac's gaze flitted over to Kit. Ryder saw the hunger in his eyes, the need for her.

"We need to talk, Ryder," Mac said.

Ryder sighed. Damn, he wasn't ready for this. "Yeah, I know we do."

"You love her," Mac said.

Ryder nodded. "Yeah. I love her."

Mac didn't react, but it was hardly news. He'd already told Mac as much.

"She loves you."

Ryder sucked in his breath. He didn't want to hurt Mac. No matter how much he loved Kit, he just couldn't bring himself to hurt a man he'd called friend for most of his life. A man who was more a brother to him than any blood brother could have been.

Mac stared at him. "It's okay, man. I know she loves you. She told me."

Ryder bowed his head. "I'm sorry, Mac. You have no idea how damn sorry I am. I never meant to come between the two of you."

Mac took a long breath then expelled it, the sound loud in the quiet room. "She loves both of us. She'd never betray me, Ryder. I know that. This is tearing her apart."

"I know," Ryder said quietly.

"We both love her. Always have. We've shared a close relationship, the three of us. There isn't any reason we couldn't continue it."

Ryder's head jerked up. He stared at Mac in shock. "What are you saying?"

Mac shifted, pain crossing his face. He looked wiped out, as if he'd exerted himself completely.

"Look, man, let's talk about this another time," Ryder began.

"No," Mac said forcefully. "We need to talk about it now. Sort it out so that when she wakes up we can make her happy again."

"Mac, what you're suggesting . . . hell, I don't even know what you're suggesting."

"Don't you? We were all happy when the three of us were together. Kit was happy. The way I see it, we could continue that relationship. The three of us."

Ryder opened his mouth then snapped it shut again. What Mac was suggesting . . . it was perhaps the most unselfish gesture he'd ever witnessed. And the most practical. For the first time, hope beat a steady rhythm in his mind.

Why couldn't they continue as before? They'd done it for months. That period had been the best in his life. Only when they'd begun to splinter had things gone into the shitter.

He looked over at Kit. "What about her?" Ryder asked softly.

Mac stayed silent a long moment. "Obviously, it would be up to her, but I know I won't be demanding she choose between us, and I don't think that's what you want either."

Ryder shook his head. "It's why I left before."

Mac nodded. "I figured as much. Look, I've given it a lot of thought. Before I went and got myself shot. It was hell watching Kit those two weeks after she miscarried. She was so unhappy, and there wasn't a damn thing I could do. But *we* could."

"I don't know what to say, Mac. This is such a gift. A gift I could never expect to receive. I love Kit so damn much. I never wanted to let her go, but I didn't want to hurt either of you."

"And I love you," Kit said softly.

Both men jerked their heads to see her laying there on the recliner, her beautiful eyes open and so full of love and joy.

She sat up, her hair sliding over her shoulders. Even as rundown as she was, Ryder had never seen such a beautiful sight.

She walked over to the bed, slipped her hand into Mac's. "I love you, Mac. I never ever want to hurt you. My commitment is to you. I'll honor it always."

Mac smiled and put his fingers up to her mouth, tracing a line around her lips. "I know you do, baby. I also know you love Ryder. We both love you, and we can make this work. It won't be easy for you, committing to us both. We both can be real pains in the ass, but we'll love you and protect you, take care of you always."

Tears shone in her eyes as she glanced sideways at Ryder. She looked to him, waiting for what he would say.

He reached for her arm, rubbing his fingers lightly up her skin. "I love you, Kit. I know I've never admitted it to you, but not a day goes by that I don't dream about holding you, touching you, loving you. I fought it. I didn't want to come between you and Mac, but I love you so damn much I can't breathe sometimes."

She sniffled, and he smiled. "I swear, darlin', you've cried more in the last few months than I've ever known you to."

She looked between him and Mac as if afraid to believe what she'd heard. Hope and relief burned so brightly, her eyes looked like a pair of emeralds.

"Are you sure, Mac? Are you sure we can do this?" she finally asked.

Mac coaxed her down to sit on the bed so she was between him and where Ryder sat in the chair. "We'll make it work, baby."

She glanced over at Ryder. "Do you want this? Do you want . . . me?"

Ryder leaned forward and tipped her chin up before capturing her lips in a deep kiss. She tasted so sweet. It had been too long since he'd touched her so intimately.

"I've never not wanted you," he murmured against her mouth.

She pulled away, her eyes shining, the biggest smile he'd ever seen pulling up the corners of her mouth.

"I'm so happy. After being so scared for so long, I am so happy right now."

Mac smiled. "I guess you like my idea then."

She started to throw herself into Mac's arms but pulled up at the last second.

"Careful, darlin', don't kill him," Ryder said with a chuckle.

She eased herself into his arms instead. "I love it, and I love you. I love you both. I'm going to spend the rest of my life proving it too."

CHAPTER 17

$\mathcal{K}$it wrapped Mac's arm over her shoulders to help him out of the truck, despite his laughing protests that he could damn well walk himself.

Ryder collected the bags, and they all started toward the door. As they walked in, Kit guided Mac toward the couch and pushed him down.

"Kit, you're not going to start fussing over me," Mac said with a chuckle. "I'm okay."

She smiled down at him. "You've taken care of me for so long, Mac. It's high time I took care of you. So shut up and let me do my thing."

She glanced over at Ryder and raised an eyebrow. He'd been quiet all the way home, and she wondered if something was bothering him. A pang of worry assailed her. Was he having second thoughts about the arrangement they'd agreed on?

"Stop your worrying, darlin'," he said as he walked by. He

stopped to drop a kiss on her head before moving over to the armchair.

"Am I that obvious?" she asked in exasperation.

"Yes," both men said.

She grinned ruefully. "Sorry. I'm in too-good-to-be-true mode. At any time I expect one of you to jump up and say it's all a big joke and leave."

Mac reached up and tugged her down beside him. "Do as Ryder says. Stop worrying. I love you, and I'm not going anywhere."

"Well, that's what I wanted to talk about," Ryder interjected.

Both Mac and Kit turned to stare at Ryder.

Ryder leaned forward, his expression serious. "How many times have we all said we were getting out of this town?"

"Only a million," Kit said, rolling her eyes.

She studied Ryder intently. What bug had he gotten up his ass now? They should be celebrating Mac's return home, not dragging up old stories.

"What would you both think of doing just that?" Ryder continued.

Kit fell silent. Mac crooked one eyebrow. "What do you mean, man?"

"Things could be hard for us here. I don't plan to keep my relationship with Kit a dirty secret, and I don't imagine you do either. None of us have ever wanted to live here. We used to swear we'd get out one day. Maybe it's time."

Kit swallowed. She hadn't considered what would happen when people got wind of their relationship. Her lips firmed. She didn't give a flying fuck. She was happy and that was all that mattered.

Ryder held up a hand. He must have seen the protest forming on her lips. "Let me finish. Mac's going to be laid up awhile. I don't want you going back to work, despite what you said about making ends meet while Mac is on disability. I have money. Money I've never cared about. Well, it can finally be put to good use. We can get the hell out of this town none of us want to be in and go someplace else. Any place and start over."

Mac shifted beside her. She turned to see him staring at her. "What do you think, baby?"

What did she think? She was stunned. She'd gone on thinking for so long that she was trapped here, she didn't know how else to think. And to leave with Mac and Ryder . . . she'd go anywhere with them.

"I think that as long as you two are with me, I'll go anywhere," she whispered.

"I could pick up another job when I've recovered," Mac said. "Cops are needed everywhere."

"And in the meantime, we could go where the wind blows," Ryder said. "Figure out where we want to settle and then do it."

He made it sound so easy. And wasn't it? What was stopping them? She'd always dreamed of leaving this town and the painful memories behind.

Ryder got out of the chair and knelt in front of her. "Would you go with us, darlin'? Would you trust us with your life and happiness? To always take care of you and love you?"

She threw her arms around Ryder and held on for dear life. She would not cry again, damn it.

When she pulled away, he kissed her, warm, passionate, taking her breath away. Behind her, Mac's hands slid up her back, curling around her neck and massaging.

Yeah, she'd go anywhere with them.

"When do we leave?" she asked.

what she craves

CHAPTER 1

*N*o guts, no glory, no orgasm. She wanted the latter but was short on the former.

Mia Nichols wiped her hands nervously down her bare legs and contemplated running as far and as fast as she could from Jack Kincaid's bedroom. But no, she'd come this far.

She'd snuck in, using the key Jack had given her for emergencies. She spared only a moment's guilt over the fact this wasn't really an emergency. Not unless you considered desperation a crisis.

The fact that she stood there, naked, couldn't really be construed so much as a crisis as it was a bold plan to take the initiative. Yes, that made her feel much better. She wasn't throwing herself at Jack, exactly. She was merely going after what she wanted. What she'd wanted for years. What she thought he wanted too when he wasn't so wrapped up in his goddamn sense of responsibility.

She knew he was just on the other side of the wall sleeping.

The soft sounds of his deep breathing filtered through the crack in his bedroom door.

You want this, Mia. You've wanted it forever. Go get it for God's sake. You won't get a better opportunity.

Summoning her flagging courage, she quietly eased into the bedroom. His body was bathed in the soft light that filtered through half-closed blinds. The sheets tangled at his hips, barely covering the bottom portion of his torso, leaving his upper half bare.

She licked her lips and moved closer. God, he was gorgeous. Hard, lean, the lines and angles of his body were just made for a woman's touch. She could spend hours exploring the muscled dips and bulges.

He faced away from her, his jaw, rough from the overnight beard, prominent against his pillow. One arm rested down his side, his hand gripping the sheets that had long since been discarded. His other arm was flung out beside him, his fingers splayed out like he was reaching for something.

She edged closer to the bed. There wasn't a time when she could remember not loving him. The years before his entry into her life faded, not worth remembering. They were a muddled mass of pain and anguish, of things she'd rather not remember.

He'd saved her. Taken care of her. Made sure she had what she needed. Except she needed *him*. Not in just the role of a guardian, someone who looked out for her and checked in on her from time to time. She wanted more than the casual conversations they had, and the occasional shared pizza on the weekend.

She was no longer the girl he'd rescued. She had long since grown into a woman. With a woman's needs. And tonight Jack Kincaid was going to see that firsthand. If he didn't toss her out of his bed as soon as she got there.

Nervously she leaned down, unsure of what to do first. Kiss him? Touch him?

The decision was made for her. She didn't get to do either.

As soon as she bent to brush her mouth across his jaw, a hard arm closed around her. His other hand slid under the pillow in one quick motion, and she found herself staring down the barrel of a nasty-looking gun.

She let out an eep of fright and tried to back away. The arm around her waist tightened.

"What the hell are you doing"—he looked up and down her body—"naked in my bedroom?" he demanded.

Her cheeks burned, and she cringed from the glitter of surprise and anger in his eyes. This wasn't going the way she'd planned.

His arms loosened, allowing her to back away a bit. Jack laid the gun on the nightstand and sat up, dragging the sheets with him.

But she'd gotten enough of a peek to know he obviously slept in the nude, and that he wasn't unaffected by the sight of her naked body.

"Mia, what are you doing here?" he asked again, his tone not as strident at it had been earlier.

"What does it look like I'm doing," she asked in exasperation.

She crossed her arms over her breasts, her humiliation growing by the second.

He cocked one eyebrow. "It looks like you were trying to climb naked into my bed."

"Observant of you," she said snidely.

His gaze raked up and down her body. "What the hell kind of game is this, Mia? Because I have to tell you, I don't have time for this."

She let her arms fall until she stood proudly before him. "I want you, Jack."

He rubbed a hand through his short hair. "Ah hell, Mia, get your ass dressed and get the hell out of here. I don't have the stomach for little girls playing at being an adult."

Her cheeks burned furiously. "I'm not a child!"

"You're too young for me," he said bluntly.

She moved closer to him, allowing her breasts to bob in front of his face. She saw how his eyes tracked downward, saw his body tighten in response.

"I'm not a child," she repeated. "I'm a woman with a woman's needs. I've wanted you so long, Jack. Don't turn me away. I can see you want me."

Jack smiled mockingly. "You've come to the wrong place, sugar. I haven't got a gentle bone in my body. Take your virginity and your dreams of flowers and sweet talk somewhere else. If we fucked, I'd ride you long and hard, and I wouldn't give a damn that it was your first time."

A shudder rolled through her body. Her nipples hardened to points, and she heard Jack swear.

She moved forward, closer still to him. She wanted to touch him so badly she ached.

"I don't want you to be gentle," she whispered. "I want you to be you. I want *you*."

"Christ, Mia. I'm too old for you. You're just a kid. Get some damn clothes on."

She ignored him, pressing her body to his as she moved onto the bed. She stared up at him, her eyes seeking his. When their gazes met, she saw hunger reflected in his dark eyes. He wanted her. He could fight it, but she could see the truth.

Hesitantly, she twined her arms around his neck. He stiffened at her touch but didn't yank away from her. Her lips hovered a heartbeat from his, and she heard him suck in his breath.

"Kiss me," she said.

She touched her lips to his and found him unyielding, resistant. Not giving up, she deepened her kiss, running her tongue across his lips.

"Goddamn it, Mia," he swore.

He hauled her up against him and returned her kiss with force-ful intensity. His hands ran up and down her back as he devoured her mouth.

She moaned against his lips as his hands tangled in her hair. He pulled her back by her hair and stared hard into her face.

"Be sure about this, Mia. If you don't turn tail and get your ass out of here right now there's no turning back.

"Kiss me," she said again.

He hesitated for a long moment, staring at her with hard eyes. Eyes that gleamed with want. She arched into him, tempting him with her body. His arms tightened around her. She could feel the flex of his strong muscles, and she knew in that moment she'd won.

He rolled her over and underneath him, reaching back to tear the sheets away. His hard body rocked over hers, rubbing and pressing against her skin. He took her hands and yanked them high over her head.

She let him have his way, a surge of red-hot need bursting through her at his exhibition of power and control. How many years had she lusted after him? She'd loved him since she was a starry-eyed teenager just feeling the first pangs of adolescence.

His thigh pried at her limbs, inserting his muscular leg between hers. His mouth moved across her like a storm. Hot, fast and intense.

"Let me touch you," she gasped out.

He fused his mouth over hers, silencing her effectively. Despite her struggles, he held fast to her hands, knocking them against the headboard when she tried to reach for him again.

"Be still," he growled.

Her head fell back as he nuzzled at her neck. His teeth grazed the sensitive skin below her ear before sinking into the curve of her neck.

She bolted forward, gasping in pleasure. He sucked at her flesh, nipping and biting then sliding his tongue over the area to soothe it. Flames licked over her body. She twisted and squirmed, but he held her tightly, not allowing her to move.

His cock nudged impatiently at her pussy. Rubbed up and down her damp slit.

"Open for me," he demanded, his voice husky and deep, the command sending delicious thrills up her spine.

She relaxed her legs, and immediately he was at her entrance, probing hotly, the swollen head of his penis spreading her tight folds.

In one strong thrust, he seated himself deeply inside her. Slight pain registered, but it was shoved aside as he began moving, the friction fanning the flames out of control. She gasped and struggled to free her arms. She wanted to grab onto him and squeeze for dear life as unbearable sensations rocked her body.

He slammed her hands back onto the mattress, once again uttering a harsh command. "Stay."

She melted into his body, her vision blurring with her desire. He bucked and undulated his hips, plunging into her slick pussy over and over.

"Please," she gasped.

He caught her lips between his teeth and tugged, sucking her bottom lip. His tongue slid over the fullness of her mouth, tasting as he rocked against her. Then his teeth sank, and she tasted the saltiness of blood. He licked and soothed, kissing the tender flesh.

"You're so fucking beautiful," he muttered as he bit a line down her jaw to her neck. "Too young, too beautiful and too reckless by far."

"I need . . . I need," she began. She convulsed wildly against him. Her body tightened, blew out of control.

"What do you need, sugar?" he asked as he released one of her arms to reach down between them.

He stroked her quivering clit.

"That, oh my God, that!"

She started to lower her free arm, but he growled in protest.

"Keep it high where I can see it."

He reached over with the hand that held her other and captured her fingers, meshing them against her other palm. He continued to finger her slick flesh as he rode her harder.

"Say my name," he demanded.

"Jack!" she cried out.

"Come for me, Mia. Come here in my hand while I'm touching and fucking you."

She rolled her hips as a huge wave began building in her belly. It spread like fire to her pussy, all her attention focused on the depths he reached with his cock.

"Come now."

She opened her mouth to scream, and he slammed his mouth over hers sucking her response into his throat. She closed her eyes and screamed again. He sucked her tongue into his mouth, and she lost all ability to breathe.

Little bands of tension began popping in her cunt. The sound of his balls slapping against her pussy—wet, erotic sounds—filled the room.

"Put your legs around me," he panted. "Take me deep."

She obeyed and moaned as he slipped even deeper. He paused, his hips quivering against the back of her legs. Then his cock jerked and pulsed, and the flood of his release spilled into her.

He lay there a long time, deeply embedded in her, her hands held tightly over her head. He relaxed his sweat-soaked body onto her already damp one. She twisted restlessly, loving how her body accommodated him, cradled him. A perfect fit.

Finally he released her hands, and she lowered her arms to his shoulders, holding him close to her.

"Did I hurt you?" he asked gruffly.

She shook her head. Hurt was the last thing she'd experienced. As far as first times went, it couldn't get any better than that.

Slowly, he extricated himself from her hold, sliding from her pussy in a wet rush. He left the bed and returned a moment later with a damp cloth.

He spread her legs until she was bared to him. Then he gently cleaned her still-quivering pussy, wiping and soothing with the cool towel. When he was finished, he tossed the cloth across the room and turned back to her.

She lay staring at him, unsure of what came next. The silence felt awkward, but she'd always known he wasn't a fan of too much talking. He tended to get things accomplished with action.

He slid up the bed until they were facing each other. Then he hooked an arm over her waist and pulled her up tight against him.

"You set your course, sugar. You're mine now, and I don't readily give up what belongs to me."

She exhaled in relief. He wasn't tossing her out as she'd feared he would. Possession burned darkly in his eyes. They gleamed in the low light, almost predatory.

"I've always wanted you, Jack," she said huskily. "I've always wanted to belong to you."

He tucked her head under his chin. "You don't know what that entails, little one. You may not feel that way when you find out just what it does mean."

She stared quizzically at him. He shook his head at her silent question.

"I'm tired, and you look like the cat who got the cream. All soft and contented. Lay in my arms. We can talk tomorrow."

She snuggled into his strong arms, laying her head on his hard chest. Tomorrow sounded good.

CHAPTER 2

$\mathcal{M}$ ia came awake, a cock deep in her pussy, Jack's mouth on her breast. She gasped as he sucked at her nipple then bit down on the bud.

"You're awake."

She opened her mouth to reply, but he slid his tongue past her lips, devouring her with his kiss. After several breathless moments, he pulled slightly away.

"We need to talk, Mia."

She panted, unable to form a response. He was fucking her in slow, deep thrusts. Talk? She couldn't even think.

"Can't we talk later?"

He kissed her again then slid his mouth down her cheek to the curve of her neck. He bit and sucked, marking her. She bruised easily, and she knew she'd have one hell of a hickey when it was over with.

"I swore I'd never touch you. Not when you were so young and had no idea what you wanted. Told myself I'd never go to you, that you'd have to come to me."

Her breath hitched and her pulse sped up. He had wanted her.

"We shouldn't be doing this. You have no understanding of how it would be if you belonged to me."

She shivered. Her heart pulsed and ached with the power of those words. His. God how she'd longed to belong to somebody. Her entire life had been spent longing for someone to love her. Her.

Jack had been her hero since the day he'd broken down the door to her dad's house in a routine drug bust. He'd saved her from her father's clutches when he would have taken her down with him. Then Jack had held her while she cried. He'd been responsible for finding her an apartment and a job. He'd insisted she finish high school. In short, he'd saved her life.

"I'm yours," she said.

He withdrew and held himself at the rim of her pussy entrance. Then he rolled his hips and sank back into her.

"I'm not an easy man to live with. You have no idea what you're getting into."

She frowned. He was so serious. Like he was an ax murderer or something.

A ringing phone distracted her from his cryptic statement. She glanced at the nightstand, but the phone there wasn't the one ringing.

Above her, Jack froze then swore.

"I have to get that," he said as he pulled away from her body.

Cold air washed over her, and she sat up, reaching for the blankets. She pulled them up to her chin and watched as Jack stumbled across the floor to where his jeans lay in a heap.

He reached into the pocket and pulled out a cell phone.

"Yeah," he bit out.

Mia hugged her knees to her chest and waited.

"What? When?" He broke off and swore. "Where?" he finally said. "Okay, I'll be there."

He snapped the phone shut then strode back over to the bed. She looked up at him, disappointment weighing heavy in her chest.

"I've got to go. Sorry." He tilted her chin up and kissed her forcefully. "I don't know when I'll be back."

She nodded and shivered as a chill took over her.

He spent a few minutes pulling his jeans and a shirt on then fastened his shoulder holster. He reached for his gun and shoved it into the holster.

He stopped long enough to give her a smoldering look then disappeared out the bedroom door.

Mia sighed in disappointment and slid her legs over the side of the bed. She stood up, a bit shaky after the night's activities. He hadn't lied. He hadn't been the least gentle. The soreness between her legs was a testament to that.

But she loved that about him. His raw, rugged appeal. The fact he didn't simper and play the understanding male. She liked him strong and unyielding. He made her feel safe.

She trudged to the shower and took a quick rinse under the warm spray. Afterward, she retrieved her clothing from the floor outside Jack's door where she'd shed it the previous night. Then she headed to the kitchen in search of food.

She spent the day in anticipation of his return. When evening fell, she wondered if she should stay or return to her apartment. Maybe he'd gotten busy with a case. She needed to get a change of clothing anyway.

But she wanted to be here when he got back. So she waited, finally falling asleep on the couch at midnight.

The next morning, she awakened to a beam of sunlight stabbing through the window across the room. It hit her square in the eyes, and she winced and turned her head away. Her eyes fell on the wall clock hanging over the mantle: 9 A.M.

She sat up, looking around the room. Where was Jack? She
stood up and paced back and forth. What should she do? He
hadn't even tried to call her. She gnawed nervously at her lip.

She hated the uncertainty she felt. Maybe she should go home
and wait for him to call.

After battling indecision, she searched around for her shoes
and slipped out the kitchen door into the garage. Her beat up
Honda Civic was parked on the apron, and she climbed into the
hot interior.

She drove the fifteen minutes to her apartment complex and
let herself in. Not wanting to miss Jack if he returned home, she
quickly packed a few changes of clothes plus her work uniform for
the next day. She got back into her car and traveled back to Jack's
house.

To her disappointment his truck was still gone when she pulled
into his driveway. Palming the spare key Jack had given her, she
walked to the kitchen door to let herself back in.

For the rest of the day, she watched TV, browsed idly through
the collection of magazines on the coffee table before falling asleep
again on the couch.

The next morning she got ready for work and drove to the
diner. After a full day of waitressing, she was exhausted and more
than ready to see Jack. She stopped by her apartment to shower
and change. She wanted to look her best, not like a wilted, sweaty
dishrag.

As she pulled into Jack's driveway, she noticed a "For Sale" sign
in his front yard. What the hell? She hadn't known he was selling
his house. Surely that would have come up in conversation before
now.

Nervousness settled into her stomach as she climbed out of her
car. Jack's truck still wasn't there, but he'd had to have been home
at some point if he managed to have a realtor out.

She took the key and inserted it into the lock. It wouldn't

budge. She stuck it in again and twisted. The key didn't work. What on earth was going on? She stared in bewilderment at the door. The locks had been changed.

She walked around to the front window and tried it. Locked fast. When she looked inside, she froze. All the living room furniture was gone. The room was completely empty. Spotless.

She stood there for a long moment, unable to process what she was seeing. Then she returned to her car. This didn't make sense. None of it made sense. Where was Jack?

Her purse lay on the seat, and she fumbled through the contents, finally yanking out her cell phone. She dialed information and asked for the number for the district Texas Rangers office.

After a few moments she was connected to Jack's office. A man answered with the standard greeting, and Mia bucked up her courage and asked for Jack Kincaid.

There was a long pause.

"I'm sorry, ma'am, there's no one here by that name."

The knot grew in Mia's stomach. Something was wrong. Horribly, horribly wrong.

"There must be some mistake," she said. "Jack Kincaid works for the Texas Rangers. He's worked there for years."

"I'm sorry, ma'am," he repeated. "We have no record of a Jack Kincaid."

"But he works there. I'm not crazy!"

There was another long pause. "I'm truly sorry. There's nothing I can do. I've never heard of Jack Kincaid."

Mia shut her phone in stunned disbelief. How could he have disappeared? What had happened? Surely he wouldn't leave town and not tell her.

She drove back to her apartment, numb, in shock, disbelieving what she'd seen and heard. Was she dreaming? Would she wake up in Jack's arms, the whole thing nothing more than a bizarre nightmare?

The tears began to fall as soon as she walked into her apartment. She huddled on her couch, drawing an old afghan around her for comfort. What had gone wrong? Had he lied to her? Was he dead somewhere? What kind of bizarre situation occurred that his house was on the market and no one at the Texas Rangers knew who he was?

The simple answer was that he'd left, plain and simple. But she couldn't face that. Couldn't face the idea that after getting close to him, finally, he was gone.

What was she going to do? She'd never felt so alone in her life. Or so afraid.

Over the next several weeks, she got up, went to work, drove by Jack's, came home, went to bed and started the routine all over again. She lost weight, knew she looked like hell. The other waitresses were casting suspicious glances in her direction.

She'd managed to thoroughly embarrass herself when she'd gone to where Jack had worked and demanded to see him. In the end, she'd been escorted out and been told none too kindly not to return.

Then three months after Jack's disappearance, Mia drove by his house, just like she'd done every day. Only today she saw a large moving truck out front. Two kids played out on the front lawn while the parents directed the unpacking of the truck. On the "For Sale" sign was a big fat "Sold."

She stopped her car in the middle of the street and just stared. Her hands shook, and her eyes stung. She wiped at her face, willing the sick feeling welling in her stomach to go away.

He was gone. Really gone.

Before now she'd hoped that one day she'd drive by and see his truck parked in the garage. Until today, she hadn't given up hope. But now . . . now she had to face reality. He'd left her and his life here behind. Why she didn't know. She was afraid to examine the reasons. But it was apparent he wasn't coming back.

CHAPTER 3

TWO YEARS LATER

*J*ack Kincaid stood staring out the window of his Dallas office. He flexed his neck and rotated his shoulder. Even after being back for six months, he still had trouble being confined to the desk again.

He's spent the eighteen months before that living a different life, one that went against everything he fought for on a daily basis, but one that had given him freedoms he'd sometimes enjoyed.

He tried to conjure guilt for the life he'd led. Told himself he should regret it. But the simple fact was, in the end, he'd brought down the biggest drug ring in Texas—hell the entire South. He'd done what he had to do, and the world was a better place for it.

A nagging sense of regret filtered through his mind. Not for the job he'd done, but for a girl, all soft and sweet. Big innocent blue eyes and pretty blond hair. Mia.

He let out a sigh and turned away from the window. He'd

known when he got the phone call he wouldn't be back. That day he'd left Jack Kincaid and his life behind. Become Todd Kirkland. Member of the most notorious motorcycle gang in the South.

Mia was young. She only thought she wanted him. She'd be pissed for a few days, but she'd go on and live her life without him. Maybe settle down with a nice guy and have a few babies. He'd fully expected to find her married when he got back. Only she hadn't been there.

He'd asked idly about her in the diner where she'd worked only to be informed she'd left there not long after he'd gone undercover. Maybe she'd gotten smart and stopped waiting around for a man she only thought she wanted to be with. Wherever she was, he hoped she was happy. She'd had too much pain in her young life.

But still, that night, the night she'd come to him, so full of fire and passion, still burned in his mind. His body still reacted to that memory. Never mind that he should have kicked her out of his bed the minute she planted herself there. He was fourteen years older than her. Almost old enough to be her fucking father.

That fact should have stopped him. He should have never taken her innocence. A selfish part of himself wasn't sorry for it. That memory had carried him through a lot of terrible times in the following months.

He sat down behind his desk shaking his head. No sense rehashing the past. Mia was long gone.

His office door opened, and he looked up to see who had intruded on his solitude. He relaxed when he saw it was Kenny, his longtime friend in the Rangers.

Kenny wore a peculiar expression. Almost wary. Jack cocked an eyebrow, wondering what was on his friend's mind.

"You're not going to believe who I saw the other night," Kenny began.

Jack grunted and took a seat behind his desk. "Who?" he asked, trying to pretend interest he didn't feel.

"Mia."

Jack bolted to attention. "Mia? Mia Nichols?"

Kenny nodded.

Jack's heart began to pound a little harder. Was she still around? Closer than he'd thought? He wondered if she was happy. He shook his head. No sense revisiting the past. Yeah, he'd spent a lot of years looking after her, but it was time he stopped thinking about her so damn much.

Then he furrowed his brows as he remembered one important fact. "But you've been out of town all week working a case in south Texas."

Again Kenny nodded.

"Where? Where did you see her, and are you sure it's her?"

"Curvy, blue-eyed girl with long blond hair? Small birthmark on the curve of her hip?"

Jack stared hard at his friend. "How the fuck do you know she has a birthmark on her hip?" His throat tightened uncomfortably. "Tell me you don't know this because she's a stiff."

"No, no," Kenny hastened to assure him. "No, she's very much alive and kicking."

Relief poured over Jack. "So how was she then?" he asked casually.

"She's a stripper."

Jack's mouth fell open, and he leaned back into his chair. What the fuck? "Say that again?"

Kenny walked further into Jack's office and settled down in the chair lining the wall.

"The guys and I went out to this strip joint in this hole-in-the-wall town a few miles down from where we were staying. And there she was. Onstage, dancing."

A sick feeling swelled in Jack's gut. A stripper? Goddamn it, was this her idea of moving on with her life? Living in some seedy-ass town stripping for a living?

The idea of other men staring at her, seeing her naked body sent a surge of anger rolling through his system.

"Are you sure about this, Kenny?"

"As sure as I could be without asking her name," Kenny responded. "She went offstage, and I didn't see her again. But I was sure it was her."

Jack's fist slammed down on his desk. What had happened to her? Why was she stripping for God's sake? Was she in some sort of trouble? Was this the only way she could earn a living? He found that hard to believe. The Mia he knew would never sell her body on a nightly basis.

Guilt and regret seeped into his chest. He'd known two years ago that she was better off without him. Now he wasn't so sure. He couldn't turn his back on the fact she might need help. Like he'd already turned his back on her once.

"Where?" he demanded. "Where is this club?"

Kenny looked strangely at him. "Look, man, I didn't mean to upset you. I just thought you'd like to know I saw her. You spent a lot of years making sure she was taken care of."

"You did right, Kenny. Now tell me where this club is. Murphy's been on my ass to take a vacation after my undercover stint. I think I'll take him up on it."

Jack entered the club, glaring around the room. The entire joint set his teeth on edge. It was small, shabby in appearance. The clientele was not what you'd call the higher end.

He took a seat in the far corner, not wanting to draw any attention to himself. He surveyed his surroundings and took note of each person. Then his eyes drifted toward the makeshift stage in the middle of the room. Basically it was an elevated platform with a few shoddy-looking steps for the dancers to get up and down.

He waited impatiently for the dancer to complete her routine.

When she was finished, she stepped down, accepted a few tips and fended off a host of seeking hands.

His jaw clenched tighter. Goddamn, the idea of Mia, *his* Mia, working in these conditions made him want to break something.

He got distracted when a waitress came by to take his drink order. He impatiently waved her away and growled in frustration when she stopped at the table in front of him, obscuring his view of the stage.

When she moved away, he focused on the stage again, and all the breath left his body. He struggled to breathe, and clenched and unclenched his hands.

It was her. Unmistakably her.

His hungry gaze devoured her. She was so damn beautiful. She was thinner than he remembered. Her eyes were haunted, not so full of shine and innocence. Though she was only now twenty-two she had the look of someone who had seen and experienced far more than someone else her age.

He ached at that loss of innocence. He should have never touched her. Never given in. If he hadn't, she'd still be in her old apartment at her old job, safe where he could watch over her. Just like he'd been watching over her since the night he'd saved her from her drug-crazed father.

When she undid her top and her breasts bounced free of constriction, his cock hardened painfully. Then he looked around to see the same desire roll through the crowd of men assembled. Rage curdled his blood, effectively staunching his own physical reaction.

The entire performance was torture for him. He wanted to jump onto the stage and wrap his shirt around her, shield her from the lascivious stares of the others.

When the music wound down and she finished her routine, he stood, prepared to confront her. She walked down the steps to the floor, pulled on a T-shirt then headed to the bar. She slid onto a bar stool next to some guy who looked like the cover model for a Harley magazine.

He sat back down to watch this newest development. The two chatted, and she smiled for the first time since Jack had seen her appear onstage. Then she leaned forward and hugged, *hugged* the biker dude.

The biker kissed her gently on the forehead and smoothed her hair away from her face. Goddamn, Jack was going to kill the son of a bitch.

Mia drew away from Ryder Sinclair's embrace and smiled up at him. "I'm so happy for you, Ryder. I know how much you love Kit. I just wish you weren't leaving."

Sadness pitted the inside of her stomach. Ryder was her only friend since she'd come to this hellhole. The only person she'd felt free to be herself with. Now he was leaving with Kit Townsend and Mac. The three of them had decided on a rather unique relationship, but Mia could see Ryder was more than happy with the arrangement.

"I hate to leave you, little girl," Ryder said, his face softening. "I don't like the idea of you being here alone."

She laughed. "I'm hardly alone."

"The assholes in here don't count," he pointed out.

"How is Mac doing?" she asked, anxious to shift the conversation from her loneliness.

"He's doing better. Kit's fussing over him, coddling him like a damn two-year-old."

Mia smiled sadly. "I'm gonna miss you, Ryder."

"I'm going to miss you too, little girl." He reached into his pocket and pulled out a piece of paper. "This is my number. If you ever need me, ever need anything at all, I want you to call, okay?"

She took the paper and folded it in her hand. "Thanks."

"You better get on home now." He smudged over the shallows under her eyes. "You look tired. Can I give you a ride?"

"Yeah, I'd like that. One last ride on the Harley."

They walked down the hall toward the dressing room, where she collected her things. Then she led him out the back entrance. It was easier than walking out front, having to pass through the hordes of horny men.

"Is Kit going to be angry that you're here tonight?" she asked lightly as she climbed up behind him on the motorcycle.

"Nah, she knows I came by to say good-bye. If I know her, she's at home fucking Mac's brains out."

Mia raised an eyebrow and leaned into Ryder's back as they started into the small alleyway beside the club. "And you missed out on all that to come see me? I feel positively honored."

He chuckled then gunned the engine and headed down the street. They rode several blocks to the shoddy, run-down apartment complex Mia called home. Her apartment outside Dallas had been shoe-box small, but it had been clean and safe. Two things she couldn't say about her current residence.

Ryder parked near the stairs, and Mia got off the bike.

"Want me to walk you up?" he asked.

She leaned over and kissed him on the cheek. "No, you go on home to Kit. Thanks for everything, Ryder. I mean that."

His dark eyes flared with emotion, reminding her of another set of dark eyes so long ago. She flinched at that remembrance and blocked it solidly from her mind.

He rested a hand on her cheek. "You take care of yourself, little girl."

She smiled. "I will. See you, Ryder. Be happy."

She turned and walked up the stairs to her apartment, old, familiar emotions rising in her chest. Ryder was just a friend, but she still felt the old pain of desertion. Things she'd rather not remember.

As she walked inside her door, she saw, more than usual, the decrepit state of her apartment. Despair threatened to overwhelm her, and she battled fiercely not to succumb.

Yes, she was in a mess, but she'd work her way out of it. Another six months and she would be free. Free to pick up and leave, go her own way, continue her solitary existence.

She tucked herself into the tiny closet that called itself a bathroom and took a lukewarm shower to remove the sweat and the smell of the bar.

When she was finished, she stepped into her bedroom—the only other room besides the kitchen—and pulled on her pajama top. She loved the silky feel of the material. It was her one luxury, ironically bought so many years ago when she'd planned to seduce Jack.

Jack. Not a day went by that she didn't think of him in some capacity. She tried to keep his image, his memory from haunting her, but she was never successful. And tonight was worse. Ryder had at least said good-bye. Something Jack had never done. Coward.

She was about to dive into her bed when a knock sounded at her door. A tingle of apprehension skirted up her spine. She never had visitors. Not any that she welcomed anyway.

The knocking grew louder, so she padded out of her bedroom and reached for the door knob. She cracked it an inch and peered into the darkness. When she saw the man standing there, her hand fell from the knob. Her heart raced and pounded, and her palms grew sweaty. It couldn't be. Not after all this time. But it was.

There on her doorstep stood Jack Kincaid. And he didn't look happy.

CHAPTER 4

"*L*et me in, Mia," Jack demanded.

Mia shook her head in denial. What was he doing here? Her hand shaking, she reached up and undid the chain. Then she slowly opened the door, her eyes eating up his appearance.

He was harder than she remembered. Maybe a little leaner. His muscle tone hadn't suffered, though. If anything he was more buff than ever. But his eyes. They burned holes right through her, eliciting a frightened shiver.

"I always wondered what I'd say if I ever saw you again," she said softly. "Now I realize I have nothing at all to say to you."

She accentuated her bold statement by slamming the door in his face and quickly bolting the lock. She jiggled the chain in place and backed away from the door.

Jack pounded fiercely. "Damn it, Mia, let me in."

She fled to her bedroom, tears forming in her eyes as she sank down beside the bed. The floor was hard on her knees, but she paid the pain no heed as she rocked back and forth. Why had he come? Why now?

She was so relieved to see him alive, but the fact that he wasn't dead meant he could have come back to her, called her, written. Anything!

In the distance, she could hear him shouting through the door. The entire apartment reverberated with his pounding. Then she heard a loud crack as the door exploded inward.

She scrambled up as Jack stalked into her bedroom.

"Goddamn, Mia, anyone could have broken in here. It was like knocking over a match. What the hell are you trying to do, get yourself raped or killed?"

Her mouth gaped open. Her cheeks burned, and anger, hot, liquid rage boiled within her. She flew at him, kicking, hitting and screaming at him for all she was worth.

"You sorry, worthless bastard!"

He caught her arms, easily holding her away from him, but she wouldn't quit.

"Stop it, Mia, before you hurt yourself."

"Fuck you!"

She twisted and writhed, kicking at his shins until finally he pulled her against him, wrapping his arms around her until she thought she'd suffocate. He held her tightly, suppressing her tirade.

Still she tried to struggle. When that didn't work, she cursed him, using every word she'd learned in her time at the strip club.

"Jesus," he bit out. "Seems the only way to shut you up is this."

He pulled at her hair, tipping her head back, then he fused his lips to hers. It was angry, hot, seething, a cauldron of fire poured over her.

She clamped her lips shut, but he coaxed them open with his tongue and teeth. He nipped and sucked until finally her mouth fell open, a soft sigh escaping her. Hot tears ran freely down her cheeks. For two years she'd dreamed of this moment, of touching him, loving him again.

She tore her mouth away. "Stop. I don't want this."

"Look at me when you say that, Mia. Because I don't believe you," he rasped. "Look me in the eye and tell me you don't want me, and I'll back off."

She stared up at him, allowing the pain and anguish from the past to come pouring out. "I—I can't."

She hated herself for saying it. For feeling like she'd die if he didn't touch her. She ached for him, hungered for him like she hadn't for any other man.

He hauled her against him again, sealing their mouths together. He feasted on her lips, licking and sucking, tasting her, allowing her to taste him.

Mia found herself backed into the bed. Jack paused long enough to rip at her pajama top, rending it in one hard pull. Then he tumbled to the bed, holding her underneath his taut body.

She didn't have time to think, to catch her breath, to do anything more than feel the tumultuous wave of passion as it rolled over them.

She whimpered as he nipped at her neck, her ear and then her jaw. He licked where he bit, alternating the soothing with the punishing.

"I can't wait," he ground out. "I've got to have you now. I've waited too long."

He raised himself off her and yanked off his shirt. His muscles bulged and rolled. Her eyes widened when she saw a tattoo on his abdomen. An intricate symbol, one she wasn't familiar with, rested to the right and up three inches from his navel.

His hands dropped to his jeans, and he slowly peeled away the material. His underwear came with the jeans, and his cock sprang from the restraining clothing. He kicked free of the pants and crawled back onto the bed, hovering over her.

"You're mine."

Fresh anger surged over her again, and he must have sensed her imminent protest, because before she could open her mouth, he spread her legs and plunged into her in one swift motion.

She moaned at the fullness, the overbearing sensation of him filling her. He rocked his hard thighs against her, flexing, pushing deeper.

He pulled away and bent his head to her soft belly. His tongue swirled around her belly ring. She flinched as his teeth grazed the sensitive skin. Kisses whispered across her flesh. He sucked the diamond stud between his teeth.

"This is new," he murmured against her navel.

"So is your tattoo," she said dryly.

He looked up at her, darkness swirling like a black vortex in his eyes. They clouded and his expression grew hard.

"I did what I had to do."

He moved up her body, sliding his cock back into her pussy. Again, she gasped as she stretched to accommodate him. Every nerve ending, every centimeter of the delicate tissue screamed for release. It had been so long. Too long without him.

"Why, Jack? *Why* did you leave?" she asked as the prick of tears stung her eyes again.

He ignored her as he sucked at her nipples. He acted like a starved man, like someone who had gone too long without the pleasures of a woman. He cupped one full breast in his hand, flicking at the nipple with his thumb. It tightened into a hard bud.

Then he bent his head and grazed his teeth over the tip. Once, twice, then he bit into the puckered flesh, and she gasped at the incredible streak of fire that blew through her body.

Her fingers dug into his hair, threading and tunneling through the strands. It was longer than it had been. He'd always worn it short, just a tad longer than military style. Now it looked wild and unkempt, like his eyes. What had unsettled him so much? What had happened to him in the last two years?

She wanted to know, but more than that she wanted the horrible ache in her body and heart to be assuaged. For tonight, she'd take what she could get. He'd used her, and she didn't feel one iota of guilt for using him in return. She'd have plenty of time to hate him tomorrow.

"Look at me," Jack demanded.

She blinked and focused her attention on him. He'd stilled within her, holding deep in her body. He held her nipple between two fingers, rolling the point back and forth.

He moved his body, stroking the clinging, wet walls of her pussy with his cock. In and out. "Who do you see? Who's fucking you," he asked, his eyes piercing hers.

"You," she gasped out.

"Say my name, damn it."

"Jack."

Approval rumbled through his chest.

"Who do you belong to?"

She froze. How could he ask her who she belonged to? The question hurt and pissed her off all in the same breath. She shoved at him, trying not to let the horrible grief completely overtake her.

"I hate you," she whispered as a tear trickled down her cheek.

He trailed a finger under her eye, catching the single tear and wiping it away. Then he lowered his lips, taking her mouth gently, unlike his forceful movements just seconds before.

He reached down with his hands and cupped her buttocks, pulling her tighter against him. He held her, cradled her as he sank into her. She shook her head. Not this way. She didn't know how to handle this side of Jack. She needed him forceful, demanding, not this tender, loving man.

She linked her arms around his neck and pulled him down to her. Her lips slid from his shoulder up to his neck. She flicked her tongue out to his ear and smiled a secret smile as his big body shuddered.

Then she sank her teeth into the flesh just below his ear. His entire body jerked and he uttered an oath. His hands gripped her ass tighter, massaging and spreading the cheeks. He rammed forward, foregoing the leisurely pace he'd set moments ago.

"You make me crazy," he muttered in her ear. "I've dreamed of this. Of taking you every way imaginable. Of putting my brand on you, so hard, so deep that there's no doubt of who you belong to."

"More," she begged. She shifted restlessly beneath him, wildness building and spiraling out of control in her.

For the first time in two years, she felt free. Her problems faded away. Nothing else in the world mattered but the two of them, right here, right now.

"Come with me, sugar," he gritted out. "Let it go. Trust me this one time."

Trust him.

Again he must have sensed she was in danger of fading. He reached between them and stroked at her quivering flesh.

"Come for me, Mia."

She arched her back, straining closer to him, trying to drive him deeper into her spasming pussy. Her stomach clenched and rolled. She closed her eyes and dug her fingers into his shoulders.

Then he withdrew, and her eyes flew open in protest. He wasted no time with explanations. He flipped her over on her stomach and spread her legs all in one motion. Then he was on her, driving into her from behind.

Her stomach pressed into the mattress. Her hands splayed out over the covers at her head, and she dug her fingers into the sheets, twisting the material as her need consumed her.

He rocked against her, driving her deeper into the bed. She twisted her face to the side, her mouth open in a silent scream. Her fingers curled into balls.

His hips slapped against her ass. Faster. Harder. He showed no mercy in his relentless assault on her senses. His hands gripped her ass, pushing upward so her pussy was more easily accessible.

"Jack, please! Please." Her voice trailed off until only a small sob escaped her throat.

She needed him, needed his control over her. Craved it for two long years. Only he could make her feel this way. So protected and cherished. For a few moments she could forget his desertion. Forget everything but the fact he was here, giving her what she needed.

He slammed into her one last time, and she arched her ass into the air, desperation lashing at her. A cascade of intense pleasure tightened every muscle in her body as she strained, awaiting release from the sharp peak she'd been driven up.

And then she shattered into a million pieces. They floated above her, she could almost see what they looked like when she closed her eyes and buried her face in the bed.

Behind her, Jack jerked and pressed his body into her, swelling within her. Hot fluid shot forward, surging into her waiting body. His cock spasmed, out of control, scraping against the walls of her pussy.

Oh God, oh God, oh God. She swallowed and tried to breathe in, trying to catch up, but her lungs felt constricted, her chest so tight it was painful.

Jack slumped over her, his warm body covering her completely. He nuzzled his face into her hair as he panted in her ear.

She closed her eyes, not wanting reality to intrude. She just wanted to stay this way a little longer. In a world where she didn't feel so much damn hurt.

Jack eased off her, sliding out of her pussy in a warm flood. He rolled to the side and pulled her into his arms. She didn't resist, closing her eyes as soon as her head met with his chest.

His hands stroked through her hair, and he murmured things in her ear she couldn't hear. They didn't matter. For one night, she was back where she belonged. It was a night she didn't want to end.

CHAPTER 5

$\mathcal{M}$ia eased from the bed, careful not to disturb Jack, who was sleeping soundly. Even at rest, his expression was not one of peace. His brow creased, and his lips were pressed tightly together.

She collected clothing from the small bureau next to the bed and padded into the kitchen to dress. A wide yawn stretched her jaw, and she flexed her aching body. Jack had commanded her body several times through the early morning hours. He'd possessed her over and over, as if he couldn't get enough.

If she didn't hurry, she was going to be late, not something Martin would appreciate. He'd expressed in very clear terms that she was to be at the club early to prepare for the evening's events.

Mia sighed. She hated the private parties her boss hosted. She hated being on display, having to put up with groping and lewd invitations.

Boss. What a laugh. The word "boss" implied a reciprocal

agreement. A boss was someone you could cut ties with by quitting. Martin wasn't her boss. She was his bloody slave.

She eyed the splintered remains of the door as she walked outside. Jack better damn well fix it because she couldn't afford to buy another. No, it didn't offer much in the way of protection, but she sure as hell wasn't going to sleep with the door wide open in invitation to whoever happened by.

The heat invaded her body as soon as she descended the shaky stairs. It was hot and humid, and she'd be a sticky mess by the time she walked the five blocks to work. She'd have to shower before she reported for duty.

She plodded down the street, her worn flip-flops not doing much to shield her feet from the sweltering heat rising from the pavement.

What was Jack doing here? It didn't make any sense. He showed up with an attitude, spouting off that she was his. Bullshit. She'd been his for the taking two years ago. That was a lifetime ago. So much had happened since then. It felt as though twenty years had passed instead of two.

She sighed, suddenly feeling so weary she could barely keep her head up. She'd gotten herself into such a mess. There were days when she wondered if she'd ever get out.

In her wildest fantasies, she'd imagined Jack storming in to her rescue, but now that he was here, she just wanted him gone. There was nothing he could do to help her, and she didn't want him to know just how far she'd descended since he'd left.

He was two years too late.

Jack pried his eyes open and gazed at the spot beside him in the bed. Empty. He turned over, his head still fuzzy from the first full sleep he'd gotten in two years.

He sat upright swinging his legs over the side of the bed so his feet hit the floor with a thump.

"Mia?" he called.

He stood up and walked barefoot across the floor toward the tiny bathroom. Not finding her there, he stuck his head into the kitchen. God what a dump this was. He couldn't imagine her living here. It was a wonder she hadn't been murdered yet.

Rage billowed over him when he realized she had gone. He thumped the rickety wall with his fist then cursed a blue streak when he put a fair-sized hole in it. What a piece of shit. The entire apartment was one big rat hole.

He stomped back into the bedroom and yanked on his shirt and jeans. He had no idea where she'd gone, but he wasn't going to sit here like a dumbass and wait for her to come back. How far could she have gone on foot anyway? He was laying odds she'd headed back to the club.

A few minutes later, he roared out of the parking lot of the apartment complex and drove toward the strip club. He came to a stop outside the front entrance and jammed the truck into park.

None of the neon signs were lit up, and a quick check of his watch told him the club wouldn't open for several hours. So why the hell had she come in so early? If she was even here.

Jack strode up to the front door and jiggled the knob. It was an old wooden door, probably not any sturdier than Mia's apartment door. It was open so he slipped inside.

The front room was empty. No one had cleaned up from the previous evening yet. Empty beer bottles, napkins and paper littered the floor and the table tops. Confetti was strewn about the stage and the area surrounding it.

A distant sound alerted Jack to the hallway and he took off in that direction. As he passed several doorways, one opened and Mia nearly ran headlong into him.

He caught her by her arm to steady her, and she made an exclamation of fright.

"What the fuck are you doing here, Mia?" he demanded.

She gazed up at him with wide eyes, but she didn't speak.

He shook her to dispel her from her daze. "What's with sneaking out of my bed and leaving without so much as a word?"

Her mouth gaped open. "You goddamn hypocrite! Fuck off. I used you, Jack. Just like you used me. I needed to get off and you happened to be the nearest cock. You were a good lay, but I have work to do. Get out."

Jack gritted his teeth as anger surged like molten liquid through his veins. She was pissed, and she was baiting him. He tried like hell not to react to her flip statement, but it hacked him off, this change in Mia.

"You're wrong. I was a *great* lay," he corrected.

She flushed angrily and yanked her arm away from him.

"Hey, Mia, this guy buggin' you?"

Jack jerked his head up to see a large man looming in the hallway. He curled his nose. The dude could use a bath. Greasy-haired fat slob. Jack didn't like the way the man was leering at Mia.

Uneasiness flashed in Mia's eyes.

"No, no, he was just going as a matter of fact," Mia said tightly.

She looked up at Jack, directly into his eyes, and he could see the stark fear reflected in her stare.

"Don't push this," she whispered. "Please, Jack, just go."

The pleading in her voice struck a nerve deep within Jack. She was scared of this bastard, and that made Jack want to take the motherfucker apart piece by piece.

He hesitated a split second as Fat Man ambled up beside them. Mia's eyes skittered back to Jack one more time before she hurried down the hall and slipped into one of the rooms.

Fat Man turned his slobbering glance on Jack as Mia disappeared from view.

"Interested in my Mia, are you?"

My Mia, Jack wanted to growl.

Fat Man took out a cigarette and stuck it between his teeth. "She can be yours for the right price."

"She wasn't interested in my offer," Jack drawled.

Fat Man laughed. "I own that piece of ass, and if you pay me enough, it can be yours. She doesn't have a say in the matter."

It took every ounce of Jack's self-control not to deck the son of a bitch.

"I'll think about it," he said instead. "What time does the show start? Think maybe I'll hang around until then."

Fat Man smiled. "Starting early tonight. Have some important customers from out of town. Reckon the other girls will be showing up soon, and the dancing will start in two hours or so. Have a seat out front. My bartender will be in soon. First drink's on me."

Jack watched as the fuckwad ambled off down the hall. If Mia hadn't practically begged him not to make a scene, he would have taken apart the bastard with his bare hands then hauled Mia out by her hair.

As it was, now he was stuck suffering through another night of Mia stripping for a horde of horny men. He didn't know what the hell was going on around here, but he sure as hell wasn't going to sit back like a moron. Mia had some serious explaining to do. She obviously still needed someone to take care of her, and he was going to haul her ass back to Dallas where he could do just that.

Mia stepped onto the stage, ignoring the whistles and catcalls. The music hadn't even started yet and there were already demands for her to take it off.

Her eyes scanned the crowd, and her heart leapt when she saw Jack standing against the wall. His arms were crossed over his chest, and his gaze bore into her. Every facet of his body screamed possession. It rolled off him in waves. He looked poised to strike at any moment.

He caught her gaze, knew she was looking at him. He raked his eyes up and down her body. They glittered with desire, with barely suppressed passion. It sparked. Arced like a current of electricity between them.

Slowly, she tore her gaze from him and took her position against the pole in the center of the stage.

Her arrangement was different tonight. Usually she went for something slow and sexy. A few suggestive turns could make up for any nervousness or inhibition. Tonight, however, the music thumped. All drums, it sounded like a wild jungle beat.

She shook and shimmied, her breasts jiggling against the small scrap of material charged with covering her. Her hips rolled, wild with the rhythm. The music invaded her body. She closed her eyes and forgot all sense of time and place.

Tonight she wasn't dancing for a crowd of strangers. Instead she imagined that it was only her and Jack. She wove a seductive spell, alluring, inviting.

She knew he watched her. She felt his eyes on her, burning, sizzling over her like a blowtorch. She undressed as *he* undressed her. Let the material slip from her body as if he were doing it himself.

Her hair fell as she unpinned it from the coil at the nape of her neck. The strands covered her breasts, and her nipples played an erotic game of hide and seek.

She closed her eyes and threw her head back in abandon. Her hands cupped her breasts, plumping them, pushing them upward. She opened her eyes drowsily then let her breasts fall. Her hands slid down her belly, dipping teasingly close to her pussy. She dipped two fingers underneath the silky scrap of material and let them linger as the noise from the crowd grew louder.

She chanced another look at Jack and shivered at the raw need in his eyes. Yeah, she'd put on a show entirely for his benefit. Given him a taste of what he'd thrown away. She hoped he had a hard-on from hell.

The heavy beat of the drums intensified. She twisted and gy-rated, throwing her arms over her head and giving herself over to the final climax of the performance. She collapsed to the floor, bucking and writhing as she faked orgasm.

Twenties rained down around her. Men surged to the edge of the stage, waving money in both hands.

She slowly rose to her feet, collecting the bills on the floor and tucking them seductively in her G-string. She walked close to the crowd, waggling her hips as fingers brushed against her skin.

When she reached the bottom of the steps, Martin was waiting for her, a wrap over his arm. She flinched when he touched her. She yanked the wrap around her and walked ahead of him toward her dressing room.

Martin hurried after her, huffing as he heaved his considerable girth down the hallway.

"You were smoking tonight, Mia. Very well-done. My visitors were very happy with your performance, and they look forward to a more private setting. Get changed and meet me in the back room. Don't dawdle. They're waiting."

Mia paused at her door and turned to look at him. "I really don't feel well, Martin. Can't we do this another time?"

His face grew red, and he shook a stubby finger in her face. "Don't give me that bullshit. You'll be there or else. You can't tell me you'd prefer the inside of a jail cell."

She shook her head. "No," she whispered.

"I didn't think so. Now hurry your ass up. I'm not in the mood for your stupid mind games tonight."

Mia ducked into her dressing room and shut the door, making sure to bolt the lock. She leaned heavily against the door and slid down to the floor, her face in her hands.

If only she could go back to that awful night. She shook her head, warding off tears. She couldn't change the past, and there was no sense acting like a freaking wimp. The best she could do was bide her time, pay back her debt to Martin then get the hell out of this life and this town.

She scrambled from the floor and quickly dressed. She knew what Martin expected. She didn't have to go naked, but she might as well be for all the skimpy bathing suit covered. When she pulled on the stiletto heels, she wavered a bit and gripped the edge of her dressing table for balance.

She was tired, her feet already hurt and now she'd be expected to serve cocktails and hors d'oeuvres in three-inch heels. Lovely.

An impatient knock sounded at her door.

"I'm coming," she grumbled.

She carefully walked to the door and opened it. Martin stood there looking up and down her body, an appreciative gleam in his eye.

"Very nice. Now come on. They're waiting for you."

"Just who is 'they'?" she asked suspiciously as she followed him down the hall.

"It's none of your concern," he snapped. "They've paid handsomely for your time, and I expect you to be polite."

"As long as that's all I'm expected to do," she reminded him.

"You'll do what you're told," Martin said in a dangerously low voice.

He stopped at the end of the hall outside the large room he often hosted private affairs in or rented out for bachelor parties. It was the one nice room in the entire shoddy building.

He opened the door and shoved Mia forward. She blinked and looked around nervously at the group of men seated at various intervals. She could see the gleam of appreciation, the spark of lust that entered their eyes when they saw her.

She looked back at Martin, prepared to protest, but his glare stopped her.

Jail, he mouthed at her.

Mia looked back again at the men assembled and wondered if maybe jail would be a preferable alternative.

CHAPTER 6

$\mathcal{J}$ack watched Fat Man hustle Mia down to the end of the hallway and all but shove her into the room. His hands flexed and curled into fists at his side. Something didn't add up here.

His instincts had never steered him wrong, and they were screaming at him right now. He forced himself to be patient. He wanted to knock the damn door down and pull Mia out of the room, but he'd seen the fear in her eyes. She was in some kind of trouble. He didn't want to get her hurt.

A few minutes later, Fat Man shuffled from the room, and Jack moved forward. They met halfway, and Jack inflected a note of casualness to his voice.

"We meet again," he said.

Fat Man looked up in irritation then smiled when he saw Jack. "Are you here to see Mia?"

Jack nodded. "I've given consideration to your proposition."

Fat Man jabbed his thumb over his shoulder. "She's entertaining some guests of mine, but you're welcome to go in. For a price."

Jack's eyes narrowed. "Exactly what sort of entertainment are we talking about, because I have to tell you, I'm not into sharing pussy."

Fat Man laughed. "You give me five hundred and she's yours for the night. She's not fucking any of the guests. I much prefer to tantalize them a bit. Dangle the carrot in front of their nose until they're so fucking horny, they'll pay out the nose for a chance to be with her. I have plans for Mia, and they don't include being a common whore."

"And yet, you'll give her to me for the night," Jack said.

Fat Man shrugged. "She could stand to loosen up. Besides, she didn't much like you from what I could tell. Will serve the little bitch right if I give her to you. Maybe she'll figure out she doesn't call the shots around here."

Jack wanted to wrap his hands around the son of a bitch's neck and squeeze until his eyes popped out. He reached for his wallet, careful not to betray his anger by the shaking of his hands. He peeled five bills off and thrust them at Fat Man.

Fat Man collected the money and stuffed it into his pocket. "Just make sure she's back before six tomorrow night. She has a show to do and an important appointment right afterward." He laughed as he said the last.

Jack nodded, his jaw clenched too tight to speak.

Fat Man gestured toward the end room. "Have at it."

Jack walked toward the door and paused just before opening it. "What are you into, Mia?" he murmured. "Why the fuck are you selling yourself on a nightly basis?"

He shoved the door open and took in the scene before him. A group of men dressed in business suits lounged in seats scattered over the room. Music filtered through cheap speakers, and all eyes were toward the front of the room. Jack followed the direction of their gazes to see Mia performing a sensual dance, using a chair as a prop.

She was dressed. Barely. Her nipples and pussy were covered, but that was about all he could say for her. She looked up and saw him. She stopped moving for a moment as she stared back at him. Shame crowded into her beautiful baby blues. Then she looked away and resumed her dance.

Soon the music ended, and Mia made her way through the seated men, smiling and flirting. She took drink orders then sashayed up to the minibar to pour the drinks.

Though she looked poised and confident, Jack could see her hands shake as she placed the drinks on a tray. He'd seen the fear and embarrassment in her eyes. Whatever the situation might be, he knew one thing without a doubt. Mia didn't want to be here.

He leaned back in his chair and tried to look no different from the other men in the room. When Mia had served the others, she walked up, her eyes hooded.

"What are you doing here?" she whispered.

He lifted one brow. "Making sure you don't get into any trouble."

"Martin won't like it," she hissed. "You need to go."

"Oh, you mean Fat Man? He knows I'm here. Be a good girl and get me a drink," he said with a pat on her ass.

She flinched and walked away. Jack winked at the other men who had been watching. He had no idea who they were or what danger they might pose, but he wasn't about to drop his guard around them. Let them think he was just another guy out looking for pussy.

The hours bled on into the early morning. Mia looked exhausted, dead on her feet, and still the men wanted more. More drinks, more dancing. As they grew drunker, they got louder and more demanding.

At one point, one of them pulled Mia down to his lap and

ground her ass into his crotch. He cupped her breast through the material of her top and squeezed.

Jack started out of his chair just as Mia dumped a drink over the guy's head. The man shot out of his seat, knocking Mia to the floor.

"Bitch! You're going to pay for that!"

The man wiped angrily at the liquid running off his expensive suit. Then he reached for his belt buckle, and Jack had had enough.

He pushed his way through the men who were all standing now, cheering Angry Man on. Jack bent down and picked up Mia, cradling her in his arms. She clung to him, her heart pounding against his chest. She was scared out of her wits.

"I'll bid you gentlemen a good evening," Jack drawled. "The lady and I have some business to attend to. Don't we, sugar?"

She nodded and buried her head in his chest.

"Wait just a goddamn minute," Angry Man protested. "We paid for the bitch's time."

"Take it up with Martin," Jack called over his shoulder as he headed for the door. "Since he promised the girl to me tonight."

Jack saw another guy put a hand on Angry Man's shoulder. "Let it go. We'll have our chance tomorrow night."

Jack frowned but continued out the door.

He carried Mia through the now-empty club and outside to where his truck was. Her small hands curled trustingly around his neck, and her face stay buried in his chest. She shook slightly, and it made him angrier by the minute.

He opened the passenger side of his truck and gently deposited her inside. Then he walked around and slid into the driver's seat.

He glanced over to see her curled away from him, her face toward her window. He bit back a curse and started the engine. He passed her apartment complex after a few minutes and kept driving toward a section of town a little less seedy.

Her head popped up. "Where are we going?"

"To a hotel. No way we're going back to that shit hole you call an apartment."

To his surprise, she didn't argue. But then she looked too damn tired to say much of anything.

He whipped into the parking lot of a chain hotel and cut the engine. "Stay put," he directed. "I'll get us a room."

Five minutes later, he returned, hotel key in hand. He pulled around to an empty parking spot and eased the truck into it. Shoving the truck keys into his pocket, he got out and walked around to Mia's side. When he opened her door, he saw she was sound asleep.

Not wanting to disturb her, he eased his arms underneath her small body and lifted her out of the truck. He walked toward the hotel room and when he got to the door, he shifted her weight so he could reach the lock from underneath her legs.

Dawn was already creeping across the sky. Soon it would be completely light. He shouldered his way into the room, glad to see the windows had room-darkening curtains. Mia needed to rest.

He kicked the door shut behind him then carried Mia over to the bed. He put her down, and she opened her eyes. Fear, confusion and uncertainty glimmered within them.

He pulled the covers back, easing them out from underneath her. Then he climbed in beside her and pulled the sheets over them both.

He could sense her uneasiness. She was tense, waiting. What for he wasn't sure.

"Go to sleep, Mia," he murmured into her hair. "We'll talk when you wake up."

He pulled her up against him, holding her tightly. Her body tucked against his like it belonged. She molded to him so perfectly. He threaded his fingers into her silky hair.

Tomorrow. Tomorrow he was going to find out what the fuck

was going on. Tomorrow he was putting an end to this bullshit. For now he was going to wrap himself around her as tightly as he could go, until she didn't know where she ended and he began. And he hoped she got the message loud and clear. She was his, and he wasn't letting her go. Never again.

CHAPTER 7

$\mathcal{M}$ia woke from a deep sleep. Her eyes fluttered then widened as she registered a hard body pressed tightly to hers. Jack.

She lay there not moving, her cheek pressed against the hard muscle of Jack's chest. Unable to contain the urge, she rubbed and nuzzled closer. She inhaled deeply. His scent filled her nostrils, warm and comforting.

His hand curled into her hair, rubbing over the back of her head. Soft spirals of pleasure radiated and hummed over her body. Her body loved his touch even if her mind screamed its protest.

"What time is it?" she whispered.

"Almost five."

She stiffened. Almost time to go into the club. There was no way she'd be able to sneak out this time, and Jack would demand to know what was going on. She closed her eyes. She had to be there tonight. There was no way she could face jail and the sneering deputy who waited for her there.

She pulled away from Jack and sat up in the bed. She clutched a pillow to her stomach and hugged it with both arms. When she chanced a glance at Jack, she immediately regretted it.

He stared intently at her, his dark eyes peeling back every single layer of her skin. She looked away.

He put out a hand and rested it on her back, stroking her hair absently.

"We need to talk, Mia."

She swallowed hard. Yeah, they needed to talk. But then she didn't really want to know why he'd left her. She'd already come to some rather unpleasant conclusions on her own. That only left talking about why she was taking off her clothes in a shoddy-ass strip club. And she wasn't in a hurry to discuss that.

She stood up beside the bed, refusing to look at Jack. "I need to get back to my apartment," she said. "I have to go into w-work in an hour."

Jack shot out of bed. He stood in front of her and gripped her upper arms in his hands.

"You're not going back there, Mia."

"I have to," she said simply.

Jack let his hands slide down her arms. "I know you're angry, Mia. I need to explain why I left."

She shook her head. "It doesn't really matter at this point, Jack." She looked up at him sadly. "It's too late anyway."

He gripped her chin in his hand and stared hard at her. "What's going on here? The Mia I knew would never take off her clothes for money. You were a virgin that first time for God's sake. I remember the Mia who snuck into my bed, and I look at you now, and I can't reconcile the two to save my life."

Tears filled her eyes. His judgment hurt. It shouldn't, but it did.

"You lost any right to judge me when you walked out on me two years ago," she hissed.

She yanked away from him and turned her back, trying to quell the trembling in her body.

"Mia, I had to leave," he said. "I had to leave, but it wasn't because of you."

She whirled back around. "Then why did you leave, Jack? I'm dying to know why you'd walk out and never even so much as call me. Why would your house go up for sale two days later, and why when I called your office was I told that Jack Kincaid never worked there?"

His expression dulled and regret flared in his eyes.

"Do you have any idea what that was like for me?" she whispered. "I didn't know if you were dead or if someone was playing a sick joke, or maybe you just indulged in a quick fuck and were too cowardly to tell me you wanted me out."

"God, Mia, it wasn't like that."

"Then what *was* it like, Jack? I'm waiting."

Tears streamed down her face. She wiped angrily at them, but they continued to slip down her cheeks. So much grief was bottled up inside her, she felt near to exploding.

He ran a hand through his unruly hair and closed his eyes.

"You've changed, Jack," she said in a low voice. "I don't know what happened, but you aren't the same person. Your clothes, your hair, the tattoo."

He held his hands out and cupped her shoulders. He pushed her gently down to the bed. "Please, Mia, just listen to what I have to say."

She looked back up at him, waiting.

"I'd been working undercover on a case. I'd been trying to gain access to a large motorcycle gang in southwest Texas. They were one of the largest drug traffickers in the entire South. They had border connections, and their network was so large, so far reaching that they were virtually unstoppable.

"Their connections made it almost impossible for an under-cover agent to break in. I'd been trying for a year. We had just about given up when the call came in. I was invited down to Mex-ico to meet the leadership. We knew this was a huge step. We also knew that while I was there, they'd launch an extensive back-ground check. Uncover every detail of my life since my birth. We couldn't chance anything. We had to make Jack Kincaid disap-pear. So I left."

She stared at him for a long moment then burst out laughing. A wave of hysteria washed over her, and she buried her face in her hands.

"What the hell is so funny?" he demanded.

He reached down and tipped her chin up, forcing her to meet his gaze.

"You left. Just like that," she said helplessly. "Glad I meant so much."

Jack knelt in front of her, gripping her hands in his. "I lived each day in a hell of my own making, doing things I'm not proud of, things I had to do to bring down a network of criminals."

She stood up and shook off his hands. She tried to control her anger, her grief. Then she turned around and focused her stare on him.

"Tell me something, Jack. Why didn't you make sure I knew what was going on? Don't you think I would have understood? That knowing anything was better than the hell of not knowing whether you were alive or dead or just didn't give a flying fuck about me? Or maybe you thought you could lay it all out to me after the fact, and I'd forgive you for being so cruel because you're a fucking hero now."

He didn't immediately respond. He looked confused by the question.

"I'll tell you why you didn't bother," she said softly. "Because you didn't love me. You didn't care about me."

He started to protest, but she held up her hand to silence him.

"I'm not playing the martyr here, Jack. I'm facing facts. If you had loved me, if I was important to you, I know you well enough to know you would have moved heaven and earth to make sure I knew something. You wouldn't have wanted to worry me. You wouldn't have allowed yourself to leave without me knowing you cared. I mean honestly, would a cop ever just leave without telling his wife?"

"Mia—"

Again she held up her hand. "I'm a big girl, Jack. I may not have always acted like it, but I'm capable of taking care of myself. I've spent the last two years hating you when I should have been hating myself for throwing myself at you like I did. I made it too easy for you, and I paid the price."

Silence crept over them, laying heavy like a blanket over the room.

Finally she broke the silence. "I need to go to work, Jack. I don't have a choice. It's not as easy as just picking up and leaving. I didn't have to run away like a hurt little girl when you left, but I did, and now I have to face the consequences."

Jack closed the distance between them. He cupped her face in his hands and stared down at her, fury in his eyes.

"What the fuck are you talking about, Mia? What is going on here?"

"Please, Jack," she whispered. "Take me to my apartment so I can change. I have to do this. I do not have a choice."

His eyes narrowed and his jaw ticked. "What kind of trouble are you in?"

She closed her eyes, wishing she could tell him. But he couldn't help her. Telling him wouldn't change a damn thing.

"Please, Jack. Don't make me beg."

He swore violently. "What is that motherfucker holding over you, Mia?"

She felt the blood drain out of her face. He was getting too close to the truth. But then how would he ever guess what she had done?

"What matters is that I get into work. Tonight is important, Jack. If I don't show up, I'll be in a lot of trouble," she said quietly.

He wavered, indecision etched in his face. "All right," he finally said. "I'll take you in, Mia. But after tonight, you're not going back. I don't give a shit what kind of trouble you think you're in. This conversation is far from over. After tonight you're going to tell me what the fuck is going on, and you're not going to leave anything out. Are we clear?"

Mia sighed in relief.

"I'm going with you," he added. "I don't trust that fat fuck as far as I could throw him."

CHAPTER 8

*J*ack glanced sideways at Mia as he drove toward the club. He couldn't believe he was agreeing to this. He should drive right out of town and keep on driving. Take Mia as far from this place as he could.

But he couldn't do that without finding out what sort of hold Fat Man had over Mia. Whatever it was, Mia feared him deeply.

Tonight, while Mia danced—her last dance—Jack was going to find out what was going on.

She looked tired. And too damned vulnerable. Her words echoed in his memory. She'd delivered the statement that he didn't love or care for her with so much hurt, so much emotion swimming in those blue eyes that he'd felt gut shot. And he hadn't even been able to respond, because damn it, she'd been partially right.

That night, the whole episode had seemed like a dream to him. It had happened out of the blue, so unexpected, like one of his most erotic fantasies come to life. He'd fought his feelings and physical reaction to Mia for so long that he hadn't been able to hold out under her direct assault. And afterward, he'd felt guilty as hell.

A part of him knew that he hadn't explained to her, hadn't made her understand about his departure, because he secretly hoped she'd move on with her life and forget about him. If he hadn't had to leave, he would have taken over her life, possessed her completely, and that wasn't what she needed.

She was young with her whole life ahead of her. She didn't need to be tied to a man who'd demand everything of her. Who'd expect her to give herself completely and wholly to him. He couldn't change who he was for her or anyone else, but he'd be damned if he couldn't protect her from him. And his needs.

Even now, two years later, his response had been to barge back into her life, take her home and stamp her his. He shook his head. He wanted her, but he knew it wasn't enough. She deserved more. More than he could give her.

Which left the question of what to do when he got her the hell out of here. Take her back to Dallas? Take up where he'd left off before, watching over her as he had since she was sixteen and homeless?

He pulled into the parking lot of the strip club and shut down the engine. Then he looked over at Mia again.

"This is it, Mia. I mean it. Last night. We're going to get this over with, and then you're going to tell me what I need to do to get you out of whatever mess you're in."

She turned her head, raising her eyes to meet his gaze. There was so much sadness reflected in the blue pools.

"There's nothing you can do, Jack. This is something only I can fix."

"Bullshit."

She opened the door and slid out of the truck. He yanked his keys out of the ignition and followed her to the door. She turned around and put her small hand on his chest.

"Don't come in, Jack. You'll only make things worse. If you want to come for the performance, fine. Come back a little later. But if you barge in with me and hang over my shoulder, you'll only make things worse for me."

He tensed, every instinct he had screaming at him to go in anyway, to not let her out of his sight.

"I need to know what is going on, Mia."

She looked down, her glossy blond hair falling over her shoulders. "I'll tell you everything. Tonight. I promise."

He nudged her chin up with his finger. "We'll find a way, Mia. I swear it. No matter how bad you think it is, I'll find a way out."

She smiled and reached up to touch his cheek. "Thank you, Jack."

He stepped back. "I won't go in until the show, but I'll be here watching. I want to make sure nothing hurts you."

She expelled a long sigh. "I'm not in any danger, Jack. There are just things I have to do. Consequences for choices I made. I don't want you to worry."

"There's not a damn thing you can do about it."

She turned around and pushed open the door to the club. She glanced back at him once before closing it behind her.

Jack slowly walked back to his truck. He didn't like the idea of leaving Mia on her own, but he did need time to do a little investigating. Primary on his list was Fat Man. A guy like that was bound to have dirt piled a mile high in some corner of his universe. It was just a matter of finding it.

He flipped open his cell phone and made a quick call to Kenny.

Mia knocked on Martin's door and waited for him to answer. He'd demanded she come in early today, despite her late night entertaining his slobbering guests. He'd seemed agitated lately, not that him being hyped up over anything was unusual. She was convinced he had a pretty nasty drug habit. Ironic that he'd saved her from serving a prison sentence for drug possession.

She opened the door when she heard him snap out the command to enter.

His expression brightened when he saw her standing in the doorway.

"Ah, there you are. Good, good. Come in."

She cocked a suspicious eyebrow at him as he hurried around the desk to greet her.

"Sit down," he said, shoving a chair at her.

"What's this all about, Martin?" she asked wearily as she sat down.

He wiped his sweaty brow with a rag then dropped it back onto his desk.

"You, my dear, are the answer to all my problems, just as I was once the answer to all of yours."

"I seriously doubt that," she muttered.

"Oh, but you are," he said, a gleam entering his eyes. "You see, Mia, there is, how shall I put this, much outside interest in a girl such as yourself. I stand to make a tidy profit from auctioning you off to the highest bidder."

She shot to her feet. "You're out of your fucking mind! There is no way I'm selling myself off to anyone. I've had enough of this. If my alternative is jail, then so be it."

Martin smiled. The confidence in his smile unnerved her. Made her afraid.

"I don't recall offering you a choice in the matter. This is no longer about your working off a debt to me, a debt that was fabricated by the way. You see, the good sheriff and I have a little agreement. I pad his pockets, and he, well, he supplies me with suitable girls for my business."

"You bastard!"

She turned around to storm from the room only to find herself barred from the door by a very large, very formidable-looking man. She hadn't even heard him come in.

She shrank back, and for the first time felt real fear. It tasted metallic in her mouth. She looked back and forth between the two men in panic.

"What are you doing?" she demanded.

"The auctioning of slaves to a master is a lucrative business," Martin began. "A business I've been involved in for some time. I hadn't planned to sell you so soon. You bring in a lot of customers to the club. But you've captured the interest of several parties. Several wealthy parties. I find myself in need of a large sum of money. A sum you will certainly fetch once I put you on the auction block. I can always replace you in the club. There's always a dumb young girl willing to get into trouble."

His gaze slid over her body, and he smacked his lips in satisfaction. "By the night's end, you will have a new master, someone who will not treat you as well as I have no doubt, and I will be free from my current money troubles."

"I won't do it," she said shakily. "I won't agree to this."

"And again, my dear, you don't have a choice."

She felt a prick in her shoulder, and she whirled around to see the man who'd stood in the doorway holding a syringe in his hand. The room swirled and blurred in her vision. Then she felt her legs give out as she sagged to the floor.

CHAPTER 9

*J*ack settled into his chair and took a swig of his beer. He tried to act casual, but his nerves were on edge. His call to Kenny had been productive. Maybe. It could mean something or it could mean nothing at all.

The little town Mia had settled in was not known for being the center of justice and the American way. The Texas Rangers had been investigating the local sheriff's department for a year, but so far had been unable to uncover anything concrete. But the alleged connection between the sheriff and one Martin Lindelle was enough to make Jack's internal radar leap off the scale.

Then there was the fact that a six months ago, Mia had been pulled over by a sheriff's deputy. No charges filed, no suspicion of wrongdoing, and yet suddenly Mia decided to stay on when she'd professed to be driving through. And ironically enough, she went to work for the man rumored to have an illegal connection to the sheriff.

It got more interesting and coincidental by the minute, and Jack didn't put much stock in coincidence. All he knew was that he wanted to get Mia out of town as soon as possible.

He drummed his fingers on the table and checked his watch. Mia should have been on by now. Instead another stripper was ten minutes over her routine and the crowd knew it.

Movement in the hallway across the room focused Jack's stare on the doorway. He saw Martin amble forward and peek out as if searching for someone in the room.

Jack stood up and donned his best asshole sneer. It was something he'd perfected during his time undercover with the Sons of Sin. He walked casually across the floor toward Martin. As he drew near, Martin looked up.

"You're looking for Mia?" Martin asked in a calculated manner.

Jack allowed his expression to grow dark. "Yeah, I'm not happy with last night's arrangement. Bitch snuck out on me after knocking me out cold."

Martin's eyebrow shot up in surprise.

Jack slid his shirt upward, just enough that Martin caught a glimpse of the tattoo on his abdomen.

"I'm not used to being ripped off. I'm not happy about it at all. What kind of scam are you two running anyway? You collect the money and she rips off the customer?"

Martin's eyes were fixed on the tattoo. Jack knew he recognized the symbol. He should. It had been on TV enough lately.

Martin ran a nervous hand through his hair. "I didn't know she skipped out, I swear it."

"Where is she?" Jack growled. "We have unfinished business."

Sweat beaded on Martin's forehead. He licked his lips nervously. "She's not, well, she's not here, exactly."

"What do you mean 'exactly'?" Jack's voice dropped to a dangerously low level. He knew it sounded menacing, and he hoped to hell it scared the shit out of Fat Man.

He closed the distance between him and Martin, and he grabbed Martin's shirt collar and hauled him up close. "You tell me where she is, you fat fuck, or I'll take great pleasure in carving you into little pieces and feeding your ass to the buzzards. I'm sure you've heard of what happens to people who cross the devil."

Martin's eyes bulged out of his head as he glanced right and left. He motioned frantically toward the end of the hall. "L-let's go into m-my office. Perhaps we can clear this little matter up."

Jack released the shaking man then followed him down the hall and into his office. Martin sat down behind his desk while Jack opted to stand. He wanted to maintain his intimidation over the sleazebag.

"I've had a lot of interest in Mia," Martin began as he mopped at his brow. He leaned forward and continued in a whisper. "The girl is being auctioned off tonight. You're certainly welcome to bid on her."

Jack swallowed the huge knot of rage building in his throat. He wanted to reach across the desk and strangle the bastard with his bare hands. Auctioned? Like a hunk of meat. It made his blood boil. Mia was his, and no one else would touch her. Or they'd die a long, painful death.

He forced himself to smile. "Indeed. A slave auction? It sounds very intriguing. Where might I find this auction?"

"I can call ahead and make sure you're given admittance," Martin said hastily. "I'll give you directions. Whatever it is you need."

Jack leaned over, his nose inches from the foul-smelling breath blowing from the bastard's mouth. "Even better, inform whoever is holding the auction that I am interested in making a preempt offer, but first I want to sample the merchandise. As I was unable to do last night. It's the least you owe me. If I'm satisfied, I'll make it worth your while. If I'm not, I'll leave her to your highest bidder."

Martin's eyes bugged out, and sweat rolled profusely from his face. "I no longer have any control over what happens with her. I turned her over to Drake. He handles the auction details. I'll give you the address and directions. But that's all I can do, I swear. You'll have to make your offer to Drake."

He scribbled frantically on a piece of paper then shoved it toward Jack.

Jack collected the piece of paper and shoved it into his pocket. "You better hope Drake will entertain my offer, Fat Man. Because if he doesn't, I'm going to hunt you down and feed your carcass to the buzzards."

Jack turned and walked out the door.

Martin heaved a great sigh of relief then reached for his phone. He punched in a number, cursing when he had to redial it three times.

He shoved the receiver to his ear and waited.

"Get me Drake. We have a big problem."

Mia opened her eyes to complete darkness. She blinked, trying to bring her surroundings into focus, but the black void was suffocating.

Her tongue lay dry and swollen in her mouth, the aftereffects of the drug dulling her senses. She swallowed then licked her cracked, dry lips.

As she slowly became more aware, aching discomfort registered in her arms and legs. She was upright, yet her legs bore none of her weight. She gave her hands and feet an experimental wiggle. Her wrists were bound together, her arms stretched high above her head. Her shoulders burned from the strain of her weight.

A bead of sweat rolled down the side of her neck then slid down her chest. Her bare chest. She was naked and spread-eagled, suspended from some sort of device.

She yanked at the ropes binding her wrists, but they held fast and dug painfully into her skin. Fear crawled over her body. Her stomach rolled and rebelled as nausea threatened to overtake her. Her encounter with Martin in his office rushed back in a flash. A slave. He was selling her like a piece of meat at market.

She gritted her teeth and fought the panic that ripped and tore at her consciousness. The little bastard wouldn't get away with this. Jack would save her. Oh God, where was she? Where was Jack? She closed her eyes and took long gulping breaths to try and steady her frazzled nerves.

She wanted to scream. Wanted to rage against the animal responsible for her captivity. But she didn't want to alert him to the fact she was conscious. Who knew what would happen to her then? So she bit her lip to staunch the moan of desperation that fought to escape her.

For how long she hung there in the dark, she didn't know. It seemed an eternity but in reality, it could have been minutes. Or it could have been hours.

Lights turned on, flooding the room and blinding her. She squinted against the bombardment. She heard footsteps, and she blinked rapidly so she could see who was in the room with her.

She finally focused on a figure standing a few feet in front of her. She forced herself to meet his gaze head on, refusing to buckle to the fear and panic clawing at her. "What do you want?" she demanded.

The man merely smiled. He pulled a whip from behind his back and slapped it against his leg.

"I'd save my breath. You have a rather long night ahead of you."

Smug bastard. If she could get her hands free, she'd delight in choking the oily little worm.

"Why am I here?" she bit out.

"You're going to be auctioned off to the highest bidder. You've outlived your usefulness at the club, and we've had a lot of outside interest in you. There are quite a few gentlemen willing to shell out a lot of money to possess you."

Mia's eyes widened in horror. "That's not legal, asshole. You can't sell a person. I'll never agree to it."

The man laughed. He walked around her, the slap of the whip against his leg echoing in the small room. She could see cameras had been set up in various positions, all trained on her.

"There is nothing more beautiful than a woman in bondage. Except a woman writhing in pain, struggling against her bonds. It's a sight men go crazy for. Submission is the ultimate turn-on. Knowing a woman is theirs to do with as they wish."

Mia trembled, her stomach in knots. She was afraid. Jack. Would he find her? Would he look for her when he didn't see her at the club? Or would he think she'd run again?

"You're a sick fuck," she said in disgust. She was careful to keep her anger front and center. It gave her something to concentrate on. Gave her a measure of control when she had none.

He chuckled. "I almost wish you were mine to tame. Ah yes, Mia, you're going to turn a tidy profit for me." He gestured toward the cameras. "Your new master is watching. Waiting for the time he can claim you. Bend you to his will. Make you serve his every desire."

She glared up at the cameras. "I won't do it."

"You have no choice."

Her chin sank to her chest. Her strength was fast failing.

Across the room a door opened.

"Cut her down and take her to the bedroom. We have a customer. Martin called over, said to give him what he wants."

Mia lifted her head in the direction of the voice to see a man in a dark suit standing in the doorway.

"Martin forgets he is not in charge here," her captor said in a silky voice.

"I think you'll be interested in his offer," the second man said.

"He has rather interesting connections. It would be to our advantage to hear what he has to say."

"Very well. Leave her here until I've spoken with our guest. The auction is set to go live in half an hour. If I have need of her, I'll summon you."

The man with the whip circled around in front of Mia. He touched the tip of the leather to her cheek and stroked softly downward. Then he turned and walked away.

Mia slumped downward again, breathing a prayer of thanksgiving at her temporary reprieve.

"Please, Jack, find me," she whispered.

CHAPTER 10

"Tell me, Mr. . . . what did you say your name was?"

Jack looked up at the well dressed man who'd entered the small sitting room. "I didn't," he replied brusquely. He eyed the whip that dangled from the man's hand and tried to control the murderous urge that assaulted him.

He glanced over to the two armed men who'd kept him company while he waited to be seen. How many more there were, he wasn't sure. The house was well guarded from the outside as well as the inside.

The other man smiled. "I see. A mysterious one. Tell me, what is it I can do for you?"

"You have a woman I want."

The man's brow arched. "I have many women."

Jack eyed him steadily. "Blond, shapely, nice tits and ass. Going to auction tonight."

The man's eyes flickered. "You must mean Mia."

Jack nodded.

"And what is your interest in her?"

"We have unfinished business."

The man sat down in an armchair and set about pouring a drink from a crystal decanter on the end table next to him.

"Would you like a drink?"

Jack shook his head.

"My name is Drake," he continued. He picked up his glass and swirled the contents before taking a swallow. "Eric tells me you have connections. Is this true?"

Jack slowly raised his shirt to bare the tattoo on his abdomen.

Drake's eyebrow came up. "You're him aren't you. The one who escaped the raid. The police are looking for you, and yet here you are, interested in a woman. Odd, don't you think?"

Jack willed himself to relax, to act nonchalant. He slipped into a role he'd played to perfection for the last two years.

"I lost my slave in the raid," he said with a shrug. "I'm looking to replace her before I head south to lay low. Isolation gets lonely, if you know what I mean."

Drake grinned. "That I do. What are you offering?"

Jack pinned him with a hard stare. "I paid for the bitch last night, and she skipped out on me. I have no intention of paying for goods I haven't sampled. I want an hour with her. If I like her, I'll be very generous in my offer. I'd ask that you forego the auction until you've entertained my offer."

Drake set his glass down and continued to study Jack. "You want to sample the merchandise? I'm sure you know that's unheard of."

"I have no intention of paying for pussy unless I know it's prime," Jack said lazily.

"I would expect some sort of deposit. Nonrefundable of course," Drake said smoothly.

Jack crossed his arms over his chest. "And I said I'm not paying a dime until I know what kind of product I'm getting. Do you doubt my word?" He said the last menacingly and enjoyed watching the smarmy bastard squirm in his chair.

Truth was, he'd love nothing more than to have blasted in with guns blazing, but he had no idea what he was dealing with. He had to play this cool. Make sure Mia was safe. And hope like hell Kenny showed up with the troops soon.

"Very well," Drake finally said as he rose from his chair. "I have a few stipulations of my own. Your 'sampling' can be of benefit to us both. I'll expect to film your session. If you don't purchase her, it will be valuable footage to show my prospective bidders. And a warning: my men will be watching. Just so you know."

Jack willed himself not to knock out the jerk's teeth. The veiled threat pissed him off. Like the sons of bitches wouldn't be watching regardless of whether they considered him a threat. He nodded his acceptance of the terms, not trusting himself to speak.

Drake motioned for him to follow.

"I'll escort you to a more appropriate room and bring Mia to you. When the hour is up, I'll expect an offer. Otherwise you'll be asked to leave."

"Fair enough."

Drake nodded to the two men standing a few feet away. One of them walked up behind Jack and proceeded to pat him down.

"Never can be too careful," Drake said with a smile as he reached for the wallet pulled from Jack's pocket.

Drake thumbed through the wallet, then, seemingly satisfied with what he saw, he handed the wallet back. "You can follow me, Mr. Kirkland."

Jack followed Drake down a long hallway and into a plush bedroom. A king-size bed stood in the middle of the room. As Jack gazed around, he saw hooks in the ceiling as well as on the bedposts. An old-fashioned wooden stock sat at the end of the bed, and a multitude of whips, cuffs, nipple clamps, beads and every other imaginable sex tool lay neatly arranged on a long table lining the far wall.

The wall adjacent to the table had a large mirror encased in it, two-way, no doubt. He looked around for the cameras and noted at least two. He would have to be damn careful not to give himself or Mia away.

His stomach clenched at what he'd have to do. It was ironic. In order to save Mia, he would have to have her in a way he'd always wanted. He only hoped she'd forgive him. That she'd understand. And if she didn't, he could live with that just as long as he got her safely out of here. Even if it meant earning her contempt.

"Wait here," Drake said. "I'll return with the girl."

Jack took a deep breath and lounged casually in an armchair facing the bed. He didn't want to appear nervous or agitated.

A few minutes later, the door opened and Drake walked in, shoving Mia in front of him. She was completely naked except for a collar around her neck. Drake held a leash attached to the collar.

She stumbled as Drake pushed her again. "On your knees, bitch," Drake ordered Mia. "Greet your temporary master. If you please him, you may find a home with him. If not, you'll be sold at auction later."

Mia slowly raised her head and looked at Jack. Her eyes flashed with rage. She was pissed. Good. They hadn't broken her spirit. She'd need every bit of her wits about her if they were going to get out alive.

As she continued to stare at him, he saw something else mirrored in her depths. Something other than anger. Relief. Trust. He didn't deserve her trust. He'd let her down, and yet she stared over at him, calm, composed, though her rigid stance belied her fear. He stared at her, willing her to understand, to continue to trust him as he did what he must.

He strode over to her, hoping she'd remain quiet until he could get rid of Drake.

"You may kiss my feet, slave," he ordered harshly.

She blinked in surprise then seemed to compose herself, hiding her emotions behind an indifferent mask. Drake shoved her down, and she caught herself with her hands, her face just inches from his feet. After a moment's hesitation, she pressed her lips to the tops of his shoes then slowly pulled away.

"Very good," Jack said approvingly. Then he looked over at Drake. "You may leave us now."

Drake looked as if he'd say something, but nodded and backed out of the door.

Jack collected the leash in his hand and pulled Mia to a standing position. He faced her away from the mirror. She stood stiffly as he walked around behind her. He pressed his chest to her back and gently brushed aside her hair. Then he bent his mouth as if he were going to nip at her neck.

"We're being watched." He waited for the words to sink in, allowing her time to digest the situation. "I need for you to trust me, Mia. Do whatever I tell you, no matter what. We're going to fuck. We're going to put on a show for these bastards. Concentrate on me, sugar. Nothing else. When I give you the signal, I want you to pretend to faint. We can't simply walk out. We're going to have to fight our way out. Do you understand?"

She nodded slightly.

He closed his eyes briefly, regret sawing through his chest. And shame. He hadn't ever wanted her to see the real Jack Kincaid. Would she hate him? It didn't matter. Her being alive mattered. Her inevitable contempt for him didn't.

He steeled himself and stopped fighting his arousal. Embraced it, allowed it to wash over his body. Images of the past flickered through his mind like a fast-action movie. Mia in his bed, his mouth on her, her legs wrapped around him. The aching desire he felt whenever he so much as touched her, thought about her. He grabbed onto that desire and harnessed it.

"Get ready to begin," he murmured as he stepped away.

He circled back around in front of her. "On your knees," he said sharply.

She sank to her knees, her eyes lowered in perfect submission. If she only knew how beautiful she looked. He should feel like the lowest scum for being so turned on, but he couldn't deny the surge of lust that raced through his veins.

He unzipped his pants and pulled out his dick. He laced one hand through her hair and pulled her forward. "Suck me," he ordered. "Take me deep. Make me like it or I'll spank your ass."

Her lips slowly parted. She looked up at him, uncertainty flashing in her gorgeous blue eyes. He nodded to her, showing her his approval. He positioned himself at her lips and plunged inside her mouth in one hard thrust.

God, she felt like hot silk surrounding his cock. Wet, hot, so erotic. He dropped his hand from his cock and wrapped both hands in her hair, holding her tightly against him.

He allowed his dominant nature to take over. This was something he didn't have to pretend. The act that wasn't an act. He called the shots. Just like he always demanded.

He blocked out their surroundings, shoved everything from his mind but the woman before him, his most precious fantasy come to life.

"When I come, I want you to swallow every drop," he rasped. "If you spill even a drop, you'll be punished. Do you understand me?"

His cock buried so deeply within her mouth prevented her response, so she nodded her head.

He withdrew, giving her time to catch her breath, then he pressed forward again, seeking more of her silken heat. One hand slipped around to her jaw until he cupped her chin, squeezing slightly.

"Open wider, relax your jaw," he directed. "You can take all of me. I want you to do it."

She struggled against him, but he wouldn't allow her to dictate the action. Eventually, she stopped fighting him and relaxed in his hand. He surged to the back of her throat, pausing to enjoy the sensation of being completely buried in her mouth.

When she started to struggle again, he withdrew again to let her catch her breath.

"Very good," he purred. "One would think you've been sucking cock all your life. Now open wide, sugar. I'm going to come."

He cupped her jaw again and began pumping deeply into her mouth. The wet sounds of her sucking and his hips slapping against her cheeks filled the room. Semen surged from his balls, tightening every inch of his cock.

He swelled in her mouth, and the first bursts of cum blasted against the back of her throat. She moaned softly as she swallowed and swallowed again.

He jerked against her, the muscles in his legs clenching as every last drop of his seed filled her mouth. She continued to suck softly at his penis, licking and swallowing the last drops from his skin.

Finally, he pulled away. He cupped her chin and forced her to loop up at him. "Did you like that, slave?"

Her eyes glittered brightly with need. Her lips were swollen from his harsh use of her. "Yes," she whispered.

He wiped at her lips with the pad of his thumb. "Stand up," he directed.

She rose shakily to her feet, wobbling a bit as she stood in front of him. He reached out to cup her full breast in his hand. He tweaked her nipple with his fingers, pulling it to a stiff peak. She shivered underneath his hand and leaned into his caress.

"Did you like sucking my cock?" he asked.

"Y-yes."

"Yes, master," he corrected.

"Yes, master."

"Very good. I'm pleased."

Jack wanted to see her bend over the bed, her pussy bared to him. He wanted to spank her, witness the red glow appear on her ass, but he didn't know what she'd already been subjected to. He couldn't do this, even though it was common practice for a master to punish a slave, and the observers might expect it. He'd never seek to hurt Mia. He wanted to bring her as much pleasure as he would find.

"You may go lie down on the bed," he said. "On your back, legs and pussy spread. Allow your legs to dangle off the bed."

She turned and walked toward the bed, her steps uncertain. He ached to reach out and comfort her, to let her know he would save her, but right now, he had to convince anyone watching that he was merely sampling the goods.

She did as he asked, lying down on the bed, scooting to the edge and letting her legs fall over the side. She spread herself so that the pink folds of her pussy were visible.

He undressed then walked over, settling between her thighs. He reached out to touch the soft blond curls, letting his finger linger over her clit. She sighed softly and jerked in reaction.

He trailed it lower until he circled the rim of her pussy entrance. Then he slid one finger in, fucking her in slow, easy motions. He pulled away, and she moaned in protest.

"You exist for my pleasure, slave, not the other way around," he reprimanded. "Remember that, and we'll get along quite well." He let the words slip from his mouth even as he sought to give her satisfaction. To make her burn for him the way he burned for her. To make her forget that they were being watched. He wanted her sole focus to be him. Only him. And the pleasure he could give her.

He lowered his head, finding her soft folds with his mouth. He nuzzled between them, licking and nipping at the sensitive skin. Her thighs trembled around his head. Her body shook and quivered, and a series of soft gasps escaped her lips.

He slid his tongue from her entrance to her clit, tasting her, loving her. He circled the tiny button with the tip of his tongue before finally sucking it into his mouth. She was close to her orgasm, but he knew he couldn't give it to her yet.

He pulled away. Then he climbed up over her body and straddled her face, placing his knees on either side of his head. "Suck me until I'm hard enough to fuck you properly," he demanded.

He leaned forward, bearing his weight with his hands. His hips arched over her mouth, and he rocked forward, sliding back between her lips. The position was erotic as hell. He could fuck her face as if he were fucking her pussy.

He slid in and out, rotating his hips and bucking forward again. His dick sprang to life in her warm, soft mouth. Soon he was hard again. He sank lazily to the back of her throat, enjoying the sensation of her tongue rubbing over his cock.

Finally he withdrew and slid back down her body until he once again stood between her thighs.

"Spread yourself for me," he said. "Use your fingers."

She hesitantly reached down, spreading the plump folds of her pussy. The rosy button puckered and strained. Her entrance glistened with her juices. She was turned on. Wanted him as badly as he wanted her.

He thumbed her clit, rolling it in a circular motion. Her hips bucked, and she let out a low wail. Holding his thumb firmly against the tiny mound of flesh, he positioned his dick and thrust to her hilt.

She gasped aloud and twisted underneath him. He pinned her against the bed, pressing tightly against her. He gave her a moment to adjust to his size. When her pussy clenched, milking him, he began pumping into her.

His hand left her clit, and she sobbed her protest. He spread her legs wider and sank deeper into her. He reached up with both hands and twisted her nipples between his fingers.

He held onto them, pulling and tugging at the tips as he slammed repeatedly into her. Her body tightened and convulsed around him. Her pussy clenched, grasping at his cock. He knew she was close to her orgasm.

He began pounding harder, and when he felt she was nearing her peak, he gave each nipple a sharp pinch.

She cried out, and he felt a flood of wetness around his cock. He continued to thrust. His own orgasm was close. Finally he ripped himself from her pussy and directed the spray of cum onto her stomach and breasts. He pumped with his hand until the last drops splattered onto her skin. Then he slid back into her and stayed there for several long seconds.

For a brief instant, their eyes connected. He held her gaze for a long second, willing her to understand. She stared back unblinking, her acceptance there for him to see. An unnamed emotion swelled in his chest, raw, hot and aching. He wanted to gather her in his arms, carry her as far from this place as he could. Somewhere he could love her and take care of her.

He pulled away from her and helped her from the bed, giving her hand a reassuring squeeze. "Go into the bathroom and clean yourself. When you come back out, I want you to suck me until I'm hard again."

"Yes, master," she said quietly.

She walked into the bathroom a few steps away, and he could hear the faucet running in the sink. A few moments later, she walked back out. He stood in the middle of the room, and she moved over to him. She knelt gracefully in front of him and put her hands on either side of his hips.

Her tongue slid over his semihard dick, and he groaned. She sucked him into her mouth, working her tongue over the sensitive head. She was an absolute goddess, and he'd give anything for them to be anywhere but in this hellhole.

He allowed her to do most of the work this time, patiently waiting as she found her rhythm. Her hands glided over his skin, each touch sending a jolt of pleasure up his spine.

Soon he swelled and filled her mouth. He'd never had such a reaction to a woman before. He was ready to fuck her again after two of the most explosive orgasms of his life.

"On your knees," he gritted out. "On the floor, face to the floor."

She released his cock and knelt in front of him, placing her cheek on the floor, her ass in the air. His hands trembled as he palmed her ass.

He leaned over her, positioning his cock at her pussy. He bent his head to nip at her shoulder. Then he murmured in a low voice.

"When I try to fuck your ass, you scream and pretend to faint. Understand?"

"Yes," she whispered, her voice trembling.

He flexed his hips forward, surging into her wet pussy. She felt magnificent. So tight. She fit him like a glove, stroking over his dick like molten lava.

He fucked her slow and easy for several minutes. His mind raced to ready himself for the coming scene. He wasn't sure how many were watching, but they'd come running quick enough. Mia was their paycheck. Hopefully he could disarm them, using the element of surprise, and at least he'd have a gun, a way out.

"Get ready," he mumbled without moving his lips.

He pulled out of her and smacked her ass crudely. "Let's see how you like being ass fucked, slave," he said loudly.

He parted her ass and tucked his cock against the tight, puckered opening. "Now," he whispered.

He rolled his hips forward, pretending to fuck her ass. She let out a scream worthy of any Oscar. Then she slumped forward on the floor.

Jack leaped up. "Goddamn it!" he roared. He whirled around angrily. "What the fuck is up with this?"

As expected, the door burst open and two men rushed in, guns drawn. Drake was behind them, his face angry.

"Stupid bitch fainted. What kind of operation is this?" Jack ranted.

"My apologies," Drake said, his cheek ticking with annoyance. "You can be sure the situation will be remedied. Immediately. She will be punished and better prepared."

Jack waited until Drake took a step closer, and then he struck with deadly speed and precision. He lashed out with his foot, knocking the gun from one guard's hand. He rotated around, kicking the other guard in the gut. As the guard bent over gasping, Jack hit him on the neck with the edge of his hand and the guard went down, unconscious.

The second man lunged for Jack, and he twisted, bearing both of them to the floor. Suddenly the man went limp, and Jack shoved him aside in confusion.

Above him, Mia stood with the gun in her hand. She'd knocked the shit out of the guy with the butt of the pistol. She raised it and shakily pointed it at Drake, who stood there, mouth open in shock.

"Don't move, fucker," she hissed. The gun shook harder as she curled her finger around the trigger.

"Mia, sweetheart," Jack began soothingly. "Let me have the gun. We don't have time. Give me the gun."

Her eyes remained steady, staring at Drake with so much hatred, Jack feared she was going to shoot right there. Not that he'd regret such a slime bucket meeting his maker, but they needed Drake in order to get out alive.

He cautiously wrapped an arm around her shoulders and reached for the gun. "Give it to me, sugar. We need to hurry. There will be others."

She turned to look at him, her blue eyes blazing with so much hurt and anguish it took the breath right out of him. She eased her grip on the gun and handed it to Jack.

Jack took the gun and walked forward, pressing the barrel into Drake's head. "Get my shirt on, Mia."

Mia yanked on the shirt. It hung to her knees covering her nudity, not that it mattered. Better naked than dead in Jack's mind.

"Now get my jeans, sugar."

He pulled them on with one hand while holding the gun on Drake. When he'd finished, he yanked Drake around and began walking toward the door.

As they passed the unconscious guard, Jack bent down to retrieve one of the fallen pistols. He handed it back to Mia. Then he wrapped an arm around Drake's neck and dug the barrel into his temple.

"You won't get away with this," Drake finally spoke. "The house is surrounded. You'll be dead before you can get off the grounds."

"Then I guess you'll be dead too," Jack said harshly.

At the doorway, Jack paused and looked back at Mia. He nodded reassuringly at her. Then he looked down at the gun in her hand. "Know how to use that?"

"I can manage," she said through clenched teeth.

"Then let's get out of here."

CHAPTER 11

*M*ia gripped the pistol with both hands and followed Jack into the hallway. She shook like a leaf, but she wasn't about to be the cause of them getting killed.

The day's events fast caught up to her, and she struggled to cope with the traumatic last few hours.

Ahead of her Jack stopped, nearly causing her to run into him. He paused then whispered back to her.

"There are more in the front room. Get ready and follow my lead."

Panic swelled in her chest, and she shook harder. Would they be able to escape?

As soon as they rounded the corner, Jack nearly dragging Drake, the room exploded into action. Three guards yanked their guns out, pointing them in their direction.

Jack dug the pistol harder into Drake's temple. "Put the guns down or your boss gets it. *Comprende?*"

"Do as he says," Drake gritted out.

One by one, the men slowly dropped their weapons onto the floor.

"Mia, get over by the door," Jack ordered as he sidled in that direction, still dragging Drake along with him.

Mia hurried toward the door, careful to keep her attention on the guards. The gun felt slick in her hand, and she gripped it harder to keep from dropping it.

"I want you to open the door. I want you to dive out, and roll down the incline. And keep going. Don't stop for anything. You understand?"

"What about you?" she asked.

"I'll be behind you. They have guards at the front entrance. There's a winding drive from the front gate to the garage. But just outside the door, there is a drop-off. You'll have to jump over a row of bushes. I'll provide cover fire."

"Okay," she said with more confidence than she felt.

"Go!" he said as he sprang into action.

As Mia reached behind her to yank open the door, Jack shoved Drake across the room toward the guards. She heard shots ring out as she turned around and dove.

She landed with a painful thud, her bare skin scraping along rocks and roots, and she slid down the incline. She threw out a hand to stop herself and crawled frantically back toward the top. She didn't care what Jack had told her; she wasn't going to leave him to die saving her ass.

She gripped the gun in one hand while she struggled for a handhold with the other. Pain sliced down her leg, and she felt a warm trickle. She must have cut herself in the fall.

Gunshots above her spurred her faster up the hill. When she reached the hedge, she tunneled through the prickly branches to peer out the other side. Lights from the house illuminated the area enough so that she saw Jack taking cover behind one of the large wooden columns on the porch.

He was taking fire from at least three locations. Bullets peppered the column, splintering pieces of wood in all directions. Mia looked frantically toward where the shots were coming from, searching for a target she could aim for.

She raised the pistol, holding it steady in both hands. When she saw one of the gunmen edge around the side of the house, she squeezed off a shot. He dropped to the ground.

"Take that, motherfucker," Mia muttered.

"Mia, goddamn it. I told you to get the hell out of here," Jack shouted.

"Tough shit," she said under her breath.

She jumped as a bullet plowed through the hedge just above her head. She scooted back and returned fire, blindly, moving her hand from side to side.

She heard a thump then found herself propelled backward as Jack pulled her out of the bushes. He rolled down the hill, taking her with him.

Pain sliced through her body. Dirt filled her mouth, and her hair caught on sticks and rocks as they bumped and slid to a stop in the ditch.

Gunshots peppered the ground around them, and she heard Jack let out a curse of pain. He yanked her against his body and rolled her underneath him.

His heart hammered against her chest, and his breath came in ragged spurts. But he didn't stop. He yanked her up when they reached the stone fence surrounding the estate. It was only about five feet high, but getting over it without getting shot would be tricky.

Jack didn't give her time to contemplate just how they would accomplish the feat. He simply picked her up and shoved her over. She landed in a heap, and seconds later, Jack fell beside her amidst the sound of gunfire. He dragged her further down the incline until they landed in the ditch by the road.

"Jack, are you shot?" she asked.

He didn't answer right away so she shoved at him.

"Be still," he ordered. "Give me a minute."

They lay there a few more seconds in the deep ditch, the ground hard beneath her back. Finally he eased off of her, rolling to the side.

"We're going to run for the woods. If we can get deep enough, we can lose them."

The thought of running through deep woods, barefooted and half-naked, frightened her. But then the idea of staying put and being shot was even scarier.

Jack rose with difficulty, and it was then she felt a drop of blood splash onto her face. Jack's blood.

"You *are* hit," she whispered.

"It's just a scratch," he said. "Come on, let's go before they make it down with searchlights."

Hand in hand, they ran for the cover of the trees across the road. They plunged into the dense thicket and ran blindly through the underbrush.

After what seemed forever, Jack slowed.

"We need to find a place to hide and regroup."

His voice sounded strained, as if he were in pain. A flash of panic speared Mia's stomach. What if he was badly wounded? There was no way she could get them both out of the woods safely.

They settled for a deep ravine, nearly dry since there had been no recent rainfall. They slid down the embankment and leaned against the hard dirt wall.

"Where were you hit?" Mia demanded as she ran her hands over his body.

"Don't worry about me," he said shortly. "Are you okay?"

He gripped her shoulders in his hands and pulled her up against his chest.

She yanked away. "I'm fine, Jack. Thanks to you. Now tell me where you're hit, damn it."

"My arm," he said. "It's just a graze. Don't even think the bullet penetrated."

She reached up, feeling her way in the darkness. His upper arm was wet and sticky with blood. Using her thumb, she gently felt for the wound. He winced when she slid over the gash.

"Sorry."

He raised his free hand up to her cheek. "I'm sorry, Mia. I'm sorry for what you had to go through."

Her cheeks grew hot. How could she possibly explain to him that what should have been the most humiliating experience of her life had been the most sexually fulfilling one? As much as it shamed her to admit, she'd forgotten everything once Jack had touched her. Forgotten they were being watched, that she was going to be sold like a piece of real estate.

For the space of a few stolen moments, she'd been his.

"I'm the one who's sorry," she said quietly. "It's my fault we're in this mess."

"And I want to hear all about it as soon as we get out of this mess alive."

A knot formed in her throat. How would he react when he found out what she'd been arrested for? She felt more shame over that than she did stripping or any of the things she'd been forced to do since her arrest. Jack would never understand.

"I think the bleeding has slowed down," she said. The blood felt thicker and stickier against her hand. "I wish I had something to wrap your arm in so it wouldn't get dirt in it."

"Too late," he said. "Besides between the two of us, we don't have a lot in the way of clothing."

There was a hint of humor in his dry tones, and she laughed. She put her hand over her mouth to quell the sound, but the laughter turned to an almost hysterical sound.

God, get it together for Pete's sake. This was no time to act like a freaking girly girl. They were being chased and shot at, and the last thing Jack needed was a weak twit.

She stifled the last of the desperate sounds, nearly choking as she swallowed them back. "I'm sorry," she mumbled.

He leaned forward and kissed her forehead, holding his lips there for a long moment.

"We should go. I need to get to a phone. I called one of my buddies with the Rangers before I went to get you. We can't trust anyone in this town, particularly the local cops."

"Tell me about it," Mia said under her breath.

"Are you hurt anywhere?" he asked as he stood to his full height.

"No," she lied.

She had numerous cuts and bruises. Knew her leg was bleeding, but it was nothing life threatening, and she didn't need him worrying about her when their priority was finding a way to elude their pursuers.

"Which way?" she asked.

"We'll follow the ravine," he said. "We can move quieter since the bottom is sandy and rocky."

Not to mention how much easier it would be on their feet.

When they'd traveled a half mile or so down the deep ditch, an idea struck Mia. She put her hand out to Jack and stopped in her tracks.

"What's wrong?" he asked sharply.

"Jack, I know where we can go. I have a friend. He lives in the next county, and his buddy is a sheriff's deputy there. We can trust them. Maybe they can help us until your people get here."

"Just who is this friend?" Jack asked. "And how do you know we can trust him?"

"His name is Ryder. His buddy's name is Mac. We used to spend a lot of time together. Mac isn't active duty because he was injured awhile back. They're supposed to leave town soon, but when I spoke to Ryder a few days ago, he said they weren't leaving for a week."

"Is he the big biker dude by chance?" Jack asked dryly.

Mia glanced over at him in the darkness, trying to get a read on his expression. "How do you know what he looks like?"

"I saw you with him that first night. At the bar."

"He came to say good-bye," she said softly. "He's been a good friend to me."

"The question is how we get to these friends of yours," he cut in.

"Ryder gave me his cell number. If we could reach a phone, we could call him and he could come get us. If Mac came with him, the local cops wouldn't be suspicious."

"Which means we still have to find a phone," Jack pointed out. "Which we aren't going to do standing here in the middle of nowhere."

"Yeah," Mia muttered as Jack took off in front of her again.

She followed behind him as they trekked further into the woods. The ravine narrowed in places, and in some areas it held water. They sloshed through the mud, and Mia was grateful they couldn't see. She didn't want to know what they were stepping on or around.

"I see a light up ahead," Jack called back in a quiet voice. "Might be a main road or maybe a business."

He reached back and caught her hand in his. The small gesture made her pulse race, this time not from adrenaline-laced fear. She felt safe, as ridiculous as it seemed. When he touched her, she felt as if nothing could hurt her.

They crept closer toward the distant twinkle. The ravine widened, and water crept up to their ankles. A distant rumble echoed, and Jack yanked her down, his body hovering protectively over hers.

"It's a car," he whispered. "We came out by a road."

They waited as the sound drew closer. It grew louder as it passed in front of them and then began to recede in the distance.

Jack slowly got up. "Stay here just a minute. Let me take a look around."

Mia huddled in the water, shivering, not from cold, but from fatigue as the last of her adrenaline-induced high faded.

A few minutes later, Jack slid down the bank of the ravine and put his hands around her shoulders.

"There's a house about a half mile across the field. No one's home that I can tell. If we're lucky, there's a phone there we can use."

"And maybe some clothes I can steal," she muttered.

Jack helped her up the steep embankment, and they staggered the short distance to the gravel road.

"We need to hurry. Can you make it?" he asked.

"Let's go," she said by way of answering.

They ran across the road and into the field. A single dusk-to-dawn light illuminated their path, and as they crossed into the ditch on the other side, she glanced at the leaning mailbox next to the long winding driveway. She committed the address and the county road number to heart before running as fast as she could to catch up with Jack.

The rocks dug painfully into the soles of her feet. Warm blood ran freely down her leg, and sharp thorns slapped at her knees. Cramps rippled up her sides, knotting under her ribs, robbing her of breath.

They circled to the back of the run-down house. An old, beat-up car was parked in a garage in the back, and a single lamp shone from one of the windows of the house.

"Do you think anyone's home?" she whispered.

Jack squatted behind the garage and caught his breath. "I'll need to get a closer look. I need to get in touch with Kenny and

give him some more information. I don't want him coming in
blind, but it's probably better to do that once we've hooked up
with your cop friend."

"So what do we do?" she asked.

"Hope no one's home," Jack said. "Come on. We're not getting
anywhere by sitting out here."

They hurried toward the back door. Jack drew his gun and
pressed himself flat against the house. He peered into the window
and motioned for her to keep still.

"There's no one in the kitchen. The rest of the house is dark.
They're either gone or asleep. I see a cordless phone on the
counter. Wait here. I'm going to go in and get it. You can use it out
here."

Mia held her breath as Jack tested the door. To her relief, it
wasn't locked, and it opened noiselessly. He disappeared inside,
and she gripped the gun tighter.

Two minutes later, he returned, phone in hand. He gestured for
her to follow him the short distance to the garage.

"We can hide here while you make the call," he said as he
thrust the receiver into her hand.

CHAPTER 12

*T*he dusk-to-dawn light over the garage cast a pale glow over their hiding place adjacent to the old building, and Jack listened as Mia spoke in low tones over the telephone. It chapped his ass to have to ask Biker Boy for help, but he also knew he didn't stand much of a chance of getting him and Mia out of this alive without it.

He was injured and so was she. He'd noticed the blood down her leg as well as the other numerous cuts and bruises. But she'd never complained. Not once. He'd underestimated her.

What had happened to her in the hours she'd spent before he'd come for her? He wanted Drake. Wanted to kill him for daring to touch Mia. He just prayed that he'd arrived in time to spare her any harsh treatment at Drake's hands.

Mia turned around, the phone in her hand. "They're coming for us," she said softly.

"How long?" Jack asked.

"Thirty minutes maybe," she said with a shrug.

"Come here," he directed.

She walked into his arms, and he pulled her tightly against him. Then he turned her around and tugged up her shirt. His hands smoothed over her body, searching for injuries, reassuring himself that she was okay. After he rotated her back around, he caught her wrists in his hands and frowned at the chafing he saw. Rope burns. He bent his neck and kissed the inside of each wrist.

"What did they do to you?" he asked hoarsely.

She looked earnestly up at him, her blue eyes shining in the dim light. "Just what you see," she said. "Nothing else."

He pressed his forehead to hers. "I'm sorry, Mia. Sorry for what I had to do. I can only hope you don't hate me when all of this is over with."

She curled her arms around his neck. Her small body melted into his, and he closed his eyes in pleasure. He loved the way she fit against him. So soft and sweet.

"I don't hate you," she whispered.

He held her tightly, stroking her matted hair. "You should. What I did was unforgivable."

To his surprise, she pulled away then slowly pressed her lips to his. Featherlight, so soft and achingly sweet. He didn't move, afraid to ruin the moment. Instead, he let her dictate the action.

"You saved me," she said against his lips. "How can that be unforgivable?"

He stared at her for a long second. She surprised him at every turn. He'd always viewed her as delicate. In need of taking care of. It was a role he was suited to play. This new look at her unsettled him. Maybe she didn't need him as much as he'd always liked to think. Far from being weak, she had a thread of steel woven into her deceptively fragile-looking exterior.

Maybe he needed *her*. And that disturbed him.

"We should get out of here before the owners return home," he said. "We can wait in the ravine again. It's deep enough that we can't be seen from the road."

She curled her hand trustingly into his, and they crept across the field, staying low to the ground. When they reached the road, he looked left and right then shoved Mia forward. They ran as fast as they could to the other side and slid haphazardly down into the gully.

He collected her in his arms and held her as they waited. After several long minutes, he asked, "What does your friend drive?"

"A red Dodge truck," she replied. "They're good people, Jack," she said as though sensing his hesitation to trust complete strangers.

"Yeah, well, let's hope your cop friend isn't in league with the cops here."

"He's not," she said simply.

As the minutes wore on, she slumped in his arms, her body wilting against his. He stroked her head and kissed the back of her neck. His arm hurt like hell, but at least the bleeding had slowed to a trickle. A good cleaning and a bandage and he'd be fine. It was Mia he worried about. He hadn't been able to do more than a cursory inspection of her injuries in the dim light by the garage.

When he heard the sound of an approaching vehicle, he tensed. Mia stirred against him, and he put a finger to her lips.

"I'll check it out," he murmured. "Stay here until I call for you."

He gripped his gun and climbed up the incline. A truck drove toward them, headlights off. Smart thinking on their part; otherwise, Jack wouldn't have been able to see anything in the glare.

But still, he wasn't taking any chances. He waited until the truck was almost on him, then he sprinted to the middle of the road, drew his gun and stood pointing his weapon at the driver's side of the truck.

The truck slammed to a halt, and in two seconds, Jack found

himself staring down the barrel of a gun. Mexican standoff. Only neither of them was Mexican.

Another man got out of the passenger seat, ignoring Jack's presence completely. Biker Boy.

"Mia?" Biker Boy called out. "Where are you, little girl?"

Jack had to hand it to him. At least Biker Boy sounded concerned. The other guy—Mac, presumably—hadn't said a damn thing. Just continued to point his weapon at Jack.

Then Mac spoke.

"I don't particularly like being drawn on, especially by someone who I left a warm bed in the middle of the night to help."

Jack relaxed his grip on his gun and tucked it into the waist of his pants. He hurried over to where Mia still hid and leaned down to give her his hand.

"It's safe. You can come on up now."

He pulled her to stand beside him, and she went immediately to Biker Boy.

Mac walked around to where they all stood, though his gun was still gripped in his hand.

"I suggest we don't stand around exchanging pleasantries. Let's get the fuck out of here," Mac said.

"You're hurt, little girl," Biker Boy said to Mia as he hugged her up tight.

"I'm fine, Ryder. Let's go, please."

Jack curled a possessive arm around her waist and helped her into the extended cab of the truck. Ryder slid into the front, and Mac hurried around to the driver's side.

As they drove off, Mac looked into the rearview mirror at Jack. "Suppose you tell me what the hell is going on."

Jack put an arm around Mia, pulling her over to lie against him. "My name is Jack Kincaid. I'm a Texas Ranger. Earlier tonight, Mia was kidnapped and was going to be forced onto the auction block to be sold as a sex slave."

Ryder sucked in his breath. "Son of a bitch!"

"How do the local police play into this?" Mac asked. "Ryder said Mia told him they couldn't be trusted."

"They can't," Mia spoke up quietly.

They drove for several minutes, turning out from the gravel road onto a paved highway.

"Get down," Mac ordered grimly. "There's a roadblock up ahead. I don't know what the hell is going on, but I hope you're telling me the truth, because I'm about to lie through my front teeth."

Jack immediately shoved Mia to the floorboard then lay over her. Ryder threw a couple of gym bags from the front on top of Jack. What the hell was in those things? Bricks?

The truck slowed, and Jack held his breath. He heard Mac say something, presumably as he flashed his badge. Then he listened to one of the cops rattle off a spiel about some crazed psycho on the loose and a woman wanted for drug possession.

In a few seconds, they drove away, and Jack relaxed again.

"Y'all can get up now," Mac called back. "Coast is clear."

Jack crawled back onto the seat and helped Mia up beside him. "Did I hurt you?" he asked in a low voice.

She shook her head and nestled into his side.

"We're not far from my house," Mac said.

Fifteen minutes later, they pulled into the driveway of a small frame-house. Mac and Ryder piled out, and Jack slid out of the back seat. He held his arms out for Mia, and she crawled out beside him. She stood, trying to straighten and pull down her shirt to an acceptable length.

They entered the house, and Jack saw a small woman hurl herself toward Mac. But what surprised him more was that after she laid one hell of a scorching kiss on Mac, she turned and did the same to Biker Boy.

Then she turned her stare on Mia, and her eyes narrowed. Jack fixed her with his most ferocious scowl. He didn't need some snot-nosed woman looking down at Mia.

Mac responded by stepping in front of Kit and folding his arms across his chest. He glared at Jack.

"Look, guys," Mia broke in tiredly. "Can we dispense with all the testosterone? I promise Kit and I aren't going to pull each others' hair out."

Ryder looked over at Mia in concern. "Why don't you go take a shower and clean up, little girl. I'll get you some fresh clothes."

"We both could do with a shower," Jack said, letting the others make what they wanted of the statement.

Ryder raised a brow. "No problem. I'll show you to the bathroom, and I'll get something for you both to put on."

Jack put a hand to Mia's back and guided her ahead of him as they followed Ryder into a large bedroom. Ryder gestured toward the bathroom.

"I'll leave some clothes out on the bed for you."

"Thanks, Ryder," Mia said.

"Anytime, little girl."

As soon as Ryder left the room, Jack ushered Mia into the bathroom.

"What the hell was all that about? I feel like I entered the twilight zone."

Mia laughed. "Mac, Ryder and Kit have a unique relationship, I guess you could say."

Jack raised a brow. "You mean they're together? Biker Boy swings both ways?"

"No! Oh good grief, no." She broke off choking with laughter. "Oh Lord, if Mac or Ryder heard you say that, they'd probably kill you. They, uhm, well, they share Kit."

Jack shot her a look of disbelief. "That is fucked up. No way I'd share my woman with another man."

She looked at him for a long moment, her eyes sparking with heat. "No, I don't guess you would."

He turned the shower on then slipped out of his torn jeans. He reached for the hem of Mia's shirt and slowly pulled it over her head. He watched carefully, examining her body language for signs that he was pushing her too hard. All he found was answering desire.

He stepped under the warm spray and pulled her inside with him. As the water poured down over them, he placed both hands at her head and lowered his lips to kiss her.

Water beaded and rolled over the tips of her breasts. Her nipples puckered and became hard points. He couldn't resist touching them, cupping the soft mounds and tweaking the nipples with his fingertips.

He poured shampoo into his hand and lathered her hair. He soaped the rest of her body, taking care not to hurt the scrapes and scratches. He cleaned the dirt and blood from her legs, and took special care to wash the large gash on her calf.

Then he soaped his own body, hurriedly rinsing so he could turn his attention back to Mia. He held her under the spray, washing the soap and grime from her body. His hands rubbed and caressed, trying to banish every touch except his.

She moaned against him, such a sweet sound of surrender. He had to have her. Right here, right now.

"I want you," he whispered in her ear. It wasn't a request. Rather it was a demand, said as gently as he could, considering his raging need.

He picked her up easily, hoisting her up his body. His cock strained and bulged outward. Holding her with one arm, he reached for his penis, positioning it at her pussy. Then he slid her down onto it.

She wrapped her legs around his waist, locking her ankles together. He cupped her ass with both hands, pushing her up and down as his cock slid easily to her depths.

He fucked her with urgency. They didn't have time for a slow round of lovemaking, not that he could promise her one anyway. They came together in an explosion of need and adrenaline. The sound of her ass slapping against his thighs rose over the rushing water.

As he felt his balls tighten, he bent his head and sank his teeth into the soft skin of her neck. She gasped in his ear and clutched him harder with her hands.

He came in a rush, filling her with his hot release. He knew she hadn't yet reached her peak. He slammed against her twice more, draining himself completely.

He reached up and turned the water off then hauled her out of the shower. Not wanting her to ease down from her impending orgasm, he set her on the counter and spread her legs wide.

Her pussy, dark pink from his thrusts, spread open to him, soft and inviting. Her damp curls, dark against her pale flesh, glistened with her moisture and his seed.

He plunged two fingers into her, using his thumb to roll over her clit. He positioned his other hand between her ass cheeks. Using one finger, he gently brushed against her tight anal opening.

Continuing his thrusts with one hand, he inserted one finger into her anus. She clenched her muscles against the invasion and let out a soft moan.

Her body writhed restlessly on the counter. She squirmed with unfulfilled need.

"How close are you?" he growled in a low voice.

"Oh God," she panted. "Please don't stop."

"I have no intention of stopping, sugar. I want you to come all over my hand."

He slid a second finger into her ass, and she went wild. She bucked against him as he drove her to higher pleasure. Her pussy sucked at his fingers and flooded with moisture.

"That's it," he purred. "Let yourself go."

He pinched at her clit, and her body spasmed and went limp. He carefully withdrew his fingers and gathered her in his arms as the last of her shudders wracked her body.

"Let's get dressed and see about getting out of this mess."

CHAPTER 13

*M*ia walked on shaky legs into the bedroom where Ryder had laid out clothing for her and Jack. She was running on empty. Somehow she managed to pull on the shirt and sweats before her legs gave out and she slumped onto the bed.

In front of her, Jack pulled on a T-shirt and a pair of pants that were a bit too large for him. He moved closer to her and cupped her chin in his hand.

"I know you're tired. Let's go talk to your friends. I need to call Kenny and see how far out he is. He should be rolling in soon. I promise when this is over, you can sleep for a week."

She tried to smile but couldn't quite muster the energy. Emitting a long sigh, she stood up and walked toward the door.

Mac, Ryder and Kit all stood in the living room and looked up when she and Jack walked out. Mac eyed them impatiently, his arms crossed over his chest.

"Which one of you is going to tell me what the hell is going on?" Mac demanded.

Jack slipped his hand over Mia's. "The asshole who owns the strip club in the next county tried to auction Mia off earlier tonight. If I hadn't shown up, and if we hadn't shot our way out of there, Mia would be well on her way to some jerk who'd keep her as a sex slave."

Mac's expression darkened. Beside him, Ryder swore softly.

"And you didn't go to the local police why?" Mac asked.

"Because they're in on it," Mia spoke up softly.

Jack looked sideways at her, his eyes probing.

Mac looked kindly at her. "Maybe you should sit down before you fall down and explain what you mean."

Kit still looked guardedly at her, but her eyes had softened some. "Can I get you something to drink?" she asked.

Mia shook her head and sat down on the couch. Jack remained standing.

"I think the judge is in league with them too," Mia said. She took a deep breath, knowing she'd have to come clean with the entire story.

"Six months ago, I drove into town. Wasn't planning to stay long. I stopped at a local burger joint and when I came back out, my car wouldn't start. One of the local cops said he had a brother-in-law who owned a repair shop. Had it towed over there, found out it was going to cost me several hundred dollars to fix. Money I didn't have," she added lamely.

She kept her gaze down, not wanting to meet Jack's stare. "The garage owner said he had a little job he needed done, and if I'd help him out, he'd wave the costs of the repairs. I jumped at it. He wanted me to deliver a duffel bag across town to an address, so I did it."

She heard a groan but wasn't sure who it came from. She didn't look up to see. She twisted her hands in her lap, and continued on.

"Halfway across town I got pulled over. By the same cop who'd arranged for my tow to the garage. He searched the car and found drugs in the duffel bag. He arrested me and took me into jail."

"Son of a bitch," Jack spat out. "Classic setup."

"Before they booked me, fingerprinted me, did anything, Martin showed up."

"Who's Martin?" Mac interrupted.

"He's the guy who owns the strip club," Mia replied. "Anyway, he showed up and made this big deal out of bailing me out, said if I'd come to work for him, he'd make sure things got straightened out. I found out later he expected me to strip for him. At first I refused, but he made it clear, as did the asshole cop, that I'd promptly be arrested and put away for drug possession if I didn't do what I was told. They hinted strongly that the judge was a 'close friend' and would render a rather harsh sentence."

"Goddamn," Jack said, slapping his fist into his hand. "I'm going to kill those sons of bitches."

Mia looked up at him for the first time. She swallowed heavily. "Jack, I knew what was in that duffel bag. I knew what he was asking me to do. I did it anyway. I'm *guilty*. If this all blows up, I'll be going to jail on drug-possession charges."

Jack stared back at her for a long time, his eyes glittering with anger.

"And I'm telling you, if I had made sure you were taken care of, none of this would have ever happened."

"So he's the asshole who hurt you," Ryder said, realization reflected in his voice. "I always wondered who put those shadows in your eyes."

"Ryder, please," she said.

Jack jerked his head in Ryder's direction. "Yeah, I'm that asshole. The same asshole who isn't going to stand by and let her be hurt again."

"Can we keep to the matter at hand?" Mac asked, holding his

hands up. "We've got problems. If old Judge Allen is in cahoots with this Martin and at least one of the cops, you can bet that the sheriff is involved as well. They go way back."

He turned to Jack. "You might want to get your Ranger buddies in here. The problem is, we have no hard evidence, and we can't go around arresting law enforcement personnel, not to mention judges who've been around longer than dirt, without proof."

"We need Martin and Drake, the asshole who was going to auction Mia off," Jack muttered. "If we can get those two, chances are they'll sing."

"I don't want to go to jail," Mia whispered, shutting her eyes tightly as the nightmare of the last six months hovered like a cement block over her head.

Jack got down on his knees in front of her. He gathered her hands in his and stared into her eyes. "You won't go to jail, Mia. You were set up from the beginning. I won't let you go. Do you understand that? I know I've let you down, but I need you to trust me now. Can you do that?"

She slowly nodded, and savage satisfaction rolled across Jack's face. He hauled her up against him and kissed her long and hard. When he finally let her go, her lips were hot and swollen.

He stood up and looked over at Mac. "I'll call Kenny, but I need to go after Martin and Drake. If we can get to them, we'll have what we need to go after the rest. Who can you trust in your force?"

"Let me make a few calls myself," Mac said. "We may not do this by the books, but we'll get it done nonetheless."

Jack grinned. "You're my kind of guy."

The next hour blurred by in a flash of phone calls and the arrival of more cops. Mia watched in a daze from the couch. She huddled there, wrapped in a blanket.

"Ryder told me you nearly kicked his ass when he walked away from me."

Mia looked up to see Kit standing by the couch. She smiled slightly. "I told him he was a dumbass."

"Can I sit?" Kit asked.

Mia shrugged.

Kit sighed. "Look, I know you don't like me, and well, I don't like you much. You're much too pretty, and Ryder has seen your tits. But I'm sorry for what happened to you."

Mia choked back a laugh. "Would it make you feel better to know half the men in this part of Texas have seen my tits?"

"I'm only letting you in my house because Mac hasn't seen them," Kit said dryly.

Mia relaxed a little. No, she and Kit would never be friends, but she appreciated the other woman's honesty. And she wasn't about to tell her that Mac *had* seen her tits. He'd been in the club when she'd danced before.

The clicking and clacking of guns, the rustle of vests, the room echoed with the sounds of a dozen men, all readying themselves for action. They talked, planned and muttered.

Finally they were ready to leave. Jack knelt in front of Mia.

"I'll be back soon. We'll get you out of this, Mia. I swear it."

She leaned forward and kissed him hungrily. "Hurry," she whispered.

Jack stood back up and stared over at Ryder. "You're staying with them, right?"

"Well, I'm not a cop," Ryder said lazily. "No way I'd leave Kit girl or Mia alone."

A look of understanding passed between the two men. Kit hurried over to Mac.

"Please be careful," she said in a husky voice. "I don't want you hurt again."

Mac kissed her, his lips roving across Kit's possessively. "I'll be fine, baby. You stay here so Ryder can look after you. I'll be back when I can."

Mia watched as they walked out the door. She couldn't help the shaft of fear that cut through her chest. Jack was going out to fight her battles. She should be with him, not here, letting him do the fighting for her.

"I'm going to fix us something to eat," Kit said as the door closed behind the men. "You need to eat something. When was the last time you ate?"

"I don't remember," Mia admitted.

Kit walked into the kitchen, leaving Mia and Ryder alone in the living room.

"You okay, little girl?"

Mia shook her head. "I'm scared. I don't want anyone hurt because of my mistakes."

They sat in silence. Kit brought in a plate of sandwiches and a pitcher of tea. Mia picked at her food, her heart not into eating.

As they sat in the living room, watching the hours tick by, a knock sounded at the door.

Ryder stood up. "Kit, you and Mia go into the kitchen and stay there. I'll see who's at the door."

Mia followed Kit into the kitchen, her pulse hammering at her temples. She went to the sink and ran water in her hands, splashing her face in an attempt to dispel the fear eating at her.

"I'm not sticking around in here," Kit muttered. "I don't know who's at the door, but I'm not about to let Ryder get himself into trouble."

Over a stripper. Kit didn't need to hear the rest. Kit's expression pretty much said it all, and Mia couldn't blame her. She wouldn't like the man she loved to risk his life for a nobody.

Mia followed close behind. When they entered the living room, Mia froze. Standing next to Ryder were two cops. Two Buford County cops.

"Mia Nichols?" one of them asked as they stepped forward.

Ryder swore. "I told you to stay in the kitchen."

"We have a warrant for your arrest, Miss Nichols. Put your hands behind your back and turn around."

Mia stared at the two officers in horror. "What are the charges?" she croaked, though she knew. She *knew*.

"Drug possession and prostitution," one of them answered.

The other walked up to her and grabbed her arm, spinning her around. He twisted one wrist behind her and clamped cuffs on her. Then he bent her other arm and secured her other wrist.

He began reciting her Miranda rights in a firm voice.

"Ryder, do something!" Kit cried.

"No!" Mia spoke up. "Don't do anything stupid. I'm not worth you getting hurt or killed. Just please, find Jack. Tell him what's happened."

Ryder looked torn between tearing the two officers apart and heeding what Mia had said.

"You can't leave Kit here alone, Ryder. You'll only get arrested. Think," she pleaded. "My only hope is if you tell Jack what's happened."

Ryder swore long and hard. "Don't worry, Mia. Kit and I will be down to stay with you."

"Stay here," Mia begged. "Please. You need to be here when Jack gets back. Don't worry about me, okay?"

The officers herded her out to a squad car and unceremoniously stuffed her in the back. Her worst fears were coming true. She was going to jail. How would Jack be able to help her now?

CHAPTER 14

*M*ia sat in the corner of the small jail cell, her knees huddled to her chest. They'd printed her, photographed her, read her rights and stuffed her in a cell. Everything by the book. She was arrested on an outstanding warrant for drug possession and a more recent charge of prostitution.

No matter what happened tonight with Martin, the sheriff or the judge, she was still stuck here in a jail cell, her sins entered in the books. She'd have to pay the piper.

A sound down the hall alerted her to another presence. She stood up and raced toward the door. Was Jack here? As she pressed herself against the bars, straining to see, her chest tightened in dread. It wasn't Jack. It was the cop who'd originally arrested her. The one who'd set her up.

She shrank back, retreating to the back of the cell. The cop—what was his name? Danny? David? Like it mattered. Dickhead was more appropriate.

"Well, well, well, if it isn't Mia Nichols."

Keys jangled and clinked as he unlocked her cell. Panic and uncertainty swelled in her throat. What was he going to do? There was no one around to stop him, not that they would. The whole fucking department was crooked.

He swaggered into the cell and shut the door behind him. He leered openly at her as he closed the distance between them.

"What do you want?" she demanded with more bravado than she felt.

"If I were you, I'd be nicer to me," he chided.

He reached and ran a hand down her cheek. She flinched away. He backhanded her, splitting her lip.

She raised her hand to her face, shocked by the speed in which he'd struck. Blood shone on her fingers when she pulled her hand away from her throbbing cheek.

He grabbed her by the front of her neck and hauled her to a standing position. His fingers pressed into her throat, and his breath blew hot over her face.

"We have some unfinished business, bitch. You always thought you were too good for me. Now you aren't so high and mighty."

With his other hand, he ripped at her neckline, tearing the shirt down the middle. She struggled wildly against him, but his hand tightened around her throat until spots danced in her vision.

His mouth closed over hers, kissing and thrusting his tongue into her mouth until she gagged. Helpless tears rolled down her cheeks as he ground his pelvis against her belly. She could feel his hard erection and knew if she didn't do something to stop him, he was going to rape her right here in the cell.

He shoved her against the wall and held her there with one hand while he ripped at her pants. If he would only let go of her throat.

Finally he released her neck as he reached down to undo his belt. She gulped in great big breaths, trying to make the dizziness dissipate. She waited, biding her time, enduring his groping, waiting for the perfect moment to strike.

When he pulled out his cock, she struck with all the pent up fury she'd been harboring for six months. She rammed her knee into his groin, sending him sprawling backward, howling in pain.

She wasted no time. She leaped on him, grasping his quickly shriveling dick in her hand and twisting for all she was worth. She doubled her free hand into a fist and punched him in the face over and over.

"Fucking bitch!" he screamed.

He threw a punch, connecting with her jaw. She fell off him and struggled against the blackness overtaking her. She couldn't pass out. He'd rape her whether she was awake or not. The bastard was not going to get away with abusing her.

He leaped on her, grabbing her arms and forcing them over her head. She retaliated by head-butting him in the nose. Blood squirted like a fountain. He let go of one of her hands and grasped his face.

Then he balled his hand into a fist and punched her in the stomach. All the breath sucked right out of her, leaving her wheezing for breath.

Sheer determination kept her wits from fleeing. She raked at his face with her nails, then she jabbed him in the eyes as hard as she could.

He fell off her, clutching his injured face. She rolled away, scrambling to her feet. She heard footsteps pounding down the hallway.

She glanced up, her hopes fading. It was another cop. Helpless rage rushed through her veins. There was no way she could fight off two of them.

"What the fuck is going on here?" the cop demanded as he fumbled with the keys to unlock the cell.

He rushed in, and Mia shrank to the far side of the cell. They may well carry out their plan, but she wouldn't go down without fighting. She waited, collecting her strength, waiting for the second man to strike.

"Fucking bitch attacked me," Dickhead said as he staggered to his feet.

The second cop looked at him in disgust. "You're a dumb son of a bitch, Moreland. Things are going to hell in a handbasket. Martin and Drake have been arrested, and you risk everything for a piece of ass."

Moreland wiped at the blood still running from his nose and reached down to hike up his jeans. "Fucking bitch needs to be taught a lesson."

"Save it," the other cop said. "I suggest you get the hell out of here and get cleaned up."

Moreland shot Mia another look of pure hatred as he started for the cell door. He stopped and pointed a finger back at her. "This isn't finished, bitch."

Mia tensed as the other cop walked over to her and got into her face.

"If you know what's good for you, you'll forget what just happened here."

After issuing the threat, he spun around and stalked out of the cell, slamming it shut behind him.

They disappeared down the hall, and Mia started to shake uncontrollably. She sank down to the floor, holding her face in her hands. Nausea rolled in her stomach, and she crawled over to the corner and retched.

Afterward, she picked herself up and hobbled over to the small cot. She hurt from head to toe. Gathering her tattered shirt around her quaking body, she squeezed her eyes shut and waited. Waited for Jack. Prayed he'd find her in time.

*   *   *

Jack stared at Mac, his jaw clenched so tight he thought he'd break his teeth. "What do you mean Mia was arrested?"

Mac ran a hand through his short hair. "That was Ryder on the phone. Two cops showed up at the house with a warrant for Mia's arrest. Drug possession and prostitution."

"Prostitution? What the fuck?"

The two stood outside the Clark County Police Station where Martin and Drake had been taken in for questioning. Jack wanted to be the interrogating officer, but Kenny had shoved him out of the building.

"Goddamn it," Jack swore. "Where would they take her?"

"Ryder said they were Buford County so I'm sure they took her to the county lockup."

Jack swore again. "We've got to get her out of there. I don't trust those motherfuckers as far as I can throw them."

"It's going to be hard unless Martin or Drake sings loud enough for us to get warrants for the arrests we need. Until then we'll have a hard time getting a judge to agree to let her go."

Jack started for the door of the police station. "Then we better make damn sure they talk. I'm not letting her spend the night in some jail cell."

He nearly collided with Kenny at the door.

"We've got what we need. I've got arrest warrants being issued for the sheriff, county judge and a few sheriff's deputies over in Buford County. We're heading over there now if you want to come."

"Mia's been arrested," Jack said. "I'm going over to see about her. I want her out. I want the charges dropped. See to it quick. They're all a bunch of bullshit."

"Will do, man. I'll meet you over there as soon as I can get a judge to sign off."

Jack nodded and hurried back to where Mac was still standing. "I need a ride," he said curtly.

Mac nodded. "Get in."

CHAPTER 15

$\mathcal{A}$s they roared into the parking lot of the Buford County Jail, Jack jumped out of the truck and hit the pavement at a full run. He burst into the front entrance, startling the cop sitting at the desk.

Jack flashed his badge. "I'm Jack Kincaid with the Texas Rangers. I understand you're holding Mia Nichols here."

Something in the cop's eyes glinted. He looked a little uneasy before saying, "Sorry, we don't have a prisoner here by that name."

Jack exploded forward, hauling the cop over the desk. "You tell me where she is, or I swear to God, I'll kill you right here, right now."

"Jack, hold up," Mac said from the door.

The cop drew his weapon, pointing it at Jack. "Put me down, asshole. I don't give a fuck who you are. I'll arrest you for assaulting a police officer."

"Shut the fuck up, dirtbag," Mac growled.

He walked forward pointing his gun at the Buford County cop. "Drop the weapon. Jack, put him down."

Jack threw the cop back across the desk. He landed with a thump in the chair, nearly vaulting it backward.

"Now," Mac said, "tell us where Mia Nichols is."

"Cell three," the cop muttered.

"Give me the fucking keys," Jack demanded.

The cop dug into his pocket then tossed a ring of keys in Jack's direction.

"You go on back," Mac said to Jack. "I'll keep an eye on our friend until Kenny gets here."

Jack raced down the hallway, bolting through the door at the end. He passed two cells before stopping at the third. His eyes jerked to the far side where Mia lay curled in a tight ball on the cot. He jammed the keys in the lock and threw open the cell.

He rushed over to where Mia lay, his heart in his throat.

"Mia?" he whispered.

He hesitantly touched her shoulder. A knot formed in his throat when he felt her shaking. He gently turned her over. Fury, hot and raging, washed over him when he caught sight of her bloodied face. Worse, her throat was one big bruise. Some bastard had tried to strangle her.

Her shirt fell open, a long tear down the middle. A fist-sized bruise covered the right side of her ribs.

"Oh my God. Mia, honey, are you all right?"

Tears streaked down her cheeks as he gently folded her into his arms. God, he wanted to cry. Wanted to howl in fury. She trembled against him, her small body shaking in his arms.

"What did they do to you?" he choked out.

"I'm so glad you're here," she whispered. "I was so scared."

Jack pulled her away so he could see her face. His fingers carefully trailed down her cheek, wiping her hair from her face. He pressed his lips to her forehead, and felt the sting of tears in his eyes.

"What did he *do?*" he asked raggedly.

"I fought him off," she said proudly. "I think I broke his nose."

Jack smiled, his breath catching as he tried to hold back the emotion. "Way to go, baby."

"Don't leave me in here," she begged, more tears filling her blue eyes.

"I won't, sugar. I swear I won't. I'm taking you to the hospital. We're getting out of here right now."

"I was so afraid," she whispered. "Now that you're here, I'm not afraid anymore."

The words said so trustingly tugged at places long ago buried. Elicited emotions he didn't know he had. Had he ever thought her weak? It shamed him to admit he had.

Now looking at her, bloodied and bruised but so strong. So very strong. He knew she was far from weak. He was the weak one. When it came to her, he felt as vulnerable as a newborn.

He carefully picked her up, cradling her to him like a fragile piece of glass. She laid her head on his shoulder and closed her eyes. A single tear slid down his cheek as he walked down the hall.

When he walked to the front, his cold gaze locked onto the cop still sitting at the desk. He worked hard to control the rage brewing like a thunderstorm.

"This isn't finished. I'll be back, and so help me, you're a dead man."

The cop blanched. "It wasn't me," he said defensively. "It was Moreland. Dumbass couldn't keep his dick in his pants. She fought him off. Broke his damn nose. I sent him home to clean up."

"Come on, man," Mac said quietly beside him. "I'll drive you to the hospital. We can take out the trash later."

Jack followed him out, his emotions that of a crazy person. He'd never felt so angry, so furious in his life. Yet, when he looked down at Mia, he was simultaneously assailed by so much tenderness and guilt, it threatened to bring him to his knees.

He got into the truck, cradling Mia to his chest. He was careful not to jar her. He didn't want to cause her any more pain.

When they arrived at the emergency room entrance, Mac shoved a jacket toward Jack.

"Wrap it around her if you want," Mac said.

Jack nodded and arranged the jacket around her so she was shielded from view. "Thanks. I appreciate the ride. Don't wait. I'm sure Kenny will need you."

"I'll get back to you and let you know what's going on," Mac promised.

Jack carried Mia inside. He never put her down, even as they waited for a room. When they were finally called back, he placed her on the bed and arranged a sheet over her.

Through it all, the exam, the questions, Jack sat beside her holding her hand. He trembled with anger as he listened to Mia recount the details of her attack. He wanted to kill the bastard. Wanted to spill his blood. Rip his dick off and shove it down his throat. He'd never felt such a surge of violence in his entire life.

When the doctor finally left, Jack traced a finger down Mia's cheek. "I'm sorry this happened to you, Mia. I'm so damn sorry I wasn't there to protect you."

She let out an indelicate snort. "I managed to take care of myself."

"Yeah, I know. I'm proud of you. The other cop says you kicked Moreland's ass pretty good."

She grinned crookedly around her swollen lip. "I don't imagine he'll be using his equipment anytime soon."

Jack choked back his laughter.

Mia's expression grew serious, and fear shadowed her eyes. "What's going to happen, Jack? Will I have to serve time? I'm so scared."

Jack reached out to cup her face with both hands. "It's not going to happen, Mia. You were set up, plain and simple. I don't care that you knew what was in that bag. You were played from the beginning. Martin and Drake sang like birds, according to Kenny. They worked the same set up on pretty girls who floated through town. They used them to make money in the strip club, then they'd sell them off to the highest bidder in an auction. Over the years, it's proved to be a profitable business."

Tears slid down her cheeks. "I was so stupid," she whispered. "If I had just stayed in Dallas. I had an apartment, a job."

Pain slashed through Jack. He knew well why she'd left Dallas. Because of him. He closed his eyes and looked down. He remembered her pain-filled statement, that he hadn't loved her, hadn't cared about her, and that was why he hadn't made sure she knew what was going on. It shamed him to his core that she'd been right.

He hadn't cared about her. Not in the way that mattered. She'd always been a duty to him, a little lost girl he'd looked out for after she'd lost her dad in a drug raid.

The night she'd come to him, so full of innocence, had thrown Jack for a loop. Then he'd been called away, and he hadn't given thought to how it would affect Mia. He'd done his job, placed her below it in his priorities.

And now . . . now he realized just how much he loved her. He loved her, but he was absolutely no good for her. He'd caused her so much pain and heartache already, and he feared if she stayed with him that he'd take the one thing he loved most about her and crush it. Her spirit. Her courage.

He couldn't do that, couldn't force her to submit to his dominant nature. He hated this. Hated the pain.

"Jack," she whispered.

He looked up at her, sure his tortured emotions were emblazoned in his face.

"What are you thinking?" she asked.

She put her fingers out to touch his lips.

He caught her hand and kissed it. "I was thinking how much I love you. How much I wish things were different. How much I've hurt you."

Her blue eyes filled with heartrending emotion. "You love me?"

He bowed his head. "I only now realize how much I love you. I wish it wasn't too late. I wish . . ."

She struggled to sit up in the bed, hissing in pain.

"Sugar, what are you doing?" he demanded as he pushed her back down.

"What do you mean it's too late?" she demanded. "You don't want me? Is it because of what I did?"

He looked at her in shock. "God no. It's because of me, Mia. I'm no good for you. Never have been. It's why I fought my attraction to you for so long. You're so sweet and innocent. You have such a fire in you. And your spirit . . .

"Don't you see, Mia, if we were together, I'd crush the thing I love most about you. I'd take you and I'd push and push until you'd have no choice but to bend or break. I don't want you to break, Mia. And I don't want you to bend."

She looked at him in confusion. "What are you talking about, Jack?"

He felt the knot of shame growing in his stomach. "Earlier, when we fucked, Mia, when we put on a show. It wasn't a show. That's how it would be with you and me. I'd expect, no I'd *demand* complete submission from you. In and out of bed. I can't do that to you, sugar."

She smiled. A big glorious smile that lit up her entire face. It made her blue eyes shine like a clear Texas summer sky. He'd never seen such a beautiful sight.

"Oh Jack," she breathed. "Is that all?"

"All?" he sputtered. "Mia, I don't think you understand."

"Oh, I understand," she said, the smile never leaving her face. "I understand that I love you and that I'm not letting you go. Ever again. Don't you think I know all this about you, Jack? I knew it when I snuck into your bed two years ago. I knew it and accepted it. Craved it. Needed it. I need you, Jack. Only you."

He swallowed then swallowed again, but the emotion swelling in his throat wouldn't go away. He'd done everything wrong and yet, he was being given the most beautiful gift in the world. She was giving him herself, her trust and her love.

"Are you sure?" he croaked out. "Be sure, Mia. I won't let you go. I'll love you always. I'll take care of you, but I'll never let you go."

"I've always been sure, Jack. I wish I had waited for you. Wish I hadn't run like a scared, hurt little girl. I've made so many mistakes. I'm tired of running. I want to go home. With you."

Jack gathered her gently in his arms and held her tightly.

"You once told me you didn't have a gentle bone in your body," she said, her voice muffled in his chest. "But you lied, Jack. You've never been anything but gentle with me. I know you'll never hurt me. I crave your dominance. I need it. I only feel safe when I'm with you."

He pulled away just enough that he could kiss her, devour her mouth. Her words set his soul on fire. He felt a satisfaction, a deep contentment he never thought he'd experience.

"I'm still too old for you," he said gruffly.

She grinned saucily. "Lucky you. When you're old and gray, you'll have a hot young chick in your bed."

He kissed her again, hungrily, trying to absorb every inch of her. "Damn right. And I plan to keep you in my bed for a long, long time, sugar."

CHAPTER 16

"*O*pen your eyes," Jack said as he moved his hands from Mia's face.

Mia opened her eyes and looked at the brick house looming in front of her. Her gaze filtered down to the "For Sale" sign with a "Sold" slogan slanting diagonally across it. She looked back at Jack in wonder.

"Is it . . ."

"It's ours," he said. "Signed the papers this morning."

She let out a squeal of delight and threw herself into his arms. He caught her, and she wrapped her legs around his waist. She peppered his jaw and lips with kisses as he laughed.

It had been a month since they'd left south Texas and all of the painful memories associated with her time there. She'd been cleared of all her charges, and there had been a veritable roundup as multiple arrests were made.

Jack had taken her back to Dallas, where they'd stayed in an apartment. He had gone back to his job with the Rangers, and he'd insisted she not return to work. She knew he still worried over her injuries, both physical and emotional.

"What do you think?" he asked as he grabbed her hand and started toward the front door.

"I love it!"

"I want you to marry me," he said in a matter of fact tone. "As soon as we can arrange it. Thought we might even fly to Vegas in the next weekend or two."

She smiled. In typical Jack fashion, he hadn't asked, he'd merely said. Not that there was any question of her agreeing. He well knew it too, or at least he should. They'd spent every minute of the last month together, exploring their newfound relationship to its fullest.

There were still times when he caught himself, when he worried he was being too forceful, but she laughed and told him she wouldn't have him any other way. And it was the truth. She loved him, loved his dominant nature, delighted in submitting to his demands. He took such very good care of her.

She sighed. After so much fear and pain, she found it almost too good to be true that she and Jack were together, that they were so happy.

"You're awfully quiet," Jack murmured beside her.

She smiled up at him. "I was just thinking."

"About?"

"Just that it all seems too good to be true. I'm so happy. I can't believe you love me."

His eyes darkened. He pulled her against him almost angrily. "It's me who is lucky, sugar. I don't deserve you. I don't deserve your trust after all that's happened. I'm going to spend the rest of my life making sure you know just how much I love you. Not a day is going to go by that you won't know how much."

She sighed against his lips and gave herself over to his kiss. "And yes, I'll marry you."

He grinned somewhat sheepishly. "I guess I should have asked."

She smiled and kissed him again. "Well you could have, but I rather liked being told I was going to marry you. I think Vegas is a great idea. Now, are you going to show me my new house or are we going to stand out in the yard all day?"